Tony,

Now you know the rest of the story.

# BrownWater III

Your friend

[signature]

# BrownWater III

---

## Time to Go Home . . .

# Samuel C. Crawford

**To order additional copies of this book, contact:**
Xlibris Corporation
1-888-795-4274
www.Xlibris.com
Orders@Xlibris.com
29644

To Pat, my loving wife and our lovely daughter Stephanie. You two have always been my biggest supporters and for that, I am most grateful.

To my mom, Vivian P. Crawford.
Thank you very much for your encouragement.
It was greatly appreciated.

To James H. Crawford, U.S. Navy Retired.
Thank you for your continuous service to our country.

# Forward

## by Joni Bour

There are many books written about the Vietnam War, written by researchers, veterans, know-it all and even know-it nothing types. Some authors approach their subject as if they are hunting their enemy, slowly, quietly and then when you least expect it— WHAM, right between the eyes with the story. Others go a long, go a long and never really get anywhere at all. Some are strictly facts and some claim the truth but clearly forgot to put that part in the book. Then there is Sam. I say this with deep reverence, and then there was Sam. I have read so many, many books about the Vietnam War and its veterans that rarely does an author or his/her book surprise me. Few and far between is the book that really makes me think it not similar to the one before. I have never read anything like the BrownWater series (I through III).

Sam will tell you if you have the pleasure to meet, that these books are works of fiction. But I would be remiss if I did not point out similarities in the lives of Sam Crawford and his main character Charles: The BrownWater series may be fiction, except for the fact they revolve around one particular young sailor during the Vietnam War and Sam is a Navy veteran of the Vietnam War. Also, many of the things Sam relates really did happen, so except for that, yep, purely fictional. Sometimes I think perhaps writing all from memory might just be too painful, just too real for a funny guy like Sam. I don't know. But that aside, Sam spent six years in the Navy, three of them in Vietnam—so maybe, just maybe even if Dan and Charles are all made up, he certainly tells the story from the perspective of someone who knows, not guesses, he is no pretender.

I don't want to give the plot away on this book if it is your first Sam Crawford experience or let the cat out of the bag if it is your second or third brush with Charles and Dan. But I will say this: If you are looking for draft dodging, blood and guts, smoking dope or post war angst, keep on looking. You won't find anything like that here. But you will get what was probably more typically the BrownWater sailor—19 years old, never been anywhere but High School, scared of everything that moves, duped by small children, standing watch every time he turned around and just trying to stay alive. This story has a lot of humor amid what you know is sad and life changing. Sam doesn't have to tell you his character is at war, you know it. Sam can get away with telling his story this way, because he lived through that blasted war. He will make you snicker all the way through 400 plus pages. But he does more than that. He transforms one young man kept alive by the grace of God and the wisdom of men only slightly older than he, into a smarter more savvy young man, much wiser than 19 or 20-something years. Charles is quite a piece of work, but you are left feeling like—if he can make it over there, he can make it anywhere and truth be known I think he did. I think he might have made it through six years of Navy service and then perhaps he went to college, married, had a daughter and lives a successful life in Delaware. In the three BrownWater books that Sam Crawford has written, I have grown quite charmed by Charles and only hope this bumbling young man grew up to be as fine a man as the author.

# Chapter 1

Beeeeeeeeeeeeeeeeeeeeeeeeeeeeeeeeeeeeeeeeeeeeeeeeeeeeeeeeeeeeep.

Beep.

Beep.

Beep.

Beep . . . . Beep.

Beep . . . . Beep.

Beep . . . . Beep . . . . Beep.

Beep . . . . Beep . . . . Beep.

Beep . . . . Beep . . . . Beep . . . . Beep . . . . Beep.

Beep . . . . Beep . . . . Beep . . . . Beep . . . . Beep.

"Wake up, Charles! It's not time for you to transfer out just yet," Dan yelled, all the while shaking me like a rag doll.

Damn, all this shaking just might kill me. I was not sure what caused him to cut loose on me like that, but I wished that he would stop. With me being in the hospital and all that, he should at least be gentle with me.

"You okay man?" Dan asked, with a touch of fear in his voice.

Beep . . . . Beep . . . . Beep . . . . Beep . . . . Beep.

Beep . . . . Beep . . . . Beep . . . . Beep . . . . Beep.

Looking at me as if I didn't answer quickly enough for him, he shouted, "Charlie!"

Beep . . . . Beep . . . . Beep . . . . Beep . . . . Beep.

Beep . . . . Beep . . . . Beep . . . . Beep . . . . Beep.

I looked up at him and struggled to get out a question. I asked, "What?"

For once, he had a surprised look on his face liked the one that was always found on mine. I loved the fact that something could surprise him. I just did not care that he was looking at me with his surprised look, as if he had that; the deer-in-the-headlights look. Damn, what did I do? I was the one hurt here, so give me a break, I whispered softly to myself.

"I thought you checked-out just then," he explained, still with that surprised look on his face.

Mentally and physically, I could only come back with, "What?"

"Right when we came back, your heart monitor went off. It looked as if you had dropped dead before you got to tell me good-bye," he admitted, as his face changed to a more normal, relaxed look.

Beep . . . . Beep . . . . Beep . . . . Beep . . . . Beep.

Beep . . . . Beep . . . . Beep . . . . Beep . . . . Beep.

I still had no idea what he was talking about as he continued, "Your heart monitor, you know, that beep, beep, beeping thing you go going."

Now that I caught on to what he was talking about, I said, "No sweat." I was going to tell him how pleased I was that I did not drop dead on him; however, he did not give me a chance to respond.

He jumped in and explained to me, naturally with a smile as if a scam was coming my way, "That was only part of it."

With not knowing what else to ask on this, I simply came back again with, "What?"

"My man," Dan said, as he started out to explain and making sure that the new guy heard him, "if you would have needed mouth-to-mouth, shit man, you'd be dead now. I don't do no mouth-to-mouth. No body, no way, no how."

That selfish remark did not warrant a response from me. So, for now, I would just ignore him on that one. I was too tired to debate with him about anything right now anyway.

With the excitement quickly over and as if there were no reason for him to stick around, Dan looked down at me, and said, "Hang in there, my man. The new guy here and I are off to the tailors for a fitting. He's not exactly dressed for the occasion. You know, you don't wear white to a war."

I was about to add in a comment just to be part of the conversation when the two of them were already up and walking on down the hall. I was a little ticked that I did not get a chance to say anything. In addition, I was not too thrilled that Dan would have let me die, rather than to try mouth-to-mouth and save me. Then I thought, nah, he would have saved me somehow. Oh well, damn, they could have waited a minute to see if I needed anything. I guessed they'd be back soon, I assured myself.

Beep . . . . Beep . . . . Beep . . . . Beep . . . . Beep.

Beep . . . . Beep . . . . Beep . . . . Beep . . . . Beep.

With nothing to do and still feeling like crap, I thought that I would attempt to nap again. Only this time, I would make sure that my hook-ups, were hooked-up. My beeps seemed normal to me now and I guessed that to be a good thing. As for me, it was my first experience with the beep machine and an experience that I would gladly avoid in the future. I didn't know which was worse, almost dying, or having Dan trying to shake me to death. Whatever, at least I was still alive and I did not need the mouth-to-mouth part.

It took a little while for me to finally fall asleep, and when I did, I was out cold. I was not sure how much time went by when I got a little tap on the shoulder from Dan. He asked me, "You asleep, my man?"

"No, not now," I replied, trying to show him that I was asleep and that currently, thanks to him, I was now wide-awake. At least this time, he came back with his new friend to see me and all I got was a little tap on the shoulder.

Dan looked over at the new guy and said, "You were wrong."

"Wrong about what?" I asked, not wanting to miss anything. I continued, "What? Did he think that I was dead or something?"

With a smile on his face and all the while holding back his laughter, Dan answered me, "We had a small bet going."

"A bet on what?" I wanted to hear about this, even as my strength was depleting and talking was still difficult.

As if he was embarrassed to explain, Dan said, "On whether you were dead or not."

A little pissed that my life had a bet on it, I asked Dan, "And how did you bet?"

"As always, I only bet on sure things," he answered, with a smile.

Realizing that sometimes Dan did not always answer completely, I asked him, "I know that you only bet on sure things. My question to you is; how did you bet this time."

"I won a free soda," Dan answered, and that comment was followed with, "Thank you Charles Edwards."

"You are most welcome. Yet, I was the one that wanted a soda and I was willing to pay for it. And here you go and win a free one because I didn't die on you," I said, and hoped that I could at least get a little swig from his soda.

"You looked dead from a distance," the new guy explained, as if he had to clarify that to me.

I was not thrilled with what he just said. I came back with, "So FNG. What does a dead guy look like?"

So, twice in one day now, someone else was looking at me with the; deer-in-the-headlights look. I could not tell if he was confused because of the question that I asked, or that he did not know what an FNG was.

"FNG," I snapped at him before he could respond. "Stands for, 'Fucking New Guy.' In addition, you be the Fucking New Guy here. You haven't been here long enough to have seen death yet, so don't be so quick to pronounce me dead."

That statement caught me off guard. I did not know that I had enough strength to say all that at one time and that I showed no compassion towards this poor sap that I just met. However, it definitely sounded like something Dan would have said. So for now, I would rather get back to my nap than to explain to this jerk that I was not dead.

After a second, he apologetically came back with, "Sorry, man. I am just so scared with being over here, that everything looks dead or dying to me."

Wow, he reminded me of me just then, like when I would say the wrong thing about something. This guy knew that he had said something wrong and was now sorry about it. Moreover, as expected, Dan stepped in to save him the way he always seemed to save me. He said, "Give him a break, Charles. He's from California."

After an awkward moment, Dan added, "Everyone from California normally looks dead. Know what I mean? Hell man, many Californians are brain dead anyway from taking too many pills, smoking pot and or from sniffing glue."

After a little smile as if he was thinking of what else to say, Dan added, "Californians take downers, upper, and maybe even some sideway pills."

Still a little pissed and ignoring his comments, I said to Dan, "Yeah, right. He's from California." That may work sometimes with some people, but not me, not now.

The new kid came back with; "I am from California. San Diego, California. No shit. And I am really sorry for what I said."

Well, after giving this some thought, and the fact that they could be telling me the truth, I might as well give him a break. I always got a break from Dan after many of my blundering episodes. I said to him, "It's cool. No sweat. It don't mean nothin."

To try to put a little humor into this situation and to give this FNG a break, I added, "So, I really looked that bad? I looked dead to you?"

He quickly responded, "No. I mean yes. No, I mean no."

Dan stepped in again to help this guy out, "Relax. Don't sweat it. My man Charles here can't die. He hasn't gotten orders for the Navy to die yet."

Because this FNG seemed upset about what he said about me, I thought that maybe he was sincere about his half-hearted apology and I would just let it go.

After a few minutes, the two of them kind of moved off slowly away from me. I figured that they wanted to talk a bit and not disturb me. I could make out that Dan was doing most of the talking, and was pretty sure that this guy was getting some pointers from Dan. I could hear Dan explain, "If an officer tells you that he needs something, then you need to tell him how he could get along without it."

I chuckled at that one as Dan continued with, "When you don't know what to do, then walk fast and look worried."

I couldn't see his face, but I could only imagine that he was taking all this in, when Dan added, "Following all the rules will not necessarily get the job done."

To change the subject and to join in on this conversation, I commented as I looked at his uniform and saw that his new/used uniform did fit him better than mine did, "You look good. You now look like you belong in The-Nam."

He seemed a little relaxed now. He said, "Hi. My name is Russo. You're Charles, I understand."

With a little trouble moving around because of my chest and stomach pains, I held out my hand for a regular handshake. Even if I could do that jive, knuckle-knocking, finger-grabbing, shake-a-ma-thing handshake, I was not in the mood. In getting into position for the shake, I looked down and noticed his shoes. He still had on his regular, brightly shined, military issued dress shoes. I could not let that one go, and I asked him, "Are you wearing those shoes to the war?"

After shaking my hand, he stepped back and said, "Yeah. Dan and I couldn't find anything in my size. He said that they had a similar uniform shop back at the Army's BEQ."

To be funny, I added, "You could have gotten a pair a size or two too big. Then you could have put on some extra socks."

"I thought about that until Dan told me about all the times you complained about wearing boots that were too big. He explained to me that he just wasn't in the mood to hear me whine about my boots being too big for the rest of the war. I figured that, according to Dan here, that we were only a couple hours away from the ship," Russo explained. "I can wait until we get checked-in to get a pair of boots."

"Not a problem. And no, you cannot have my boots if anything happens to me," I said, and hoped that I made that very clear. No way was I going home without my boots. That comment surprised him and I did not take it any further.

Dan broke in and said, "Listen Charles. We have to be going here. Anything you need me to do for you when I get back?"

"You are assuming that I'm not going back?" I questioned him, not thinking that I might be going home. Then just maybe he knew something that I did not. Such as, that I might die here. Nah, my injuries did not seem to be very bad. I was going to be okay.

"Not with your injuries. You will probably get a ticket home and that's a good thing. At least this way, you won't have to wait around for the next eleven months to see how you're going to be sent home."

It sounded good the way he explained that and I was better off going home. Maybe not out of the Navy, but no longer in a place where people were always shooting at me.

"Anything I can do for you when I get back to the ship?" Dan asked a second time. However, he asked in a way as if suggesting that he really did not want to do anything for me. He was just being nice and thought he would ask.

He should do something, anything for me, we be buddies, and he was never that busy anyway. Whatever, at this point, I did need his services, I did not know what for, but because he asked, I would ask him. "Just tell the Master-At-Arms that I'll be back soon and then he can assign me something to do. You can tell the Captain that I was shipped home. That way, he will not be spending anytime looking for me."

Dan smiled and said, "Yeah. He'll find out that you are not from California and he'll send you home for sure."

"I was thinking the same thing," I responded to his very true statement. I continued, "Whatever, I will be back, so do not send my stuff home. My parents will get my things and think that I was killed or something. My little sister will want my room then."

"No sweat. I won't send your stuff back home," Dan assured me.

"Other than that, I can't think of anything else," I said.

"No sweat. Can do, my friend," he answered, and I could tell that he was scamming up a way for someone else to do it for him. This guy the asked Dan, "Do you have a lot of stuff?"

Dan looked at him as if he was doing an inventory list in his head before answering him, and or, to explain his theory about stuff. You remember, the stuff you left home, the stuff you bought with you and then the stuff that you take with you when you are gone for a few days. I waited for Dan to give him that story, but instead, he said to him, "I started out with nothing, and I still have most of it."

Russo looked around as if he wanted to increase the amount of stuff that he had with him, my boots for example. As he, Russo, stepped up and was about to ask something, I butted in this time and said, "And no, you cannot have my boots or anything else that's mine."

As if this thought had crossed his mind, he stepped back, and like a child, held his head down and looked at the floor. Oh well, that was not a problem with me. He could look down at the floor all the day long if he wanted to. Just leave my boots alone.

With that little detail taken care of, it was time for them to leave. Dan apparently was not much for good-byes, because he simply shook my hand and told me, "Take it easy."

That was it? Nothing more? I was not expecting a hug, a kiss, or anything, but more than a handshake after what we had been through in the past two or three weeks. I would have even appreciated a jive handshake with all the extra knuckle-knocking and finger-grabbing that went along with it.

Same thing from Russo, a handshake, and they were ready to head out and before I could say anything else, the two of them had turned around and were heading on down the hall. I figured that Dan would at least turn around once more before he turned the corner and disappeared forever. Just as he approached the corner and as I expected to see him turn, I was tapped on the shoulder and told to lie still and that I was being taken to my room. By the time I looked up again for Dan and Russo, they were both out of sight.

I was already missing them, well Dan a little more than Russo. Yet, with the way I kept meeting up with everyone else over here anyway, I would see him again soon, for sure.

I was going to miss that guy. Not a, 'tear in the eye' kind of misses, just that I was going to miss his humor and lack of compassion for others. He was a good example to follow. Some of his examples were bad and those I will avoid copying.

It only took a minute for them to roll me into my private room, a private room with about a dozen beds and patients. It was an odd-looking hospital ward. Not odd in the type of furniture, sick an injured patients that were there, only odd that it looked as if it was built in an airplane hanger with the high, rounded ceiling and walls. One a good side note, it was a good thing that it did not look like an intensive care unit and with that, I could only assume that my injuries were minor. Speaking of injuries, no one had told me how I was doing. Hell, the only thing that I knew for sure was that my heart worked fine and that my stomach did not hurt as much as it did before. My vision was okay and I could hear normally again.

I was no sooner moved into my bed, when that lady nurse stopped by for a visit. I asked, "How am I doing?"

I only received a smile back as she examined my injury. After a minute of careful study that led me to believe that, I had many problems, she told me, "You will be transferred out tomorrow with orders stateside."

"Stateside where," I asked.

She gave me an odd look, and asked, "You are more concerned about where you are being transferred to than you are about your injuries?"

Damn, that came out wrong. Let me try this again. "How are my injuries? And . . . am I being transferred home?"

"Your injuries are minor. You have some bruising and that should be healed in a few weeks and some cuts that are not likely to leave a scar. You are not being shipped home, just stateside. I would assume that you might be transferred somewhere near your home," she explained, as she completed her examination.

"Sounds great, Doc," I said, forgetting that she was an officer. I quickly came back with, "Sorry. I meant, sounds great, doctor. Thank you, sir."

Damn it. I just sir'ed a woman and by her little smile, I believed that she would let that one infraction go for now.

"You will be fine, young man. I'll send someone by to explain to you what will happen next."

I was about to ask her some additional questions, but she had already turned around and headed away. With that, I just laid back down and closed my eyes. A moment later, I received a tap on my shoulder. I turned around and saw an orderly, a nurse, or someone with a pole and an IV bag wanting my attention. I did not know if the IV was for me or not, but the only thing that I was sure of, was that this guy was no nurse's aid and I was not in the mood for an enema.

"Lay back for me. I need to get this IV started on you," he explained.

I figured, no sweat, and complied. This was over in a few minutes and he too walked away, leaving me alone. Now that everyone had walked away from me, I was left with some free time. I looked around my room to see who was with me. To my right, there was a guy lying on his back with his penis all taped up with bandages. Wow, what a place to be shot I thought. This guy was going to get a Purple Heart and a purple penis. I asked him, "What happened to you?"

He sat up on one elbow and said with some embarrassment, "I decided to get circumcised. I sort of thought it was a good idea at the time."

Just the thought of that got me to close my legs together really tight as if some imaginary person was going to reach down, grab me, and clico and dico my oxooos.

"It wasn't all that bad. Except for the stitches," he explained, as if I really wanted to know about that. Besides, no. No need to show me your scar, I thought to myself.

I could only make a face as if I was in a great deal of pain just thinking about his, his, thing that was sticking out in the open. He continued, "Yeah. I got over twenty stitches."

"Stitches?" I questioned, and thought that when you were circumcised, that it was just a little snip here, a little clip there, and then you stick it in a bucket of ice for a few days.

"Do you want to see," he asked, as if he was going to be selling tickets.

"No thanks. If you seen one circumcised scar, you've seen them all." I could not believe that I said that, or could I believe that he wanted to know if I wanted to look.

"No sweat," he answered. "I haven't even looked myself. I'm a little too scared to look."

After saying that, he laid back in his bed and I could swear that, he had a tear or two running down his face.

The guy on the other side of me asked, "Hey man. What's ya in for?"

"Stomach wound. I'm going to be fine. Going home for this," I answered, and turned around to see him. After I said that, it dawned on me that I was really going home. Well, at least back to the states.

"Me too. I might be out of here today. Hope so anyway," he said, indicating that if he were not the one going home, that he would be greatly disappointed.

Before I could continue with our conversation, an officer came in with a clipboard and a small duffel bag.

He stood at the foot of my bed at attention, and asked, "You Edwards? Charles Edward, Seaman, U. S. Navy."

I answered quickly with, "Yes sir."

Showing no emotion or even the fact that he cared about what he was doing, he marked-off something on his clipboard. He then reached into his duffel bag and pulled out a small box.

"Here you go, Seaman," he said, as he handed me this little brown box.

As I took it, he added, "It's your Purple Heart from the President of the United States and your Commander in Chief, Richard Milhous Nixon."

I looked in the box and as I went to look back at him, he had already headed away. Oh well, so much for an official ceremony and there goes another person that did not spend much time with me. Maybe these things were handed out so often that it no longer mattered to those in charge. Well hell, it mattered to me. Every time I go to put suntan lotion on my stomach, I will always be reminded about how I got those scars, assuming that my scars do not go away. Then again, maybe girls will like it that I have a little battle scar. If anything, it would make a nice conversational piece.

"Congratulations," quickly then came a remark from the guy with the stitches in his britches.

"Apparently, giving those things out, well, it's not that big a deal around here. In fact," he continued, "I almost got myself a Purple Heart until that same officer asked me about how I got wounded."

To be funny, I said, "I would have given you one just for surviving the operation."

He chuckled and responded, "Maybe so, but it hurts so bad that I wished that I didn't volunteer for it."

"I can understand that," I answered, and turned to gloat over my new medal. At least with my scars, I can show them off. His, well, nothing to brag about there.

A moment later, I looked up and saw that a Marine Chaplain had entered our room and was talking to my neighbor. After he prayed with him for a minute, he came over to me and asked, "How are you doing, my son?"

Well, I knew enough not to call him 'Pop.' However, I did not know if he was a, 'Father' kind of Chaplain or a, 'Brother,' Chaplain. To be safe, I answered with, "I'm doing fine, sir. Apparently my wound was not all that serious."

He smiled at me with one of those smiles that can only come from Christians that really know Jesus. His presence made me feel a little better. It was hard to explain, but I felt better just because he smiled at me. Anyway, I added; "I'm getting orders to be shipped back to the states. Hopefully, close to home."

I waited for him to sit down and talk with me, or at least pray something, but he moved on to the next guy. Maybe he was a Jewish Chaplain, as he could, or should be able to spot a new circumcision from a distance and that he wanted in on the details.

After he spent a few minutes and a prayer with this other guy, he was off to ignore and/or pray with others. I looked over at the guy the Chaplain just left, as he said to me, "He does this every day about this time. He's just making the rounds."

I did not know what to think about that. When watching WW II movies, Chaplains were always around when someone got hurt out on the battlefield. This chaplain, well he apparently made his house calls in a more secure area. Whatever, I was not dead or dying and I was not very religious anyway. But still, he did look like someone that knew Jesus.

As things calmed down a little and because I was more in the mood to take a nap than to talk with anyone, I decided to take a nap and hoped that my beeps keep a beeping. With little trouble, I fell asleep.

# Chapter 2

"Get up, Seaman. You're not that bad off," then came this unknown, unfriendly, and uncaring voice that caught me totally off guard. I was under the impression, and belief, that anyone in a hospital should automatically, and without reservation, receive tender loving care. Granted, I was not shaken to death as I was yesterday by Dan, but this person's tone was not very professional for a hospital employee. Then again, this was the military, and I was in The-Nam.

I looked up towards this, this little irritation of mine and opened my eyes the best I could for such an early hour. What I saw was a sight that will give me nightmares for the rest of my life. Standing next to my bed was Mr. Circumcised Man. He had tapped me on my shoulder with his left hand as he held in his right hand about two hundred feet or so of bandage that was wrapped around his newly acquired stitches. I could only respond, "Would you mind pointing that thing in another direction?"

"Sorry man. I forgot that I had it out," he said, as he took a few steps back. Clearly, he was embarrassed. Not as embarrassed as me, but he was embarrassed just the same.

Didn't know that he had it out, yeah right, and for some reason, I didn't have any compassion for this guy. Anyway, I blurted out and said, "With twenty some stitches on that 'bad boy' of yours, how you could forget where it was? Do you normally take it out like that for some fresh air and sunlight? You two going for a walk or something?"

After I said that, and in a small way, I felt sorry for what I said and how I had said it. But hell, those were his problem and not mine. Besides, he would get over it and Dan would have made the same comment.

He took another step back, aimed it towards his left, and repeated, "Sorry man."

"What's going on?" I asked him, as I sat up and rubbed my eyes trying to get that visual out of my mind. "Well, I'm awake now. What the hell do you want?"

A little taken back by the way I jumped on him, he apparently had a hard time even to say anything to me at all. He gave me the impression that he was about ready to cry and walk away. Whatever, just as he was about to say something to me, an officer came in the room. The officer looked over at him, then down at his bandages, then back up at him. If I had been that officer, I would have told him to, "Zip it up mister, and keep it out of sight." The officer said nothing, looked over at me, and asked, "You Edwards?"

I figured great, I was going to get another medal. How cool this was starting to be. I did not know what for, but I had been getting a new medal every few days or so anyway and that maybe, I was due again. This was really cool; the girls' back home will just love me in my spiffy uniform loaded down with medals like a real war hero.

"Yes sir. I'm Edwards. What do you have for me? Sir." I did not mean to sound so Gung-Ho, but this was The-Nam. He did not know that I was already heavily decorated and had seen combat a number of times. Not bad considering that I just turned nineteen years old yesterday. In addition, I was in the hospital with combat injuries, and because of that, I should receive special treatment.

"Here are your orders back to your unit. You leave immediately," he said this in such a formal, military tone, that I could do nothing but respond, "Yes sir."

Without ceremony, without any new medal, without a smile, he handed me my new set of orders, smartly turned around, and left the room.

That was it? There was not even a plane ticket for me to get back home? I thought that I had completed my tour of duty here. I thought I was headed stateside. Damn, this ain't right. In The-Nam or not, it just ain't right.

I looked over at Mr. Circumcised Man who had taken a few additional steps back and saw that he looked rather sad. I did not know if he looked sad because of what I said to him a few minutes ago or sad because I was not being shipped back to the states. And yes, maybe he was sad because he was all bandaged up and unable to go out for a walk. In addition, no way would he be allowed to ride in a crowded elevator with that thing of his sticking out the way it was.

I said to him, "I'm going back to the war. I thought I was going home. Shit."

Still, he stood there and did not say anything. He appeared to be the kind of person that wanted to start a conversation up with me. Yet, he did not know how to continue one once it got started. Whatever, I did not want to be bothered by him, not now. I got up; left my orders on my bed, got myself dressed, and just headed out of the room and into the hallway. I needed to take a walk.

After a few minutes walking around in the hallway and giving this some thought, I felt that there was really no reason why I should not be reassigned to my unit. I was healthy and could do whatever duties they handed me. Oh well, I must follow orders and this was the military.

As I continued my way on down the hall, I turned a corner, passed two doorways, and soon found myself in a very crowded courtyard. In the middle this courtyard and next to a water fountain were a handful of young ladies, maybe a half dozen or more. To top it off, each one of them was very stunning. I mean these ladies were enormously gorgeous. Yet, somehow, they seemed different and a little odd by their dress in that they were all dressed identically, as in same-same. Nice, very short mini dresses, but they all had on the same nice, very short mini dresses with little while tennis shoes on instead go-go-boots.

Yet these short mini dresses were most acceptable by me, in fact, I really liked it. However, these ladies kind of reminded me of the two girls that were at Bertha-Butt's birthday party a few weeks ago and that would make them a pack of 'wild women,' that came over here to pick up service guys. I mean, why wait until the fleet pulls in when you can go to the fleet. It must be for them like visiting a candy store. They would just walk in, smile, and show a little leg and bingo, wall-to-wall guys. Or, wall-to-wall peter.

Apparently, Bertha-Butt must have some friends here at the hospital and it must be these ladies. I said to the guy next to me, "I wonder if these young ladies are counting how many 'feet of peter' there is in here today?"

He gave me a response of, "What?"

"Yeah. They are probably calculating their count by the number of guy's, times nine inches, to give'm a total count," I said as I chuckled a little. I added, "It'll be easier for them, I guess, if all of us guys would just line up, nuts to butts for a head count." I said this and believed that I was one funny guy.

He turned to me and I assumed that he would agree to what I said, and possibly add in something funny himself. Or at the very least, express a smile at what I said about the character of these ladies. However, before he could respond, I noticed that he was an officer and I quickly concluded with, "Sir."

He looked me straight in the eye, only the way an angry officer could do, and questioned me without even a hint of a smile; "Do you know who these ladies are?"

I figured that I could say about anything that I wanted because I was in the hospital from wounds that I received from the VC. I effortlessly returned a comment of, "Sir. Don't know. Don't care. But hell, let me know what bar they work out of and I'll be glad to go there and buy any of them a drink or two. Sir."

I could not tell what he was thinking and I could only assume that maybe he somehow or some way, knew Miss Bertha-Butt. Oh well, apparently that was not a good move on my part and it was very clear by his facial expression that I was now in trouble. His officer's training on how to crush young enlisted guys like me was to be tested out on me, I feared. Sure enough, he came back, and questioned, "I say again. Do you know who these ladies are?"

"Well, they might be Donut Dollies. I mean, we are in a hospital, sir." It would appear to me that these ladies were Candy Stripers. A little old to be Candy Stripers, but Candy Stripers that needed a little more respect than I was apparently handing out.

Oh my, wrong answer. The officer came back and said, "Think again, mister."

Here I was, again looking, as a deer-caught-in-the-headlights, with another officer on my case and in my face. I did not know how to respond this time, so I didn't respond at all. Well, he asked that question again and it was best that I come up with something, and soon.

"Sir, no sir. I just thought they were here to pick up guys." Not a good response, but one that I hoped would keep me out of trouble.

He turned towards them, pointed to the one closest to us, and said, "Miss Virginia. The one beside her," he continued, "is Miss Florida and walking toward us is Miss Maryland. These are ladies and not the kind of ladies that you have been spending your time and money on over here."

Oh, shit! I just ran right into the middle of an USO Show. "I didn't know, sir. My first time here and I didn't see Bob Hope anywhere, sir," I answered, not knowing what else to say. Now I would have expected that these ladies would at least wear a banner across their chest making it clear to me just who they are. You know, shouldn't that be a rule or something?

I heard a voice, a crystal-clear, very Southern-Drawl voice, behind me say, "Hi. And where you' all from?"

I turned around and hoped that she was speaking to me. To my disappointment, she wasn't. To make it even more disappointing, she had the attention of a marine, a damn marine grunt at that. So, for now, I could only look at her and feel a little sad that he had her attention. Anyway, with her close to me, then maybe this officer would leave me alone and not belittle me in front of Miss Virginia, Miss Florida, and or Miss Maryland. Well, to my good fortune, he did not say anything else to me. He was too busy checking-out Miss Maryland to be troubled by little oh me.

Without realizing that I was again unable to speak in a whisper, I said aloud to myself as I looked around the courtyard, "I would love to take any one of them to the beach and use up a tube or two of sun tan lotion."

A sweet voice from my left side, answered, "Is there a beach around here?"

"Damn, damn, damn." I did not mean to say that to where anyone would hear me, but someone did and I might as well turn and see whom it was. I turned and there in front of me was a beautiful blond, one of the Miss America Misses, with an empty glass and a full smile.

She continued, "I could use a cold drink and a walk on a nice beach right about now."

I looked behind me to see if she was speaking to anyone else, not to be funny; it was just that I could not believe that she initiated a conversation with me. In addition to that, and to top it all off, she apparently gave me an opening. Naturally, I had no idea about any beach around here so one of her requests would go unanswered. I reached out for her glass, and asked, "What are you drinking?"

To my surprise, someone beside me had said the same thing exactly when I did, "What are you drinking?"

Damn, I turned and it was the officer from a minute ago. The one that wanted to shoot me for what I said about her and the other USO girls. She said, "Coke," and handed the glass to him. I could do nothing but to put my hand down and step aside as if

I was in the way. Damn, I would have thought that the wounded in a hospital would have gotten their attention, besides, isn't that why they were here in the first place.

Just as I was about to walk away with my head down and tail between my legs, she turned to me and said, "Would you get me a drink, please?"

Great, I was back in. Maybe it was just that I was better looking than the officer was. I mean, I was taller than he was. He also had a hump back, which caused him not to stand up very straight. All I had to do now was to find a beach for us to walk on. In addition, of course, a way for us to get there.

I gave her a smile that outdid hers. Miss USA could have taken a lesson from me on my performance as a smiler. I took her glass with pride, excitement, and I had a feeling of happiness all over. However, as I was about to go and get us, yes, her and me, as in us, as a couple, a drink, she added, "If you wouldn't mind, one for the Lieutenant also, please."

Damn! Shit, shit, shit, shit! Wow! In a fraction of a second, I went from lover boy to waiter, what a let down.

"Yes. Coke for me," the Lieutenant said with the tone that suggested, 'kiss my ass, sailor.'

Without thinking and using poor judgment, I looked at the Lieutenant and quickly replied, with an attitude, "What's the matter with you? Got a broken leg or something? Sir."

He might be an officer and all that, but I happen to be a patient in this hospital and not a maîtred. On top of that, this officer could not even stand up straight. I was taller, good-looking, and I had just received a Purple Heart.

Well, sure enough that was the wrong thing to say. Anyway, here it comes, her smile dropped and I could tell that her anger was a building. Before she could respond, the Lieutenant spoke up and said, "Not, a broken leg young man. I'm just missing a leg."

Oh my. I was so busy checking-out the girls when I came in that I failed to notice that he was on crutches, which explained his poor posture, and most importantly, he was missing part of his leg from the knee down. I could only respond with, "Sorry sir. Didn't know, sir."

Go figure, I just turned down getting a drink for a one legged officer. So for now, I turned to her, took her glass and then his. In the most humbled posture that I could muster up, I said, "I'll be right back."

Before they could respond, I was off and looking around for a place to get drinks. Maybe I could find one in Dong-Tam, Can-Tho, or Baltimore, Maryland. No need to find them drinks and return to face additional embarrassment. I was just going to di-di-mal myself right the hell out of Dodge. In addition, with that in mind, I simply walked away and just kept on walking. No way was I going to return to the arena of my stupidity. I figured that he had the girl and that he could get the drinks.

I made my way to the other side of the courtyard without offending anyone else or whispering aloud. I even made it a point to stay away from anyone on crutches. I had always thought that USO gatherings were to be a good, fun thing to attend. Whatever, I might as well head on back, pack what little I have, and return to my unit.

On the lighter side, as I made my way back to my room, I gave some thought about what Dan would have done here. Then it dawned on me, he would have gone and invited Mr. Circumcised Man to the USO show. Probably would have told him to cover his eyes for a surprise and guide him down to the courtyard. Take him to the middle of everyone and leave him there, hanging out all by himself. But hell, I could do that. I could just tell him to head on down and see how his stitches hold out with all the excitement that the girlies would surely create.

Having those thoughts, I must have generated a smile that caught the attention of some guy sitting in a wheel chair. I looked over and down at him and after he displayed a big smile, and spitted right at me. Damn, out of nowhere, I had run into Murph, Mr. Beer Spitter himself.

"My man, Murph! How you doing?" I questioned as I wiped what appeared to smell like beer from my face.

He was unable to respond because he still had a mouth full of beer. Well, I assumed it was beer. Anyway, after a quick spit down the hall at a couple of officers sitting in a row of chairs, he answered, "Doing just fine. Heading back in about an hour."

I asked, "How was your friend that was wounded the other day?"

"He's also fine and heading home. In fact, because he was going home, he was doing much better than fine. What about you?"

"Heading back same-same. Going to pack-up right now," I answered figuring that we could team up and head back together.

He quickly responded, "Cool. See you back at the ship."

With that, he simply turned around and headed away. Damn, guys are always turning around and walking away from me. Oh well, I was on my own anyway, so no sweat. Beside, I do know how to get around. I should be able to get back by myself.

I walked a few feet, turned the corner, and could clearly hear; "Your girlfriend's breath smells so bad that when she yawns, her teeth duck."

"Is that right, nigger? Your girlfriend be so stupid that when she's stopped at a stop sign, she would wait for it to say go," was his quick response.

I was thinking that it just could not be the same two colored guys from before. No way could they have all new jokes about each other. As in most of the time, I was wrong again. Sure enough, there they were and still going at it and going strong.

"Shit, man. You be so ugly that when you were born, the doctor looked at your ass, and then your face, and said, 'Siamese twins!'"

I knew not to say anything to these guys and that I should just walk on by as if I did not hear or see anything. No needs to get them ticked off or to have them make fun of me. Anyway, I tried sneaking by and I was successful. I did make it past them without being noticed.

I did make it a point to listen in to hear at least one more insult before I was out of hearing range. "Your girlfriend be so fat that she be taller when she lies down," was the last thing that I heard and I liked that one.

With my mind on getting back and packing up, I did not notice my name being called out. Well, not exactly my name being called, it was the colored guys yelling, "Hey, Dan's little buddy. Hey man, you be hard of hearing?"

Well, that got my attention and I turned back to see them before they yelled even louder and causing everyone to stare at me. "How you guys doing?"

"You dumb ass white trash. What you think? We be in a hospital, don't you see," was the somewhat humorous response from Monroe, the president's grandson.

I could only muster up a response of, "Okay. I see that you be okay." Great, now I was talking the way they did. I sure hope that they would not ask me anything else.

It was most helpful to me when Monroe spoke again and said, "Sorry man. Be cool, we be cool. My man here be a heading home. You be heading home?"

Here I was with a one-word response, "No." Then I figured, what the hell, I could talk. These are not bad guys and with that, I added, "Got to report back. Got my orders a few minutes ago."

"You see," Monroe added, as he pointed to his friend, I meant brother. "He be going home because our unit has reached its quota of the dead and wounded."

I must have looked puzzled because Monroe answered my question before I even asked it. He answered, "Once a unit be at quota for dead and wounded, that unit be have a 'stand down' until another unit reaches its number."

I was not sure on exactly what they were talking about and they apparently didn't want to take the time to explain it to me, because before I could ask a question, the two of them turned and walked away. I didn't know why, but I will most assuredly meet up with those two guys again.

I made it back to my room to collect my things when Mr. Circumcised Man came up to me and said, "That officer who gave you your orders earlier."

"Yeah, what about him?"

"He was here a minute ago looking for you," he explained.

"Which way did he go," I asked, and hoped that he would just point with his free hand. It was very strange to walk into a room and see a guy standing there with his Crown Jewel sticking out and all bandaged up in a little turban. Just to make this a little more interesting, I could see that there was a little red dot on the top of it. Not that I was staring at his thing, but it was very challenging not to look down. Anyway, with his thing wrapped up the way it was along with that little red dot on the top, well, it looked to me like he had a little Indian guy stuck between his legs. Wow, that image will surely give me nightmares every time I see some 'Rag-Head' on the street. Same-same vision with the Push or Pull-start Rag-Heads.

"Left. He went left," he explained. "I was surprised that you didn't bump into him when you came in."

"Thanks," I replied, and back out into the hallway I go and I was able to catch up with the officer who was just twenty or so feet ahead of me.

"Sir. Excuse me, sir. Are you looking for me? Seaman Edwards."

He turned and officially said to me, "Yes. You have a new set of orders. You are to report stateside for thirty days medical leave."

This was great news, as I was, all smiles, from ear to ear. "Don't be that excited, Seaman," he told me breaking my spirit.

"Sir?"

"You're not getting out of the Navy, you're just getting out of Vietnam," he explained. I got the impression that he did not like giving me those orders.

Then I said under my breath, "Tough, so what, no sweat."

I was lucky that he did not hear me. On the other hand, maybe he did and I was just not enough of a big deal for him to mess with and waste his time.

He handed me my orders without any expression at all. After that, he simply turned around and headed on down the hall. I figured so what, he has his orders for places to go and things to do, and I have mine. Only that my place is home and my, to do, is to take it easy for thirty days. With much excitement, I rushed back to my room to pack up my things.

While I was looking for things to pack, it dawned on me that I didn't have anything to pack. So not to appear stupid in front of Mr. Snip & Clip, I made my bed instead.

He just stood there and watched and it appeared that he wanted to either tell or ask me something. I broke the silence and said to him, "You should head on down to the courtyard."

"What's down there?"

I stood up from making my bed and took a step back before I answered him. It felt odd to be standing next to a guy with his thing sticking out the way it was. Anyway, I said to him, "There are some USO people down there talking to everyone. Your operation might be a good conversational subject and I would think that you would have a fine time. You would most definitely be the center of attention."

He gave me a look of appreciation, thanked me, changed hands for a better grip, and made his way out the door and I assumed that he was heading that way. I headed out close behind him because I did not want to miss out on all the excitement that he was about to create.

Walking behind him, well, I had to walk behind him because it was too dangerous to walk out in front. I did not want to walk beside him because everyone might think that I was with him. Anyway, walking behind him was an amusing event all by itself. As people would pass him, they would stop, stare, point, and then make a joke about it. Everyone gave him a clear path to walk by them, assuming that no one wanted to bump him, or be bumped. With the way he was walking and holding himself, the back view gave the appearance that he was looking for water with a divining rod.

As we neared the courtyard, I could hear all the normal sounds of many groups of people, about fifty or so, talking and joking. All the attention was focused on the USO girls who were now standing on a set of steps for a photo opportunity.

As he stepped into the courtyard, all the sounds in the world clogged-up and everything became totally silent. You could have heard a mouse fart it was so tranquil

I did peek around him and looked inside. The entire area looked as if I just arrived at a mannequin convention with everyone looking his way. I almost felt sorry for this poor sap, but I didn't. I was enjoying myself and thinking of how proud Dan would be of me today. Dan hell, I was proud of myself for what I just did. There was nothing like watching something dumb happening to someone else for a change. This was cool, very cool and if I were ever to get around to writing a book, this would be necessary to include. Sure wish I had a camera, however, if I did, it would not be developed.

Slowly but surely, sounds began to stir. Some whispers at first, then some low talking and without warning, extreme loud laughter. One voice did stand out as someone, who must have been an officer by the way he barked orders, said, "You! Get that thing wrapped up and out of here."

Another officer, I assumed, jumped in, and asked, "Who invited you?"

Well, here is where I come in. He, the guy with his lightening rod sticking out, turned and pointed at me and said, "He invited me. I would not have come here if it weren't for him. He made me do it."

Oh shit, I was in trouble now and I had nowhere to hide. Naturally, and as my bad luck continued, it happened to be the officer that I ticked off moments earlier. The guy with only one leg and still waiting for his drink that was standing next to my face. What was I going to do?

Anyway, before this Lieutenant could say anything and as everyone, and I mean everyone, stared at us, Mr. Circumcised Man quickly exited the courtyard and ran past me. Just as I was about to make my exit, the one legged officer stuck out one of his crutches against the wall and pinned me in.

"Is this your idea of a joke young man?" He quizzed me.

"Sir. No sir. He needed an excuse and to blame someone, anyone and I was it," I said, and then realized that that happened to be a good answer and that I was rather proud of myself.

"Wrong answer," he snapped back, as he lowered his crutch.

Well, now was my chance to make my move. I darted down the hallway and made my way outside and I did not look back. I figured that with only one leg that he would be unable to catch up with me. Officer or not, he still only had one leg.

Once outside, I noticed a chopper pad not to far from where I was. I made my way there and took up a good hiding spot. It was time for me to maintain a 'low profile,' and I made myself invisible.

I waited for a while and no one came after me. I waited a little longer and as I built up a little courage, I decided to checkout my new surrounding, still maintaining a low profile. I realized that this was the chopper pad where all the injured would come in and that this was probably the way I arrived yesterday. I sort of missed that chopper ride and I'd bet that if I were to ask anyone else that was onboard with me, they would have stories on how we flew over an aircraft carrier.

This was certainly a very busy base and as with most bases over here, in The-Nam, helicopters were everywhere. For example, not that it was hard to miss with all the noise they created, but there was a V shape formation of choppers flying right above me. It looked nice, organized, and military like and maybe there was an air show going on right now. I doubt it, but this would be the place to hold an air show because all the planes, choppers, and pilots are already here.

Okay, getting back to my situation, there were two choppers sitting there with engines running that I assumed could be my ride out of here. Besides, I knew how to get a ride; I would just simply walk up to a crewmember on the first chopper and asked if he was heading to Tan San Nut Air Force Base. I did and he responded by saying that he was not but that the other chopper was going that way. I thanked him and repeated my question to the other crewmember on the second chopper.

"Yes. If you want a ride, get onboard now," he yelled at me so that I could hear him over all the noise. With little fanfare, I was off and heading home. Well, at least heading to the airport and that would be followed by a flight home. No need for me to hang around right now and take the chance that the officer that was handing out orders earlier would find me, and make another change to my next duty station.

Anyway, after we took off and with nothing new for me to see, other than looking past the M-60 mounted in the doorway, which now was nothing special; and knowing that I was not going to see an aircraft carrier this far from the ocean, I was soon into a nap.

# Chapter 3

Without any warning, my ride on my escape chopper landed and everyone was ordered to disembark. You would have thought that flying around in a military aircraft in a war zone would have kept me awake anticipating some type of action, or at the very least a little excitement along the way with great views of the country side. Oh well, I guessed that I was just an old salt now where riding in choppers was no longer as adventurous as it once was when I first arrived in-country. Besides, I did not think that I would be getting my view of an aircraft carrier flying over these jungles hundreds of miles from Yankee Station.

Everyone exited the aircraft immediately and I found myself on a pontoon. Not in Saigon mind you, but just some pontoon that happened to be a chopper-landing pad right in the middle of the river. I really could not tell where I was because most every part of the rivers that I've seen so far had looked same-same to me where everything was brown and green. Even the water was just as brown here as any other place. This was not much of a photogenic country for anyone who likes to take color shots.

The flight crew didn't seem to be in too much of a hurry themselves in getting out or anything. With that in mind, I decided to stay close to the chopper believing that I could leave with them when they were ready. Besides, it was not as if I could head off in any direction with water being on three sides and the stern end of some ship on the fourth side.

One crewmember finally did exit the aircraft and I noticed that he was looking towards the stern of this ship as if he was expecting someone. A moment later, an officer approached, and the crewmember yelled, "Let's go, sir. We have a schedule to keep. Please sir, get on board quickly."

The officer said nothing as he boarded the aircraft and this was apparently our reason for stopping here in the middle of nowhere. Everyone else got back onboard and as I made my way to the doorway and was about to enter, I noticed that our new passenger looked familiar to me. In fact, he looked extremely familiar. Not familiar as if he was a friend of mine, but familiar as if he was someone that I should avoid.

Oh shit! I had run into this officer a number of times before and this was someone that I most certainly should avoid. This particular officer was the same-same officer that was on the flight deck when Dan and I escaped from a supply ship a few weeks ago. I crossed his path again getting a haircut a few days ago and he remembered me then. Well, no way was I going to be taking this flight with him with no escape route. I decided not to board the aircraft because I figured that this was a helicopter pad and that another helicopter would be by eventually.

I waved at the crewmember indicating that I was not going with them and with that, he said something on his radio. A second later, the rotors picked up speed for take off. As if this was planned, the officer that I was doing a good job avoiding up to now, noticed me standing there. Well, his mouth dropped down as he took off up-up, and away. I believed that he was prepared to start yelling and screaming at me, but it was too late and I had gotten away from him once again.

The chopper continued up and it was soon on its way. As I watched the chopper depart, I was thrilled that I had escaped his wrath. However, when I realized that I was left behind, I was afraid to look around to see exactly where I was. Then I figured that it did not really matter where I was because it was not as if I was going to call someone to come and get me. Hell, 'what's the big deal,' Dan would have said to me. This was a no sweat, in The Nam situation. I was only trying to get halfway around the world and I was doing it without any luggage.

Okay, so for now, I should head onboard this ship and find anyone that might have a schedule of outbound flights—the Comm-center for example. This way, if I have the time, I could get something to eat or just hang around the flight deck for a little while. Of course, I knew enough to avoid working parties.

Up the gangplank I go, and the first person that I came across, was some guy getting a suntan and reading the newspaper. I started up a conversation with him and in the process; I asked him where I was. He answered, "USS SUMMIT. Where do you think you are?"

"Damn, damn, damn," I said this very loud this time as I turned around and looked at the ship. How could this happen to me? I had spent days and days trying to find this place and the one time that I was trying to make it somewhere else, damn, here I am. Dan would have been proud of me for getting here in record time. Then again, he would have criticized me to death for being this stupid.

It was doubly clear to me where I was because a minute later, that damn monkey, Bullshit, ran past me with the dog, Pisser, in close pursuit. Yep, I was back. Anyway, because I was here, I might as well check-in with the Ship's Office. I could get my orders stamped and have them assist me in getting to Tan San Nut Air Force Base for my flight out now that there was a chopper pad attached to the back end of the ship. But then again, I could be kept here. Nah, no way I have orders. Crap, I have two sets of orders. One for staying and one for going, and I best get rid of the ones for staying.

Without having to ask anyone for directions, I made my way to the Ship's Office and stopped just short of the door. I was going to leave my sea bag outside when I remembered that I did not have one. Speaking of my sea bag, with some luck, Dan remembered what I had asked him, and that he did not send home my stuff and that my things are still here. Hopefully, I will still have a set of clean clothes to put on for the trip home.

I boldly walked inside and made my way up to the first desk. I've been here before and I knew what to do and who to see. The Petty Officer behind the first desk looked up and said with a confused look, "I thought you were dead."

He made it appear that my being alive was going to generate extra paper work for him. So what, I thought, and I came back with, "Sorry to disappoint you, but I got better."

The Petty Officer looked pissed that I answered him that way and pointed for me to proceed to the desk behind him. Whatever, I moved on and around his desk and stood in front the next desk behind his. This Petty Officer looked up at me and said, "I also heard that you were dead."

Before I could muster up something polite and non-sarcastic to say, the guy behind me that I just left, added, "The man told me that he got better. Lucky for us."

This guy looked at me as if I said that smart remark. So far, I have spoken only once and gotten two guys upset with me. Isn't it enough that I was alive? Shouldn't they at least be happy that I got better? Again, I thought, whatever. I'm not going to be here all that long anyway. These guys are just jealous that I was going home and that they must stay here.

I was motioned to check in with the officer behind his desk and I immediately did just that. Now this officer, he's the one in charge of personnel, looked up at me, and said, "I heard that you were killed. I recently heard that you got better. Which is it?" He asked and showed genuine concern for me, I thought.

Now what do I do? Was this a joke of his and now it was up to me to respond in like manner? Or, that he was serious with his questioning and a joke from me right now would be in bad taste? Hell, I had never seen officers joke around with enlisted crewmembers before and I don't believe that it will start with me. Well then, what should I do?

In only a second, I had calculated all the worst things that could happen to me. I was not going to get a dishonorable discharge for however I answered; they can't send me home because I already had orders for that. They can't send me to Vietnam because I was already here, but they could keep me here if they wanted. What's the problem with that? I was already planning to put in a full year tour of duty anyway. With that reasoning, and thinking like Dan, I said, "Sorry to disappoint everyone here with my good health. Next time I get killed, I'll stay dead."

His face turned from his soft, caring, and concerned look to the face of one angry man. He stood up and in a soft, but loud speech, explained, "People die around here all the time, mister. Even some of those get better. So wipe that stupid-ass smile off your face before I send you back for immediate facial first aid."

I could only stand at attention and stare at the wall behind him. No way did I want to make eye contact with him. He continued, "After I'm done with you, you will not, I say again, you will not want orders to go home anytime soon."

"Yes sir. Sorry sir," I said with some embarrassment. Shit, officers sure have a way of making themselves kings around here.

He sat down and composed himself. It took a minute, but he looked back at me and said, "Because we thought that you had 'checked-out', your things were boxed up and sent home to your parents. Your buddy Dan took care of that."

"I told Dan not to send my stuff home," I blurted out quickly and remembered to add in, "Sir."

Again, the officer stood up, leaned over close to my face, and said, "I told him to pack your things. I am an officer and you are a Seaman—a Seaman that is apparently looking to be demoted to Seaman Apprentice. Now, which set of orders would you obey?"

"Yes sir. Sorry sir," I humbly responded, as those behind me snickered at each other, over my time in the spot light.

The officer sat back down and composed himself. I sure had it in my favor, or not in my favor, to affect negatively officers. He thought for a moment, and with his own snicker, as if he knew something that he was not telling me, he suggested, "You might want to call your parents and make sure that they do not, I say again, do not open your things. There is no telling what Dan placed in your bags."

The Petty Officer behind me spoke up and added, "Yeah. The last time Danny Boy sent some things home for one of his friends, we got a letter from a Congressman asking a lot of questions."

The sailor at the first desk added in his two cents, "Yeah, then remember we got a second letter from that same Congressmen after they had some film developed."

The officer showed agreement by shaking his head up and down and that was quickly followed by laughter from everybody here. With everyone having a good time at my expense, I figured that I would stop by the Behawah and attempt a telephone/radio call home using it to warn my parents and save them confusion and me some embarrassment.

"I have nothing here, Sir?" I asked, knowing clearly, what he just told me.

"I say again," he repeated after his laughing stopped. "Your things were boxed up and sent home to your parents. What part of what I just said didn't you understand?"

Damn, even when I was dead, I could still screw up.

The Petty Officer from the first desk came up beside me and handed the officer a message. He told the officer, "Read this sir. It just came in this morning."

He snatched it from the Petty Officer and read the message. He looked confused, then angry, and that was followed by a smile. Looking up at me, he said, "According to this message from the hospital, you were cut a set of orders to report home for thirty days TAD medical leave before being re-assigned to another duty station stateside."

"Yes sir," I said, knowing not to make it appear that I was too excited.

He handed back the message to the Petty Officer and said, "Cut the orders. We do our own orders around here."

"Yes sir," returned an answer from the Petty Officer, who quickly returned to his desk to cut me a new set of orders.

"Add in that he is not authorized to make a layover in Cam-Ranh-Bay," the officer said, trying to get in one last dig at me.

The Petty Officer responded, "Yes sir. No layover in Cam Ranh Bay, got it. I'll place that little note right on the front of his orders."

I was about to ask how long this was going to take when the officer ordered me, to "Take a seat Edwards. It'll be a few minutes."

Not wanting to cause any more issues, I did just that. I sat down quickly and sat smartly at attention. It didn't take long and my orders were cut and handed to me. I could only respond to the Petty Officer with, "Thank you," and "Thank you, sir," to the officer.

Then I remembered that I was almost out of money and today was payday, I asked the officer. "Sir. Could I get paid today?" I had about forty dollars in my pocket but I cannot make it home on that little bit of money. Granted, my air fair and food, and lodging was taken care of as long as I was in-country, but I will need a little more cash to get across the states to Maryland.

Looking irritated, he answered me explaining, "We sent everything out. Pay record, service record, medical record, and most importantly, your shot record. So Seaman, before you can leave, you must get your shots all over again."

Damn, damn, damn. Not those shots again. "Sir," I pleaded, "Didn't they keep a copy of my medical records here?"

I got the impression that my getting my shots all over again would help make his day. However, my questioning him just pissed him off all the more, as he jumped back with, "Seaman. What part of, 'we sent everything of yours home,' didn't you understand?"

"Yes sir," I answered.

"Got it now? No pay today, but do leave sometime open for your shots before you leave," he suggested, and it appeared that he was done with me and that I should move on.

I did not respond, because what could I say? The officer then picked up a sheet of paper off his desk that appeared to be a copy of the POD. (APPENDIX A) He glanced over it and said,

"You can get your shots today. In fact, you can get your shots right Now. Unless of course, you have additional questions to ask that I've already answered."

As I was considering what I was to do or say next, the ship's Captain came in and joined us. I was about to shout, 'attention on deck,' when the Captain spoke right up and said to everyone, "As you were."

He was about to walk past me when I apparently caught his eye. He looked down at me and said, "Thought you were dead."

Luck was with me because before I could respond, the Captain then said, "I see that you got better. Getting orders state side I understand."

"Yes sir. Heading home sir," I answered.

Just as I realized that, I should avoid talking to the Captain and to above all, not to mention anything about home, he quickly came back with, "Going back to California? You and I still need to touch bases on California. You have some time now?"

With that comment, I could tell that everyone in the office looked up at he and I as if everyone was thinking, who was going to tell the Captain that he was wrong about California.

Luck was now in my favor, because before I could answer, a radioman came in and made his way to the Captain. He had a message with him on a clipboard for the Captain to review and initial. At least this way, I was no longer the focus of his attention.

"Captain. Flash message from COMNAVFORV," the radioman informed him in a most serious way.

After the Captain read the message, he initialed the message and said under his breath, "Another damn mining attempt."

The radioman, with a look of fear in his voice, shook his head north and south before he turned to head out.

The Captain then tells him before he was out the door; "I'll meet you back at the radio shack in a few minutes. Call the Comm. Officer, have him meet us there."

A moment later, as if nothing important just took place, the Petty Officer that handed me my orders said, "You are to report to your home of record. If you do not hear from anyone or you do not receive anything in the mail within twenty-one days from BUPERS, you are directed to give them a call. Better yet, you can stop by because you live so close. Unless of course, you move to California."

I could leave now and now would be a good time, but I wanted to give the Captain a few minutes head start. "Yes sir. No sweat," I answered trying not to make eye contact. No reason to tick him off any more than I already had.

I reviewed my orders expecting to see some instruction on how to get home when the Petty Officer spoke up and said, "Look man. Just make it to Tan San Nut and check-in with the Duty Officer. He will assign you a flight out to Travis Air Force Base. You'll be on the 'Freedom Bird' for your return trip to the real world. There are always empty seats going home. Right now, we have more guys checking into The-Nam, than we have checking-out."

"Does anyone here have a flight schedule? You know, for anything going to Tan San Nut," I asked, because if anyone was to know, it should be someone in the Ship's Office.

My question was answered with laughter, but no flight schedule.

The officer spoke up and suggested, "Look, our landing pontoon is new. We do at times have a lot of flights in and out. You are better off getting something off the Behawah. She's close by and has flights all day long."

I thanked him and not expecting any long good-byes from this group, I repeated, "Thanks."

The Petty Officer that typed my orders made one last comment as I opened the door to leave, "Don't lose your orders. It's a real pain in the ass to do over."

"I'll do my best," was the only response that I could come up with right then.

"You're best to do what? Your best to lose them," asked the now apparently irritated guy that must be having a bad day. Then, in all fairness, I thought that to be his problem, and not mine.

"Not to lose them," I shouted. I did not mean to shout back that loud, but it felt good. Besides, I was never going to visit them again anytime soon anyway. With that, I walked out the door with my orders in hand and my head held high, I was going home.

To my surprise, another chopper had just landed at the chopper pad where I came in. As I noticed that it had cut power, I figured that, with a little luck, I could get my shots, make it back before it took off, and save me a trip to the Behawah.

In my attempt to hurry down to sickbay, I dropped my orders on the deck. They just slipped out. To my misfortune, surprise, and out of nowhere, that damn monkey dropped down and grabbed my orders before I could pick them up. Well, off he goes with my orders in hand. I figured that I could easily catch him because he couldn't go very far and that he probably couldn't swim. However, he was making good time swinging and jumping from the overhead pipes. Every so often, he would stop and tear a piece of my orders and throw the pieces at me. This was a time that I wished that I had my M-16 with me. Loaded and the safety off.

This damn monkey, with me in close pursuit, came up on two guys tanning in their hammocks. The monkey ran across one guy, scared him a little, and jumped onto the lap of the other guy that was sound asleep. This uninvited intrusion startled him to react as if a ton of bricks landed in his lap. Instead of grabbing my orders for me from the monkey, he knocked them both off his stomach and out of his hammock. Then once again, the monkey and I were off on our little adventure with him in the lead and me taking up the rear.

I would get close to him and as I reached for my orders, he would tear off another piece to throw at me. Then he would take off and go about ten or twenty feet and wait for me to catch up. It was almost as if he was teasing me and I didn't know why. Why me? I was never mean to this damn monkey. I didn't like him but I was never mean to him. Other people would throw stuff at him, but I never did.

However, this time when I catch him, I will be mean to him. I wanted to grab him by his tail and swing him around a little, or at least, tie his tail to a hand grenade. Anyway, he was off again and I was close behind him. He did leave an easy trail to follow with torn pieces of my orders every few feet. Sort of like leaving me a bread trail to follow.

By the time that I did catch up with him, he threw the remaining pieces of my orders at my feet. I picked up the large pieces of my orders and wanting to do something to him, I took off my boot and threw it as him as hard as I could. I missed badly and got it hung up on one of the overhead pipes. That damn monkey, as if he had done this kind of thing before, took my boot, and threw it over the side. I watched as it hit the water and before it sunk completely, it was hung up between the aft pontoon and the ship. Now I really wanted to kill him, no more mister nice guy.

Hopping around on one foot, I continued to follow that damn monkey and it didn't take long before I lost him. So, with that, I made my way down to the pontoon and was lucky enough to retrieve my boot.

I was about ready to head back to the Ship's Office, when I saw that damn monkey. Only this time, he had taken refuge on one of the VN boats tied along side the pontoon and had made a friend with one of the VN crewmembers. I decided not to do or say anything because as long as that monkey stayed on that VN boat, he had a good chance of being dinner tonight for the crew. With that, I felt much better now that he will soon get what he deserved, and with one wet shoe, I walked back to the Ship's Office anticipating that all of them would be giving me a hard time.

I humbly walked inside and made my way up to the first desk. Naturally, I've been here before and I knew what to do and who to see. The Petty Officer behind the first desk looked up and said with a confused look, "You back already?"

I showed him my orders, well, only the large pieces. He must have seen something like this before as said, "You gave the monkey your orders?"

"Not really, he jumped on me and grabbed them from me," I explained.

The Petty Officer looked pissed and pointed for me to proceed to the desk behind him. Whatever, I moved on and around his desk, just as I did earlier. I stood in front the desk behind his and that Petty Officer looked up at me and said, "I thought you transferred out already?"

Before I could muster up something polite to say, the guy behind me that I just left, added, "Lost his orders. He gave them to the monkey. He's been gone for less than five minutes now and he had already lost them. Hell, and the man isn't even a marine."

This guy looked at me as if I said that smart remark. With that, I thought, whatever. I was not going to be here all that long anyway. These guys are just jealous that I was going home already and they only wanted to take it out on me—second set of orders or not.

I was motioned to check-in again with the officer behind his desk and I slowly did just that. Now the officer that was in charge of personnel, looked up at me with a surprise look, and said, "I heard that you lost your orders."

I tried to answer before he quickly cut me off.

"It wasn't enough that your things are not here. Medical records, shot records and even your pay records are not here. So you decided to trash your orders and have nothing?"

"Sir, it was that damn monkey. I attempted to explain as I was cut off again.

"Let me guess. You walked out the door, what, maybe five feet, and you then handed the monkey your orders?"

"No Sir. That was not how it happened." I said, and maybe I was being a little too bold with my answer.

"Relax Edwards. That damn monkey does that to everyone."

I questioned in amazement, "He likes to trash-up everyone's orders?"

"No ass-hole. He doesn't just trash orders. Anything that falls on the deck he will grab up and if he can't eat it, he'll tear it into many small pieces."

I mustered up a smile that, if anything, relaxed me some. At least I felt a little relaxed.

"No sweat, Edwards. Take a seat and I'll have a new set of orders cut for you right now," he informed me as he barked orders to the poor sap that had already done that for me earlier.

It wasn't long, maybe five minutes, and I was in receipt of my new, undamaged, untorn, and most readable set of orders. I headed out the door and leaving behind a small puddle of water under the chair where I was sitting from my water soaked boot. The last thing I heard as I left and after I said, "Good Bye," was, "Did he piss himself? Damn, he left us a piss-puddle to clean up."

Someone else remarked, "He's worse than that damn dog."

I just kept on walking as if I did not hear anything. My only concern now was that I not create any reason for me to return to that office. Never ever again.

With my new set of orders, I figured that I would just get my shots over with and out of the way. The chopper, that was there the last time I left the Ship's Office, was now gone. Whatever, I headed on down to sickbay. I might luck out and there would be no line and the corpsman would be there, reading a book, and would not mind giving me my shots all over again. Better yet, remember that I already had the shots and that I could miss out on getting them again this time. As long as he handed me an updated shot record, hell, he could do what he wanted.

I turned into the passageway near sickbay and noticed that there was a line of about five or six guys. I asked the last guy in line if he was in line for sickbay to get his shots.

He turned, looked at me, said, "Yep," and turned back around. He was not very friendly and that was okay with me. I was just pleased that he wasn't Louie-Louie or Washington.

The line went quickly and it was soon my turn. The Doc looked at me and said, "I heard you were dead. I can't give a dead man shots."

He appeared to be joking with me and that was a good thing. I came back with, "No sweat, Doc. I'm heading back to the states to catch up with my shot records. Can you make me up a new shot record so I can get out of the country?"

The Doc looked at me and smiled. I was unable to tell if he was smiling because he was going to stick me in the ass or save my ass. He said, "Give me your name and service number. I remember you." He walked over to a file cabinet and added, "I'll make you up a new record."

"Thanks, Doc," I said with great joy.

"No shots for you today and no charge," he announced as others in line behind me wondered why I was getting preferred treatment.

It was only a minute later and I was heading out of sickbay, without getting any shots. I had my orders in one hand and a current shot record in the other. But I really appreciated the fact that my butt was not sore. For me right now, life was good. If only I could just get a few things that I needed for my journey it would be even better. I could use some cash and dry boots.

# Chapter 4

Just outside the Ship' Office, I noticed that a ship, LST I think, had just tied up along side us. Tied up as in very, very close. I did not hear any announcements about a working party to off-load supplies and if I did, or, if I was to hear about it, do I take part? In one way, I was no longer a member of the crew and with this not being my duty station; I would luck out and not have to participate.

With the LST alongside and plenty of helicopters coming and going, getting a ride out of here should be easy.

With that frame of mind, I planned just to continue on my way. I was no sooner five feet from sickbay when I ran right smack into the Chief Master-at-Arms. He gave me a look as if he had just seen a ghost. It was my guess that he also thought I was dead like the others. Wanting to take the chill out of the air, I said to the MAA before he had a chance to say something, "Good afternoon, Chief. As you can see, I got better."

He asked, "Better from what?"

Oh my. I guessed that he was not up to speed with my getting better from being dead. Anyway, I said, "Didn't you think that I was dead? Everyone else seemed to think so."

"Well, young man," he started to say, giving me the look of a disappointed parent. "From the work you do around here, if you would have been dead, that would have explained your poor performance."

I had no response to that. I was even doing a poor job at being dead. I could only give him the look; as if I was a Special Ed student and that, I didn't understand the question. However, I just thought up one excuse that I could use, and with that, I just blurted out, "But Chief, I've never been assigned a job. You and I never got together on that."

Instead of jumping in my case, he simply questioned, "Did you ever complete your Check-in-Sheet when you checked-in?"

"No Chief, I've never even seen a Check-in-Sheet," I answered. I knew full well that this to be something that I should have taken care. Taken care of when I checked onboard.

"And here I thought you were skating your duties and goofing off," he informed me, as he placed both hands on his hips. At least he didn't reach for his side arm and lead me toward the fantail to test the theory on whether his weapon performs properly or not.

Still, I had nothing to say. I was not about the blame the people in the Ship's Office for overlooking that detail when I checked-in. Without waiting for me to respond, which would have taken a long time, he continued with, "SOP mister. Standard Operating Procedures require that you, along with everyone else that checks onboard, to complete a Check-in-Sheet at check-in time."

Taking a deep breath and not allowing me to respond, he continued, "And do not give me that song and dance story about not getting one from the Ship's Office."

My only response was not to respond. Then, as if all the angels in Heaven felt sorry for me, a voice from above spoke up and said, "It's okay, Chief. That damn little monkey Bullshit took it from him the day he checked onboard with me."

I looked up expecting to see God; or at the very least, a light at the end of a tunnel. However, standing against the railing on the next level above us was my buddy Dan. Once again, he was there just in time to save my butt.

The MAA looked back down at me and asked with skepticism, "Is this true, Seaman? You and the monkey had a skirmish?"

"Yes sir, we did. I realize now that I should have gone back and gotten a replacement," I said, understanding that I was again being dishonest to someone in authority. Not a very good habit for anyone to pick up. Yet, one that evidently worked well over here, in The-Nam. Besides, I only needed a little lie to get past the Chief before I was off this ship and heading home.

"Very well then. Report to the Ship's Office and have them issue you another one," he commanded just as he turned and headed away.

After the Chief was out of hearing range, Dan said, "Don't sweat it."

Naturally, I stared up at him with my, 'I am an idiot' look, as he added, "Check-out-Sheet, it don't mean nothin.' Not now."

Dan, before I could muster up anything as a response, had turned and walked away, "Catch up with you later. I got something important to do right now." With that, he was soon out of sight. Now what do I do?

Whatever, I might as well make a head call before I try to bum a ride over to the Behawah. At least that was something that I could do without getting into trouble or offending anyone. A minute later, I was at the head and before me was a small crowd. Seeing a small crowd on a small ship with lots of people onboard wasn't all that unusual; however, it was just that everyone was staring at one of the stalls with its door closed. Not everyone here just could be in line waiting for his turn with other stalls available.

As I was taking all this in, the MAA came in behind me and said, "Make a hole."

With that said, he shoved us aside. He was apparently not in a very good mood. At least he was in a bad mood with someone else and that was fine with me.

A couple of guys that were standing next to the closed stall door made a large, 'hole' and gave the MAA plenty of room. Still not knowing what was going on, I decided just to hang around and see for myself. Yet, I did not see or hear anyone hanging onto the overhead pipes peeing in pain as others made fun of him for making the most of a free hooker. No one was taking a shower and washing their hair with Brill Cream or Nair. Other than a crowd being here, everything seemed normal. Well, in The-Nam normal.

The guys up front made some comments to the MAA that I did not hear and that seemed to have angered him a little. Again, at least he was angry with someone besides me. I must stay now to see how whatever this, was turns out.

"Crapper. Let's go. You're done in there. We have a war to fight," the MAA commanded with others mocking and repeating what he just said.

"Let's go, Crapper. Wipe up and zip up. Wipe up and zip up," others kept repeating.

The MAA put his arms up indicating that everyone should be quiet so he could hear what Crapper had to say. Well, what he, Crapper, said to the MAA was all that the crowd needed to hear that would have them burst out in laughter. He said, "I'm short of toilet paper. I need another roll."

A moment later, no less than ten rolls of toilet paper come a flying across the room and all of them landed inside his stall. Two guys up front were able to slam-dunk their rolls, as one of them must have bounced off Crapper's head because it bounced right back out. Without missing a beat, that roll was rebounded and slam-dunked right back in for two points. With the way Crapper screamed in shock and pain, someone should have gotten a foul.

"Crapper. Time to go. Get your ass out here and get it out here now," the MAA screamed. He was obviously ticked with the delay and the circus atmosphere that was going on strong here in the head.

"Give me a minute, Chief. Just a minute," Crapper cried out.

"You don't have a minute. Come on out here now," screamed the MAA as he reached for his pistol.

This just can't be right I thought. He just can't go around and shoot someone for taking too much time on the pot and using too much toilet paper. Well, I must still be the FNG here because the guys up front knew enough to back away from the door as if the MAA was really going to fire off a shot to unlock the door.

This I must see. No way was I going to leave now. Just then, as two guys passed me in a hurry to vacate the area, one said to the other, "Remember the last time the Chief fired off a couple of rounds in the head?"

The other guy responded, "Yeah, Johnny Boy was shot right in the left nut by accident. Not a pretty sight, but he did get shipped home."

He then added one more comment, "On a side note if you remember this. After that, he was not able to walk a straight line again. He kept pulling towards the left."

"Yeah, I remember. We told him that he needed a front end alignment and that would always piss him off," the first guy responded jokingly, but it did sound true.

Yet, I was thinking that this just could not be true; however, I decided to leave because it would be my luck that I would get hit. With that, I was close behind everyone else that was quickly leaving the area.

I was no more than one compartment away when a shot did ring out and I wanted to go back and see the damage. However, others that stayed when I left, well, they were now quickly running past me, and they did not mind knocking me out of the way for not moving fast enough.

Having gotten the hint that I was not to hang around, although I wanted to see what had happened, I just left with everyone else. With nothing else to do, I figured that I would visit the chow hall now for lunch because it was lunchtime. No reason to go hungry when meals are provided free. Besides, I could hit the head at another time. So with that, I made my way to the chow line and it was a little crowded. Not a big deal as the line moved rather quickly. The first cook dropped a grilled-cheese sandwich and asked if I wanted a second one. I shook my head no and moved away before he could unload a second sandwich on me.

The second cook laid on me about two pounds of french fries. Macaroni and cheese was my third entree and all this together looked rather appetizing. I could clearly smell the cheese from my sandwich and even the steam from my fries smelled very good. This simple meal looked most enjoyable and I might even want seconds.

My next move was to make it down the ladder to the dining area and as before, it was a trick not to fall. At the bottom of the steps, someone was passing out copies of the POD and even this guy was very unhappy about his duties. Damn, what could be so hard about passing out sheets of paper? At the very least, he's not passing out ammo or medical supplies. Anyway, I found an empty table. I made myself comfortable and eagerly looked forward to enjoying my scrumptious looking meal.

Two guys sat in front of me that I've never seen before. The two of them smiled and said hello. They seemed friendly enough and I returned them a, 'hello grin' of my own. I didn't exactly do a Miss America kind of grin, but a friendly grin just the same.

One guy, with blond hair, looked at his food and smiled. He apparently was pleased with lunch today; however, his smile dropped away as he searched the table for something. In a panic move, he snapped at me and asked if I had the salt and peppershakers. I shook my head no and continued with my meal. His buddy, wearing glasses that were too big for his face, said to me, "He really loves to dump salt and pepper on everything that he eats."

I responded, "Sorry. I haven't seen the salt or pepper shaker." I did make an effort to look at the table behind me, just to be polite, but there were no salt and or, peppershakers to be found.

The blond hair guy looked around at the table behind him and he too didn't see any salt or pepper on any nearby tables. He seemed a little pissed and it appeared that he was willing to skip his meal until he found the salt and peppershakers. His buddy started in right away and dove into his french fries as if this was his first meal in days.

"You been here very long?" I asked the guy with glasses because he seemed the friendlier of the two.

"I just sat down, or didn't you notice? You've been longer than me," he answered in a, not so friendly attitude, as his friend placed one folded napkin in his lap and an unfolded another napkin under his neck.

"I meant, you know, here in Vietnam," I clarified.

"Almost a year now. About ready to mail out my letter home to warn my parents and friends of my return to the real world," he explained with much enthusiasm as his, not so friendly attitude changed.

Before I could respond, his friend mumbled to himself, "Crumb catcher for my shirt, crumb catcher for my pants. No need to be messy."

I ignored his friend and said, "Oh, you mean that joke letter? You know, the Notice of Return. (APPENDIX B) I've seen that one before." I was happy that I already knew what he was talking about this time. It felt cool with him being here a year and me just a few weeks and that I was current with what was happening.

He looked at me as if I had two heads and asked, "Are we talking about the same letter?"

I questioned, "How many letters are there?"

"Well, mine is a warning letter. Titled Indoctrination for Return to Zone of America. Here, check it out," he said as he reached into his pocket and handed me his letter. (APPENDIX C)

Oh well, I read it and it was a different letter. In fact, it was a lot funnier than the other one that I had read. I handed it back and thanked him. Wanting to be funny, I recalled what I heard from another short-timer and I said, "So, if you were to mail your letter home today, you would get there first. You'd be getting home faster than First Class, U. S. of A. mail."

"My man, you be right," he answered after a chuckle.

I just said, "Okay," and continued feasting on my grilled-cheese sandwich and pleased that I was a funny guy.

After taking a bite of his sandwich, he came back, "My home town is Eastover, South Carolina. I will meet up with my girl friend once I get to California."

After a short pause and a big smile, he continued with, "Now let me tell you something, my girl Joyce is hot. When she gets decked out in her hot pants, go-go boots, and halter top, there is nothing as hot as my Joyce."

Again, another short pause as if he just got excited thinking about her and that he wanted a paper towel. "After we meet up, we'll drive across the country together. Want to see America and all that. Hell, I might even get us a motorcycle for the ride back."

Just then, both guys stopped eating, stood up, and got heavily involved in handshaking with that knuckle-knocking and finger-grabbing thing and that was followed with much laughter. They did everything except hug and kiss. Myself, I didn't see were what he had said was all that exciting to go through all that commotion, but then again, I've never seen his girl Joyce.

Before I could respond to his excitement, because it was catching, the one guy that I remembered would eat his meals in a habitual routine walked past and sat down behind me. Wanting to be cool, I said after the two of them had calmed down and taken their seats, "See that guy that just sat down behind me?"

They both looked around me and said, "Yeah. So?"

"This guy is a real bookoo dinky-dau looser kind of a sailor. You should see how he eats his meals," I said, wanting to be the bearer of cool news.

The two of them just gave me the deer-in-the-headlights look. They didn't say anything, but their expressions told me that they were both thinking, 'What?'

"The last time that I saw this guy eat, everyone was singing at him," I said with some excitement.

"Singing," they both answered at the same time as if thinking, what's the big deal.

"Yeah, singing. They would sing, 'One bite, swallow, turn the tray. Two bites, swallow, turn the tray,' and so on," I explained, with much animation.

Still, the blond guy looked at me as if I had two heads and said nothing. His buddy stopped eating, stared at me, but continued to chew his food. The way they were looking at me was most uncomfortable and I was afraid to say anything else. Maybe the guy behind me was their friend or something. On the other hand, maybe I took the wind out of their excitement.

After swallowing his food, the guy wearing the glasses placed his hand on the other guy's shoulder to get his attention and asked me, "Could you show us what you are talking about? About this loser guy behind you."

His buddy nodded in agreement and the two of them waited patiently for my demonstration.

That was cool, I thought. Odd, but cool just the same. They were just confused with what I was talking about and I could be a cool guy and show them an example. I assumed that after I gave them a little demonstration, that it would be clear to them that the guy behind me was crazy. That would open a little conversation, which would be even cooler with me having some time to kill.

"Okay. I can tell you in advance, how this guy will eat his meal. He has a whole system down pat and it's a real hoot to watch," I explained, remembering not to talk loud enough to be overheard by the guy behind me.

The two of them asked in unison, "Like what?"

Well, that response seemed rather odd. They both talked as if they were one in the same, or at least, two people sharing the same mind. Anyway, I continued with, "He'll look down and smile at his food."

"Yeah. So what? Maybe he is just laughing at his food. That's not odd, not odd at all," responded the guy wearing glasses.

His friend said, "Possibly he saw something move in his cheese. A cooked fly in his fries."

"Okay. Maybe not that part, but he'll do a look-see for the salt and peppershakers," I added, and somewhat defending myself.

The two just stared at me as if I was the crazy one.

"Okay. You're missing the point," I interjected before they got me too far off track with this little exercise. "Now, he'll grab the salt and peppershaker and see if the tops are on right."

"Yeah, what's wrong with that? A lot of people check that out," snapped the guy with glasses with his buddy in agreement. He continued, "Especially around a bunch of guys in a place where everyone likes to play practical jokes on each other. Sometime the tops are not secured and that shit will dump out right in your meal."

This was not going well for me. Instead of being a cool dude, I was getting frustrated with the two of them as if they were trial lawyers and I had done something wrong. However, I will move on and try to salvage this endeavor.

"Hang on now. Now watch. He will grab one of the shakers and count aloud to three as he adds salt and pepper to whatever it is that he's eating."

Again, they both looked around me and said at the same time, "Not today, my man."

Now they were giving me a look as if I should explain myself. It dawned on me that there were no salt and peppershakers on any of the tables. Relieved with that issue solved, I said to them, "No sweat. Watch and this time he will unfold a napkin under his neck and say something like, 'Crumb catcher, crumb catcher, catch my crumbs.'"

At least now, I was getting a smile from these two. An eerie smile, but I was still cool.

"Anything else," the blond hair guy asked as his smile changed into a look of anger.

"Oh shit," I said softly to myself. Situation not good here. Yet, I thought, how could this piss anyone off? I mean, everyone in the chow hall before was getting into it and no one seemed upset with anyone. Whatever, I will keep on being cool and these two sissy boys will just have to catch up.

"Yeah. There's more," I said, as if I was someone in authority. "He will take a bite of his food and then turn his tray around. He'll do this until everyone in the room starts to sing, 'One bite, swallow, turn the tray. Two bites, swallow, turn the tray,' and so on."

Neither one of them seemed amused with what I was telling them. At this point, nothing these two did together made any since, until; the blond hair guy removed his napkin that was tucked in under his neck.

Watching him do that wasn't all that unusual except for the fact that he made a production out of it. It got a little scary as he mumbled to himself, "Crumb catcher for my shirt, crumb catcher for my pants. No need to be messy."

The guy with the glasses said to me, as I witnessed this unusual act, "You mean like what I am doing?"

I made a quick turn around to look again at the guy behind me. Well, it was all coming back to me now. The guy behind me was not, and I say again, was not who I thought he was. Damn, damn, damn as I was thinking as I realized that I was sitting with the bookoo dinky-dau looser kind of a sailor. Now everyone onboard will think that I was a friend of these two guys.

Sure enough, he took a bite from his tray and turned his tray around. Well, before anyone could start to sing, 'One bite, swallow, turn the tray. Two bites, swallow, turn the tray,' et cetera, et cetera, I picked up my tray and vacated the area. I figured that I could eat later, much later, and alone. I could eat a grilled-cheese sandwich and fries most any time.

After dumping off my tray and once topside, I made my way down to the pontoon to see if anyone was heading towards the Behawah anytime soon. Well, no one was. With that, I figured that I could come back down a little later and again ask around.

Back onboard, I sat myself down on one of the bitts with a view of the landing pad pontoon to see when the next chopper would be in. So, for a little while, I sat there, relaxed, and daydreamed of going home and all the while, letting my one boot dry a little. At least I had a nice spot to relax and air out my foot, and to enjoy my picturesque view of the river. Browns and greens, but still it was a picturesque set of browns and greens.

Two guys came up beside me and one of them sat down on the bitt next to mine. The other guy was carrying a radio that had a baseball game playing. I could not tell anything about the teams. I picked up nothing from what little I could hear. It would have been nice to know what teams were playing, the score maybe, or who was winning.

Wanting to hold a conversation to help pass along the time, I asked the one sitting next to me, "What's the score?"

He looked at me as if I had two heads. On the order of the line that I had interrupted his quality time with the radio. Well, he did answer, and he answered offensively, "Five to Three."

I didn't see anything for him to be offensive about, hell man, it was just a game. Figuring that I could be rude back to him, I asked a second question anyway. "Who's winning?"

Simple enough question. Not that hard, but I'll just wait and see what he does.

"The five."

Okay now, time to cut my losses and move on with my life. Besides, I had had enough of the side of this boat anyway. I ignored him and after a few minutes, I put my, almost dry, boot back on and made my way to the starboard side and there was a floating pontoon filled with ammo and sandbags being towed up river, or maybe it was down river. It appeared to be an officer standing at the highest point. I assumed that he was either giving directions or enjoying the view. After some thought, with him being an officer, it had to be for the view only. At least I had the sun in my face and it felt good just to relax here for a little while longer.

# Chapter 5

After thirty or so minutes of taking in the beautiful view of the river, I looked down at my boots and realized that I sure could use a new pair. Now reason for me to keep and wear wet boots. I have the time now and with that; I'll just make my way to the ship's store and see if they carry boots, I said to myself, believing that I just came up with a great idea.

At the ship's store, I found it opened and awaiting my business. "You have any boots in stock," I asked the clerk behind the counter. He was a Third Class Petty Officer and his name was Tony as indicated by his non-military style nametag hanging from his shirt.

Not being very polite, he gruffly asked, "Size?"

"Eleven," I answered.

It felt odd giving away your shoe size and not the shoe or boot style that you would like him to bring back for me to try on. Now that was just as odd as by the way he walked. He walked in a hip-pity hop-pity kind of way. As if he was a white guy trying to walk like a colored person and that he needed more practice or a better teacher. After about ten or so steps, he stopped and scratched his butt a few times. Then he held up his right leg and did some digging as if he had a wedgie.

Now that was something that I really did not need to see. Besides, if he was not trying walk like a colored person, then maybe he and Louie-Louie had spent some time together. No way, he didn't look queer. He did not have that girlish gay guy kind of queer smile.

After disappearing behind the wall, or bulkhead, for a few minutes, he came back empty handed, and said, "No got."

Before I could ask if he possibly had other boots in different sizes, or to say thank you, and without thinking, I asked him, "What happen to you? You look like you have difficulty in walking."

His sternly looked at me as if he did not want to answer. I didn't know he walked that way normally and that he was not in pain, or that he had answered that question a million times.

Before he answered, his face softened up a little. "Yeah man. It hurts a lot and it's hard for me to walk normal like. Of course, it will be harder explaining this to my girlfriend Joni back home."

I didn't know how to respond to that, so I didn't. It was just as well because he came right back with, "I got my left butt cheek all cut up by some F'en little gook kids."

For the next few seconds or so, if was impossible to tell if he wanted to tell me about his girlfriend Joni, or on how he got cut up. He looked like a talkative sort of guy; so again, I waited for him to respond.

He went right to his girlfriend and explained, "No matter what I write about, she always sends back my letters with the misspelled words all circled up in red."

Lucky for you, at least you have a girlfriend I thought to myself. I asked, "How did you get all cut up?"

With a sigh and the drooping of his shoulders, he went into some detail about the time, date, and place of his injury. As for the time, date, and place, I didn't care about all that, just tell me about what happened.

"Little F'en gooks kids work in pairs. One would bump you to get your attention while the other would use a straight razor to slice through your pants pocket to get to your wallet. Only this time, the little shit sliced too deep and cut me a cut that took nine stitches to close up."

After he said all that, he again went up on his right leg for a little tug of war. At least this time I knew what he was doing and I was most grateful that he didn't need any help from me.

At this time, I didn't know what else to ask him. He didn't have any boots for me in my size and it didn't appear that he wanted to talk anymore about his little pain in the ass. Then again, I was not sure if his pain in the ass was his cut, the kids that cut him up, or his girlfriend Joni's grammar checking.

Tony, seeing also that we had nothing else to discuss, suggested that I checkout the ship's supply locker. I thanked him and off I went.

The clerk behind the counter at the supply locker informed me that they didn't carry boots and that I should check with the Ship's Office and see if they would order me a pair. Well, no way was I going back there and figured that I would just be contented with what I had. Besides, I should be home long before they even came in.

After I made my way back topside, I figured that I would try to find Dan before I escaped. However, after a few minutes or so of just walking around, I could not find him and everyone that I asked didn't know where he was. Well, half of them didn't know where he was and the other half didn't know who he was. Then the last guy that I ask suggested that I check for Dan at the USO show on the forward pontoon.

Wow, another USO show? Hell, how did I miss that? On this little ship. There was a show going on and I missed it? Great, I might even meet up with the Miss America group again. Quickly, I made my way to the stern and looked down onto the pontoon. Sure enough, there was a small crowd around a little makeshift stage and right in the middle of the crowd, was my man Dan. However, instead of a group of round-eyed beauties parading around in short skirts and little tennis shoes, there was just one Vietnamese girl doing a strip tease show. It didn't seem right, as she didn't have a pole to stroke or spin around on.

Listen to me, as if I've been to a place like that. In reality, I've only seen things like that on TV or at the movies. Anyway, getting back to Dan, I tried a number of times to get his attention. Dan had a front row seat and he was not looking up here where I was. His seat was right at center stage and that show had his full attention.

Now, she wasn't all that good looking but who was looking at her face. Some of the guys there were making all kind of nasty rude remarks and she was doing a very good job ignoring them. Or, maybe she didn't understand English, which in this case, it may have been a good thing for her.

I wanted to take a trip down and sit next to him but because it was crowded where he was, I just took a seat next to a loaded M-60 and waited for the show to end. Near by, there were a few guys drinking something that apparently made them feel little or no pain and that it had placed a pretty face on the stripper.

I get a tap on my shoulder from a Third Class Petty Officer. He offered me a drink and I asked, "What is it?"

"It's free," was his drunken response.

Reviewing my present situation, here I was at a strip tease show, around a bunch of drunks, and all the while, standing next to a loaded M-60. Well, this was The-Nam and I was apparently the only one here concerned about it. So for now, I would just blend in and make an effort to be cool.

A Second Class Petty Officer that was drinking with him explained, "Acadoma Rice Wine in that bag, and behind me here is a couple of bottles of San Miguel beer. Want some?"

"Sure," I responded, making a motion indicating that I wanted a beer and not the rice wine.

The Second Class Petty officer explained, "I traded two cases of C-rats for this bottle of wine. Try it."

After downing half of my luke-warm beer, I took a swig from the wine bottle and did everything I could not to spit it out on anyone. That was some nasty stuff. "Thanks, but I'm not a wine drinker kind of a guy. Beer, give me beer anytime."

I really should not have said that because the next thing I knew, I had a freshly opened, warm beer, placed in my hand. Damn, damn, damn, I did not have any plans for me to get drunk today, and never any plans for me to get sick and getting sick with this warm beer was my next move.

For the next hour or so, the three of us watched this strip tease show and finished off the rest of the booze. Well, we really spent that hour drinking and talking about going home and paying little attention to the show. She was unattractive and wasn't doing anything exciting that kept our attention.

The show ended and instead of making my way down to try and find Dan, I followed these guys to their berthing compartment and it was there we had more to talk about and even more to drink. The next thing I realized was that we had drank the entire day away, even to where I missed dinner and the night's movie. Even more disturbing, I missed any chance of leaving here today and now I had expanded my odds of meeting up with the Captain.

Nah, no way, I thought. Anyway, so for now, I would just find a place for me to pass out and enjoy a good night's sleep. I would simply get up bright and early and get off this ship tomorrow at 'zero something early.'

"Is that rack empty," I asked, as I pointed to the second rack from the bottom as I held in my urge to throw up. Not a good move if I wanted to sleep here where I was.

"Yeah, you can have it, but you might want the one that's below it," replied the guy that was in the rack above the empty one.

"Thanks," I replied after looking at the one bunk that he selected for me. I didn't see a difference, but I decided to take his advice.

His friend in the bunk beside him added, "Yeah man, you don't want that bunk."

After his comment, the two of them laughed. I took a second look at the, 'forbidden bunk,' and they looked same-same to me. It was at this point that I wondered if something was unusual about the bunk that they wanted me to sleep in, as if, Dan, had put them up to it.

The first guy then said, "Look man, you can sleep in that bunk if you want to, but it hasn't been vacuum up yet today.

I looked again at the bunk and sure enough, there was dirt in the folds of the sheet. There was so much dirt there that small children could play with their Match Box cars and make little roads from the layer of dirt on the sheets.

Okay then, no sweat. I thanked them and moved into the bunk beside the dust bowl bed. So for now, all I needed was one good night's sleep to sober up before I could head home to the real world.

No sooner than after my bed was made with fresh sheets provided by my new drinking buddies, I was face down in my pillow and sound asleep.

I was not asleep all that long, or it might have been a few hours, don't know for sure, I was tapped on my shoulder and asked, "You have a watch to stand the midnight watch. Get up. You D'Antonio?"

Now, what a dumb-ass way to ask those questions. What kind of idiot would ask such a thing? Shouldn't it have been something like, "Are you D'Antonio?" Then say, "Get up," and that could be followed by, "You have a midnight watch to stand." But no, and to top it all off, I wasn't D'Antonio, I didn't have to get up and I didn't have a watch to stand.

I was not even going to turn over and answer this guy face to face. I've seen enough idiots in my life and no need to see another one. I answered him sharply with, "You got the wrong guy. Now go away, you bother me."

He didn't respond right away and the silence was uncomfortable. Still, I made no effort to turn his way and pretended as if I had fallen back to sleep.

"You meant to say, 'Now go away, you bother me . . . sir,'" he finally spoke, and I knew that I was in trouble. Of course, my trouble happened to be with an officer.

I didn't have a choice now of what to do, so I turned around and mustered up the courage to apologize to him face to face. "Sorry sir. Didn't know that you were an officer, sir."

Before my eyes could adjust to his flashlight in my eyes, he said to me, "I know you. I've been hunting for you."

Oh crap, who was this officer? It could not be the Captain, because the Captain was much older and no way would the ship's captain be running around people for watches. It just could not be the same officer. The same one that had been looking for me from before. He was not the same one from the supply ship a few days ago. I saw him depart on a chopper earlier. With that, I came up with, "Do I know you sir?"

Before he could respond, the guy above my bunk, butted in, and said, "I am D'Antonio. Which watch do I have sir?"

As if I didn't exist, the officer stood up and answered, "You have the stern watch in fifteen minutes."

"Yes sir," he replied. "I'm going there now. Thank you sir."

For a moment, and only for a moment, I thought that maybe I was all but forgotten about. However, no way, no how, because this officer leaned back down and said, very close to my face, "I will talk with you later. I know where you are now."

Damn, he did return on that chopper earlier. I'd bet that he had been spending an awful lot of time trying to find me.

Next, he smartly stood up and marched away. He was apparently very proud of himself for finding me and believing that he knew where I was staying. Well, luck was on my side because I was out of here tomorrow and all he will find will be an empty rack.

So for now, I turned back over and made an effort to fall back to sleep, convinced that I was a winner over this situation. However, the longer I lie there, the more I felt that I must get up and move to another location. There was no telling exactly when he would be back to rip me apart. You know, the way that officers seemed to enjoy ripping us enlisted guys apart. Anyway, with that thought, I packed up the few things that I had, folded up my bedding, and headed towards another berthing compartment to search for an open bunk.

In the next compartment, there was Dan talking with a few guys and it looked as if he was taking up a collection. Everyone, about five guys, were giving him something. Before I could say anything, Dan looked at me and asked, "Your girlfriend's picture. Do you have a photo of your girlfriend?"

Guessing that this was a scam, I was slow to respond. Then, the one guy closest to me asked, "How about a picture of your sister? You got a sister, right?"

"For what," was the only thing that I could come up with thinking that Dan was probably making up a Mail Order Bride catalog or something same-same.

Dan came back with, "It's for Butch here."

"Yeah man, cough up one of your pictures for Butch," everyone responded in as if this was an order.

Still, with my ever convincing, deer-in-the-headlights look, I responded with, "Okay." Now that was not a, 'for sure,' okay, I just wanted to show that I was in with what ever they were doing, but not totally.

Dan, once again stepped up and explained, "My man Butch here got a Dear John letter from his woman, Karen."

"Okay?"

Taking a big breath as if this was going to be a long lesson for me, Dan continued, "Here, in The-Nam, when a guy gets a Dear John letter, we have a standard response."

"Okay?" Was this another one of those joke form letters to send home, I questioned myself?

"We gather up a collection of as many pictures of girls as we can," Dan explained, as everyone chimed in with total agreement. In fact, it almost seemed like a football rally where the entire town showed up with one purpose, kill the other team, or kill this Karen girl.

"Okay?"

"Then we mail off all the pictures to this bitch Karen, that sent in this here Dear John letter," Dan concluded, with everyone giving each other the high five as this one colored guy made an attempt to show those who tried to do that hand-shake thing, how it was done.

In addition, and for a moment, everyone seemed to have put too much focus on the hand-shaking thing with that black guy before Dan piped up and said, "Gentlemen. We have a mission to complete."

Well, that got everyone back to the subject at hand, as I stood there not completely understanding what everyone was doing and unable to submit a picture for this soon to be completed mission.

Dan, as always, noticed my continued confused look and said, "Along with the dozen or so pictures, Butch here will add in a little note that will say something to the effect, 'Sorry that you want to break up. Because I can't remember which one you are, please select your picture from the pile, and mail the rest back.'"

Now that was cool and very clever. With everyone there, I got in with all the high-fivin', and for a moment, I was everyone's friend. Everyone's friend until I was unable to cough up a picture for Butch's collection. And with that, any additional high-fives from me would go unanswered.

"What else should I say in my letter," Butch asked the group.

Dan jumped right in, and like this was the norm, everyone looked his way awaiting his words of wisdom. Dan said, "Say something like, 'are you the one that is so ugly that when a dog humps your leg, he keeps his eyes closed?'"

Well, that was funny as the high-fives went to everyone around me. Okay then, I could add something to this crew. I was a funny guy back home and I could be a funny guy here with these guys. Hell, the one that was getting all the attention just got dumped by his girlfriend. How cool could he be? With stupid boldness, I suggested, "How about telling her that you only wanted to date virgins because you can not stand any criticism?"

For that suggestion, my only response from them was somewhat cold. As if this was a postcard from hell, or a photograph from National Geographic, I got a frozen moment in time of a bunch of guys giving me the deer-in-the-headlights look.

Quickly, I responded before any of them could, "Sorry. That made a good punch line in a joke that I heard yesterday. Apparently not for this situation or this crowd."

"Apparently not," answered Butch, and again, with high-fives going on all around me again.

The one guy standing beside Butch, asked, "Didn't you say that she had huge tits that hung down to her waist? Didn't you also say that her bra size was a 48 long?"

"Yeah, when she lies on her back, they fall down to her sides and with her arms sticking straight out, you'd think that she was making an angel in the snow."

Oh my God, what a visual. Dan spoke up and said, "Ask her then, if she's the one that has her belly button between her nipples."

High-fives made their way around the group and because the focus had not been on me, I moved my right hand up above my head expecting someone, anyone to return my high-five. Well, when no one did, I did the next best thing; I slid my hand across the top of my head to smooth out my hair as if that was what I wanted to do all along.

The guy next to me, his name was Malcolm, he piped up and questioned, "Ask her if she would like to have her name removed from the walls in the head."

I turned to this guy, wanting to join in, and asked, "Did you add to the collection a photo of your girlfriend."

"No you ass hole, I only have one photo of my wife, Sharlene, and that ain't going no where man."

Okay, I think I will just ease myself to the other side of the room before this guy gets even madder at me. Crap, I just never, ever, fit in.

"Sometimes I just call her Shar. What you think about that," he asked me.

"Shit man, I don't know. I would think that if Shar was my wife and that I only had one photo of her, that I would not send it in either."

"You be right, give me five," he asked with a huge smile on his face.

Okay now, I was fitting in. We did the high-five and with my new friend, I didn't move over to the other side of the room.

Butch acknowledged what Malcolm had said and with a huge smile on his face, as if he just had the greatest come-back to this

Dear John letter of his, announced, "Tonight I will mail this out, along with the comments about her tits and all the pictures."

High-fives started up again and I had no desire to try to join in this time. Then, as I should have expected, the guy to my right was going to give me the high-five and so was the guy to my left. Because I was too slow to respond, they both ignored me. This was followed by high-five's with my face only inches from their hands. Naturally, the connection created a loud smacking noise that caused my eyes to blink.

Then, before I could say something to Dan about finding a place to sleep for the night, he and Butch were off to find more pictures. I believe that Dan said something about getting some pictures of Louie-Louie for this collection along with some colored girls. Wow, this episode of military life could be a book all buy itself.

As everyone dispersed, I was unable to make it passed these guys in time to catch up with them. Anyway, for now, I was alone with a single mission to find a place to sleep tonight. Because I was unable to contribute to this worthy cause, I figured it best that I find another compartment to sleep and without any fanfare, I simply exited the way I came in.

Moments later, I found what I was looking for, an empty bunk with a lot of distance from my last known location. In no time at all, I was sound asleep and dreaming about going home.

Just as before, I was tapped on my shoulder and asked, "You have a watch to stand. The 0200 bow watch. Get up. You Stewart?"

How many dumb-ass people are there on this ship? Here was another idiot asking me the same thing as the last guy. I was not going to go over the part about how it should have been asked in a more proper order, but I was going to assume that this person was an officer and that I would answer him accordingly.

"I am not Stewart. You have the wrong bunk, sir," I said without turning over to face him.

There was silence and the only thing happening was that he kept shining his flashlight in my face trying to see who I was. I laid still like a possum and hoped that he would just go away and wake someone else, hell, anyone else and leave me alone.

Well, the silence and flashlight in my face continued a bit longer, before he spoke up and said, "I know you."

Oh crap, this officer was the very same officer from a little earlier. I was sure of it and I knew that I was in real trouble now. Yet, before I responded, I must think same-same about what Dan would do in a situation like this. Then it came to me, I said, "Sir. Sorry sir, but I don't know you, sir."

He stood back a bit and questioned, "Didn't you and I just speak at the last change of watch over in the R2 berthing compartment?"

"Sir, no sir. I've been here most of the night, sir," I said, realizing that I was lying to an officer, but not completely. I have been here, most of the night.

He was now giving me the deer-in-the-headlights look and I might as well see how much I could get away with. I said, "Sir, I have a very common, everyday kind of face. I am always getting mistaken for someone else."

Still, I was getting a stare from him as if I just might be getting away with this. Not using common sense, but enjoying the moment, I continued with, "Sir. If you have me pegged for someone that's in trouble, well, I'm not him. However, sir, if you owe this guy some money, then I am your man."

I thought that was funny and I got a few chuckles from the other guys in their bunks who couldn't help but to overhear us.

Before he could respond, the guy above my bunk butted in and said, "I'm Steward. I know sir, I have the stern watch."

"Very well," replied the officer that I now had totally confused.

Steward quickly jumped from his bunk and was soon on his way to stand his watch. Now this left me here alone with the officer and neither one of us obviously knew what to say next.

With the officer not wanting to appear stupid, he apologized for waking me and followed Steward out. Before I could pant a sigh of relief, the officer returned and said, "I'll check back with you in the morning. There are a couple of issues that I would like to clear up with you and I don't have the time right now."

I could only respond with, "Yes sir."

Again, I knew that I must find another place to catch a few hours of sleep before I escaped from him again. Whatever, with that, I was up, packed, and looking for another place to sleep. In my search for an empty bunk, I made my way through the crew's eating area and saw Billy-Bob writing a letter.

"Mr. Charles. How you doing my man?"

"Fine, Billy-Bob. Who you writing to?" I asked, because I did not think that he knew how to write and if he did, I did not think that he would have known anyone that could read.

"My girl back home. Her name is Bunn," he answered most proud of himself.

"Bunn."

"Yeah man. Bunn, and she be hot. Know what I mean," he expressed himself with a big smile along with his head bobbing north and south.

Now I was confused, and with that, I asked him, "Didn't you buy a wife over here once before?"

"Hell yeah. But I had to give her back, don't you know," he reminded me.

"But what about this girl, Bunnie?"

With a huff and a puff, he came back with, "Her name is Bunn. Bunn, not Bunnie. I just told you that my girl was hot and I did not say anything about her being no rabbit."

"Sorry. Didn't mean to offend you," I apologized quickly, so as not to have him pissed at me. I didn't feel like hiding from him and that other officer all in the same night.

"Like I said, my girl Bunn be hot. Blond hair," he said, and then paused as if he was thinking what else to add to her description.

He paused for a few more seconds before he came back with, "Blond hair. Hell man, that's all that I can remember."

I kept silent with his last remark and not attempted to question him more. Still looking confused, Billy-Bob added,

"Look. It's just fine with me that she's hot. I don't know the color of her eyes or even remember how tall she is or what she weighs. She's just hot and that's all you need to know. Know what I mean?"

"Yeah, no sweat with me," was my response and hoped that it would end with that.

However, and as I should have assumed, Billy-Bob continued with, "Now. That's just one of my girls with the designation number of 1A."

He doesn't know the color of her eyes, her height, or her weight, but he had given her a draft status. "Don't you mean, A1?"

"No man. Listen up. Did I not just tell you that she was 1A? A1 is a damn steak sauce. I gave her 1A status because she's number one with me."

Oh well, I might as well ask. "So what does the 'A' stand for?"

"You see, I have a second number one girlfriend. She'd be my 1P girlfriend," he said, expressing himself, as if he was the richest and the smartest person in the world. He made it sound like everyone should have a number of girlfriends and a number scheme for them also.

Well, with me already into this conversation, I might as well see how it ends up. "So, stud man, tell me about this 1P of yours. Do you know the color of her eyes?"

Looking at me as if he was almost pissed for how I asked that question, Billy-Bob answered, "Not sure about her eyes either. The only time that we were together was in the back of my dad's car. It was usually dark and all that I can remember is that she has strawberry blond hair."

"Is she hot?"

"Oh yeah. I may be a little slow on the uptake according to some peoples standards, but I be only dating the hot girls," he explained, and for a retard, he most definitely had something going for him that was not very apparent.

"Does she have a name like Bunn," I asked, because I just had to find this out.

"Leslie. My girl, '1P,' Ms Leslie is tall and has long legs and long strawberry blond hair," he explained as if he was a proud new parent and was describing his first new born.

Damn, what does this guy have going for him? "So Stud Man Billy-Bob, which one is the hottest? Bunn or this Leslie girl?"

"Didn't I just tell you that I'd only date the hot girls," he explained, raising his voice up a little.

"But, but, but," I stuttered. "You have one as an 'A' and the other as a 'B.'"

"P," he snapped back at me. "My Leslie is a 'P,'"

"Okay, 'P.'"

"Hell man, that's right, 'P'. But they are both number ones. The 'A' and 'P' be there just to help me decide when they are in heat. My '1A' is the hottest in the AM. My Ms Leslie is the hottest in the PM. Know what I mean, don't you know."

"Heat, hot? Hot, heat?" I answered him and hoped that if I were lucky, he would not have a comeback.

Well, he did, as he added, "The girls that you date back state-side, they aren't hot?"

Great, now I was in competition with a retard about my dating habits back home. "Well yeah, they are hot. Not all of them, but most are."

"So, when you are ready for a slam-bam, thank you mam, it doesn't matter if it goes better for you in the AM or PM?"

This conversation was giving me a headache, as I had had about enough of this as I could stand. Between listening to Dan and his words of wisdom, sending off a dozen photos of pretend girlfriends, and now listening to Billy-Bob, the Stud man of both the AM and PM period, I must get myself out of here. And, all the while trying to avoid the ship's captain and an officer bent on getting even with me.

"Cool," was the only response that came to mind and I really, really did not want to ask or find out anything about the AM or PM details.

"Have a seat," he suggested, as he pointed to the open seat in front of him.

Now what do I do? If I do not take a seat, then he might get upset with me, and that was not good. If I take a seat and stay, that one officer may come by and see me, and that was not very good. But wait, I was tired and I want to get some sleep. I should do just that, find a bunk, and get some rest. Tomorrow may prove to be a long day like this is becoming a long night.

"Sorry Billy-Bob, I need to find a place to catch some sleep," I explained, trying to show that I was saddened that I could not join him.

Billy-Bob, showing me a facial expression heavy with thought, tells me, "Try the new Tango boat, port side. Everything's new and it hasn't been assigned a crew yet."

Sounds good to me, I thought. I'll be off the ship and out of site. "Thanks Billy-Bob. Later," I answered, and with this new piece of information, I was on my way for an un-disturbed night's sleep.

Billy-Bob yelled, "Tango 220."

I returned his yell with one of my own, "Thanks. 220. Got it."

Finding my way topside without running into that officer was not an issue. However, finding Tango boat 202 wasn't as easy. Tango boat 202 was not port side, but was tied up on the starboard side on the aft pontoon. I made my way down there and for a new boat; it didn't look all that new to me. Well, maybe it had a difficult delivery or it was just new to the unit and not new, as in brand new-new. Whatever, and not a big deal and surely nothing to sweat over, I simply made my way onboard, made myself comfortable after I found an unoccupied bunk. After a few seconds, I was soon sound asleep.

After, I think, an hour our two, I heard a loud Boom!

I didn't know what that was but it was sure loud and very close. "Damn, damn, damn," I said loudly to myself thinking that no one was nearby.

"And who are you," came a voice out of the darkness. At least it was an American sounding voice and not the VC.

I didn't answer right away, because I wanted to see to whom I was speaking. I looked up and in the darkness, I could see some big guy holding out his 45 and both of them were focused on little oh me. Before I could answer, he asked, "What are you doing here?"

Believing that I was on the wrong boat, I came back and answered, "Isn't this Tango boat 202?"

"Yep," came the reply and because he didn't tack on the 'sir' part, I assumed that he was not an officer.

"I thought this was a new boat that didn't have a crew assigned to it. I was using it to catch up on sleep," I said as I got up to face this guy and hoped that he would lower his 45.

"This is not a new boat. Now," he added after giving this some thought, "Tango 220 is the new boat around here and she's on the other side of this ship and it's still tied up. And it's without a crew."

Damn, I'm on the wrong boat. "Sorry about that. Can you let me off?"

"No," was the reply.

"Okay. When can you let me off," I asked, not sure if this guy was teasing me or not. No need to tick him off and then end up here as a part of his crew.

"We're on Bid Patrol for the next four hours and you can get off when we have finished."

I could only look at him and express approval because he was in charge and I was here until his watch was over. With that, I laid back down and figured that I could resume my sleep. However, before I could get all the way down and under my blanket, he instructed, "No way man. You're here and you're going to pull your weight like everybody else onboard."

With that, I got myself back up and asked, "What would you like me to do?"

"Make your way to the stern, you can man the concussion grenade station," he instructed as he pointed in the direction he wanted me to go.

So, for the next four hours, there I was, standing the stern watch, pulling grenade pins and throwing them in the water as I prayed that we didn't hit a mine, or worked ourselves into a firefight. I just wanted to go home.

Our assignment was to patrol around something with YRBM painted on the bow. Not sure what kind of ship this was, but there was a lot of helicopter coming and a going. Hell, with that much activity, you would think that it could patrol itself. You know, when a chopper pilot was landing or taking off, have them look around for the VC and knock off this Bid Patrol stuff.

While making one of our many patrol rounds, around the YRBM, a towboat passed us by and was towing a large barge that was set up as a fort. This portable fort, thing-of-a-gig, was going somewhere for placement as an ambush or something. Other than that passing us by, this was an uneventful evening.

Hours later, and before the storm hit us, we tied up along side the aft pontoon as we had completed our Bid Patrol. I was happy, tired, and most hungry. With little delay, I worked my way to the chow hall for the standard egg cube, bacon, and home fries with a warm bowl of canned milk.

My breakfast was rather good, but would have been wonderful if they would have served up some grits. I'll just make it a point for when I get home to visit Howard Johnson, Bob's Big Boy, or my favorite breakfast place, my Mom's kitchen table. Now when she cooks, she'll make a large pot of grits for my brothers, my one little sister, and me. And between us, we have never left anything for her to throw away.

After a thankfully, uneventful breakfast, I made my way topside to work on my plans to get home, I heard my name over the 1-MC. "Seaman Edwards. Report to the Ship's Office."

Well, no such luck that there are two Seaman Edwards onboard, so I might as well stop by and see what's up. Then again, maybe I shouldn't go. What if my orders have been changed and I was not going anywhere? Then again, there was the possibility that I was getting another promotion with a new medal or two. Maybe you are not allowed to be a Seaman and wounded at the same time. I remembered that you had to be at the pay grade of Seaman or higher just to be in a war zone.

Anyway, I best go and see what's up. No need to have them send the marines out to drag me back. So, with little delay, I found myself at the Ship's Office.

I walked in and announced to the guy at the first desk, "I'm Seaman Edwards. Someone here wanted to see me?"

He looked confused and yelled to the guy behind him. "You looking for Edwards?"

"No. Not me," he answered and he did not even bother to look up. With his head still down, he yelled to the guy behind him, "You looking for Edwards?"

"Yes," then came the response. "Come on back and take a seat Edwards."

"Yes sir," I smartly answered seeing from here that he was an officer, the same officer that I had spoken with yesterday. At least I was off to a good start with remembering to 'sir' him.

"Be with you in a minute," the officer assured me as he completed whatever it was that he was doing.

A minute later, he pulled out a small box along with a certificate that looked military and official like. He explained, "We, as in you and I, have been authorized to wear the PUC for Extraordinary Heroism. As you can see, it was signed by the President of the United States and our Commander in chief, Richard Milhous Nixon."

He passed the ribbon and certificate along with something to sign. "Sign here Seaman."

I didn't know what to say and I figured that I could read the certificate later. For now, I just wanted to get off this ship and head home before they decided to keep me. I signed the form and before I could retrieve my ribbon and certificate, it was snapped away from my reach.

He explained his actions with, "Because you don't have your records with you, these items will be mailed out to catch up with your records. Besides, we only have a few medals and certificates available for the crew of over 200 personnel."

Without keeping my mouth shut and just accepting the situation, I asked, "Can't I just have my ribbon for now?"

Well, you would have thought that I was trying to borrow a thousand dollars from a poor man. The look that he was giving me would make water boil.

"And tell me, Seaman, which uniform would you want to wear your ribbons on?" He asked, knowing full well that I didn't have an acceptable answer for him or a uniform to wear it on.

Knowing when to leave, I stood up and thanked him for what he did. Without waiting for permission to leave, I smartly turned and left the Ship's Office hoping that I would never be back here again.

Outside, I wanted to tell someone, anyone of my cool news that I'd just received another medal. For today, I was starting out with a hangover, a new medal, along with a sore finger from pulling grenade pins for four hours. However, I still wanted to go home and my plan for now was to get over to the Behawah and make a call home. From there, I could always find a ride to Tan San Nut on one of the many choppers that lands and takes off from her flight deck all day long.

Anyway, with little delay and with a huge smile on my face, because I now have an itinerary, I worked my way down to the forward pontoon and started asking for a ride to the Behawah.

Luck was going my way today because the first crewmember of an Alpha boat that I asked was doing just that, heading to the Behawah. This crewmember explained to me that they had just one thing to do first and that would get there right after that and that I was more than welcome to join them.

I did not really care what it was that they had to do first; I just wanted to be on my way and off the USS SUMMIT. I thanked him, jumped onboard, made myself comfortable, and sat back to take in a little sun with the time that I had to kill for the ride over to the Behawah.

In a matter of minutes, we were freed from the pontoon and on our way. And, in a manner of a few minutes more, I will be making a phone call home. With those thoughts, I was happy until I looked back at the USS SUMMIT, and for a moment, I was sad. I was sad until I turned around forward and saw that we were headed directly at the Behawah. My short life here on the muddy rivers of South Vietnam for me was almost over. All we had to do was to find a place to dock as that might be a problem with all the Stab boats and crew that were tied up alongside the Behawah, but that was not my problem as I was only a passenger, so for now, I was just going to take in a little sun.

Wow, the sun really felt good beaming down on me. Yet, I knew that this wasn't going to take very long, so I should enjoy what little time I had until we tied up. However, after tanning for a little while longer than expected, I looked up and noticed that we had almost passed the ship. I was about to ask the crewmen near me about our status, when he threw a concussion grenade in the river, which was followed by two quick blasts from his shotgun.

Now, there was nothing new about anyone blasting away at debris in the river, especially with a concussion grenade and shotgun, but couldn't we just work our way towards the pontoon so I could get off first? Hell, I had a telephone call to make.

Then it dawned on me. I was on a Bid Patrol and I would be on this Bid Patrol for the next four hours. Damn, damn, damn. It was 'this' that was the one thing that they had to do first. Okay, I decided that I would just sit back and enjoy the sun for a few more hours. However, before I could work up a good sweat, the Boat Captain came over and told, I meant ordered, me to take the bow watch and to throw a few concussion grenades in the river every five minutes or so. Anyway, here I was, again, with four hours of grenade pin pulling which was not a pleasant way to spend the morning.

# Chapter 6

With my Bid patrol over and sporting a new blister on my second finger from my second of a four-hour duty of pin pulling, I jumped the last few feet onto the pontoon. I wanted off that Alpha boat as quickly as possible. No need to have them change their minds and then decide, at the last minute, do a second watch.

Anyway, knowing where I was going, I made my way up to the radio shack and it was same-same as before. It looked like the same-same guys were here that were here the last time I was with Dan. I completed my Telephone Request chit, turned it in, and took a seat. In fact, I had the same-same seat as before.

Five minutes went by and the guy behind the desk called out the name Ben. Ben somebody, I did not get the last name. Anyway, one guy shot up like a bullet and raced over to take a seat at the desk. Now this guy, Ben, whatever his last name was, looked very familiar to me. I was not sure from where, but he looked familiar just the same. Then again, everyone over here dressed alike anyway so sometimes, it was hard to tell.

I heard Ben explain to the radio operator, "I got to speak to my wife. I think she hates me. Put me through now, please."

The guy behind the desk ignored his request completely and moved on with his instructions, "When you finish talking say, 'over' and flip this switch."

"Okay, okay, okay. I got it. Make the call," Ben said, showing no manners. In fact, he was so rude to the radio operator that Ben could have been an officer.

"Listen up, man. I must give you these instructions. That's SOP and all that," the radio operator explained to an impatient Ben somebody. "Everybody gets instructions. You're in the Navy my man. Either you give instructions or you follow instructions. Dig it?"

Ben held his head down a little as if rethinking his rude attitude. "Sorry man. I just have to talk to my wife. You just don't understand."

"I don't need to understand your personal problems," the operator explained as he added, "I just need to give you instructions."

"Sorry," replied Ben.

As if the apology meant nothing to him, the radio operator continued his instructions with, "When you hear them say, 'over,' flip the switch. Then wait a second or two before you respond. Got it?"

"Yeah, no sweat. Got it. I've been here before," Ben answered, as if getting these instructions all over again was a waste of his time and that would cut into his time with his wife that was apparent to be most important to him.

The instructions continued, "You are not to mention where you are, what ship you are calling from and don't mention anyone's full name or rank."

"No problem," Ben responded, as he squirmed around some in his seat and doing everything in his power not to say anything rude that might cause his call not to be put through.

"No unit ID's, don't mention your full name and rank. And don't be a smart-ass and try and use code. If I detect anything that resembles code, I will 'over and out' your ass right out of here. Got it?"

"I said no problem already," he answered, a little louder this time and then realizing that he just might lose his turn if he kept his attitude up. "Sorry," he added.

From what I could tell, things were not going well for this guy Ben what's his name, and he just had to speak with his wife.

Out of the large speaker behind the desk, blared, "This is KAFW0799. Go ahead, over."

"Hello Eva baby. This is Benny Boy. How's my girl doing? Over."

The switch flipped and then silence.

The radio operator snapped and said, "Cool it. This is my radio. I'll tell you when to start talking."

"Sorry. I just got a little excited. Sorry," Ben responded apologetically.

His squirming increased as this guy Ben, sat there waiting to speak to Eva. Then it hit me, I clearly remember this guy now. He's the one whose wife didn't like the idea that a bunch of us guys were listening in on their intimate conversation that last time I was here. Oh well, I'll get to see how it goes this time.

After what must have appeared to be a lifetime for Ben, the speaker squelched with, "Is this you, Ben?"

Again, silence and then static. Apparently, the radio operator must have clicked the switch, because the static stopped and Ben exploded with, "Honey. I love you. For your next birthday, I'll get you an even bigger fan over our bed. I got us a box of those glow in the dark rubbers that you asked me to get. I got your favorite colors, banana yellow, and the one with the red fire balls on the tip. I even got us a can of that spray that smells like cotton candy. Can't wait to see you. Can't wait to party with you with all this stuff. Over."

Now this conversation had everyone up and turned in his direction as if he had these items out for display.

Silence, then a little static before a response of, "This is your mother-in-law. There ain't no party here. Over and out loser."

Wow, that was it? The line went dead and that was the end of Ben's telephone call for today. Life must be a real bitch when your own wife won't talk to you. An even bigger deal when your mother-in-law has the power to hang up on you and your free, long-distance telephone call. Poor Ben may be in a combat zone over here, but there was a real war going on at his house back home. I imagined that he hated his mother-in-law right now more that he did the VC.

Well, he did the only thing he could do. He requested to make a second call and that was declined. Ben then simply got up and left the room. Now there goes a guy that would volunteer for a suicide mission or at the very least, walk point.

After his sad departure, everyone went back to his naps as if nothing happened. Before I could get into a sound sleep, "Edwards. Is there an Edwards here?"

Lickety split; I jumped out of my seat, flew over to the chair, and waited for my instructions. However, instead of instructions, I was told that no one answered at the number I requested and there would not be a second attempt anytime today. Yet, I was informed that I was welcome to return tomorrow and submit another request chit.

I must have looked like a little kid that had lost his lunch money, as I was about to cry. I thanked him for trying and sadly made my way out. I could not think of what was worse. Having a call not go through, or having it go through and being hung-up on. Knowing my parents the way I did, they would never have hung-up on me. No matter how mad they were at me and there were times that I got them really mad.

Oh well, for now, it was time to head on home. I could always call my parents from the airport and tell them to, 'come and get me.' Now that would be a good telephone call.

Finding the flight deck on this ship was a non-sweatable situation. Hell, you just find a ladder or stairwell and head up until you see sky and a large flat area with a big circle painted in the middle.

The flight deck was just as it was the last time I was here. About a dozen or so guys were spread out over the flight deck tanning away. Everyone had a radio, but unlike being down the beach at Ocean City, Maryland, all the radios here were tuned to the same-same station. It wasn't as if we had many choices to pick from, you know what I mean. However, there was this one guy near by who had his portable 8-track player blasting away. The only tape that he apparently had was a tape by Iron Butterfly, and it was very loud.

About the only place that I could sit down and wait for the next flight out, was off to one side with a couple of other guys that were sitting in the shade apparently waiting for a flight out also. I grabbed the last spot that had shade and as with most meetings of guys over here, we all introduced ourselves and went into a little detail as to where we were from and where we were going.

When it was my turn, I explained how I was heading home and about how I was wounded. That seemed to spark some interest with these guys. Because I was doing most of the talking, I just kept on talking. I started to brag about my trips to Cam-Ranh-Bay and how I even had orders ordering me not to make any layovers there. Naturally, I had to add in the part about the girls and my little visit to the beach. I made it a point to cover the birthday party at Big-Ass Bertha-Butt's place and our escape from certain death. I covered the different bar stories that I had and went into details about Juicy-Lucy. Well, it was at this point that everyone seemed to believe that I was full of it and that they had heard about enough of my adventures with women.

I toned down what I was telling everyone as they started to talk and interject their adventures. I did pick up that their stories were nowhere close to mine. It appeared to me that most of them had been here for a year now and that they had never left the ship. In a way, for my short time here, I had covered a lot of territory and had many stories to tell. Hell, I might even write a book about all these stories of mine.

The timing of the next chopper to land was perfect because we had covered about all that we were going to cover at this sitting. As before, we were chased off the flight deck along with everyone else as the chopper touched down without landing on anyone. I was the first to make my way to the chopper and I asked the crewmen, "Saigon, Tan San Nut?"

He responded by shaking his head up and down and I assumed this to be a yes. With that little piece of good news out of the way, I was the first onboard and had my pick of seats. Naturally, I wanted a window, I meant, door seat because I wanted to take in my last view of this part of the world. I felt sorry for the guys that got in second, third, and fourth, because they were crammed into a very small space without a view. Damn I thought. I did good this time. I was going home and I have a first class seat.

A few more guys did get onboard even after I assumed that we had a full load. This chopper had landing skids and not wheels and with that information, I knew that we were not going to get a running start. These pilots knew what they were doing and it we were too heavy, they would throw a couple of people off. I was thinking about my business class in high school on the stocking inventory, in that if guys were going to be kicked off, that it would be last on, first off and not first on, first off.

The power increased and we lifted off about one foot when we landed quite hard back down on the chopper pad. I noticed as the crewmember got off and walked around the aircraft. The way we took off and landed so hard, I would have thought that we were still tied down to the deck. Well, we weren't and to my misfortune, the crewmember pointed and signaled me out as someone that had to exit the aircraft. Damn, damn, damn. I was the odd man out.

As I was getting off, I was about to say something to the effect that I had just recently received a Purple Heart and that I was being sent home to recover from my injuries. However, I decided against it. I was not hurt all that bad to receive any special treatment.

It only took a second and the chopper was up-up and away without me. My ride to Saigon was gone, shit. As I started to feel bad for myself, I could see another chopper coming in. It didn't take long to land and soon I was onboard that chopper for a ride to Saigon, and it was not packed with people and cargo. In fact, it was just the door gunner and me. The only problem was that in my excitement to get onboard, I forgot to ask the door gunner where we were going. Oh well, it just might be a new place for me.

We took off slow and didn't gain altitude very fast which seemed rather odd, but it was cool because we flew right over the SUMMIT and right there on the fantail was Dan looking up at me. Well, not at me, but at the chopper. Yet, he did see that it was me and he waved. That was somewhat exciting to be recognized and I waved back. Remarkably, at the same time, we gave each other the peace sign. It was a cool feeling to have seen him for one last time and a sad feeling, for seeing him, for one last time.

I'd bet that he'd be a good friend to have back home. A good friend, not an, 'every-day' kind of friend. The kind of friend that would do more than just show up for a party, but to stay behind and help clean up. Not a friend to hear about your problems, but a friend to help solve them, or at very least, offer some sincere suggestions. An 'every-day' friend can only wonder about your love life, a real friend can blackmail with it. An 'every-day' friend will drop you as a friend after an argument, but a real friend will call you later and try to work the issue out.

Than again, it really does not matter, it don't mean nothin', as I will never see him again. For now, I'll just sit back and enjoy my, hopefully, last chopper ride. After a few minutes of looking at all the browns and greens, I must have fallen into a little nap.

# Chapter 7

Once again, I was awakened with a jolt. Getting up and over here was not easy. Not as easy as my Mom yelling at me to get up for school. It was either a jolt, someone tapping me on the shoulder, or someone screaming in my ear, "Reveille, reveille, all hands reveille. Sweepers man your brooms. The smoking lamp is lit. All hands must turn too. Reveille, reveille." I never did find that damn smoking lamp. Maybe they'll have one at my next assignment.

Okay, back to my jolted wakeup call. We had landed at some air force base and I was sure about that because I was not surrounded by water. As I looked around a little more, I noticed that we were parked in a row of about a dozen other choppers.

I stepped out and the first thing that I saw was a sign stating, 'Welcome to Cam-Ranh-Bay.' Oh crap, I must find a way out of here. It would be my luck that someone would check my orders and probably take away one of my stripes. With my luck, they might even take away two stripes. Besides, and because I was headed back to the states, then there would be no reason to keep me a Seaman. They might even take away a medal or two. Anyway, for now, I would just find the next chopper out of here. I was lucky enough be standing in the middle of an airport and finding a ride out of here should be simple enough.

With that in mind, I would just mosey on down to the next chopper that had a crew and started asking for a ride to Saigon.

As my luck would have it, I had caught up with the chopper that I was kicked off earlier and as I passed everyone that had gotten off, a few of the guys were taunting me with, "Ladies man. What are you doing in Cam-Ranh-Bay? Aren't you afraid that you'll get into trouble for being here or that you'll meet up with too many women for you to handle?"

These comments got everyone laughing, laughing at me. I figured, screw them. What I said to them earlier was true and that they were just jealous.

"Okay," I said aloud to myself. "I'm in Cam-Ranh-Bay and Cam-Ranh-Bay is a cool place to be. This may be my last time here and what the hell, I might as well stay."

With my thinking like that, I should find a place to stay the night and work on getting to Saigon by tomorrow. I've been to this town before and I know my way around almost as well as I did in my hometown of Baltimore. Hell, Dan or no Dan, how hard could this be? As long as I do not check into any military installations that will need a copy of my orders, I should be okay, and no one would know nothin anyway.

First item, I would just give that unfriendly little group a little head start before I catch a bus ride to town. If I remembered correctly, the bus stop was near the main gate and that was my second objective. Sure enough, at the main gate there was a bus just sitting there as if it was waiting on me. Then I thought, I best be careful that I don't mess up this simple task. It might be going downtown and maybe not. There was also the possibility that it was broken down. Nah, it'll just be an enjoyable ride into town.

I made my way to the bus and asked the driver, a US Army private, if his bus was heading downtown. I should have figured that he wasn't going to be kind to me because he just shouted back at me as if I was a child, and said with meanness in his eyes, "Now what do you think?"

Well, I looked at him and before I could rephrase my question, he snapped back, "This is not the bus heading to a shopping mall nor is this the bus that will be heading to a football game. This is not the bus for the football team or for the school band. This is not the bus heading to Cleveland and all points west. And, this is not the bus that takes you to your car at the airport parking lot,"

After a pause to catch his breath, he added, "And one more thing. This is not the bus that will take little old ladies with their dead husband's retirement payments to Atlantic City to gamble with."

Great. I found a bus driver that did not enjoy his assignment. Maybe he could change duties with the guys that handed out the POD's. And anyway, so much for thinking that this was going to be fun or an exciting ride to town.

I could only return a look of confusion to this driver and he had not answered me on where he was heading, only that he was not heading every place else. I thought up something and came back with, "Okay, that be cool. So you are heading downtown?"

He answered me a little more civil this time with, "Ain't that what I just said?"

This was a time for me to accept him for what he was, keep my silence, board the bus, and sit in the back. I remembered not to sit next to a window, but I sat in the back of the bus just the same. Besides, I would like some distance from Mr. Happy Driver in case someone else that he should snap at doesn't appreciate him and use him for target practice.

Just after I took my seat, another person, an Army Private, asked the driver the same question as I did. "Are you driving downtown?"

"Yes we are, my man. Step on board, the ride is free," the driver explained, in a very kind and civil manner. Damn, it wasn't as if I forgot to say please or anything. Whatever, I must let that go.

A guy sitting across from me that was already on the bus, said, "Don't sweat it, man. That driver always gives you Navy guys a load of shit. I heard him say that all swabbies are lost when there're on dry ground."

I came back and said, "I thought that he had a problem and that it wasn't just with me. Thanks."

The guy beside him, another Army guy, said, "I see that you have been in-country for a while. This can't be your first trip to Cam-Ranh-Bay.

"No. This is my third time here in Cam-Ranh-Bay," I came back boasting, as if I truly knew what I was doing and where I was going.

Before we could continue with our conversation, the bus leaped forward as if this was the first time our driver had driven a stick shift. It knocked everyone awake that was sleeping and stopped all the conversations that were going on. Everyone onboard kept his eye on the driver expecting him to crash into something before he shifted into second gear. However, our drive was uneventful, rocky every time he shifted gears, but uneventful and we were soon downtown.

I stepped off the bus in anticipation of finding a hotel because this was the stop where I thought I had gotten off before with Dan. I was looking for the hotel that we stayed in before. Without any trouble, I did find the same hotel with the same old man behind the counter.

Even the Bellhop girls were same-same and offered to take my bag upstairs to my room. I only had my one little bag with me and I could handle that by myself, thank you very much.

It must have been a habit with them. You know, someone checks-in, you ask to carry their bags, and then work on some extra items that will earn you a good tip. Naturally, I declined their help and found my way to my room alone. Once inside, I hid my one bag of all my worldly things behind the tub and headed out for a little walk around town.

Next door to my fine, five star hotel, was a small market. It had the same smells and look as the market that I visited with Dan a few weeks ago. Also, it had the same head count in that there were mostly women and children working there. It was my understanding that most of the men in this little country were in the military and off fighting the war.

The first sales lady I came up to was selling snakes. She had a whole bucket just full of dead snakes and a second bucket with live snakes. Well, I didn't have a need or desire to purchase any snakes today. Then again, I could always send one home to my little sister.

"Move Joe. You move now," someone said behind me as I was bumped from behind. I turned to see what the problem was when to my surprise, there was a little old man pushing a cart full of dead pigs.

There were four pigs in his cart, two white, and two black pigs and immediately, I moved out of his way. Just as the cart moved passed me, the snake lady came over and held up a live snake to my face. She repeated, "Joe. You buy snake. You buy snake now."

I took a step back to get her snake out of my face and in the process, I fell back over the pig cart and down I go. It was a little embarrassing falling down, but it got worse, because one of the pigs fell on me. A little black pig, a dead little black pig and for such a little pig, that damn thing was heavy.

Okay, now I have this little old man yelling at me because I knocked over his, cart and the snake lady is still trying to sell me a snake. So for now, I could only muster up enough to get up, brush myself off, hand the old guy his pig back as I told the snake lady, "No thank you."

Outside I go and I did not look back. I had had enough of people yelling at me today and I was just going to take a little walk. I walked and walked and walked and I was very tired and was about to head back when above all the traffic noise, I could clearly hear someone yelling, "Charles! Charles! Over here."

Great, my assumption now was that the snake lady and pig man knew my name. The snake lady was still trying to sell me a snake and the pig man wanted me to pay for his damaged, dead pig. Because of that thinking, I chose to ignore them yelling at me.

Their yelling continued and it was still loud enough that it was easily heard above all the traffic noise. Hearing them again yelling at me this time, they sounded American, "Charles! Charles!" Moreover, it was more than just one person doing the yelling, it was a bunch of girls yelling. American girls!

I looked all around but couldn't see anyone. Well, I couldn't see any women that knew me.

"Over here," shouted one of them again. "Over here, man."

Wanting to see what was going on and not miss out on anything, I started to checkout the other side of the street. This was not as easy as it might sound. There was a lot of traffic crossing here, where I was, and the other side of the street. Where I wanted to be. It would figure that right now, about a dozen or so large dump trucks would go zooming by blocking my view and kicking up a cloud of dust.

"Charles over here," shouted one of them, and it did appear that it was directed at me.

Damn, they were definitely American girls and there were three of them. If they were calling for me, then for sure, I was going to have a good day. After a closer look, I saw that it was Denise, Rose, and Betty. The girls I spent the day at the beach with a few weeks ago. Damn, I was a popular kind of guy here in this town. Cool. Now if those guys from earlier would walk by to see this, but they won't.

"All right," I said aloud, with a smile that spread from ear to ear. Betty noticed and she smiled back at me. Denise pointed towards her left, my right, indicating that they were headed that way. It appeared that they were in a hurry, but wanted me to try to catch up with them. I looked at all the traffic that I had to negotiate to cross over and I figured that I would never get across. However, for them, I would make the attempt. For them hell, I was going to cross over for me. At least if I was to be killed crossing the street, it would be for a good cause.

Denise yelled over again saying something like, "You best hurry up if you want to go with us."

I eagerly yelled back, "No sweat, can do, can do." Damn, and I had better do, I had better do this, and I had better do this right now.

I then thought to myself that maybe I couldn't do this. Plenty of traffic and there was no traffic light to hold up the traffic for me to cross. To top it off, I was in the middle of a very large city block and a long way from the nearest corner. Then like an idiot, I looked for a crosswalk or crossing guard as if I really expected to find one.

After a few more dump trucks roared between us, along with twenty or thirty bikes and two-dozen or so taxies, I lost sight of them. Damn, damn, damn, this was not fair. Not fair at all.

Then I heard a faint call of, "Charles, Charles. Over here. Let's go boy!"

They were already half way down the block and if I was going to make a move, I best do it now. Anyway, I did just that. I worked my way out one lane, then two. Because of the traffic and all the dodging that I had to do, I was turned around and had to back up one lane. After two dump trucks, three jeeps and an ox pulling a cart past me, I made it over two more lanes. I got spun around once more and backed up one more lane before I crossed back over two more. Only two more lanes to cross. Then, I was going to party with some women. Naturally, I believed that one of them might even like me a little. Didn't really care which one, I just wanted to catch up with them and this time, I had the time to kill and no competition with Dan. If Billy-Bob can enjoy an evening with a lady, so could I.

I was so busy daydreaming about all this that I lost focus on what I was doing and had to back up one more lane because of on coming traffic. As luck would have it, a military convoy passed right in front of me and took a long time for them to go by. Then with courage and stupidity, I darted across the last three lanes and made it onto the curb without a scratch. I grabbed a pole to hold me up as I caught my breath and as I thought to myself, 'Damn. That was more daring and dangerous than when I was in a firefight on Jersey Joe's boat a few weeks ago—even worse than being wounded.' But for right now, the only thing that could be worse for me would be for me to lose sight of the girls.'

So, let the excitement begin. I was going to party and partying I will be a doing. However, my excitement quickly vanished when I had forgotten which way they went. I had been turned around so many times and in all the excitement, I had lost track of where

I was and most importantly, which way they went. Damn, damn, damn, I was so confused that I was not sure if I had even made it across the street. I looked up and down, left and right, port and starboard, north and south, and even east and west with no luck.

All I could shout aloud was, "Screw me. Damn, damn, damn. Screw me."

As I was catching my breath and deciding which way I should go, even if it was a guess, a voice from behind me, asked, "Charles. Is that you?"

It almost sounded like a girl's voice. Not quite, but almost. I turned and saw nothing until I looked down and there, of all people, there was Louie-Louie. He gave me that little queer smile of his and said, "When you said, 'screw me, screw me,' I thought that you might have wanted some help with that activity."

I could only respond with, "What?"

His smile got wider and he came back with, "You want me to lend you a hand?"

Well, I was really ticked off now. Not only had I lost the girls, but also I was about to end up with this little fag. The only response that I could come up with was one that truly expressed my feeling. I looked into his little itty-bitty eyes, and said, "Screw you. Go away. Go away and get yourself a shoe shine or something."

That little turd spoke up and said, "You mean the kind that Dan takes everyone to?"

Not wanting to start a conversation with him, but I had to say something, I came back with, "Yeah, that's the kind. Go away."

Now, before I heard his response, because I did not want to hear what he had to say, I headed away and hoped that I was going the right way. The 'right way,' that I could catch up with the ladies and lose him at the same time. I made it to the first corner and looked both ways, and nothing. I didn't see them. As I had said earlier, I could only muster up, "Screw me. Damn, damn, damn. Screw me." Only this time, I said it much louder than before. And, as if this was my lucky day, a woman's voice from behind me asked, "Joe. Help Joe? Show you good time?"

With that, I figured that somehow Louie-Louie caught up with me and was hitting on me again. I turned around and shouted, "What you need is a good woman to teach you a lesson."

Well, it wasn't Louie-Louie. In fact, it wasn't even a man. Of all the people in the world, it was the same-same hooker, which had ignored me a few days ago. It figured that of all times that she could take with me, that she would choose to talk to me now.

"Joe. What name? My name Peggy 'C.'"

As usual and without thinking this out, I questioned her, "C?"

Well now, I got a response from her as if she just made her first sale of the day. "That's right Joe, 'C.'" As if I wanted to stay and hold a conversation with her, she continued with, "The 'C' for Cash and Cool. You show me the Cash, I show you Cool time."

Her explanation kind of caught me off guard. Then as usual, and before I could respond, she added in, "The more Cash you have, the Cooler it be."

After that piece of information, I didn't know which was worse, talking with her on a first name basis, or spending time with Louie-Louie. Then again, maybe I could introduce them to each other and I could be the third man out and exit the area.

Wow, stop thinking those thoughts right now. I must get those two out of my head, as both of them are bad news. Just as I was about to turn and run away, I almost ran over another woman who happened to be standing right behind me.

"Where you go Joe," she asked. Now, I thought that she was somewhat cute until she smiled and I only counted four teeth in her mouth. One upper and three lower and the three lower teeth were not even next to each other. They were straight, white, and without broccoli, cheese balls, or potato chips stuck between them.

"Excuse me," I said, as I took a step back to get her out of my face only to step on Peggy 'C's' foot.

Before I could turn and excuse myself to Peggy 'C,' the woman that I bumped into grabbed my belt buckle and said, "Joe. My name be Carol. Carol 'M&M.'"

Great, another hooker with initials for a nickname. Okay, I'll bite. "Carol. What be 'M&M?'"

"That be 'M' for Money and 'M' for motion," she explained making her body move in all kinds of directions. For a moment, I thought that I was at the circus and she was the rubber woman.

I gently grabbed her hand and moved it off my belt buckle that she had already started to unbuckle. "No thank you," I sheepishly explained. Then I noticed that she was able to unbuckle and half undo my belt with just one hand. Hell, I can't even do that with only one hand and these are my pants.

Anyway, after I said 'no thank you,' I must have hit her Motion button, because she gyrated her body into all kinds of shapes. And, some of those shapes would have been hard to do even for those long skinny balloons that those clowns use to make dogs and hats out of for little kids.

Rubbing up against me, she said very softly, "The more Money, the more Motions I can do for you. I make you scream for Mercy. I drive you so wild, that you pay me more Money to spare your life."

"No, no, no, thank you," I said and realized that this situation has gotten me to stutter.

"Ms M&M," I said, looking at her, "No thank you. Not today."

I turned to Ms 'C,' and said in a child like voice, "Bye-bye." I took a few steps away from them and figured that I would just turn around, head back to the hotel, and call it a day. Now, if I could just remember which way it was to the hotel.

Because this was not a tourist town, there were no signs posted stating where you are. I might as well take the easy way out and simply catch a taxi. I wondered what the driver would say if I was to tell him to take me to Baltimore. Anyway, with my second choice being the hotel, I stepped to the curb and hailed a taxi. Well, that part was easy and I jumped into a little blue and white cab and said, "Hotel."

"Okay Joe. What name hotel?"

Damn, damn, damn. I don't even know the name of the place where I was staying.

The driver seeing my deer-in-the-headlight look, asked, "Okay Joe. Which way hotel?"

I could only give him another one of my deer-in-the-headlights looks. His response was very helpful because he instructed me, I meant, ordered me out of his taxi. "Get out Joe. You numba ten thousand bookoo dinky-dau. You di-di-mal out my cab."

Oh well, you didn't have to tell me more than once that I was not welcomed here, I thought.

As if screaming at me once wasn't enough, he repeated, "Get out Joe. You numba ten thousand bookoo dinky-dau. You di-di-mal out my cab."

In a panic mode, I almost broke my neck getting out of this little piece of shit taxi of his. On the sidewalk, I stood up to compose myself when no more than one inch from my face was the hooker lady that I spoke with moments before.

"You want good time Joe? I see you come back again. You good-looking Joe. I have hotel room. You come, you like."

She had apparently forgotten about me from just a few minutes earlier. Then, it came back to her, Ms 'C' because she started to yell at me to get away from her. I had just made two steps to her left to get away from her when I could see Louie-Louie heading towards me. Shit, I turned around and headed to my right, away from the both of them.

Anyway, same-same, no need to tell me twice to go away, however, before I could get by her and flee, she yelled again, "Go away Joe. You number ten thousand, dinky-dau dumb ass. Go away my corner."

Okay, no sweat, I know now that this was not a good corner for me to be on right now. I did successfully make it a few feet from them and out of hearing range, however, before I could catch my breath and or my location in reference to my hotel, I heard someone say to me, "What? You didn't get her telephone number? A good looking woman like that?"

Guessing that I must be on Candid Camera, I could only turn and smile looking for a camera crew. Yet, in keeping with how my day has gone so far, it was Louie-Louie and his little smile.

Now how in the world did he cover so much ground and end up right next to me? This kind of action reminded me of those old movies where some girl was running away at full trot from a monster or crazy person. Naturally, she would fall down and this crazy person, who was just limping along, would end up right on top of her. It didn't seem possible but it made for a good story. So there we were, together. I was smiling because this was funny and he was smiling because he was just plain queer.

"I'm having a bad day. I only want to get back to my hotel," I said, and then realized that I had said too much to him.

"You need directions?"

"Yeah. I didn't know what to tell the driver," I explained. "I'm just lost."

He pointed to my left and said, "Three blocks that way. At the third light, go left for two blocks. It's on the corner."

Giving him my deer-in-the-headlights look and before I could say anything like, "Thanks," or "how did you know," Louie-Louie spoke up and said, "I saw your name on the registration book at the hotel. I checked in there right behind you."

Not wanting to appear rude and still wanting to get away from him, I said, "Thanks for the info. Gots to go."

Now before he could respond, I was on my way and heading on down the street. I planned to check back into my room and never leave. It didn't take long and his directions were good, and I was soon on the elevator heading up to my floor. This time, I shared the ride with one kid with his motor scooter, two marines, and two young lady bellhops. These two lucky marines were having their bags taken up for them and apparently; they were expecting to have more than their bags unpacked.

At my floor, we all got off at the same time. Great, I could only hope that we weren't sharing the same room. Anyway, we didn't and the marines were next door to me and to make it a little more interesting, the guy, and his bike had the room on the other side.

Once in my room, I decided just to take a nap. With that, I just fell face first onto my bunk and closed my eyes. For now, that seemed like an ideal way to kill sometime without provoking anyone.

I was almost asleep when to my horror; the guy next door with the bike had started to perform a tune-up. The engine would race up and then back down to idle. This repeated a number of times and I wanted to pay him a visit, but decided against it. He would probably be in some VC Hell's Angel gang or something similar.

Well, his tune up was soon completed and things got quiet again. Not too long after that, I was soon again face down and about ready to pass out. Yet, a second later, I could hear the two marines and the bellhop girls going at it. Something about price and this lasted for only a few minutes because they must have come to an agreement. Okay, that little matter out of the way, I was going to try again and catch some sleep.

Oh well, minutes later, there were the sounds of two couples making love and each pair were trying to out-do the other. Between the screaming, hollering and hearing the head board bang up against the wall, there was no way I was going to get some rest today.

With all this going on and as I laid in bed, I was thinking to myself that I should be thrilled to be heading home. However, I was a little ticked that I was stuck here right now with nowhere to go and no one to go with. I did come very close to spending the day with three, count'em, three American girls. They might have been heading toward the beach, going to a party, or simply doing lunch somewhere. Then I thought, nah, it might have been worse. I could have become attached to one of them and have to tell her good bye all over again.

I could be spending time with Louie-Louie and or the hooker, then nah, no way, no how. I was heading home and to spend any amount of time I wanted with a local, round eye girl.

For now, I figured that I would just take a nap as the noise from 'both' of my next doors calmed down and that I would head out later. As before, I turned on the TV. I was going to watch anything that was on, just to kill time, and before I took my nap.

I had to use a new pair of vice grips to change the stations, an upgrade from the last time I was here when all we had were an old pair of pliers.

I clicked from channel two to thirteen and then back to channel two. Nothing was on but another old rerun of the Tonight's Show. It was hard to enjoy the broadcast, as it was not in English. Not even sub titles. So, for now, I was just going relax and put my mind in neutral. However, before I could do all that, there was a knock at the door, and I quickly got up to see who it was.

"Who's there?"

A Vietnamese sounding girl, "I from Welcome Wagon. How we help you?"

"Damn," I thought to myself. It's the same girls from before. I might as well open up and see what my surprise would be this time.

Sure enough, it was a surprise. It was a different young lady and she was much nicer looking than the other two put together.

"I help you. Show good time. You no be lonely. Make you happy. I come in now? Yes?"

"No thank you. I okay. No need anything today," I said kindly. Good looking or not, not tonight, no way, no how, and not with me.

She questioned, "You no want girl? You queer sailor boy?"

Quickly I responded with, "No queer. No want girl. No want guy. Just want leave alone."

All I got for my polite explanation, was a puzzled look from her and right now, I didn't care what she got from me as long as it wasn't me or any of my money.

I continued politely and informed her, "I close door now. You go away. Good bye."

I did just that, believing that she understood what I wanted and I went back to watching the TV to help me fall asleep. It didn't take long before I was sound asleep, even with the sounds of motorcycles continuing going up and down the hallway.

I was awakened late at night, or maybe it was early in the morning, by the loud noise from the room next to mine. I could easily hear the two ladies of the evening earning their money with the two marines, making sure that they got their money's worth, or maybe they were on overtime as those two marines kept repeating, "Simper Fi, and Hu rah."

Moreover, the girls, well, they just kept repeating repeatedly, "You number one. Wow, you number one. I love you Joe. You love me. You no butterfly."

As for me, I only wanted to sleep and this was in no way an easy task with all the excitement the four of them are causing in the next room. I couldn't understand it as I could sleep if a firefight was going on next to me along with some concussion grenades going off below me.

A little while later, the noise not only calmed down from next door, it appeared to have stopped. No problem, I thought to myself, I could get some shuteye now. However, another couple must have just checked-in on the other side, as they were ready to party. They were just as loud as the first couple was and I might just be the only guy here not having a good time. But, no problem, one night with one of those ladies and I might be a scratchin' and a drippin' for many nights to come.

Whatever, I turned up the volume on the TV. I didn't know why I did that; hell, I couldn't understand what they were saying right now anyway. On the TV, it appeared to be the local news. I didn't know for sure that it was the news until the weatherman came on. He did speak in English and he acted just as the weathermen did back home. Back home, they always dressed fancy and nine times out of ten; they had the weather reports wrong. They would always say and put the forecasts in vague terms. Nothing was ever 100% this or 100% that. They always had their asses covered with 30% for this and the possibility of 50% for that. I mean, what was the difference between partly cloudy and partly sunny? Does 30% of rain mean that the odds of it raining are 30 to 70 or that 30% of the country will see rain and 70% will not. In addition, to top it off, they would never-ever come back and say something like, "Remember, yesterday I had a perfect weather forecast. I was 100% accurate."

With nothing on TV, nobody at my door, the tune-up shop closed, the two wild couples in rest mode, and not in the partying mood, it was sleep time and I did just that, fell sound asleep.

Later that night, some screaming, and laughing awakened me. As far as I could tell, it was a woman's scream and a man's laugh. This was not the way to get a good night's sleep. My only assumption was that the two marines next door and the bellhops were on phase two. To add in additional noise, the motorcycle guy on the other side of my room was again tuning up his motorbike.

With nothing that I could do about any of this, I reached over and turned on the TV. Maybe, to down the out, I would turn it up very loud. Then maybe not. It'll be my luck that the guests above, and below me would complain. Even to have me kicked out of my room. For now, I just wanted to go home.

A knock at my door, now what? Sure enough, it was two girls wanting to make some noise of their own with me. Again, no way, no how, and I just said, "No thank you," and closed the door. No need for me to hold a conversation with them as that would just end up frustrating me.

After about thirty minutes, TV was off the air, the bike was tuned-up, the marines were happy, the girls paid, and all was quiet. I left the TV on allowing the static to drown out any noises that might come up. I was soon asleep and stayed that way for the rest of the night.

# Chapter 8

I finally woke up and it appeared to me to be the middle of the day. I was so used to being wakened by all kinds of people, announcements, and explosions that when nothing happened, I had slept the entire morning away. Not wanting to pay for an extra day, I completed my shit, shower, shave, and was down stairs at the front desk to check out in record time.

The clerk behind the desk asked me, I assumed just to be friendly, where I was headed. I came back with, "Trying to make it to Saigon. I need to catch me a flight home."

"You have way to Saigon," he asked, as if he had a suggestion for me.

"You can help me?"

"No can do. No can help. Just being polite, Joe," he explained to me as the two marines from last night walked up behind me and laughed at our conversation.

I looked back, not in an angry way, but in a way as to suggest that I didn't think that they were funny. The shorter of the two, spoke up and asked, "You have a ride to Saigon?"

"No. Not yet," I answered.

The short guy added, "No sweat, man. Just make your way down to the docks and bum a ride on one of those riverboats. Hell, you're in the Navy aren't you? You should be able to find a boat going your way."

"That's faster than catching a flight out," I question.

Giving me a look as if I should pay attention, he came back with, "There are more boats going to Saigon than you have flights. Your choice."

"I think that I will do just that. I haven't had much luck with flights lately," I answered, giving him a smile showing approval for his idea.

With that out of the way, I paid my tab and headed out. After getting direction from about five different people, I found the piers and made my way down to the water to see if any of the boats were going anywhere near Saigon. The first three or four boats I passed that were tied up at the pier seemed empty or maybe everyone was below deck sleeping. The last time I woke up one of these boat crewmembers, he wanted to kick my ass. Well, I did throw a concussion grenade below his bow. With my luck, he'll be the same guy and of course, he would remember me.

The fifth boat at the end of the pier had its motors running. I figured that someone had to be onboard and that I would simply try it. It was an Alpha boat with a very unusual set up attached to the forward gun turret. It appeared to something that could be used to shoot down aircraft.

One guy was sunning and reading a newspaper and I figured that I would just up and ask him. "Excuse me."

Still reading his newspaper, he said, "What do you want? I'm very busy here."

"I was looking to bum a ride to Saigon. I need to be there tomorrow for a flight home out of Tan San Nut Air Force Base." I asked him very politely and hoped for an answer such as, 'yeah, sure thing, hop onboard, can I get you a cold soda?'

However, he responded with, "Yeah. I guess we could." After a short pause as if he had to finish an article that he was reading, he continued with, "Yeah. No sweat. You can put your things down over there. We leave in a little while."

"So, when are you heading out," I asked.

"We leave in a little while," was his response, as he was the sort of person that didn't like telling anyone, anything twice.

Not wanting to tick him off and then not getting a ride, I didn't say anything in return. It was just as well, because he came back with, "Now, you're welcome to ride along with us. Just bear in mind that we won't be getting to Saigon until tomorrow morning," he explained, giving me the option to find another ride if I wanted.

"No sweat. I have some time to kill anyway," I answered, making sure that I showed him that I appreciated the ride. A moon light ride down the Mekong River, or up the river, might be a peaceful experience. At least I could leave Vietnam with my last night being a pleasant one. I've heard enough of concussion grenades and hookers with marines at night to last me a lifetime. I was looking forward to the soft hum of a diesel motor with the slow, 'a rockin' and a rollin" while cruising up the Delta in my private pleasure craft.

My vision of a peaceful cruise on the delta was soon upgraded after I took a second look at the stern of the boat. This was one mean looking boat. There were a number of weapons of all types and each one of them was loaded for war. I believe that I might have made a mistake here, however, before I could say anything like, 'I'll catch the next ride,' he shouted at me, "We're leaving in thirty minutes."

Wow, I soon came out of my daydream as he added, "If you must tell anyone good-bye, now would be a good time. I'll be back shortly." He said nothing more; he just simply turned and walked away.

I could only assume that he had a girl friend to tell good-bye, as for me, I only wanted to get home and tell everyone hello. "I'll just wait right here until you get back," I shouted, as he kept walking away. He was in such a hurry that maybe he had two girlfriends to go and tell good-bye.

The other guy that was sitting there with him said to me, "Well, if you're going to sit here, then you can watch our things while I go and do an Erin."

"Sure thing," I responded, feeling rather good that they trust me to watch their things. "What kind of errands," I asked, just to be polite.

As he got up and with a smile on his face, he told me, "Have you ever seen Erin? She's hot and I'm going to go and 'do' her good."

It only took me a minute, but I got it. Oh well, then good for him. I would just make myself comfortable and kill half an hour or so. Maybe he had one up on me with someone to say good-bye to, but I was one up on him because I have someone to tell hello.

Then again, maybe not. It was just a few short months ago that I enlisted into the Navy and I essentially told everyone good-bye. In some cases, good-bye forever. Hell, by the time I was to get out of the military, most of my friends will be moved, married, or messed up on dope. Wow, nineteen years old and already I have friends that I will never see again.

Anyway, whatever, for now, I was just going to focus on getting home in one piece and then I could make new friends. With that in mind, I looked around my new environment and noticed that there was another person here. He was an older guy. Not that older guys were a big deal; it was only because there were so few older guys over here, in The-Nam. I had always thought this to be a young man's war. Most of the old people were back home in Washington making up laws that gave us the rules for us young kids to follow for this war.

"Our orders are to take up a position and create an ambush on a bridge near Rocket Alley," he started to explain to me as if he knew what I was thinking. "It's my understanding that a Marine unit will attempt to flush out some NVA Regulars and force them to cross this bridge. Our job is to keep them from crossing the bridge."

Pointing towards the gun turret with the unusual attachments, I asked, "Going to use that? I bet that it makes one hell of a frightening noise."

Looking over at the weapon, he answered, "Can't use that gun. Not there anyway."

"Broken?"

"No man. It works just fine," he said apparently saddened that he can't use it for whatever reason.

"Ammo?"

"Nope. We have plenty of ammo. You see," he continued. "It's the ammo that's the problem."

I didn't have another question for him and my confused look must have given him the hint to continue, because I still didn't get it.

"The ammo that we use is so powerful that it has the tendency to start at one end of town and not stop until it slams through the rest of the town."

"No kidding?"

"Yeah man. If we had our own men on the other side of town, well hell's bells, we'd be a shooting the hell out of our own guys. We'd be so far away that we wouldn't see who we were shooting at and our guys would have no idea where it was coming from."

"Really," I answered with another one-word response.

"These bullets will travel through these little hutches in no time at all. Hell, even concrete walls don't stand a chance."

"Why not just use it to blow up the bridge," I asked, believing that I had generated a reasonable question.

He just looked at me as if I was crazy or something.

"That way, we can keep them from crossing?" I suggested, and then remembered that I was only going along for the ride here and that I was looking for the easy way out. No need for me to be shot at again.

Still looking at me as if I was a sissy, or worse, a coward, he came back with, "We want to kill as many as possible. If we blow up the bridge, then we won't have anyone to shoot at. And if we have to, we'll take some prisoners."

Here comes my deer-in-the-headlights look. Without waiting for me to respond, he added, "Killing is easier than capturing. Keeping those little Commie-bastards guarded and fed is a lot of trouble and more trouble than they are worth."

In a way, this was very interesting hearing this from a seasoned veteran. He added as he pointed to two small boxes on the deck, "We get to hand out this crap to anyone we question, keep, or kill."

I reached down and collected one item from each box. On the lids, there were two-taped hand written notes. One box was filled with Surrender Passes, and the other box was half filled with Safe Passes. (APPENDIX D) I understood the Surrender Pass, but not the other. "A Safe Pass," I questioned.

He chuckled at me and responded, "Ass-hole. No way do we give 'Charlie' a Safe Pass. We give'm the Surrender Pass and wait for him to make a decision. Then we either shake his hand or shot'em."

I quickly dropped the Safe Pass back in the box and spent a little more time looking over the Surrender Pass. Beside the Surrender Passes, there was some Vietnamese money. (APPENDIX E) A few bill and no coins.

The Boat Captain complained, "Even in combat, we have paper work to fill out. Makes no damn since to me."

I placed the Surrender Pass back in the box, making sure that it was the correct box, and secretly hoped that I would not have to hand out either one. Then again, this had to be more difficult than passing out the POD.

"No sweat from me," I answered sincerely. If I wanted this ride, then I best go along with the program. So for now, I took a seat near the forward gun turret and settled down to enjoy the peace and calm before we headed out to kill the enemy. And, as he had made it clear to me, if we must, take a few prisoners, but apparently, only a few.

A short time later and with everyone back onboard, we were soon on our way. I did not know what to expect, but I was prepared. Well, as prepared as could be with not knowing exactly what to expect, other than we are going to some old bridge.

After about an hour or so, we pulled over and tied up to this old, rickety, and falling apart pier. I did not see any bridges nearby and this did not appear to be a place to pick up supplies and top-off the gas tanks.

I was up on the bow, just looking around, when the Boat Captain approached me and said, "We are only going to be here to drop off a Vietnamese Officer and then we'll be on our way. Keep an eye out on surrounding area for me."

No problem with me looking around for him, as I was already doing that. I nodded in the affirm as he headed back to whatever it was he was doing,

I didn't know that we had a Vietnamese Officer onboard unless one of the American looking crewmembers was Vietnamese. Well, my question was quickly solved when a Vietnamese Officer came out from below deck and with his suite case in one hand and an M-16 in the other. He jumped off the boat and headed up the hill to board a bus that was waiting for him. Not a military bus, with screens and all that, but a local bus filled with civilians and chickens.

I assumed that this officer was below decks taking a nap all this time, something I could completely understand and he was bumming a ride, just like me.

Getting back to my duties, I looked over the area and found this to be a very interesting location. Not the place for a tourist stop, but an interesting place just the same. Across the river, there was a small village with some buffalo sunning and looking at me. Children played near them and neither paid any attention to the other. I assumed this to be the norm to have a few buffalos tanning in your front yard.

Down river from where we were, I could see some more kids playing in the water while their moms did laundry. Just like in the National Geographic magazines, they were a smacking and a banging their clothes against a rock.

I looked up river and to my surprise, and this was a surprise even to The-Nam standards, was a little row of outhouses where the dropping would fall right into the river. As in up-river from where the kids were a playin and laundry was being a launderin.

I knew that the droppings would drop right in the river because the outhouse nearest me was occupied at the time and I could hear, and see, the droppings being dropped. This certainly gave credit to banging the crap out of your clothes.

Oh my, what a nasty little country this was and before I could give this any more thought, we were off and on our way up river again.

# Chapter 9

The one crewmember standing on the bow with a shotgun watching for debris in the water, shouted, "Bridge up ahead."

I assumed that this was our bridge for tonight and after our long, slow ride up-river, well it must have been up-river because the engines were going at full throttle and we were not making much headway, we had arrived.

Looking at this bridge, well, it looked familiar. I believe this to be the bridge that Dan and I had to cross on foot awhile back.

As we neared the bridge, but still a ways off, the Boat Captain handed me a set of binoculars and asked, instructed, or ordered me to, "Scan the far side, and tell me what you see."

Okay, can do, but what was I scanning for? Was I looking for a place to pull over and park? Were we to meet up with someone and he would be looking at me, looking at him? Do we have another passenger to off-load and we need a place to pull over? And worse yet, was I on the lookout for the VC? Not knowing what I was looking for, I placed the binoculars to my eyes and commenced doing my little look-see.

I looked and looked and looked and the only things that I saw were river bank, that it was all shades of brown. There were many trees and bushes, and they were all different shades of green.

Until I was asked, instructed, or ordered to stop, I kept looking. Then, after about ten minutes or so, I did spot someone.

Spotting someone was not all that unusual, I mean people do live here, but I did not know how to respond. This person was too far away to tell if he was pointing a gun at us or something similar. I, with calmness and I made it a point not to overreact, informed the Boat Captain with, "Got a gook over there. Can't tell if he's friend or foe."

Quickly, he made his way beside me, to my right, and after a little focusing to his binoculars asked, "Where?"

I knew that by just pointing, that that alone would not be good enough, and the by simply telling him his location by using the time reference from the face of a clock, that that would work. Which by the way, was the military way.

Before I said anything, I reviewed in my head what I was going to tell him. From my point of view, this unknown gook person was at my three o'clock position. Now, was this three o'clock position from where I was, going to be the same three o'clock position from where he was? Or, because we were side by side, was my three o'clock the same as his nine o'clock?

Crap, if Dan had to answer this, he would say it in a way to cover himself. With some thought, and quickly, I pointed and answered, "He's at 'my' three o'clock."

"Got'em," he responded.

'Hallelujah,' I thought to myself. I did good, damn good.

I waited for him to evaluate the situation and I had no idea on the outcome. If this gook was VC, do we take him out? And, how do you tell from this distance, the difference between a good gook, and a bad gook? At least this was not my call to make.

Feeling good that this was not my decision to make, well, that did not last long as the Boat Captain asked me, "What do you think?"

With my mind going a million miles a minute, I remembered a few things that Dan taught me before. I answered, as I kept my eye on this gook, "He seems to be walking away, and he is not carrying a weapon. If he continues on his way after he spots us, then let'em go."

After a pause to think this out some more, I added, "If on the other hand, after he spots us, if he changes direction and moves a little faster, then we might want to take him out."

What was I saying, 'take him out.'

Well, luck was in his, the gook, and in my favor, as he kept walking in the same direction. I did not believe that the Boat Captain would have taken my suggestion to take him out. Besides, the Boat Captain would have, should have, known the correction action to take. I supposed that he was just playing with me and would not have taken me seriously. No way could he have forgotten that I was FNG, FNG. As in new, new.

The Boat Captain lowered his binoculars and informed me to, "Keep an eye on him. Keep me updated if anything changes."

"Can do," I answered, and the Boat Captain went back to whatever it was that he was doing.

Nothing changed with this guy that I kept my eye on and we soon slowed as we approached the bridge. Slowing down was not all that big of a deal, but, when your top speed was less than five miles an hour, how much slower could you go? Anyway, the Boat Captain and another crewmember shinned their flashlights up and examined the bottom portions of the bridge as we passed under. This old bridge did not look all that strong to me and that it just might fall down all by itself by just walking across it. At least, I surmised, that if the VC were to cross this bridge that they would not cross all at the same time. It appeared to me that if more than one person were to cross this bridge at the same time, the weight of everyone would most certainly bring it down. Hell, I probably could have brought it down with a dozen or so cherry bombs and a hammerhead or two that I got the last time I passed the fireworks stores at South of the Border just off Interstate 95.

After our quick look-see under the bridge, we picked up speed and made our way about 100 yards or so up river. I did not know if it was 100 yards or not, but saying 100 yards was much easier than saying 90 yards, 105 yards, or whatever yards it was.

After the crew secured the boat up to a few trees, everyone went about the business of getting set up for our ambush. I asked the Boat Captain, "Is there anything that I can do?"

I mean, give me a break, as this was my first ambush.

He responded quickly, "You know how to operate the PRICK? I have my RTO busy right now with other things."

As if I knew everything that there was to know about the PRC-25 radio, I answered, "You want me to report on our location? Can do."

"Excellent," he responded, as he reached behind me for a green satchel bag that was packed away next to a cooler. A beer cooler I assumed, as that must be a required piece of inventory on these riverboats. His cooler looked new in that there were no bullet holes, or even patched-up bullet holes.

I had second thoughts now on about what I just volunteered to do. Then again, I knew generally how to work the radio. Hell, it was just a radio. However, I assumed that it was already properly set up for me to operate, as the on and off switches were the only knobs that I knew how to operate. No way could I calibrate it myself.

With some reservations, I took the satchel from the Boat Captain just after he pulled from it a small notebook. With a small, chewed up pencil, he wrote down some notes for me.

As I examined the radio, I found it already turned on, and because of that, I assumed that it was ready to go. Standing next to the Boat Captain, I placed on the headsets, as that seemed the next logical step for me to take. Well, it was not to my disbelief.

First off, I was unable to hear what the Boat Captain was trying to tell me. I normally, in the real world, would have thought that he could easily have raised his voice for me to hear. Then again, raising your voice in a combat zone may not be such a good idea.

"Get in the corner and duck down man," the Boat Captain snapped at me after I took the headsets off.

"Once you put on those headsets, you become the numba two target around here for snipers," he informed me. Not in a nice way, but in a way to keep me alive. I was most grateful for that until I realized that if I were to be placed out of action, and then his regular radioman would be pulled off from what he was doing to replace me. Not that it was a big deal to replace me with a real radio operator, but with me being replaced, I must have gotten hit or something. Oh my, and damn, damn, damn.

Understanding exactly what he meant by what he said and how he said it, I quickly dove down into a small, dark, out of sight, corner of the boat. Oh well, I saw that I was off to a good start with my new assignment and already making a good impression on the Boat Captain. Would have thought that with me being his numba two target, that it would have given him better odds of not being hit. Crap, what was I saying?

"Relax man," the Boat Captain said gently to me, as he took note on how I almost broke every bone in my body diving into my hiding place. Oops, not hiding place, I meant a secured location in which to operate the radio.

He seemed a little too much at ease with my situation, especially with him being the numba one target, in my opinion. "Send this off ASAP," he ordered, after he handed me his notes.

"No sweat. Not a problem," was the only answer that I could come up with at this time. I noticed that after going over his notes before I transmitted, I appreciated that they were complete and readable. With the details out of the way, I was ready to, 'break squelch.'

Reading from his notes, I transmitted, "Charlie Brown, Break. Betty Boop, Break. Over." Naturally, I assumed that from his notes, that we were Charlie Brown and they were Betty Boop.

This was starting out well, because I was not smacked on the head and that I did not stutter. Then before I could gloat in my success, my radio came alive with, "Betty Boop. Charlie Brown. Go. Break, break, break."

Okay, here I go with our location. "Charlie Brown. Betty Boop. Delta, Oscar, Golf. Charlie, Oscar, Charlie. Oscar, November, Alpha. Charlie, Hotel, Oscar. Break."

Wow, this was going rather well I thought. I added a smile to my face because I was doing a good job; the location of the bridge came next, "Objective. Delta, Oscar, Golf. Sierra, Charlie, Oscar. Oscar, Tango, Echo, Romeo, Zebra, Zebra. Over."

I liked this radio operator's job. Maybe, when I get back to the states, I could ask and be assigned to a Class 'A' Radio School or something similar, as I am already good at it and this little adventure could be added to my resume.

Waiting for a response, it didn't take long as the comeback was quick with, "Betty Boop. Betty Boop. Charlie Brown, Break, Break."

I did not know what to say now as I had kind of forgotten what I did the last time I had this role. Anyway, I just spoke up and transmitted, "Charlie Brown, Betty Boop. Go ahead. Over."

A few minutes of quiet with a little static mixed in go by before I heard, "Betty Boop. Betty Boop. Charlie Brown. Good hunting. Over."

What a good piece of news that was. Wow, I did it right. Can't wait to tell Dan that I could do some things right, and without his guidance. I gave the Boat Captain the message and that created a smile on his rugged face. At this point, everyone was happy. Everyone except the VC who were going to die tonight.

I now knew that there was nothing for me to do but to watch the boat crew set up shop and wait to kill some VC. Besides, they, the VC, had already injured me once and now it was payback time.

Just then, I took a moment and recalled what I just said to myself, 'waiting to kill some VC,' and, 'payback time.' I was not very sure of just what I meant by all that. I just knew for sure that I was not a killer of babies and old people as was quoted by the news people back home, but that I wanted to kill the VC just the same. This was my job, right?

I believed that what I was now thinking was right and that we were at war with these people. With that, well, that made it sort of legal. In fact, if I did not kill the VC, as ordered, I could spend a couple of years in the great state of Kansas doing time in Leavenworth making little rocks out of big ones. And with time served, I'd get no vacation time built up.

Just then, as I sat back to enjoy doing nothing but looking around at the scenery, the Boat Captain handed me a M16 rifle, and said, "Keep the safety on until I order otherwise."

"Unless he gets hit first," joked loudly a crewmember that was standing next to him. "Then I will order you to take if off safety and empty your magazine."

I didn't know if I should have laughed at the remark or not, however, I made it an issue to respond to him the same-same way as the Boat Captain. Well, he smiled at the crewmen and all seemed well.

With that, I smiled and added, "No sweat. Can do, will do."

I sounded like I wanted to get into action and in reality, I only wanted to get to Saigon and make it home in one piece. No need to find myself in the middle of a firefight and getting myself hurt.

Before the Boat Captain could give me any more additional words of wisdom, the PRICK kicked on and we could hear, 'Winner Nine Nine, Winner Nine Nine, come back.'

That must have been us, as the Boat Captain made his way to the radio and he responded with, "Bad Boy One, Winner Nine Nine."

Didn't know that we had more than one call sign, but apparently the Boat Captain knew.

I wanted to listen in just to keep myself informed on what we were doing here. However, the Boat Captain placed the headsets on and the only thing that I could pick up about his conversation was the serious look on his face. Not that a serious look on someone's face during a communication conversation in a war zone would be unusual, but he seemed to be very nervous right now as he broke out into a sweat. Not the kind of sweat found in this tropical heat, but a, 'I am scared as shit,' sort of sweat.

This went on for about five minutes with the Boat Captain taking plenty of notes. After his 'over and out,' he called together his crew and just as he was about the have his little talk, he looked over at me and said, "You best listen in on this."

He was right, as I should listen in as I was here and now a member of his crew, if only temporary. The Boat Captain did not waste anytime, as he got right into it.

"We need to guard this bridge tonight," he explained, as he utilized the most extreme hand, arm, and facial visuals, as if this was the most important assignment that he had even been given.

One crewmember, the Gunner's Mate Second Class, chimed in, and asked, "All the way up here to, 'baby-sit' a bridge? A bridge that is already falling apart."

The Second Class then looked down towards the bridge, looking as if to describe in detail how broken down this bridge was and to reaffirm to himself that this was a stupid mission. He added, "For real. We gots to guard this?"

"Shut up and listen up," ordered the Boat Captain. "Simple orders and they are just that, orders. When it gets dark, we can take out anything that crosses the bridge."

I was not sure what he meant by all that and I was not going to ask. Crap, all the way out here to be toll takers. I was starting to agree with the Gunner's Mate and my appearance must have gotten the attention of the Boat Captain.

"You, new guy," shouted the Boat Captain, pointing at me. "Translate those orders for me. What do you think they mean?"

Damn, damn, damn. I could just stand here, look stupid, not do anything, and still get into an issue with someone in authority. Before I could make up something and respond, the Gunner's Mate whispered to me, "We kill anything that crosses the bridge. Ask questions in the morning."

Not thinking, just repeating what he said, I answered, "We kill anything that crosses the bridge while we are here. If any questions need to be asked, we'll ask them in the morning."

"Very well. Good answer," complimented the Boat Captain.

I looked over at the Gunner's Mate and asked, "How do we tell the difference?"

"Difference in what?"

"Us, the good guys, and them, the VC," I asked in a voice not overheard by anyone else.

"A very simple thing," he started to explain. "Only the bad guys will cross this bridge tonight."

Finally, I believe that I just might know where he was going with this, but I decided not to interrupt him with any of my additional questions.

Before he continued, he asked me, "You have any idea where I am going with this?"

Crap, even not saying something, I found myself disciplined. Getting penalized with everyone watching us and paying attention.

"A good guess would be that the VC would be hard to hear when they cross the bridge," I said as if I had the right answer.

"Good answer and a correct one," he replied, acting as a third grade teacher that had just gotten her first correct answer from a student after months of teaching.

Because he seemed friendly enough, and I might as well take advantage of this OJT. I asked, "How quiet are they?"

"The wind makes more noise than these little pricks."

I really did not want to hear it put that way. "Won't they make noise tramping around at night," I asked, and waited for an answer.

"Noise," he questioned.

"Yeah, noise, you know. Going across a wooden bridge in the middle of the night. How quiet can that be?"

After putting his hand on my shoulder, giving the impression that he was some kind of father figure or that he was showing off for his shipmates, he continued, "For the most part, most of them are bare footed. The ones that can afford shoes, well, they are wearing army issue flip-flops."

"Then," he continued. "The ones wearing American made boots are seasoned solders and had gotten them off a dead GI."

What he was saying was important, but he was just too serious for me. Trying to respond the way Dan would, and wanting to make a joke out of this, showing that I was not scared or an FNG, I came back with, "Maybe we will get lucky and one of them will get a splinter in his foot crossing the bridge. Then maybe he'll scream or yell something loud."

He gave the impression that what I just said was not funny, not funny at all. He came back with, "They may be little yellow bastards, but they are not sissies. It will take a great deal of pain for anyone of them to make a sound at night when they are in transit."

Okay now, even if what he said was true, I just did not like hearing anything on how they just might win this war. We are Americans and we win everything.

The Boat captain butted in to stop this 'show and tell time,' and said, "Enough already. Let's check our gear and settle in for tonight."

I didn't have anything to check and I didn't know where anything was anyway. I made it a point to stand back, behind everyone as they browsed through the many large and small compartments on this boat.

I over heard one crewmember tell another as he picked up a green, army issue, flashlight, "Flashlight. Nothing more than a case for holding dead batteries."

The one he was talking to had just picked up a hammer and answered, "Hammer. When the only tool that you have is a hammer, then every problem looks like a nail."

The two of them just nodded approval over what they just said and then placed the hammer and flashlight back in its assigned place.

A few minutes later, and with everyone having completed their inventory check; I heard another boat off in the distance.

This was an odd-looking boat and one that I had not seen before. The gun placements, radar and radio antennas were not in the normal places. As if I knew what the norm was, however, it looked more like a spy ship than it did as a man of war ship/boat.

I kept staring at our new neighbor that was now tied up on the other side of the river, just under the bridge as we were.

The Boat Captain came along side me and said, "Nice boat."

I thought that it was odd-looking, not necessary a 'nice boat.' Then again, when he said, 'nice boat,' it came out okay, but when I told a Boat Captain before that he had a nice boat, it seemed like a stupid thing to say. Maybe I was correct all along and just did not know it.

Before I could respond, and I had nothing to say anyway, he added, "Their radar is so fine tuned, that it can spot a soda can at 400 yards."

"Wow, 400 yards," I answered, as if that was important to me.

The Boat Captain picked up that I was not all that impressed. He added for my benefit, "That's about the size of a swimmer's head sticking out of the water. Also, it's about the same size as the part of a mine that's above the water line."

Ah shit, I almost forgot where I was. You know, war, killings, bombs, guns, and bullets. After that mental adjustment, I did muster up enough to ask, "Would it be better for us to anchor in behind him or to have him move over in front of us?"

"No son, we'll guard this side of the bridge tonight, he'll guard the other side."

I must have given the Boat Captain a look as if I wanted to be on the other boat, which was true, as he informed me before he walked away, "Tonight, it will be your job to be on the look out for anything floating towards us. So you best be as good, if not better, than their radar."

Okay, no sweat, this will be just like being on duty back at the Summit. I answered, "No sweat. Can do. Anything in the water coming our way, I'll just shoot it up and throw a concussion grenade at it."

It felt good at what I just said, as it was a good, 'Gung-Ho,' sort of response. However, I was chastised when he, the Boat Captain, responded with, "Ass hole. You making all that noise with your shooting up and blowing up stuff in the water will not be a positive action as we are sitting here setting up and trying to maintain an ambush. A quiet ambush."

Oops. Now how do I respond to that? I could not, so I did not. Yet, I should have as the Boat Captain looked at me the same way that a parent would after a child after you said something stupid.

Even with the way he was looking at me, expecting a response, I had nothing to say. If something was floating our way, what do I do? With him wanting me to keep the noise down, yelling that a bomb was coming our way would be out of the question.

Then, it came to me. He's the Boat Captain, the man in charge, the big cheese, and with me being on the bottom of the food chain, why not ask him.

"What would you suggest I do," I asked.

"When you see something, inform me. I'll decide what actions you will take," he instructed, as he again walked away.

Crap, it would be my luck that he'd throw me in the river to better review the situation giving the true meaning of, 'to sink or swim.'

For now, I would forget our little conversation. When the time comes, and it just might, I hoped that he was not very busy when I needed him. Anyway, for now, I'd just keep an eye out for anything in the water headed our way. Everyone else onboard had something to do, except for me, and if I looked busy, I'd be left alone.

I was so busy looking busy, that I did not notice that a PBR had tied up along side us. Granted that it did come up from behind us, but if I was here to look out for the VC, I messed up. The VC would try and sneak up on us and not be detected. Here a boatload of guys just came onboard completely unnoticed. Well, maybe only un-noticed by me.

Now that they had my attention, I had to check these guys out. They were four mean looking guys that got off and boarded our boat. Mean looking by the way they carried themselves and meaner looking by the way their faces were painted with green and brown jungle stripes. And after a second glance at them, they looked even meaner because of the numbers and types of weapons and ammo that each carried.

This must be a SEAL Team and even that fact that I had never been up close to a Navy SEAL Team before, it was apparent. If these guys were just a sample of what we had as trained Special Forces, no way should we lose this little war. Hell, if I were to even think, that they were after me, I'd throw down my weapon and throw up my hands quicker than anyone in the French Army.

Now, that would be for either war, WWI or WWII. Or, I could pull what the Italians pulled in WWII half way into the war and simply change sides.

Once everyone was onboard, the PBR took off, back down the river in the direction that it came. With these guys onboard, I felt a little bigger and stronger. Almost to the point of saying, 'Come on Charlie. Give it your best shot. I'm here with my big brother.'

Naturally, after saying this to the VC, I'd be sure to stand real close to these guys. The way a little kid would do with a brother around and some bullies wanted to pick on him.

The other members of our crew, including the Boat Captain, knew enough to give these guys some walking space. They were given the utmost respect, all the while leaving out the, 'yes sirs,' and 'no sirs.'

After a few words with the Boat Captain, a conversation that he did not initiate, the four SEAL members had a seat on the deck, sitting crossed legged and in a small circle. The only thing missing from this photo op, was a campfire in the middle of them and a coyote howling off in the distance. This seemed to me to be a, SEAL Team Powwow.

I was lucky enough to be close by and could easily overhear what they were saying to each other. These SEAL guys were all business. It was entertaining to hear them talk in SEAL talk and they did this with no expression at all. I was able to pick up a few things that they were talking about, such as, 'Field of Fire, Synchronized Fire, Pucker Factor, and Cook-Off Mad Minute.'

At one point, one of them, the meanest looking one, looked over at me as if he was going to say, "What?"

Naturally, I had nothing to say, as I was afraid to say anything. I looked down at the deck and completely avoided any eye contact with him or anyone in that collection of men. With that, he ignored me and their conversations continued with, 'GSW-TTH, Muzzle Velocity, Hara-Kari, Gun Salute, and Rock & Roll.' This by the way, had nothing to do with music I assumed.

'Suicide Squads, Cyclical Rate, Pop Smoke, Shake and Bake,' were other colorful words and subject that they covered. Even

'Water-cooled' something or another was discussed and with that one, it made no mind to me. 'Thumper,' was another subject that they covered and I can assure you that this was not about the rabbit in the Bambi movie.

Everything they talked about was serious. No joking, or cutting up between them as they loaded, checked, and doubled-checked their weapons. Then, at the sound of the last magazine that was smacked in place, they each appeared to be relaxed a little. Like the calm before the storm and they were going to storm something, somewhere and afflict harm and death to someone.

The oldest of the group and apparently the one in charge, they called him 'Boss,' said, "How about that Lieutenant Kerry?"

One guy responded, "Isn't that the Lieutenant that got a hang nail and a Purple Heart all in the same day?"

The guy in charge responded, "Yep. He's that Boat Captain of one of those Swift boats."

A third guy spoke and added, "Didn't he jump off his boat and run into the jungle after some VC a little while back?"

"Yeah, that's the guy. Imagine that. A Boat Captain leaving his boat in the middle of a firefight and running off into the woods."

Every member of this SEAL team shook their heads in both confusion and discuss about this Kerry Lieutenant. I wanted to hear more about this guy, but they moved on to the details of their operations tonight.

There were some comments going back and forth between them about cutting off the ears of the dead VC, but I must have heard that wrong. Without question, I didn't expect anything to be said about the killing old people and children. Even with what some of the anti-war protesters back home claimed happened over here, I never heard anyone talk about it, even in jest. That type of action was just not in the program—especially the American program.

The one member, the one that I still believe to be in charge, the Boss, looked over at the youngest of the group, and said, "If you are going to fall asleep tonight, don't fall asleep with your finger on the trigger."

The guy sitting next to the youngest one, I believed him to be a colored man by the sound of his voice, jumped in and said, "Yeah you ass hole. The last time you did that, you farted and fired off a shot that almost hit me."

Without any self-control, I yipped out a yell of laughter that immediately caused the four of them to turn and give me a stare that came close to causing me to piss in my pants. You must understand, as this was no ordinary stare by four ordinary men. These were very mean looking men, with faces all painted up in jungle-animal-like face paint. What I could make out in their eyes, was that they were the predators and that I might end up as the pray. If they were smiling, I was unable to tell because of all the makeup. There was so much green and brown face paint, that the one guy that sounded like a colored person, hell, he could be yellow or green for all I knew.

Getting back to my, current time and place, and because they kept staring, I figured that it was up to me to say something and I best think up something fast. "Is that a true story?"

Not much of a statement, but I had death, times four, looking right at me. As their stare kept up, it appeared to me that if they were only going to cut off one of my ears, that I should consider myself getting off lucky.

Apparently, I was a 'no sweat,' 'he don't mean nothin'' kind of guy, as they turned back to face the center of the circle to continue with their conversation.

"Who's got the Comic Books," one of them asked.

Damn, now this will be a sight. These guys have enough spare room to carry around a comic book to read between firefights.

"I got a Funny Book right here," responded the little guy, the one that farted in his sleep.

Maybe when they are done with them, I could borrow one to help pass the time until it gets dark. Only to my surprise, Comic and Funny books were not books at all. They were maps, military maps and they went over them in impressive detail making 'O's and 'X's like a play that was designed for first and goal.

"Same rules," asked the colored guy. Maybe he was yellow or green, but he sounded like a colored man. He was asking the question.

"You mean the, 'kill or capture,' question, asked the Boss.

"Yea man. That be the one."

"No change. Kill first, capture wounded second, and capture the uninjured as a last option." After a pause, suggesting that he had to clarify what he just said, he continued, "If he be VC, then he be dead VC. I don't have the time, nor do I have the manpower to baby-sit the bad guys. Especially if he was wounded and needed medical attention. That my friend was taking medical people and medical supplies out of my inventory that might be needed for one of us."

He joked back, "Hell yeah man. That be cool. He can have all my supply of ammo that I have on me."

I thought that was amusing and only amusing enough for me not to make a sound in response.

The SEAL Team members, just as they were ready to go ashore and into the jungle, took a minute for a group prayer. I was not a churchgoer, but anytime someone, or some group, moved into prayer, I would fold my hands together and lower my head. Naturally, I wanted to be in agreement with them, assuming that they were praying to Jesus and not some witchcraft mambo-jumbo chicken head or chicken feet worshippers.

Overall, this was a very touching sight as well as an amazing sort of a frightening sight. What you had here was four; very mean looking guys preparing to go off to war. With what they were and what they were into, not to forget how they looked, I was most pleased that I was an American and on their side, and not on the side of the VC.

Once they left the boat and within a few seconds, they simply disappeared into the jungle. Their disappearance may not seem all that unusual, however, this looked almost like it was a movie and that they were using special effects to cause them to blend quickly and completely into the jungle. It was like a dream and their disappearance was magic. This dream like circumstances will most likely, if not most definitely, set off nightmares some time in the future for me.

For us now, it was just for us to sit here and wait. From what I understood about this ambush, the SEAL Team will flush out the VC towards us. Then it will be my job, or our job, to stop them in their tracks. Crossing this bridge did seem like a logical choke point. At least, I'd rather be the one running an ambush than the one running into it.

My duty for tonight was now to spend the next four hours throwing concussion grenades in the water or using a shotgun or M-16 to blow things away that would be floating towards us.

My assumption was that if nothing happened tonight, that we had a good night. Dan, however, would see this in a totally different way, a warrior's way. He'd inform me that if nothing happened tonight, and that we did not find the VC, that they would live to kill an American or two some other night.

Okay, without question, I wanted to save American lives and see that we kill VC, but I needed to find a way that did not place me in the middle of a negative situation. Not that I was a coward and that I didn't want to be here, it was just that I sort of strongly believed that anyone getting hurt over here should be allowed to only get hurt, just once for each tour. Even with this being a short tour for me, I got hurt and that should count as extra credit.

The Boat Captain approached me and asked, "You okay with tonight?"

"Yes, it's not that big of a deal. I've done something similar to this before when I did a couple of BID patrols. You know," I continued with confidence, "If I see something in the water, I would either throw a concussion grenade at it, or blow it away with my shotgun."

He looked at me as if I was the VC. Not a very comfortable feeling and I only surmised that he knew that I did not have a shotgun and that I only had an M-16. Before he could respond to correct me, I finished with, "I meant, my M-16. I know that I do not have a shotgun."

With one hand on my shoulder and in a low, but firm voice, he asked, "Do you understand the main function of an ambush?"

"Sure," I responded, and assumed that this would be one of those little one-on-one, on-the-job training seminars. With that, I confidently displayed the appearance that I was prepared to be all eyes and ears for this little class of his.

"In an ambush, we are not to be seen and just as important, we are not to be heard."

I knew that. Are we starting with Ambush 101, I question myself making sure that I did not voice my concern for him to hear.

My lesson started with a question, "Ambush. How will the throwing of concussion grenades in the water and the firing off of your M-16 to blow things away that would be floating towards us be a good move in an ambush?"

"I see your point. This is my first ambush. I got it," I answered, and hoped that this conversation/class would end soon. Even with only a few people around, each member of the crew was listening in on this conversation. On a good note, I will learn this now and bypass him having to smack me on the head later on for messing up.

After we had our pep talk and a review/correction of my orders, the Boat Captain made the rounds to verify that every man had manned his station. Mine was easy in that I was just to sit here on the bow and watch for anything floating our way. My orders were that if an item was to, casually, drift on past us, that I was to ignore it. If on the other hand, if it was doomed to hit us, I was to ease it away with this long pole thing-a-ma-jig that I was issued.

Giving this some thought, it seemed like an easy enough set of orders to follow. I did have an M-16, loaded with me in the event that we found ourselves in a firefight along with a bag of ammo. Moreover, as with most things that I did dealing with military issued orders, I tried to think of it in the way that Dan would see it. I should have a warrior's frame of mind being that I was in a warrior's way of life. I mean really, I was working along side a

SEAL Team. Realizing that I was not a SEAL Team member and that in no way could I ever suggest that I was. Besides, if I claimed to be one and a real SEAL Team member found out, I'd be in a world of hurt and deservingly so.

Thinking like Dan just now, caused me to rethink how simple my orders really were. If I was to spot something floating towards me, and if it was going to hit us, that I should poke it with a stick to shove it away.

Poke it with a stick! Poke it with a stick! Warning, warning Will Roberson. Not a good idea.

If this were a bomb or mine, would not I poking it with a stick, make it go off right in my face? I was not in a Road Runner cartoon, or a member of the Three Stooges. I'd get more than a darken charged face and my hair messed up if it went off. I could very easily lose my eyesight and arms. I'd have a hard time going to pee with no arms, but really, it didn't matter, as I could not see to aim it anyway. Then, instead of giving it a shake two or three times before putting it away, I'd just bang it against the wall.

'Wow, back up Charlie,' I said to myself, and this time, no one heard me. I now realized that I had the worst duty station for tonight, and this was going to be a long night. Just maybe this was to get even with me, as I was not going to serve a full year here. Hell, looking at this assignment for tonight, I'd rather spend two or more tours just to skip this duty.

"Doing okay son," asked the Boat Captain.

He scared me a little when he asked me that, as I did not hear him approach. At least I did not call him 'Pop,' as I did the last Boat Captain I talked with. Then, before I could respond, he asked a second question, "Did I catch you off guard?"

Wanting to answer properly and not show him that I was scared, I answered, "Nope, I had all my concentration on the debris floating our way. Doing my part, know what I mean?"

Well, he seemed impressed with my answer as he patted me on the shoulder and went back to whatever it was that he was doing.

Glad that he had faith in me and that I had been properly trained for this hazardous duty. But wait, I had not be trained on how to poke a stick at mines. Great, here it goes again with another letter on how I lost my life in, The-Nam, to my parents. "Mr. and Mrs. Edwards, your son lost his life today treating a mine as if it was a Mr. Potato Head."

It was no wonder why my paycheck had an extra $50 in it a months for combat pay. I wondered if there was something, I could get extra for being stupid?

Oh well, I was in the military, I was in a combat zone and I had a duty to perform. The other crewmembers had their assignments that came with its own set of hazardous duties, and I was not a member of the SEAL Team that headed out a bit ago. All in all, my duty was not all that bad. Then again, who back home would believe that I would, or could, spend a night armed with a long stick?

At least, I was not in a situation that I could start a fire and burn up a helo. Juicy-Lucy did not have me held captive and Bertha-Butt was not chasing me down a hallway looking to give me a death hug and kiss. Louie-Louie was not standing behind me, so all in all I was doing okay.

Over the next four or five hours, things were low key. The only sounds that I heard for those hours and hours were the sounds of the river, or delta. No birds, frogs, or cricket sounds, just the sounds of small waves that, faithfully, would splash up softly against the hull.

Every twenty minutes or so, a crewmember would quietly walk by to make sure that everyone was alert. For a moment, I felt as if they were checking up on me, then I considered that they were insuring that I was still on duty and that nothing happened to me.

Thinking the, 'Dan way,' had changed my way of looking at life. You don't sweat the small stuff, and everything was small stuff. Just do your duty, when you need to, and do it well. Then you won't need to worry about any stuff, large or small.

Before I could get into any deep sociological conversation with myself, I could hear gunfire off in the distance. I looked to see if I could see any muzzle flashes or tracers. If I could, and when I did, I would count the seconds between the flashes and when I heard the sound to determine how far away, it was. For each second, I'd figure that they would be a mile away.

More gunfire now and it was starting to get close enough to tell that it was coming from two different locations and that they sounded different. Sounded different in that they were different types of weapons, mostly rifles and machineguns. I had spent so much time looking off in the jungle to see about this firefight, that the Boat Captain must have picked up that I was not manning my post properly. He came over and softly said, and reminded me, "Son, keep an eye on the water. I have others checking out the firefight."

"No sweat, can do," I responded, and immediately went back to looking at the water a few feet out in front of us.

"Stay alert. Got a report that we may have something coming our way," he whispered in my ear before he headed back.

Ah shit, so much for a peaceful night. Yet, I best do my duty and keep an eye on the river as I was assured that other crewmembers were doing their duty and watching out the other areas of interest and importance.

The firefight went on for a little while longer. Could not tell just how much time passed, as the passing of time was hard to figure. There were times of silence only broken up with brief moments of rifle/machinegun fire. As before, they were firing from two locations and when I did catch a glimpse of muzzle flashes, I calculated it to be two miles away. Something, it was two and a half seconds away and then it would be three seconds away.

From my position and lack of knowledge to tell the difference between the sounds of gunfire, I was not able to pick which side belonged to us and which side belonged to the VC. Yet, if this does keep up, I will soon learn the difference.

Now that would be a good thing to know in the event that we must get involved and pick sides. If we had any big weapons and

I was in charge, I would have no idea where to aim my guns to help our guys out. Maybe that was why I was not the one in charge. But, and this was a big but, in the military, as those in charge get knocked out of action, the next highest person by rank and time, would be put in charge. If everyone here gets knocked out of action, I'd be in charge. How could that be? A few months ago, I was in high school and granted that I graduated, but still, it could be said that I could still be in high school or at least in summer school.

My training in boot camp was on how to march and tie knots and nothing was ever discussed on how to lead men in battle. It was true that what they say about the military in that you grow up very fast and would be in situations that people in civilian life never get to experience. Well, this was an experience, which I would gladly allow to pass me by, anytime. Not that I was a sissy or anything, I would like to have a little more training before I was placed in charge. It was enough for me right now to be in charge of myself. I realized that I was nineteen, but a, less than one month, nineteen year old.

Speaking of being in charge, I'd best get back and give my assignment 100% of my attention as I just noticed something floating our way. It was not coming at us real fast and I had plenty of time to check it out before responding. It looked like a large, bloated, dead pig. I didn't want to stick it as I figured that my stick would get stuck inside and I'd lose my stick. I was able to place my stick alongside it and inched it hard enough away to one side to miss us.

Inside, I patted myself on the back for doing that without screwing it up. I didn't panic or yell for help. However, before I could add in a few high-fives for myself, I heard more gunfire and it was a lot closer this time.

It was not hard to miss the muzzle flashes and now the tracers were very easy to pick up. I could easily pick out now who was shooting at whom. I could see flashes at the far side and clearly see tracers going away from the side nearest us. With a little concentration, it was possible to see that the side, from where I could see the tracers, was backing up towards us, or towards the bridge. The flashes seemed to be moving towards us and from what I knew about our operation tonight; it was our Navy SEAL Team members herding the VC towards the bridge, our ambush, and me.

At times, it would get very, very quiet. A sort of stillness with complete peacefulness in the darkness that would make you yell out, "Who's there? I know that you are out there. Show yourself," at the first inclination of anything near by or the slightest of noise.

Then again, being in a combat zone, with a little combat coming my way, puts a little damper on me wanting to yell out anything.

The Boat Captain made his way from person to person telling each of us to, "Stay calm. Stay alert and don't fire at anything until I tell you to."

Well, that made it all better for me. Then only thing missing from his little speech was a hug and three pats on the back. I didn't mean to be cynical about this, but there was a battle going on out there. It was dark and I could not tell exactly them from us. I was not going to fire at anything until I saw which direction the Boat Captain was shooting. Yet, I still think that it was us herding the VC towards us.

At least I thought I found myself to be in a safe spot, you know, behind good cover and with plenty of ammo near by until I noticed that I was sitting on top of a box of grenades. This was one sure place to be sitting to get your ass blown up.

Speaking of getting your ass blown up, I wondered if after this box of grenades did blow up, would there be anything left of me to send home?

Well, I was not going to move from here because I surmised that the odds of me needing grenades to throw were better than that of a stray bullet hitting this box. Besides, if a stray bullet were to hit this box, I'd never know.

Okay, back to the war. As projected, the gun battle made its way closer to the bridge and us. They were so close now that when a bullet made it way through the tall elephant grass, you could hear it passing from one end of the field to the other. Sort of like dragging a stick down the length of a picket fence.

It was at this time that I was trying to figure out how much time we had left before they actually made it to the bridge. My calculation gave me about 15 minutes, but after waiting 5 minutes, they no longer seemed to be working our way.

At first, they were at a standstill, both sides staying in place and just shooting back and forth. Like an old cowboy and Indian movie. The cowboys were all encircled behind wagons and horses as the Indians just ran around them, neither side gaining or losing any ground.

For now, that seemed fine with me with everyone staying in position. The more shooting the VC did, the less ammo they would have when they made it to the bridge. At first, it didn't occur to me that the same-same would be true for our SEAL Team members and as this little battle continued on for another 30 minutes or so, I felt rather uncomfortable with that scenario.

I picked up from the corner of my eye that the, real radio operator, was picking up something on his PRICK and it did not appear to be a take-out order. Well, maybe not take-out as in a pizza, but take-out as in, take-out the VC.

Even in the darkness, I could make out the fear in his eyes. The fear in his eyes was so overwhelming, that I do believe I will never forget it. The Boat Captain also picked up on this as he calmly made his way towards him for an update. As we were already in small quarters, it was easy to hear anything that was being said, even in a whisper. I overheard the radio operator inform the Captain that it was the SEAL Team on the line. Apparently, they were running out of ammo and that they were probably outnumbered.

With that information, I'd bet that I had the same-same fear in my eyes. Situation not good right now and it appeared to my non-military, non-combat training, non-take charge kind of guy in a combat situation that they, and now that we, were in trouble. Big trouble. Life and death kind of trouble. It might be that we were getting out asses kicked and that we were not kicking ass this time.

Crap, I was scared and I just wanted to go home. Not a coward, kind of scared and wanting to go home, as in leaving people hanging, just wanting this to end in our favor, then I want to go home.

It was at this point, that the Boat Captain was looking around at everyone. Looking at his inventory of men that were presently onboard, as in, who to send out and who to keep. I knew that he would want to keep himself onboard, along with his radio operator and engineman. With me being an extra guy anyway, I guessed that I would be called to do something. If I were in charge here, I would most certainly send out the experienced people. Keep the FNG's back here. Then, that would not make any sense. Send out the FNG's and keep the experienced people back here with me. No need to be short handed in a combat situation with only FNG's at your side.

Before the Boat Captain could explain anything, the radio chirped again. The radio operator looked down at the deck, as if looking down made it easier for him to hear. Then, with both hands holding his headset more securely to his head, he intently listened up at what was coming in. By his facial expression and mannerism, it was very clear that this was bad news, or maybe his favorite team had just screwed up a five run lead in the ninth inning. Maybe not.

He took part of his headset off, the left earpiece, and motioned for the Boat Caption to come over and listen in. Reluctantly, must unwillingly, and with caution, the Boat Captain did as suggested. It appeared that his hesitation was that he was in no hurry to hear bad news, or awful orders, or maybe it was both bad news and awful orders. Crap, I sure don't like it here.

As he and the radio operator listened in, this gave me, and the rest of the crew, an uneasy feeling as to what was going on and what we would be doing next. I sort of wished that they would put this on the speaker box for all of us to hear. Then again, the VC would be hearing the same-same information. Presumptuously, that this information was about them.

They both sat there for almost four of five minutes. Maybe it was only thirty seconds, but it seemed like four or five minutes.

The only movement that they did was to; simultaneously blink their eyes, as if they heard a loud noise coming over the radio. After a few blinks, I picked up that they seemed to be timed with the gunfire going off in the, now very close, as in nearby, distance.

From what I could summarize, it looked bad; however, I didn't know if it was bad for the SEAL Team, bad for the VC, or bad for us.

The Boat Captain stepped away from the radio operator and even in the darkness; I could tell that he was pale, very pale. After placing his hands on his hip and staring at the deck for a moment to collect his thoughts, he reached into his side leg pocket and pulled out a map. My first hope was that he was looking for the shortest/quickest way out of here. My second hope was that he was looking for the shortest/quickest way out of here.

He placed the map on the deck and reached in his other side, leg pocket, and pulled out a flashlight. That did not seem like a popular idea until I noticed that the flashlight had a red lens on it. My assumption was that the red light was not detectable at night. Then, if it wasn't, then how could he use it at night? Shit, I didn't know this stuff, as I was only a sailor that learned how to march and tie knots in boot camp.

After a review of his map, the Boat Captain called over one of his crewmembers and they had a detailed conversation. Not that I could hear or anything, but detailed in that they pointed to the same-same part of the map a number of times as if making sure, double sure, that between them, that they were giving and receiving the same-same orders.

The more the Boat Captain talked and explained, the more scared the crewmember looked. Even with me being the FNG here, I knew a bad situation when there was one.

The crewmember, after getting a pat on the back from the Boat Captain giving the impression that now that he had the bag, his orders, he looked around at everyone, and then he pointed at me. It was then that he motioned for me to join him. The other crewmembers that were not selected, looked relieved and that in itself was a bad sign that I picked up.

Doing my best not to give the appearance, or impression, that I was scared, I boldly made my way the few steps towards the crewmember. Outside appearance was that I was, 'Ready Eddie,' yet, on the inside, I was wet at both ends. Tears at one end and pissing myself at the other end.

He then tells me, "The SEAL Team is about out of ammo."

Before he could continue, my mind raced ahead and I was about ready to suggest that, 'Okay, we're out of ammo. Let's pack up and head back. Game over.'

"We need to load up some ammo for them and we'll meet up at this location," he instructed, as he pointed to a place on the map that didn't mean a thing to me. It didn't mean a thing to me in that I had no reference points to go by. Yes, it was obvious that north was up and that south was down, making west-left, and east, to the right, but I needed more than that.

In addition, I was unable to tell if the distance from where we were to where we must go was near by, or far away. Was an inch on the map one mile, one click, or one hundred feet? I figured that, no sweat, this was his operation and that it would be something that he would calculate, and then inform me.

He added, "It's just a little over a click. We'll take the long way around, and then we will meet up with them. After we re-supply them with ammo, together, we will fight our way back here and take no time to get prisoners."

"Just you and I," I asked, thinking that more was better than just the two of us. With more guys, we each won't need to carry as much ammo, I thought. Along with the numbers part, as the more of us over the number of them, that that would be in my, our favor.

"Nope, just you and I."

"Okay," I answered, realizing that I now had a new friend. I'm Edwards, from Baltimore, Maryland. Trying to get to Saigon." Wanting to be funny, I added, "This for me is just a slight layover."

"Glad to meet you. I'm Steven S. McAvoy. I'm from Brooklyn, New York. This is a layover for me also," he said, putting his hand out for a regular handshake. "I'm trying to get to the Satyr. It's an ARL. Have you seen her in your travels?"

Not knowing what an ARL was and not having heard anything about a Satyr thing, I came back with, "Sorry man, I've only been onboard one boat, and it was the Summit."

Before he could start to respond, or explain anything, the Boat Captain butted in and said, "Gentlemen, social time is over. It's time to get back into this war."

We looked at each other as if we had forgotten entirely where we were and what we were about to partake. For a minute, it almost felt as if we were just two guys that happened to be in the same class in school.

The Boat Caption continued with, "Now that you two had been properly introduced, do you mind getting back to your job?"

I didn't respond verbally, but I did shake my head up and down and with that, we were back into the war.

Again, not giving the impression that I was unwilling, or worse, afraid, I responded, as I looked over at this guy Steven and said, "Okay, let's do it."

Maybe my smile and extreme eagerness was a little much, as this guy looked at me as if I was a little too, 'gung ho' for this simple, but dangerous operation of his. Hope he didn't think that I was going to be in charge of this mission.

Well, in no time at all, he and I had our flack jackets tightened securely, adjusted the chin straps on our helmets a little tighter, and filled our side pants pockets with clips of ammo.

Not knowing exactly what to do, I inconspicuously watched Steve to see what he was going to do with his three things and two hands.

Not missing a beat as if he had done this before, he snapped a clip in his rifle. Then flipped the switch to safety, auto, or semi auto mode, don't know for sure which one, but he did switch it to something. This was then followed by him slinging the rifle over his shoulder and grabbing a satchel in each hand. Or maybe he was just like Dan and just gave the impression that he knew what he was doing. After some thought, he must have as he did not wait to see what I did with my three things and two hands. He most definitely gave the impression that he was prepared for a long run through the jungle, even his smile turned into that of a warrior.

Damn, damn, damn, no matter what I copied from this guy; I was still very new at this crap. I was the amateur here. Yet, in the back of my head, I heard a message or voice, as if Dan was trying to tell me something, or that I was learning as I go. The message to me, from me, was two parts. One, 'never be afraid to try something new. Remember that a lone amateur built the Ark. It was a large group of professionals that built the Titanic.' And, 'no one cares that you can't dance, just get up, and dance.'

Okay, I didn't know exactly how those two things would fit in with the, 'here and now,' as my thoughts and fears were current with the now, 'here and now,' now.

As all this was going on with being issued instructions and supplies, the firefight was still fully engaged. I did pick up that the firefight seemed to be in the same place or location for some time now. I figured that out by the loudness of the noise of gunfire.

My new fellow comrade in arms was reviewing the map once more with the Captain. I didn't see why they were spending so much time reviewing the map, as we could almost see where we had to go. I spoke up, not a good move apparently, and suggested, "We are here. We got to go there. Isn't it just a straight shot from point A to point B?"

He and the Boat Captain looked at me as if I had not paid any attention to what was going on. Steve was going to say something to me, but the Boat Captain placed his hand on his chest, giving the impression for him to be quiet as he, the Boat Captain, would say something to me.

Well, he did, and he said, "True, we are at, as you say, point A. And yes, we must get to point B. But, my good man, you must have forgotten that the VC are well armed and grouped in the middle here, between point A and point B."

Crap, that was some minor detail for me to overlook. I responded, thinking as if I was not the FNG here, "Right, I remember that part. Just thinking that it was a shorter route and the VC would not be expecting anyone to come in from their rear."

Well, not only were they surprised at what I said, I was equally surprised at what I said. Now I see that to be a rather stupid idea and I wanted more than anything, to suggest that my suggestion not be looked at or taken seriously. I believed that my suggestion to be a suicide mission. I wanted to go home instead.

The Boat Captain thought out loud for a moment, as if he was in a conversation with himself thinking that to be a good plan. And that was quickly followed by my partner, who was trying to convince him that it was a crazy scheme. Lucky for me, and my partner, my plan was scratched and it was decided that we were to go the long way around.

Once again, we looked over the map and it was apparent that we had to make our way on the east side and work our way north. With the river on the west side, no reason to put our backs up against the river, should something go wrong and we needed room to maneuver.

Moments later, we were ready to head out on a very dangerous mission and that I was not qualified. This had to be another one of those OJT things that I heard about in the Navy. On the Job Training and this OJT will have little room for error.

My partner said to me as we readied to leave our boat, "You know where we are going right?"

Without giving this much thought, I responded with, "Sure, I'm right behind you."

He gave me a look as if I was the last guy to choose for a ballgame and that he really didn't want to be stuck with me. He answered back with, "And if we get separated?"

Quickly, I came back with, "No sweat. I know the mission. I know I can keep up with you, will you be able to keep up with me?"

Wow, where was I coming up with this shit? Either having Dan on my mind was causing me to think like Dan, or there was always the possibility that I was a fast learner and knew the short cuts on survival. Whatever the reason, it made a good impression on this guy and the Boat Captain looked as if he approved my volunteerism for an assignment that he selected for me.

All seemed to be going well at this time, even with me being nineteen years of age for just a few days now. My parents would be so proud of me for doing well, but not very excited that I was going up against traffic in a firefight. Dan would just shrug his shoulders and make it appear that he was not impressed at all. Well, I was impressed that I was even here, much less what I was about to get myself into.

Before I could daydream and slap myself on the back for a job well done, Steve motioned that he was ready to go and with that, we were off.

We ran a little while, as the terrain was flat and without much vegetation. There was some elephant grass between the river and us and as I looked over in that direction, I could imagine that there were a few VC in the grass, looking at me, looking at them.

After thirty or fifty yards of running, we took a breather beside a pair of trees. He stopped at the second tree, as did I. He looked back at me as if suggesting, 'you need to go and stand behind your own tree. There was just room enough for the one of us.'

Quickly, I did step back and crouched in behind the first tree that was near by. My heart was beating so loud now that if this were to continue, I'd for sure get a headache. My rapid breathing was also an issue that was taking a lot of my thought and effort to calm myself down. It I was in any other place on the planet under these physical conditions, I would call for an ambulance or at the very least, check myself into an emergency room.

With all of this heavy thought and self-health awareness, I almost forgot about the war that was going on right in front of my face. I'd best think about the war or my personal health might take on a few more serious problems or issues.

Regaining a clear head, I reviewed the firefight that was still in process and it was easily spotted by the tracers going back and forth, or left to right, then right to left.

At this point, it appeared to me that, as I looked towards them, that we were right in the middle of this little war. Not in the middle, as in 'the middle,' but as in having front row seats and the VC were Stage Left and the SEAL Team cast members, were Stage Right. This was some show, and there was soon going to be audience participation, and I'd be a participant.

As my breathing returned to almost normal and I was able to ignore the sounds of my own heartbeat, the firefight was unbelievably loud. It was very loud and I could even smell gunpowder. Maybe the smelling of gun powder was impossible and that I only imagined it, but it seemed that I should be able to.

I looked over at my partner and noticed that he had an uncertain and unsure look about him. He seemed to view the firefight as if thinking, 'which way do I go, which way do I go.'

Well, that would be a most important decision to make and it best be the correct one. As he kept on with this hesitant way about himself, I stepped up to the plate, got in beside him, and said, "The VC be on the port side, and our guys are starboard."

His hesitant look did change to that of someone that realized that it was he, and not me, that had to make the next decision. I just knew that I was accurate with what I said, even though I could not believe that I said port and starboard, rather than left and right.

With a nod of his head, he indicated that it was time to head off in the, starboard direction, to make our encounter with the team. However, before he could take off with me in tow, I asked a very important question. I asked, "How do we make our greetings?"

I got a look from him as if that was a stupid thought and dumb question to ask. Then after he gave this some thought, he came back with, "Don't know. Never gave that a second thought. Good question."

Crap, here we were in the middle of a firefight with front row seats and having no idea what to do next. Well, we knew what we must do next; it was on how we did that, that we had to decide. Damn details.

I asked again, "We just can't run over to them and yell out that, 'we are here with the ammo. Don't shoot us.'"

"I see your point."

"Did you bring a radio," I asked.

"No, I thought you did," he answered.

Well, it was too far and too late to turn back.

As we faced each other as if expecting the other to have answers, I did pick up that there was not as much gunfire going back and forth over the last minute or so as there was earlier. I hoped that they were low on ammo and not low on personnel and whatever the reason, we need to find them soon.

"Look," I said. "Why not just go down a little father and come up to them from the rear. We can simply yell out something like, 'Don't shoot.' 'We are the good guys.' 'We got the ammo you requested.'"

After a moment, he responded, "Your plan sucks, but it's a workable plan. Ready?"

"Ready," I answered a little too quickly, yet, we must take care of business with little time to waste.

So, off we go in the same direction, which was not towards the firefight. We ran, I don't remember, one hundred, two hundred, three hundred yards, or so. From the sounds of gunfire and the location from where we last noticed tracers, we had pretty much decided that we had gone far enough and that we had to be in the rear. And, most importantly, the rear of our guys and not the VC.

We stopped for a quick rest and a regroup of our thoughts. We looked each other in the eyes and without saying a word, or making any signals, we knew at what moment that we were to takeoff in the direction of the SEAL Team.

We took off, but not running as hard and fast as before and after we had covered a little distance, he yelled out, "Don't shoot! We got your ammo. We got your ammo."

We did freeze, or Laid-chilly, in place and waited for a response. No response, but the gunfire from this end of the battle did stop.

He yelled again, "Don't shoot! We got your ammo. We got your ammo."

I did see a muzzle flash go off and it was directed at us and it came from where we thought our guys were. The good guys of all things. I did notice that the shot was way, way, over our heads as I could hear, and feel, the round pass through the branches above our heads.

I immediately took that to be a warning round and for them to see how we would respond to being shot at. I surmised that if were to fire back at them, that we were not who we were claiming to be. If again, we yelled out, 'Don't shoot,' again, they might not.

On the other hand, what it they were the VC, the bad guys. Damn, damn, damn and even if I had had some combat training, I'd bet that this part of the fighting was not covered in combat 101. I could not decide what to do and that was a good thing, as I was not the one in charge.

He yelled out again, "Don't shoot you ass holes! If you don't want this ammo, I'll take it back."

Great, he might have just pissed them off. For now, I could not tell if he did or not as our little part of the war had come to a most uneasy silence. It appeared to me that both sides were reviewing the situation and waiting to see who would make the next move, or deciding on what their next move would be.

As for me, I was not going to make a move and I wished that my heartbeat and breathing were not so damn loud. I even attempted to silence the breathing part as not to breathe too deeply to a point that I wanted to hold my breath all the while trying not to pass out.

It was silent for a very long time and possibly, in reality; it was less than thirty seconds or so. Then, a deep voice came from the darkness. If it were not for where we were and what we were doing, I would have sworn that it was the voice of God. It was a very deep, authoritative, and maybe even a voice with a southern drawl.

Anyway, the voice said, "Over here. Over here."

That sounded good to me as I was giving validity to the voice of anyone with a southern drawl, especially if that southern drawl sounded like God. Didn't believe that a Vietnamese could talk that deep and with a distinctive southern drawl. Not to mention that the Communist VC were not Christians and would not sound like God.

Apparently, my buddy had the same feeling and after gaining our strength, catching our breath, a better grip on our supplies, we were off again in the direction of the voice. Then it flashed in my head! What if that voice was really God? Would this be how and when I die? Should I stop and turn back?

Well, I kept running towards the voice anyway, and soon, we were only a short distance from the voice. I thought this to be within a few feet of where I needed to be, when I tripped over something big and this time, my pants did not fall down. I dropped my satchel filled with ammo and after I hit the ground hard, my rifle banged me on the back of my head, and that did hurt. At least it did not go off and shoot off a round in my ass.

As I raised my head to check out my surroundings, I saw a SEAL Team member standing right above me. Even in the middle of the night, and as dark as it was here, I could tell that it was one of our guys. From down on the ground looking up at him, he seemed so huge, not like the little VC guys that I remembered from the nightly news.

Feeling relieved that I had made it safely to the correct group; I looked back at what I tripped over and saw that it was a body. A dead body and by the size of it, it was one of the SEAL Team member and not that of a shorter and thinner body of a VC. Damn, damn, damn, as I had never even touched a dead person before, much less tripped over someone. I meant no disrespect, and my first reaction was to apologize for tripping over him, but I didn't know whom to make the apology out to. The body that I just tripped over or the guy standing right above me.

Quickly and without giving this any additional time, I apologized to the guy standing over me. "Sorry about that. Didn't see him there. I was just in a hurry to get you the ammo."

He didn't thank me for the ammo or accept my apology; instead, he grabbed my one satchel and tossed it to a team member to his left. Took the second satchel and tossed it to a team member to his right. He went to reach down for a third satchel and realized that I had only brought the two with me. He seemed disappointed in that I only had the two bags and that he had already given them out. Now, he had none.

Just then, Steve threw one of his satchels right at his feet. At least the focus was off me and on the pouch of ammo. He opened the satchel and loaded up his pant pockets with ammo. I didn't know where the last satchel bag went, but knew that it would not go to waste or be left behind.

With me no longer the focus, I did get up and remembered not to stand too tall, thus maintaining a low profile. I swung my rifle around, slipped the strap from over my head, and prepared myself for battle. It was clear to me that I was not the one in charge and that single fact, created an issue for me. Not that I wanted to be in charge, I just needed to find out who was in charge if I was going to fit in and not get myself, or someone else, hurt or killed. Hell, I didn't know what to do other than I needed to pay attention and follow orders. It surprised me to no end that I knew enough to ready my rifle and stand fast, waiting for instructions. As this was not the time and place for proper introductions and to attempt that jive, knuckle-knocking, finger-grabbing, shake-a-ma-thing handshake. Finding out who was in charge was easy as the guy that was standing above me, the Boss, instructed, "Stay behind me. Stay always to my right. When I move, you move. When I shoot, you shoot."

He looked me in the eye in a way that only a veteran that had seen, well, more than just seen, had been involved in combat could do. What I saw was a combination of coolness and clear thought and vision. You must add to that, they the eyes of someone that had seen many deaths, from both sides of the war—the eyes of a young man that are aged with blood and death.

Anyway, after he gave me my orders and I indicated that I understood him by a simple up and down nod of my head, fear soon overtook me and that I knew that I was in deep shit.

There was no time for a, 'group hug,' or to get into a question and answer period; we had a battle to win and VC to kill. However,

I wished that I had an idea as to what the plan was, and a few details would help. I mean, the last plan was to get here with the ammo, and we did that. My guess now was that we still had to herd the VC towards the bridge. At least we had two more souls with guns to help with the shooting. Then again, we were one body short and someone had to carry him. That would leave us with minus two, plus our two pluses and that makes us back to being even from when this whole thing started.

There was so much for me to comprehend right now, that I almost forgot that we were also currently targets for the VC and that they were not too far off from where we, and most importantly, where I was. I got in close to the Boss and stayed to his right, which was where I was. I now spent my time collecting on what information I could. I was fully aware on what was going on around me.

In one quick move, the Boss started shooting away at his three o'clock position and just after he finished off a quick burst of about six or nine shots, I did the same.

I recalled my one firefight where I was on a PBR with Jersey Joe. At least there, we had a ride out of the area and my ride now, was a few thousand yards away and with some VC between us.

Again, a burst of about six or nine shorts went out at the same three o'clock position and I followed his example, and fired off a few rounds of my own. Then for some unknown reason, I found that I was a little angry at my situation. Not angry with the Navy, any of the SEAL Team members, or anyone else, just angry at being here at this current time and place. I figured that as soon as we wipe out the VC, the sooner me, and everyone else over here could go home. It was this situation that provoked the anger in me, or was I being gung ho?

This attitude continued the next time I fired off a few rounds. When I reloaded with a new clip, I did so with much determination that I was going to make every shot count and not waste even one shot. Besides, if we wasted our ammo, then someone else would need to bring us some more ammo because I was not going head out on my own to get more, and then bring it back.

The muzzle flashes that were once going from left to right and right to left, were now straight ahead of me. Tracers also that were going left to right, and then right to left, were heading away from where I was. Only now, there was not as much going on with muzzle flashes pointed towards us.

I could only imagine what had happened. One, we knocked off a few of them, or they were now positioned closer together and that they themselves, were low or out of ammo. I wanted to think and believed that we knocked off some of them.

Just then, and to my right, another member of the SEAL Team came up beside me. He then started firing at the same-same three o'clock position. To his right, was my buddy from the boat and he had taken up a position next to the guy who was next to me. I felt safe with having so many guys and guns around me. It was like being at a firing range with all of us firing at the same-same targets.

Our shooting went on for just a few more minutes and it worked out that between the four of us, one of us was always firing, not giving other side the opportunity to take position and return fire. Then, after a few more minutes of this, and because they had not fired back at us for some time now, the guy to my left, the Boss, ordered us to cease fire. I had hoped that we gotten them all and that the battle was over. Not that they had gotten away and we must fight them again at another time and place, or even worse, they had laid a trap or ambush for us.

The next set or orders that we received was to lay still, very still and very, very quiet. The beating sounds of my heart were again so loud that it was starting to give me a headache. For every beat, I'd get a thump or thud running through my head. I could almost feel the nerves, or blood vessels or veins going from my heart to my head and it felt as if they were going to explode.

Part of that could be nerves as I was simply scared to death right now. The only thing that I had going for me was that I was not out of breath or breathing extremely hard and loud at this time. Another thing to add was the fact that I was not hurt of wounded. Better yet, I was not the dead American that was lying a dozen or so feet behind me.

For now, we laid-chilly as instructed. I did make it a point to look over at the area that we fired upon to see if I could make out anything. The moonlight was not behind us, but rather behind them. So looking in that area was not easy. It was not a full moon, just a little bit below half and the light that it did produce was like having a 25-watt bulb in a 200-watt fixture. Anyway, each time that I stared at one particular location, I must have stared at it too long because things started to move around. I could not tell if this movement was real or not or that this was purely my imagination, as if I wanted to see something. I didn't fire my weapon as I waited until the Boss instructed me to do so.

This whole ordeal of looking over an area, well, it was like looking at one of those drawing/paintings that you had fifteen things or so to pick out. I only wanted to pick out one item, the VC, and preferably a dead one. You remember, it was like looking at one of those children magazines at the doctor's office where you were to find a spoon, candy cane, apple pie, and/or a boomerang. As for me, I was looking for VC with one of those pointed hat things on his head.

We were lying here, chilled, for a long time. Maybe not a long time based on the actual time, but a long time to be still and looking into an area where everything was brown and green. Dark browns and greens, as this was nighttime, but that same-same old brown and green for which this shitty little country was famous.

The Boss made a motion that caused all of us to look over at him. Without saying a word, he indicated by visual hand motions and the moving his lips as if he was yelling, but not makings a sound, that we were all to fire at this location at the same-same time, but with just a few bursts. As for us not to overdo it. Then, we would rush the area, still bursting off a few rounds as we go. Then to regroup at that location some fifty or so yards away. Basically, it was just to the next group of trees.

All that sounded simple enough and something that I could do, I just didn't want to be the first guy in. Not that I was scared, just that I didn't know what I would do if someone was still there. If the Boss's leadership style was to lead by example, then let him take the lead and I will follow his example with courage and commitment. Still remembering that I was angry that I was here, and let's not forget that I was still a FNG.

Thinking that I didn't have it so bad as I remembered the dead American behind me. With a slow turn, I looked over in his direction. What I saw was another team member going and retrieving his ammo out of his pockets and putting the clips in his. This guy looked over at the Boss and nodded, as if he was ready for our next move. I didn't know exactly when our next move was to be, but he was ready.

It was at this time that the Boss got our attention again, and with the show of his left hand, counted down from five to zero fingers. At Zero fingers, we headed out after a few bursts of gunfire. Man oh man was I scared. If I had to crap or pee, I would have done that right then and there in my pants.

On our way there, no one fired back and when we did meet up, what we found was four dead VC. Not that I had any training on how to tell if someone was dead or not, but with the amount of holes and blood on each one, well, they just had to be dead, or they would be very soon. Okay, with four dead VC, was that a good number or not? What I meant was, were there four VC to start with, and we got them all, or, there was five or more and they are still out there.

The only thing that I could do right then was to stare at them. With that many dead people, that much blood, at night, twelve thousand miles from home, a few days after my nineteenth birthday, and a rifle in my hand that was still smoking, I didn't know what else to do. Before now, my military training was on how to tie knots and march like everyone else, and now, I was a big deal. Maybe not that big of a deal here with these guys, but back home, I'd be a big deal. Then again, maybe not, as the folks back home didn't want us over here to start with.

Bang! A shot rings out from off in the darkness, and at that same-same moment, the guy standing next to me swung around as if someone hit his left shoulder with a baseball bat, and down he goes. Not down as in dead, just down as if he was caught off guard with the hit. It then occurred to me that he was just shot. Without thinking, I immediately pulled up my rifle and fired automatically my entire clip in the area where this one shot came from. Before I was just somewhat angry, now I was angry and really, really pissed.

As I replaced my clip with a fresh one, and after the Boss emptied his clip, he motioned for me not to continue, to cease-fire. Damn, damn, damn, I had more clips, so why not let me empty them out, I thought to myself. However, he was the Boss and just maybe, one of us got'em. Besides, no reason for me to run out of ammo.

He looked over at me, and with a smile, he said, "I think we got'em."

Oh shit, did I just kill someone? I knew that to be the most correct, legal, proper, and as ordered thing to do, but still, someone was dead. I didn't feel like jumping up and down celebrating, but after giving this some thought, damn, it felt good, real good. Even if it was not my golden bullet, at least another VC bit the dust thus getting it a little closer for us all to go home after we win this little ugly war.

Okay, back to the guy that just got hit. Apparently, he was not injured as in, a bullet hitting and breaking the skin. His flack jacket took the blunt of the impact and it only caused him to swing around and drop. Another guy, the one that was giving attention to our guy that was killed, was looking over at his shoulder, as if checking for himself at what had happened, and just how injured he was. At this time, I could safely assume that he was the medic here. Now if I could just stay between him and the Boss, I'd be okay and safe.

Other than a sore shoulder, he was apparently all right. Just then, we heard automatic gunfire coming from a little distance off. At the same time, our radio operator was holding a conversation with someone, and I assumed that someone to be from our boat, that I also assumed to be where the automatic gunfire came from. I wanted to listen in on this conversation, but was unable to do so.

After a few minutes of radio traffic and after the Boss was briefed by the radioman, he informed and instructed us as we gathered around him. "We are to head back to the boat and we believe that there is one remaining VC between us. We'll do what we can to move him towards the bridge."

Well, that seemed simple enough, but what do we do with the four VC bodies that we had piled up here? Do we carry the bodies and shoot our way back to the boat? Didn't think so.

I knew about our fellow team member that was killed, as he was already here with us and would not, no way and no how, be left behind.

Well, as I mentioned before, I was not the Boss here and if I was, I still had no idea on what to do. As if the Boss was answering my question that I was thinking, he instructed, "The gooks stay here. The dead VC in the bushes, we'll ignore him for now and we'll make a run towards the bridge."

Nothing more needed to be said and after we waited for our fallen comrade to be hoisted up on a team member's back, the medic, we were off to finish our business. After only running a few feet out from where we were, we heard the automatic gunfire from our boat. I must be a seasoned combat veteran now as I could tell the difference in gunfire. You know, the difference between theirs and ours.

This time, I did not hear any return fire, which may be a good thing. My question now was, how do we communicate to the boat crew that we are headed towards them? Another question that I had was where was this elusive sixth VC? Was he headed back our way or did our boat take him out? Therefore, for now, I left those questions up to the Boss, who was presently traveling at a fast walk, or a slow run towards the boat and bridge.

I did my best to keep up with him for a number or reasons. One, he was in charge and knew what to do. Two, I was too new at this to make any decisions on my own. If I were to get separated from this group, I'd be in a lot of trouble. As long as I kept him in front of me, and everyone else behind me, I'd be good to go. I just hoped that he doesn't give orders for half of us to go one way and the other half to go the other. If he does this, I will fall in behind him and everyone else could divvy up between themselves as to which half they wanted to be in.

We were now in some tall elephant grass. The ground below us was sometimes hard and dry, then wet and muddy. The only real notable thing about this elephant grass was that it would be extremely easy to hide in. With that in mind, the more I looked around, the more my eyes were starting to dry out as I had them opened all the way and I did not want to blink as not to miss anything. With what little moon light we had, that didn't help much either. Only that it made us a little harder to see. Then again, you really didn't need to see us as we made all kinds of noise tramping over this hard, then wet ground. The Seal Team members had all kinds of gear attached and hanging from all types of places on them. I didn't know how they did it, but from what I could tell from the nightly TV news, the VC only carried their rifle and some rice as they traveled around.

After being here and being involved in this fight, that just simply cannot be true. From what I'd learned tonight, they had plenty of ammo and apparently, more ammo than our guys did. In addition, our guys only had to carry it to here from our boat, and not all the way from North Vietnam.

More automatic gunfire and it was coming from the same-same place. I was expecting it to be high above our heads as my warning shots were a little bit ago. I had no idea as to what they were shooting at and because I didn't hear anything getting hit around us, I assumed that it was not directed our way. It could be just shots to keep the bad guy or guys on their toes.

The Boss raised his hand in the universal sign for everyone to stop in place. I did, we did, and waited for his next move. It took him a while before he did anything. I didn't know if I should be watching him or looking around. If I looked around, I might pick up whatever it was that he was looking for, and then I would miss out if he were to issues any instructions. Then, if I were only to watch him, I'd miss whatever it was that was out there, that I should not miss.

All the times that I watched old WWII war movies, I'd never in a million years think that all these thoughts and questions were on the mind of soldiers in this same-same situation. Well maybe I would if I'd had any formal combat training. Damn, if someone wanted a knot tied or get a lesson on how to march and look nice for your parents to see at boot camp graduation, I'd be the man.

The Boss motioned for his radio operator to step in beside him. He then whispered something into his ear. I didn't hear what was said as he, the Boss, knew how to whisper. I had a good feeling that in combat training, there had to be a few hours of class on how to whisper.

The radio operator dropped down at the feet of Boss, and was soon into a conversation with someone, and I assumed that someone to be the radio guy on the boat. Anyway, I hoped so, so they'd stop shooting at us until we got back onboard.

This conversation went on for a few minutes and during this time, I kept one eye on the Boss, one on the radio operator to see when he completed his call, and my third eye out looking around at my surroundings. I realize that having three eyes was impossible, but I will say, put yourself in this situation and I guarantee that you will develop a third eye.

Thinking ahead, my guess was that my, our, next set of orders was to quickly head towards the boat, shooting and killing anything between us.

I was apparently catching on to this combat stuff as the Boss explained, and ordered us by saying, "We'll make double time towards the boat. We'll blast at anything in our way."

Well, that made it okay for me, as I want to return to the boat as quickly as possible so we'd get out of here. Even with being here and with what all was going on around me; I still wanted to go home.

Everyone, except me and the guy that came with me for the ammo run, was checking their weapon. One guy went as far to see how many rounds was still in his clip. I noticed that the Boss was a pickin' and a pulling' at his rifle. He didn't seem very pleased at what he was doing.

Without thinking, I asked him, "Your rifle jammed?"

He looked at me at first with anger in his eyes, then, that was followed by a most satisfying smile that almost turned into loud laughter as if he was at the circus and a clown just pulled a rabbit out of his ass.

He replied with, "Nope." A little smile and he then informed me, that, "Your gun is jammed."

And before I knew it, we had exchanged rifles. Any other time, I would have said something, but with him, the Boss, a real live SEAL team member and team leader, I knew enough to say nothing other than, "Okay." I almost added in the, 'sir' part, but was able to think far enough ahead not to, sir, and enlisted person, even if he was the Boss and that now, he had my rifle.

I looked down at my new, jammed rifle and tapped and picked at a few spots of my own, as if I knew what I was doing. I was just careful that with all my tapping' and a pickin,' that I did not squeeze the trigger. It would have be my luck that it would go off.

Crap, I came to a shoot-out and my shooter be broken. Now I'd make it a point to stay close to the Boss man, as he surely would not forget that I was firing blanks.

It didn't take but a minute and we were off, running, and a shooting our way back to the boat. In no time at all, I could see our boat and not only was I looking for our boat, but looking to make sure that they were not going to take a shot at us. It was a wonderful sight as I noticed that the boat crewmembers were standing up with their guns, not at the ready position. It was obvious and appreciated that they knew that it was we coming up to them.

Nothing more was said about the illusive VC that might still be in the area and it was not my place to ask. After I was onboard, I went back to the Boss and asked that we again exchange our weapons. He did and did so without any issues. If he would had said something against it, no sweat with me, as I would take a seat and forget the whole thing.

Our fallen comrade was gently placed down on the deck. With much care, the Boss, with the help of the one who carried him, spent time adjusting the body. What I mean was, his legs were straightened, his shirt buttoned correctly, his arms were folded across his chest, and a cap of some type was placed over his face.

As expected, remembering what they did before they left, they gathered around him and prayed. Nothing was said, as in a verbal prayer, but each member of the team laid a hand on him and apparently prayed silently. I didn't know what to do, other than to do nothing. I realized that this was not a photo op situation nor was it a time to ask any questions.

The Boat Captain was standing near by and he too, must have been in prayer as he stood there, with his head down and his hands in the position of prayer. The one SEAL Team member, the colored guy, kept his one hand on his fallen comrade, raised the other hand and his head as if he was talking face to face with God. In his eyes, I could see anger and peace. In a way, that seemed spooky but, when talking to God, I believed that it was best to say what you have to say, and that God will listen.

All I could think about right now was that this poor guy had a family back home and that they were soon to be notified of his fate. I didn't know him but I hoped that he was single and not leaving behind a wife and a few kids. Most assuredly, I did not have the same feelings for the VC that we left dead in the jungle. Strangely enough, I hoped that they also were single and not leaving behind a wife and children. Not necessarily for the same reasons, but figured that their children would grow up wanting to get revenge and kill a few Americans.

Without saying a word, the Boat Captain walked over to the wheel and started up the motor. In no time at all, we were heading back. Not sure if we were going back to where we came from, or that we were continuing on with our original destination. I was just happy that we were headed away as there was still that possible one VC left behind. This situation of us leaving a VC behind reminded me of an old WWII move where as everything calmed down after a battle, the last bad guy fired off one more short burst that resulted in someone getting killed. Without going into a panic mode, I lowered myself down beside a strong looking bulkhead. I was now cowering down into a corner, just taking a defensive position.

It was still very dark, especially when the clouds came between the moon and us as we traveled up, or down the river. Two hours later, we were still traveling the river at night. During this time, members of the SEAL Team took turns maintaining a presence next to their fallen team member. At times, different ones would talk to him as if he was still alive. Other times, it was just the laying on of hands with silent and audible prayer. The colored guy, well, he seemed to be doing the most in praying and talking to his buddy. This was a very moving sight and sadly enough, it goes on every night all around in this little shitty country.

I had a tear in my eye and it was not because something had gotten into it. Man oh man, do I want to go home.

Steve came over, sat beside me, and asked, "In your opinion, do you think I should stay onboard here or try and find the Satyr."

Crap, I didn't want to answer him on that. For me, I wanted to go home and not be in either place. "I have no idea buddy. I don't know anything about the Satyr and I've only been onboard here for a day. It might be best for you to contact your unit to inform them where you are. No need to have this time counted as vacation time."

"No shit! You mean I can get shot at and have it count as vacation time?"

Thinking to myself, you dumb ass. "Man, I don't know for sure. Ask the Boat Captain."

For now, I wanted to take a nap. Maybe not a nap, as in nap, but at least to get some sleep. Hell, it's been a long night.

He did step away and approached the Boat Caption. Quickly, I closed my eyes and forced myself into a nap. Even with a fallen sailor nearby, I knew enough to get some rest. I was not being cold, or uncaring, just that we were in the Nam and things here are not as they are at home. There is always the possibility that we might come under attack again, or be called away to another firefight.

After two hours or so without any interruptions, I noticed that the sun was coming up and, off in the distance, I could make out that a military base was dead ahead. It was not hard to figure this out, as everything was painted green and brown with sandbags surrounding each building with a little open space at the doors. The American flag blowing in the breeze was another good hint. I was extremely pleased that my temporary additional duty assignment was ending for me. Some guys and units over here had it bad all the time and they did this sort of stuff daily. Don't know how they did it and I could see clearly now where the, 'death stares' in their eyes comes from.

# Chapter 10

$S$tepping off my latest pleasure craft of the delta, I walked the long length of the pier and once I made it to solid ground, I noticed a sign that simply read, Welcome to Long-Xuyen. The good news was that I know where I was. The bad news was that I didn't know where Long-Xuyen was. Was Long-Xuyen just outside of Saigon, or, was Long-Xuyen 100, 200, or even 300 miles from Saigon. Hell, for all I knew, this little place could be in Thailand or Cambodia.

Okay, this was a no-sweat kind of situations. If I wish to get a flight to Saigon, then it really would not matter how far away it was, a flight to Saigon was a flight to Saigon. This was no different than catching a flight to Boston. You would not ask the ticket agent how many miles it was to Boston, you'd only care about how much it would cost. At least over here in-country, all my travel expenses had been free.

Now, getting back into the present time and space, all I needed to do was to find a building next to a runway that, with luck, would have a few helos and small cargo planes nearby. Simply go inside and request a flight out. I've done this a number of times before and I should have it down pat by now. With that, off I went looking for a small building near some military aircraft. I will avoid finding the motor pool because I had no desire to sit on the hood or back bumper of a jeep for a ride anywhere. A flight out of here, wherever here is, will be just fine with me.

After a short walk, I had passed the post office, chow hall, transit barracks, PX, before I found just what I was looking for. Without delay, and acting as if I knew exactly what I was doing, inside I went.

At the counter, there were three navy guys in front of me and they appeared to be together. They were definitely new in-country, still sporting dress whites. I surmised that they had been in-country for a few days by the unkempt appearance of their uniforms. You just cannot wear an all white uniform and expect it to be clean, and sharp looking, for more than a day. After they stepped aside, I worked my way to the counter and asked about anything that was going to Saigon.

I was told that nothing would be available until tomorrow morning and that there was room available at the transit barracks. As he attempted to give me direction, I spoke up and said that I knew my way around and that I was okay. I then thanked him and turned to leave.

"Seaman," he said before I could turn around and head out. "You can show these three FNG's how to get there."

Before I could think this one out, I replied, "No sweat. Can do." Then, as I started to give this some thought, I really did not need to have these three, or any three FNG's following me around and asking many questions. I only wanted to get some sleep. I wanted to be rested for tomorrow's trial and error of getting a flight to Saigon.

"Thanks mister," replied the shortest of the three that were now apparently in my care.

I placed my hand out for a handshake to the shortest guy and he mistook my jester for a salute. Hell, this little shit of an FNG wanted to salute me. Granted I was a Seaman and he was only a Seaman Apprentice, but if he only knew that in a matter of days, which he would also be promoted to Seaman and that he and I would be same-same in rank. What a way to start out a new friendship as he first called me mister and then saluted me.

The other two of this trio, were in mid-stream between a handshake and a semi-salute. It was somewhat humorous to see three guys fumble themselves around little oh me. Then again, this was The-Nam and anything and everything was possible.

I told the three of them, "My name is Edwards, Charles Edwards. I am from Baltimore Maryland."

As if I had set the standard for greetings and salutations for these three, they all responded in the exact same-same mannerisms and style.

"My name is Tom and I'm from Fort Worth. Glad to meet you." He was a little heavy for someone in the military, but then again, maybe by now, everyone that could be drafted had been drafted and we were now at the bottom of the barrel.

The second guy stepped up to the plate and introduced himself as, James Harden from Columbia, South Carolina.

We shook hands, the normal way, as the last guy spoke up and introduced himself as, Billy, from Southwest Philly. "How long have you been here," he asked.

Not wanting to be a smart-ass, but it just came out that way, I answered, "Only got here a few minutes ago. A little bit before you did." I did not like it when someone would answer my questions that way, the way Dan always did, but then again, it was somewhat cool being the one giving out the smart-ass answers.

"No. I meant here, in Vietnam," he quickly corrected himself. He had a nice smile that reminded me of the little character, Speedy; on the TV commercial, that does the Alka-Seltzer spot. You know, 'Plop, Plop, Fizz, Fizz, oh what a relief it is.'

Anyway, realizing that I was being a jerk, I quickly apologized for my rude answer. I explained that I had only been here a few weeks and because of my injuries suffered in combat that I was going home. At least, trying to get home.

All three of them, as if they had rehearsed this move, opened their eyes and mouth at the exact same-same time and stood at attention. I had their complete, undivided concentration as if I was the President of the United States or even the Pope preparing to address the nation or the world. I could have told them to sit down in a little circle, cross their legs, be quiet, and pay attention and that I was going to tell them a story. And . . . they would have done so.

"Just a little stomach injury that I suffered in a mortar attack. I'm heading home for thirty days medical leave before being reassigned," I explained, trying to keep it short.

By the look on their faces, it appeared to me that they wanted to hear more, but that they did not know how to ask. I broke this silence by suggesting, and more importantly, I changed the subject, "Follow me. I'll get us to the barracks so we'll have a place to stay for tonight."

Well, it worked and away we went on down the street to the transit barracks. In no time at all, we had all found our assigned beds, I meant bunks. They started to unpack, and after only a minute or two, they realized that there was no place for them to store their items. It was amusing to see that Billy from Philly had walked in a circle a few times looking for a place to unpack his things. With a look of confusion, he looked over at me and asked, "What do we do?"

Wanting to be gracious and polite, and still give the impression that I knew what I was doing, I had instructed the three of them to lock their sea bags to the bed. It was somewhat funny, because they never did ask why they had to lock up the bags. They simply followed my suggestion as if it was an order that was given to them by a superior officer.

This was cool having my own little army of guys following me around doing what ever it was that I said or suggested. Still in this frame of mind, I said, "Okay men. I'm going to get myself a bite to eat. Care to join me?"

I got a look from them as if this was not dinnertime and that I should have known that already. I explained, "Listen up. There was no telling if and when the VC might try and blow up the chow hall and render it useless, and right now, I am hungry."

With that suggestion, Larry, Moe, and Curly lined up in inspection formation and waited for my next set of instructions. I did not know what the big deal was here. We were only going to get some chow.

A few other guys that were also there. Apparently also in transit as we were and I didn't know what to think about my little following and me. Naturally, there were a few veterans here and they knew enough to ignore me completely, which was fine with me and appreciated. I did not need the competition from guys that really were veterans here, as I knew that I was just a few weeks over being a FNG myself. On these senior veterans, you could almost look into their eyes to tell how long they had been in-country and how much combat they had been involved in. Not a very pretty sight. Not only could you see it in their eyes, it was obvious to me that they hadn't smiled for some time now.

Billy, from Southwest Philly asked, "Can we tag along? Do you mind?"

Trying to sound most important, most irritated, and most pompous all at the same time, I said with authority, "No sweat Boot. You guys can tag along. Just keep up."

Well, everyone was happy. They were happy to have a place to stay and now they were getting a free meal. I was happy to have my own little fan club. I felt a little like the way Dan must have felt about me, only times three more with Larry, Moe, and Curly. Hell, I was the cool one now and I liked it.

Looking toward the doorway and before I started to lead my little parade to the chow hall, I said, sort of to myself aloud, "It'll be a good move to see if the guy that was on guard duty here at the barracks would like anything brought back for him."

"Why, can't he take a break," asked Tom, the guy from Texas, as if this was not our problem. "Everyone deserves a break you know."

Tom made it sound as if the guard was a union worker, and that he would and should get a break, because it was in his contract. Even if the barracks came under attack during his watch, he was due a break.

The other two looked at me as if my answer was as interesting as me pulling a rabbit out of my hat.

Trying to put on a face that showed that I was very mature and most serious, I answered my little group with, "I'm just going to do a good deed. Besides, it's nice to know who's on duty guarding my stuff."

The Three Stooges looked confused and they did not have the courage to ask me a second question so close to the asking of their last question. But hell, I had to tell them. I never liked being left in the dark so I was not going to promote that with these guys. "Simple arithmetic my new friends. He now knows that I know that he was the one on guard duty if any of my things were tampered with. You know what I mean?"

All three heads bobbed up and down like the little toy dogs that people had in the back of their cars. At least they were paying attention and agreeing with me.

We headed out and as we neared the doorway, we came across the guy that was on watch. He sort of reminded me of the chief that I saw with Dan when we got our tickets at the BEQ in Saigon my first day here in-country. There he sat with a cigarette in his mouth, coffee cup in one hand and holding a Mad Magazine in the other. All you had to do to make him a twenty-year Chief Petty Officer, was to add about fifty pounds and swap his Mad Magazine for a well-worn out pocket book. Naturally, the additional fifty pounds would be assigned to his stomach, below the belt, and you would have the chief's twin. Then it hit me; this was the same-same guard that I saw on duty a few weeks ago. He was still reading the same Mad Magazine. I assumed that he was a fresh cup of coffee that he was nursing and that he was working out of a fresh pack of cigarettes.

I told the other guys, "Check him out. He's a brand new lifer."

One guy agreed with me as the other two shook their heads both yes and no. When they caught on to how they responded, as if they were a comedy team, they shook their heads again. Only this time, they shook their heads no, then yes. It was going to be a long year for those two.

I asked him, the guard, "How's it going?"

He gave no verbal response, as he just shrugged his shoulders and said, "All right I guess."

Again, just like before, he did not look up and he just kept on reading his magazine.

I was going to ask him if he wanted something brought back from the chow hall, but I decided against it and I had no idea why I decided that. Maybe it was enough just that I was taking care of these three FNG's and myself.

Outside, the two guys that shook their heads north, south, then east and west and then shook them, east, west followed by north and south, asked, "You didn't ask him if he wanted anything. How come?"

"Well my inquisitive friends, he didn't seem all that hungry and his magazine seemed most important to him. I didn't want to interrupt him and his reading."

The three of them just acted as if what I just said meant something. I probably could have convinced them that he was a VC POW on a work detail and that he did not deserve to eat.

I asked myself, did I appear that dumb when I first arrived in-country? Probably, I answered. Well that was smart. I just asked and answered my own question. Hoped that no one noticed that little odd moment of mine.

I was able to direct my little following right to the chow hall without getting lost. Our meal today consisted of hot food, cold drinks, sweet desserts, with clean tables and floors. As we got up to leave, I jokingly suggested that someone leave the cook a tip. Well, not that I should had been surprised, but Billy from Philly did just that, and he did it with American green back. Only a dollar, but an American green back dollar just the same. Not wanting him to be taken advantage of, I said to him, "Billy. Don't do that. You keep it. I was just joking."

A little taken back by my change of orders, I meant suggestion; he snapped up his dollar and made a face to his two buddies believing that I did not see what he did.

Back at the transit barracks, there was nothing for us to do but to pass some time. For me, I only wanted to kill some time until tomorrow. For the other guys, well, I didn't know and didn't care what their plans were. As for me, I was just going to lie in my bunk, day dreaming about going home. Well, the triplets came up to me, broke my concentration, and asked, "So what's it like over here? You killed any VC? Any of your buddies get killed? How often does it rain?"

Trying to put on my, know it all, serious, mature face, I came back with what Dan told me only a few weeks ago. "It's fear and fascination. Sometimes it's a little more of one than the other is. Other times, it's just the opposite, with everything else mixed in."

"Really," James came back with a quick question as Tom and Billy rocked back and forth as if waiting to shoot up their hands for me to answer their questions next.

"Yeah, really. And I cannot leave out the death and mass confusion that goes on," I answered, as if I was at a podium answering questions during a press conference. Well, this continued on for most of the evening with me telling everything I knew about Vietnam along with a few things that I just made up. Soon it was dark outside and I had had their undivided attention for a few hours now, and as long as I was on a roll, I kept it up.

"When do you think we'll get to fight the VC," asked Billy from Philly.

"Don't know," I answered quickly. "No need to rush it."

I believe that I made myself sound like a real veteran that had been in-country for a long time.

As my luck would have it and just as I finished up with my little episode that happened the one night that Dan and I were mortared, the call went out for us to take cover. We were having a mortar attack right then and now. Naturally, as if I really knew what to do and where to go, I shouted, "Follow me. I'll take care of us."

Well, the three of them were up and got in behind me so fast that they ran into each other as if we were the Keystone Cops. Correction, not we, as the Keystone Cops, just them. I did catch a glance of the veteran guys that were ignoring me earlier and not only did they ignore me still, they even went out the other door as if they truly knew where to go at a time like this.

No sweat, it don't mean nothin, I thought to myself, but made it a point not to say it aloud. I led my small group, along with some others, to the front doorway. As before with Dan, I looked to see which way everyone was running. Remember, ones with guns running one way and everyone without a gun running the other way. Oh well, not tonight. It was 50-50 on which way everyone was running. This was not starting out the way had I planned it, the way I bragged about, and the way I wanted to lead everyone. Then I figured, just as I had a shove from the group of followers behind me, to go right. No particular reason, just right. I sure hope this was right, not so much for them, but for me.

Okay, so we ran for a couple of hundred feet and I did pick up that most everyone was running towards this one building. And, most important, no one running inside was carrying a weapon. With no one coming out carrying a rifle, this had to be the bunker. No sweat then, I had found the bunker and I was going to be one cool dude tonight. With a little luck, we'll be back in our bunks in thirty minutes or so.

One guy behind me, I did not know who, shouted, "Do you know where you are taking us?" His voice sounded very authoritative and not a hint of fear, well, that gave me the impression that he deserved an answer. However, wanting to maintain my being, 'cool' status, and to respond the way Dan would have, I shouted back, "No sweat. You don't have to follow me."

I did not hear a response. A second later, we entered this building, the building that everyone seemed to be in a hurry to get to for good reasons. This was not the bunker complex that I had hoped. There were no steps going down to a safe and secure area to hide out until the shooting stops. Damn, damn, damn, we had entered the armory and everyone walking into these doors was issued a rifle and then guided out the back door. An M-16E to be exact and after closer examination, they were not new. Along with the rifle, we were each issued three clips of ammo. This was not good, not good at all.

I went and did it now. Not only was everyone ticked at me for getting them into this current situation; we were under attack and we must take an active role. Then again, whatever, we were in the military and this was a military moment, and now it was time to earn our pay.

"You guys, you're with me," shouted a First Lieutenant that apparently knew that we didn't know what to do or where to go. For now, we had a plan. It was simple as we were to follow the Lieutenant and to bring our guns and bullets along with us.

The guy that asked me earlier if I knew where we were going was now asking, "Do you know where he is taking us?" His voice didn't sound all that authoritative now. His voice displayed the same fear that I now had.

"You wanted to fight the VC, well, you're going to fight them now," I said this to Billy from Philly, even though I didn't think that he was the one that complained before.

Billy came back with, "Cool. I can do that."

Well, for now, Billy was happy. At least one of us was happy. Whatever our feelings were right now, we have found ourselves heading for battle and I was the one leading the way. Well, maybe it was the First Lieutenant that was in the lead now, but it was me, that got us in this predicament.

All the while as we were being issued a weapon and getting in behind the First Lieutenant, there was the sound of gunfire off in the distance. Along with that, there was the occasional explosion that did not appear to have hit anything but dirt. As I kept up step for step with the First Lieutenant, I realized that I was trying more than normal to listen to all the noises and sounds. One reason for paying attention was that I did not want to miss out on any instructions or orders given out by the First Lieutenant.

Right in the middle of my listening up for orders, we arrived at this fence. Not a very big fence, and not one topped off with the usual barbwire on both sides and across the top. Without the barbwire, I assumed this not to be the main fence that surrounded the base, but then again, it was important enough fence for us to guard.

"Half of you guys to my right. The other half, to my left," shouted the First Lieutenant, as he pointed to his right side, then his left.

Crap, crap, crap. Which half was I? Shit, was I part of the left half, or the right half. What happens if we had an odd number? Do we include the First Lieutenant in the count? Do we sound off a count? You know, 1, 2, 3, 4, and so on and do I assume that the odd numbers go right, or should I assume that the odd numbers go left? This Army stuff is hard. Put me on a patrol boat and give me a box of grenades to throw anytime.

Well, it worked out okay, I don't know how, but it did and the First Lieutenant ended up in the middle of us all. As for me, I was face down in the dirt with my clip snapped in and the safety off. For now, I was ready to get even with the gooks for trying to kill me earlier.

I had Tom on my left, Billy on my right, and James was on the other side of the First Lieutenant. With Tom and Billy lying there in their dress whites, I felt like I was in a parking lot lying between two curb stops. Wanting to say something, I asked Tom and Billy if the safety was off on their rifle. Billy from Philly said, "I'm from South Philly, we don't have no safety buttons on our guns."

I didn't know how to respond to that, so I didn't. Tom spoke up and said, "I hunt a lot back in Texas, and even though I am laying here looking like the Good Humor Ice Cream Man, I know enough to set my rifle on automatic."

Okay, I was in a good spot for now as both guys on my flank knew how to shoot, and they could probably shoot a little better than I could. At least these guys were on my side and would always look out for me. I thought this to be true until Tom said to Billy, "Remind me later to thank Mr. Charles Edwards here, from Baltimore, for this fine predicament he has gotten us into this evening."

Billy came back with, "he did take care of us. We now have a place to sleep tonight and we did get something to eat."

Tom thought for a second before he responded with, "What's so wonderful about having a place to stay and a full stomach if you have a good chance at getting shot and possibly wounded?"

Now it was Billy's turn to think up something to say to this response. It didn't take long as he, Billy, added, "I see your point. We might even get killed laying here in the dirt."

I started to explain myself only to be told to shut up by the First Lieutenant. This was followed by a little, but softly spoken, rebuke from him. I was going to explain that these two guys were doing all the talking. Then I figured against it. No reason to have Tom and Billy pissed at me for something else.

It seemed to me that Tom, Billy, and James were madder at me than they were at the VC. I was going to explain to them, that it was the fault of the VC, that we were all here. Not only here at the fence lying in the dirt, but because we were here in Vietnam. Not only that, it was because of the VC that we were in the military. However, I decided just to keep my mouth shut and follow orders and my orders now were to protect this fence and not to allow the VC to get past me.

Giving this some thought, that scared the piss out of me. I didn't wet myself, but if anything was to catch me off-guard right now, I just might.

Looking out at this open field, and in my untrained military opinion, this was not the way that I would choose to attack a military base. There was nothing there but a lot of open space. If anything was to approach us, we would be able to spot it a rather long ways off, and to be a good thing. Then, giving this some thought, this just might be the main fence and out there was no-man's-land. Crap, oh crap. I, I meant we, are the first line of defense for this base.

Lying here, my mind is running a million miles a second. I was trying to figure out what the VC were doing right now. What was it that they were thinking? With the mortar rounds going off at the other end of the base, would they attack from that direction? Then, what if they decided to attack from this side? As in this side, where I am.

Damn, damn, damn. Situation not cool I was thinking when the First Lieutenant spoke up and said, "Well men, this was what you trained for."

Not me, I thought and was pleased that I did not say it to where he could have heard me. My boot camp training consisted of marching and tying knots. Nothing was told to us in boot camp on how to defend a base during a mortar attack.

Just then, I figured that I best stop feeling sorry for myself
and get myself 100% into saving this base from attack. As I had
said before, I am in the military and the military was a job that
was war related.

Now that I was giving my present duties my undivided
attention, then let me attend to my present duties. I spent the
next hour or so looking at every inch of ground between the
fence and the tree line a ways off. A ways off, what an informative,
military description that was.

I could see it now. I'd be asked on the radio, "how far be the
VC from your position?" "A ways off sir." Damn, damn, damn, I
never even knew how far away a click was. I heard tell that a
click was same-same as a mile and I had heard that a click was
same-same as 1000 yards.

Then I figured, why worry. That was why there was a 1st
Lieutenant here with us to answer questions like that.

So, right how, I was ready to kill some VC and to protect the
base. My spirit was up and I was ready for war. Come on VC;
come pay me a visit I repeated in my head. Yet, before I could
kill some VC, a siren went off and it must have been the 'all
clear,' because the First Lieutenant stood up, brushed himself
off, and said, "It's over men."

We all did same-same, stood up and brushed ourselves off.
The only thing funny about brushing ourselves off, was that the
ones wearing their whites, well, it only made it worse. It did nothing
short of spreading the dirt around some creating a grey dress
white uniform. The First Lieutenant ordered us to follow him back
to the armory to return our weapons and we simply complied.

On our way back, and wanting to break the silence, not to
mention, to try and keep the subject off me, and how mad they
were that we spent our time at the fence instead of the safety of
some bunker. I mentioned, "I hope that our bed and things are
all right. If not, then we can gather our things together, if we can
find them, and we'll need to find another place to sleep tonight."

This caught their attention as the three of them looked at me
for clarification.

I came back with, "If our things got blown up, well, that will ruin the rest of our night."

Cool, I was able to create three, count them, three; deer-in-the-headlights look at the same time.

Tom asked with Billy and James equally and eagerly waiting for an answer, "What? What do you mean? Blown up?"

"What, I mean blown up, that's what," I answered knowing that they wanted to hear more.

Confusion was all around, except for the First Lieutenant and me. I, with some simplicity, came back with, "Bombs are to blow things up, and that means that things are blown-up."

"Really," answered Billy and James at the same time as Tom just stood there with his mouth wide open.

"What is it that you think bombs blow up," I answered Billy and James as Tom kept his mouth opened.

Still, no one asked anything. Being cool again, I said, "If our shit was blown up, this will create a small problem. The Navy will issue us new shit that can be blown up some other evening."

"Blown up," Tom finally said something and closed his mouth.

"Did you guys think that bombs only destroyed jeeps, tanks, ammo dumps, bridges, planes, and not personal stuff like our beds and sea bags?"

James asked, "You mean that there's a possibility that my stuff is all gone?"

"Yep. Welcome to The-Nam boys," I responded.

Nothing more was said or asked until we returned to the transit barracks. These guys were so happy to see everything undamaged and not on fire, that you would have thought that they just won a car or something. However, in no time at all, all was back to normal as the one guy, Billy from Philly, was bitching about not having any TV to watch. Tom started to complain because he wanted to go out and find a 7/11 to get himself a Slurppy. James started to complain on how much the other two were complaining. This soon built up to where Billy bragged on how huge his TV was at home and that it was the biggest TV on his block. Tom missed his daily Slurppy trip to the 7/11 because this was a hangout for all the kids in his neighborhood.

All this got James bitching even more because he wanted to sleep and not hear about Billy's TV or Tom's Slurppy run. I was about to add in my two cents and my suggestion for them all to shut up. I was tired and wanted to sleep but figured that if I said anything to them at all, that they would just take out their frustrations on me.

At least for now, it was late and I had made a good decision not to say anything, as in before long, I was sound asleep, and if they were to talk about me or complain about anything, I never heard a word. Besides, they apparently didn't like me anyway.

# Chapter 11

"Can I have your attention please," shouted someone standing in the doorway to our dorms, I meant barracks. I looked up at him with my sleep filled eyes and the only thing that I could make out clearly was that he was holding onto a clipboard. A working party was the only thing that I could think about right now and I wanted to get a flight out, and not be a part of his working party, especially at zero dark early.

"How many E-2's do we have in here?"

Well, lucky for me, I was an E-3. It didn't matter than I was promoted to E-3 just a few days ago, but I was an E-3 just the same. Manny, Moe, and Jack, my boys from the fence fight last night, raised their hands as if they were in the first grade with an answer for the teacher. There were two marines in with us and they responded with, 'Hu Rah.' Whatever 'Hu Rah' meant, but it sounded Gung-Ho and all that. Anyway, these two Marines were the first two in line awaiting their instructions. Marines, those guys were really something. It appeared to me that they just sat around all day long waiting for instructions or orders for them to do stuff. Even with the potential of being assigned to a working party, they were Gung-Ho. Well, for me, I was Gung-Ho when I enlisted into the Navy, but after being sent here and being shot at, my Gung-Ho had Gung-Gone.

Anyway, within a few minutes, about seven E-2's were rounded up and away they went with the clipboard guy. It felt rather good that I was able to skip out on a working party and that I was not doing anything illegal, or against orders to avoid this work detail. No way could I get into any trouble this time, unless of course not enough were available guys to do the job, then someone would be back to get us E3's.

For now, I was just going to wash up, head out, and acquire my ride to Saigon. No need to have a working party slowing things up for me. However, just as I was about to head out, another clipboard army guy came in and announced that he was putting together a working party crew. He looked right at me and snapped, "You, you available?"

Without giving this any thought or concern, I came back with, "Sorry, can't help you out. I'm heading to catch a flight to Saigon. I'm heading home. My time is up."

Crap, I lied. Well, almost. I don't have a flight yet, but I was working on it. With that little detail worked out and remembering what to do in a time like this, from the Book of Dan, I turned and headed out and away from the clipboard guy and hoped that he would say nothing else to me. Well, it worked as I assumed it would. Then, by the time he figured out what I did, I would be out of hearing range from him if he were to call me back to verify my flight.

After a short walk, I had found a row of choppers and two of them had their engines running. I didn't know if they just landed or if they were ready to fly me to Saigon. Walking around them as if I knew what I was doing, I made a few inquires as to where they were off too. One had just landed and was shutting down. The other one was headed to Saigon, but was not willing or able to take me along. Two other nearby choppers had crewmembers on them and after asking for a ride, I found out that they were headed for some towns that I could not pronounce or spell their names. Because of that, I didn't want a ride with them not knowing where I would end up.

"Remember us," up and came a question from behind me. I looked and there goes the three guys from the transit barracks, James, Billy from Philly and Tom.

"Where you guys off too," I questioned, as the three of them, along with another four or five other guys headed towards a parked, but with motor's running, C-130

James answered, "Don't know. Just something to do with that cargo plane."

Great, I was not going to be a part of that working party of unloading or loading up that cargo plane. Yep, today I was cool. Just as I was about to comment, the second guy that had started up a working party also walked past me with a few guys trailing behind him. I didn't need to ask him where he was headed as he was also headed toward that same-same cargo plane.

Double great news for me today. Two working parties that were back to back that I was able to skip out on, count'em, two. This was such good news that I wanted to get Dan's mailing address so that I could tell him all about this.

So for now, I simply stood there and watched everyone board the C-130 for a little while, as I basked in my own glory. Within a few minutes, both working party teams were onboard the C-130 and they were no sooner onboard, when she upped and took off.

As I watched the plane fly out of sight, the second person that collected up the working party members that apparently did not board the aircraft, said to me as he passed, "You missed your flight? You're not in a hurry to get to Saigon?"

"Excuse me," I questioned him.

"You missed your flight out."

"Excuse me," I questioned him a second time.

"Yep, that flight is making a beer run to Saigon with a four hour layover. Wasn't that your ride to Saigon?"

"Excuse me?"

"If you were to ever volunteer for a working party, that would have been the working party to volunteer for," he explained for my benefit. "They are making a beer and pretzel run to Saigon."

Damn, damn, damn. There goes my ride to Saigon. No way was I going to write Dan about this little screw up of mine. In fact, if I ever do write a book about my time in The-Nam, I must make it a point to leave this stunt out. Boy did I screw up on this one.

"You okay," he questioned me.

"Yeah, I'm okay. I avoided your working party so that I could catch the next flight to Saigon. Going home you know."

"No sweat. You want a ride to Saigon, I'll get you a ride to Saigon," he convinced me with a sight hint of uneasiness as if this was something that was illegal or that it would cost me an arm and a leg.

I quickly came back with, "How much is this going to cost me?"

I didn't mean to sound untrustworthy, but he did have a, 'con man's smile.' In fact, if you were to look hard enough, you probably could have seen a little devil on his shoulder whispering in his ear.

"What? You think that your getting a ride to Saigon is going to cost you something?"

"Excuse me?"

He then gave me a look along with the crossing of his arms as if he was imitating Jack Benny and said, "Well!"

However, at this point, I didn't know if he was acting, if he was queer, or that he was really upset that I insulted him. Anyway, away he goes and with the possibility of the only way for me to get to Saigon before my year tour is up.

Crap, here I stand as I missed out on a flight to Saigon, and now, this guy was walking away from me and he probably really did have a way for me to get to Saigon. Hell, I was nineteen years old, I graduated high school, a combat veteran, and getting a flight to Saigon should not be that big of a deal for me. Damn, even Billy-Bob knew his way around this little, backward, country. Hell, this country was so backward, that you didn't always call it by its full name. The Nam, not even, The Vietnam. Shit, it would be the same as calling America, Amer. Alternatively, The-Amer. Stupid little country. No wonder the French threw in the towel.

With a new attitude, or an adjusted attitude with a plan, I walked right up to the first chopper that I saw with a crew and asked for a ride to their next destination. I didn't care where, just away from here. I had asked with such authority, that the airman simply said, "No sweat my man. Get on board and buckle up. We're leaving in five."

Well, for now, at least I was off this little base and heading away. Not sure just where I was headed, but away from here and with 50-50 odds that it just might be Saigon.

The door gunner leaned over to me and said that it was going to be a few minutes before we get to land in Cam-Ranh-Bay.

I answered, "Great. I love that place. The beaches are beautiful. I love lying around getting a tan with some of the Navy Waves. I've been here before," I bragged. "I know a couple of Navy Waves."

"Not today," he responded with a smile as if he had a secret to tell me or maybe he didn't care to hear me brag anymore.

My deer-in-the-headlights look prompted him to add the following. "The reason for our delay is that the base is right now under mortar attack. We don't have any ammo onboard so we must stay up here and kill some time instead of going down there to kill some VC."

Well shut my mouth. For now, Saigon was not my next port of call and my belief that Cam-Ranh-Bay was a safe place, had just blown up, or is blowing up right now. I hoped that Denise, Rose, and Betty are safe and sound. And, just as important, that they are not busy with treating the injured from this attack.

For now, our pilot cruised high enough to avoid being hit, which was a good thing, but high enough not to be able to see the action below. Which, giving this some thought, was probably a wise move. Anyway, it wasn't long before we landed and off I go again looking for a flight to Saigon, as I had no desire to spend any extra time here. I just wanted to get home.

As usual and now forming into a habit, I just moseyed on down to the next chopper that had a crew and started asking for a ride to Saigon. As luck would have it, I had quickly found my next ride out to Saigon and, I got myself onboard quickly.

After I had buckled in and made sure that I was secured, I looked and saw that I had company. These were the same-same guys from before where I bragged about my good time in Cam-

Ranh Bay and how I was not allowed to visit that, not so safe anymore town.

"What are you doing here? Thought you had orders not to show up in this town," the one asked as if he had caught me in a lie.

I responded quickly with, "Just making a transfer. Was never told, or ordered, that I couldn't make this a transfer stop."

Lucky for me, this seemed to satisfy him and the issue was dropped. As always, it was more interesting to look out at the base and all the sights than to engage in another conversation with me, about me.

We rose up and hovered about six feet above the tarmac and after the pilot stabled his aircraft, he backed-up and out from the revetment. From there, it was a slow turn to port as he then moved on down the taxiway. Moments later, we came to a hover at an intersection. This stop gave me the impression that we just came to a stop sign and the other taxiway had the right-of-way. Looking out at the helo that was taxing across from us, well, of all the people to see here in The-Nam, it was Denise, Betty, and Rose. For real, the three Navy Waves from before. No shit.

I said aloud, "I know them! It's Denise, Betty and my girl Rose."

As I tried to wave to them and get their attention, the other guys on the helo looked at me as if I was full of it. From their point of view, and I could understand that, but, damn, damn, damn. I did know these girls. I really, really did!

Well, naturally, they didn't see everyone else and me on the helo noticed that they did not see me. Even the pilots noticed that and they had no idea that I had said anything about the girls.

With nothing else to do but to hold my head down in shame and embarrassment, I did just that. For the next twenty or so minutes, I did nothing except to examine the deck of the aircraft. However, as soon as we landed, and I was sure that it was Saigon, I was the first person to exit the aircraft, and I was at front, leading the pack towards the terminal.

# Chapter 12

Finally, I had made it to Saigon. With a childlike skip and ignoring what had happened on my flight, I danced my way to the terminal. I didn't spend any time looking around at any of the sights; I've seen them all before. I wasn't looking for a, 'cool ride' in a helo; my ride today was to be on the Freedom Bird. I wasn't even worried about avoiding a working party, my mission was clear; I was to get a ride home. And in the closing stages of my, in The-Nam tour, I wasn't looking for a bar to get a beer or two or for a shoeshine place to see boobs of various sizes. I didn't need to get drunk today; however, my shoes could use a shoeshine. Nah, not today. There should be nothing in my way to slow me down now.

Once inside the terminal, I witnessed an odd, but a very understandable sight. I could tell by looking into everyone's eyes, their status. Wide-open eyes, with a touch of fear in their faces, well, they were the new guys arriving in-country. They were filled with curiosity and questions. They were the ones with 365 days to go. Yesterday, they were with friends, family, and nowhere near any bullets and body bags.

Ones with half-opened blood shot eyes, along with a facial expression of, 'don't mess with me,' they were the ones that were going home. There was no need for them to ask anyone about anything. They either had the answer or did not care one damn bit if they didn't. Tomorrow, they will be home with their friends, family, and they will be nowhere near any bullets or body bags.

Another, very clear, observation that I made was that the in-coming boys looked young, very young. Still in high school, kind of young looking boys. These boys should be pumping gas at the corner gas station, not pumping out bullets from an M16. The out-going men, not boys, but the out-going men, had a hard look about them. I assumed that I did not have this look because I hadn't been here very long. I haven't suffered many nights on patrol; I haven't been under daily mortar attacks, I haven't spent much time with my hand over an open wound to keep a friend from bleeding to death, and I haven't had to send any friends home in a body bag.

It was very easy for me now to understand why the ones going home weren't skipping around in happiness as I was. I best tune down my excitement.

Well, I must have tuned it down enough because I got this tap on my shoulder and asked, "You're new in-country. I have a pamphlet for you. Something that you will need."

Damn, I knew who this was and I knew that he was going to give me a repeat performance with the, 'free' Vietnam Phrases pamphlets that will cost me a dollar. Now was the time to say something to him. I snapped around quickly and said in a very stern and serious voice, "I don't need to purchase your damn little pamphlets. As you know, everyone who reports in-country gets them free."

Oops, it wasn't him. Not only was it not him, it wasn't even the same pamphlets. "Sorry. I thought you were someone else trying to sell me something that was free," I said sincerely, not wanting to hurt his feelings.

"No sweat. Don't mean nothin. I know the guy that you're talking about right now. He's been giving us good guys a bad rap," he explained all the while, looking over his shoulder.

Well, I might as well see what he had to be polite. I was not going to buy anything anyway; I only wanted to check it out. "Let me see one," I requested, with my hand out.

He handed me a full color pamphlet titled, A Pocket Guide to Vietnam. (APPENDIX F) I could see where this would be helpful for anyone arriving in-country. Also, no way was something this professionally printed, and in color, could be printed by the military. Not only that, after browsing a few pages, I found that I would like to take one home to show my parents and to anyone else that would be interested.

"How much?"

"One dollar, two for two dollars, or three for three dollars," he quickly answered, while he looked around again as if he was being watched. Yet, what could be wrong with this? Besides, he had something to sell and I had a dollar to buy one. Well, I did purchase one, only one.

After he thanked me and looked both ways and he asked, "You feel lucky."

"Lucky?"

"Yeah," he responded, pulling something out from one of his many pockets in his camouflage utilities. "You want to take a chance on some lottery tickets?" (APPENDIX G)

Without thinking, I answered, "How much and for which state?"

"State?"

"Yeah, I know that New York has a lottery," I said assuredly, because I knew that much about lottery tickets. Even though I was only nineteen, I had been to New York City.

"No man, listen up. What I have here today, and for today only, is some local lottery tickets. These little puppies are easier to buy and to cash in. No state or local taxes to pay. Cool huh?"

"Okay," I responded, not indicating whether I wanted one or not.

At this point, he again looked around as if he was a street pimp attempting to avoid the police as he showed me his lottery tickets. He had them fanned out like a deck of cards and that I was to select one as part of his magic trick.

"Where did you get'em at," I questioned, believing that just maybe, these were fake or outdated losing tickets.

"The local Cao-Bois sells them," he answered, picking out one from the middle for me to examine, which I didn't.

"Nah, don't think so. I'll be gone and out of the country by the time the number comes out," I said this so convincingly, that he thanked me, and as if he was an illusion, he quickly disappeared. In fact, his disappearance was so quick, that the only thing missing was for him to have said, "Scotty, beam me up." Anyway, I did find this a little unusual, but gave it no additional attention. Hell, I was going home and that was my winning ticket.

I gave my little pamphlet, A Pocket Guide to Vietnam, another quick glance and stuffed it in my pocket. Within a minute or two, and without difficulty, I found the information desk and a Master-Chief Petty Officer manned it. As expected, as must be the custom, he had a cup of coffee in one hand and a lit cigarette in the other. He seemed bored with his duties and gave out mean looks to everyone that came near him in an attempt to ask him something, anything. He'd make a good poster boy for an earlier American flag that simply said, "Don't tread on me." Damn, damn, damn, and I had to ask him something.

Whatever, I stood in front of him waiting for his attention. I placed my orders on the ledge between him and me and to my surprise; there were two piles of pamphlets on the counter ledge. Two piles of FREE, I say again, FREE pamphlets with a little sign that said, "Only take one please."

These items were stacked up very nice and neat like those Apartment Search or Auto Parts pamphlets that you would find in every sub shop and Chinese carryout back in the states. One pile had the pamphlets, Vietnam Phrases; from the last time I was here, where I had paid a dollar. The second pile had the pamphlets, A Pocket guide to Vietnam that I just purchased for a dollar. I've been taken again and now that I thought about it, that it may have been the same guy from before. I gots to look in the mirror to see if the word, 'stupid' was tattooed on my forehead. Hell, there might even be a sign taped to my back that said, "I have plenty of ones and I will buy anything."

I could do that later, but for now, I needed to ask the Master-Chief a few questions. Just as I was about to ask him something, he opened up to what appeared to be a phone book and I could hear him mumble under his breath to himself, "BUREAU, BUNAV, BUNO, BUWEPS, CIB, CINC, CINCLANTFL, CINCPACFLT, DCNO, DEROSE, DOD, JCS." He turned the page and continued with, "GVN, MARKET TIME, OPNAV, PCU, RAG, SECDEF, SECNAV, along with VCNO."

He looked confused for a moment, took a sip of his coffee, and continued with, "SAR, SIT-REP, TDY, TF, TG, VNSM."

I said, "Excuse me," and that was returned with a successful facial expression suggesting that if anyone had a question, that it would be to everyone's benefit for him to come back and ask his relief.

Not me, because I had a question and it was his job to provide me with an answer. I boldly stood up straight and tall and asked in a deep voice as if I was a big deal or something, "Excuse me. I have a question. I could come back at another time if you're too busy right now."

After I said that, I realized that I was not the, 'big-deal,' that I thought I was. My question started out mature and bold, like I wanted, then I gave in and it ended up with me being a sissy boy with me saying, "I could come back at another time." I may have looked bold, but I wasn't. Not now anyway, because he was a Chief and that I was just a lonely Seaman. And, that I was at the bottom of the food chain with him being quite near the top.

Oh well, he looked at me as if he wanted to hurt me. "Your question Seaman," he asked in a most gentile way. This Chief had a mean look but was apparently a good selection with his gentle manor for someone to be posted at this information desk.

"I would like to be on the next available flight to Travis Air Force Base in California."

"Let me have a copy of your orders, please," he asked, as he held out his hand.

I did as instructed and watched as he took off a copy for himself and then he stamped the original. His next step was to look into a folder that apparently held flight schedules and possibly information about available flights and seating. After finding a certain page, he ran his finger down one side of the page then up the other. Turned the page over and repeated his search. This went on for a few pages and it was starting to take an awful long time for such a simple task.

I assumed that a line was developing behind me because I could hear others making comments like, "Let's go already," "the war will be over by the time I get to ask my question," and, "any time now."

One comment, from the guy right behind me, was, "I can't stand here all day like this."

Being that this was not my fault and that I was simply in line just like everyone else, I responded to this latest remark, without looking to see whom it was, with, "My legs are just as tired as yours. Don't sweat it. Relax man."

The line behind me got very silent. The kind of silence that did not give me a good feeling all over. I just held my place and waited for the ax to fall, and of course, to fall on me. Well, it did with, "Relax man, sir."

Go figure, it had to be an officer. With that, I turned around to apologize and to add in, 'sir,' when to my shock and horror; it was the officer from the other day. The officer that had only the one leg.

Before I could muster up anything that remotely resembled an apology with, 'sir,' attached, he jumped in, on, and all over my case. "Correct me if I'm wrong, Seaman. But, don't you own me an apology and a couple of drinks."

Okay, I escaped once before pretending that I was the wrong guy and for the most part, I got away with it. I might as well try it again. Besides, I didn't have anything to lose. "Sir, sorry sir. I do owe you an apology, sir, but a drink, sir. I don't understand."

Wanting to keep talking and not to allow him to answer back, I hurriedly responded with, "If you want a drink sir, I'll find a soda machine and get you what you want. Sir."

Good, I had apparently caught him off balance. Oops, catching him off guard would be better than catching him off balance.

It just might be working because he was now sporting the deer-in-the-headlights look. In fact, that looked good on an officer, especially this officer and on this officer right now.

He questioned me, "Do I know you Seaman?"

"Sir. No sir," I answered with a smile trying my very best to indicate that I was not scared or lying. Well, it apparently was not working well because he asked, "You sure?"

"Yes sir. I'm sure. I believe that an officer in your condition would be hard to forget. Sir." I kept up my smile and asked a second time to move things along, "What kind of soda would you like sir?"

Not looking totally convinced, but almost, he came back with, "RC. I'll take an RC Cola." After a few, very long, seconds, he added, "Yeah. That'll be nice of you."

"Yes sir. Not a problem, sir. Just as soon as I get my seat assignment for my flight home," I assured him. "One RC Cola coming right up, sir."

I turned back around and all I wanted was a flight and seat number, and quickly. I did however; plan to retrieve an RC Cola for the officer. I just hoped that I could easily find a soda machine that takes MPC. Damn, that's right. I didn't have any coins, American or otherwise. Damn, damn, damn, I didn't need to be running all over Saigon looking for an RC Cola.

The Master-Chief spoke up and said, "Tomorrow. I have you a flight out for tomorrow. Flight number 230 at 3:15."

I was, all smiles, as the Master-Chief handed me my ticket home. It was just a blue ticket with his sloppy handwriting, but it was my ticket. "Thank you very much Chief. Got it, flight 230 at 3:15."

I was going to ask him which 3:15 this was. Should he had said, zero 3:15 for an AM flight out, or should he had said, 15-15, for an afternoon flight? Damn, damn, damn, are we discussing Eastern Standard Time, Central, Mountain, or Pacific Standard Time? I gots to know, can't screw this up, nor can I assume anything. The military was so organized, but I don't know the organization.

I looked back at the Chief and he had already picked up my confusion and anticipated my question. He quickly said to me, "In the afternoon Seaman, in the afternoon."

Now that I had what I wanted, a ticket home, and the correct time, I wondered if I could even ask for a window seat. What the hell, "Chief, excuse me. Is this a window seat?"

Looking at me as if I should be grateful and just move along, he snapped back my ticket and give it a look-see. "Sorry son, it's an aisle seat. Is that a problem?"

Crap, yes and no, but I didn't think that he cared one way or another. But, then what the hell. I could always ask. "Chief, could this be exchanged for a window seat?"

"Hell no. Anything else," he questioned me as if I was to ask for anything else, his answer would be, hell no.

"No Chief, this will be just fine. Thank you," I answered trying to express to him that it really was okay with me. No need to get him ticked off, especially now that I did have a ticket in hand.

I turned and said to the one legged officer behind me, "Sir, I'll be right back with your soda."

No reason to have him jump on me for anything. And before he could respond, I did my own disappearing act and was off looking for a soda machine. Well, to make a long story short, nearby was a little shop that sold cigarettes, chewing gum, and to my good fortune, cold sodas. To make my good fortune golden, they also sold RC Cola. As expected, I purchased the soda and quickly returned to the information desk.

I had hoped that he was still busy with the Master-Chief, and he was. With one smooth move, I placed the RC cola on the counter next to the free pamphlets and clandestinely disappeared.

With that little excursion out of the way, it appeared to me that I would have no new issues in getting out of the country. I must wait until tomorrow, but tomorrow was a lot shorter than having to wait 11 months.

Immediately, I made my way out of the terminal and worked my way to where I thought the buses would be parked. Anyway, with no buses there, I found a bench and made myself comfortable believing that the buses would be there soon enough. A moment later, two guys that were apparently fresh from boot camp sat down next to me. With them wearing their dress white uniforms, it was, as you can visualize, a single bright spot in a country filled with greens and browns. Dirty greens and browns, but greens and browns just the same.

The one who sat on the end of the bench, looked to me to be scared of everything that was near us. As someone walked by, he would scrunch up in a fetal position as if he was trying to hide in the cracks of the bench that we were sitting on. His partner, the one sitting next to me was just the opposite. Someone would walk by, he would very comfortably sit up and say, "How you doing?" Or, "What's going on?"

The scared one would give him a look as if suggesting that he should keep quiet. They made up a kind of an odd couple. Yet, I must remember that over here, you didn't really pick your friends, that have like interests with you, and that you usually hung around with someone, anyone, because he was just simply going your way.

Getting back to the other one, he would then return a look of his own to his buddy suggesting that he should lighten up a little. In that, not everyone in Vietnam wanted to kill them.

The guy next to me looked over and asked, "Is this the place to catch the bus to go downtown?"

Before I could answer, his buddy said in a feeble voice that most assuredly, fitted his outward appearance, "That's not where we want to go. Just ask him about the BEQ thing-a-ma-jig. Don't go and get directions now that will get us lost."

I was thinking how I hoped that I didn't seem like this to Dan when I first landed in-country. Nah, no way was I that rude or stupid. Stupid maybe on some things, but not rude.

The guy next to me turned towards his buddy and said something that I didn't hear. As he turned back to me and before he could say anything, his sissy pal grabbed his shoulder and said, "Remember, we have to get checked-in. I don't want to be late checking in. We have orders. Remember that, okay?"

Irritated by his friend, he turned back to me, and asked, "We are trying to get to the Navy BEQ. We missed the last bus because my friend here spent too much time in the men's room cleaning off the toilet seat before he could sit down. I told him that all he had to do was to hover, but no, he had to wipe it, spray it, and scrub it clean first."

Before he could continue with, this tall tale of his, and before I could answer, the guy on the end knocked him on the shoulder again and said, "He doesn't need to hear all that. He's a Marine. I heard tell that they don't use toilets. Don't know how."

He again ignored what his friend just said and repeated his question, "The Navy BEQ. Do you know anything about it?"

I gave the rude guy a look of my own, which suggested that he should just shut up and relax. He did sit back in his seat and tried very hard to blend in to the bench. Him I decided to ignore, for now. Looking to answer the question, I responded, "Yeah. Every time a flight comes in, buses will pull right up here to take everyone to either the Navy and Marine BEQ or Army BEQ."

Mr. Irritation sat up, spoke up, and said to me most rudely, "What about the Air Force BEQ. You didn't say anything about them. Do you know what you're talking about my man? Is there an Air Force BEQ bus or not?"

For someone that I just met, I could see why someone might want to smack him around a little. I sure felt like doing that to him and right now would be a good time. Whatever, not letting this bother me, I came back with, "We're on an Air Force Base, and Air Force guys can just walk to their BEQ from here. Even a Marine knows that much."

Wow, I did good with that answer. I just made this up and it sounded as if I knew what I was talking about this time. It's somewhat scary that I am beginning to answer questions the way that Dan did. Whatever, I be cool.

Too bold, or too stupid to apologize, he sat back in his seat as if I never said anything. Oh well, I'll just mark him up as a jerk. Not even a likable kind of jerk. Just a plane old nasty jerk, which I hoped to be nearby when someone does smack him around.

The guy next to me continued as if his irritating friend was not there, and he said, "We're going to the Navy BEQ. You going to the Army BEQ? You're Army, right?"

"Yes and no," I answered, as the sissy boy spoke up and added, "What? You army guys aren't smart enough to answer a simple question?"

Having already had about enough of this jerk, I said as I pointed to him, not meaning to put my arm in front of his friend's face, "You shut up. I have nothing to say to you and you have nothing that I would consider important enough for you to tell me."

He quickly sat back on the bench and said nothing more. Well, nothing for now anyway. I looked back over at the guy asking the normal question, as if I didn't do anything and added, "I'm in the Navy, just like you guys. However, I'm going to be staying at the Army BEQ."

The guy next to me said, "My name is Mickey Horne, and I'm from Allendale, South Carolina. And that's one damn pretty state with lots of pretty women."

I told him my name and hometown, as we didn't include his friend with our introductions. He didn't seem to mind that his friend was ignored, but his friend did lean our way to, more easily, hear our conversation. Not a problem with me to be leaving him out.

"You staying at the Army's BEQ," questioned Mickey.

After a short pause for effect, because I was cool and I've been here longer than these new guys have, I continued with, "I get a better deal there."

"You said that you're in the Navy? You're traveling and you're not in your dress whites, and you're not checking into the Navy BEQ," was a set of questions from someone that should have been silent.

Because I wasn't in the mood for this guy's attitude, I quickly shot back; "I said shut up. Sit back and wait for your bus."

I could not believe that I was being so bold with this guy. Naturally, it was easy with him being half my size. When I said that to him, he shyed back and blinked his eyes as if he was used to being smacked in the head. I have a Boat Captain that I would like him to meet. He'll smack him plane silly.

The guy next to me must have thought I was a bully or something, because he sat back and didn't ask anything more about what I just said. If it would have been just him, I would have suggested that he could follow me. Like what Dan did with me on my first day here in-country.

The rude guy was now chomping at the bit to say something. I could only look at him as if he was white trash, stupid white trash at that. Yet, I just had to say something. It was just that I was being cool and I wanted them both to see that, especially the rude one.

"When I stay at the Army BEQ," I added, speaking to the guy next to me and purposely not making eye contact with his stupid friend. "I get to miss out on standing watches."

I paused for effect and continued with, "Now when you guys get checked into the Navy BEQ and after you are assigned a bunk, you will be issued instructions, a weapon, and a time for your first watch."

"I've done watches before in boot camp. It wasn't that big of a deal," he explained, as the rude guy looked on, and to my pleasure, he didn't say anything.

I came back with, "You stood 'Fire Watches' in boot camp. You're right; they are not that big a deal. However, over here, you stand real watches with real guns. I'm talking about being issued a loaded weapon and then realizing that you're a sitting target."

Fortunately, this made sense to the two of them.

"Trust me on this one," I added, "You will not enjoy being on watch over here. They'll have you pulling four-hour watches sometimes a couple of times a day. Snipers here shoot at people on guard duty at least twice a week. That means that a guard or two is hit every week here in Saigon."

"I'll tell you this," I continued, "Let the guys that will never see action pull some guard duty while they are here in Saigon."

Mickey asked, "You don't stand any watches?"

"Not at the Army's BEQ," I said with pride.

His friend, not up to speed with our conversation, said, "I've done watches before. I can handle a watch or two over here."

As if he didn't say anything, Mickey added, "Yeah, we're headed out to sea. But first, we got to make a stop over at Binh-Thuy."

"You ship is at Binh-Thuy?"

"That was what we were told when we checked in," he answered with a confused look on his face. More like a deer-in-the-headlights look.

"What's your ship?" I asked.

The other guy spoke up and said, "My name is Clarence, and we're going to report to the USS SUMMIT. It's an ARR. Have you ever seen her?"

Wow, three surprises at a time. One, he was being civil and two, for all the ships over here in-country and out on Yankee Station, the SUMMIT would be their new duty station. Now, for the third part that surprised me, his name was Clarence. He seemed like someone that would have a name of Clarence.

I answered Mickey and still ignoring Clarence, I said, "Yeah. Not only have I seen her, I was assigned to her before I was wounded."

My response from them was both scary and comical. All four eyes opened wide with the white showing all around as the two of them sucked in air in an attempt to catch their breath. It was extremely obvious that someone had not explained to them where they were to go and failed to explain the dangers of being assigned to a combat unit.

"What?" Questioned Mickey, and that was followed with, "Say again. You know, that little part about being wounded. You remember? You just said something about that."

"Oh," I exclaimed, trying to sound like I was surprised. "You must have thought that you were being assigned to a silver navy ship, sailing on the ocean blue water in the South China Sea. And . . . that you would get to wear your little white hats and bell-bottom pants."

"Well, yes. I thought that was about right," Mickey said, with Clarence in agreement. "What else could there be?" He continued, "I did join the U.S. Navy and that was what I joined up for."

Clarence, looking more confused, asked me, "Why are you dressed that way?"

Well now, my man Clarence needed some answers. With him being reasonable still, I would give him a break. In fact, I could recall exactly what Dan had told me on my first day here. I explained, "Navy personnel serving in-country are authorized to wear greens. Once you get in-country, you don't want to be walking around in your dress whites. You make a nice target in a place where everything is either brown or green. Even the water is brown. Everything over here stays green and brown, year round."

Both of them were absorbing every word I said. I could only imagine that I looked that young and immature when Dan explained all that to me. Damn, and that was only a few weeks ago.

Clarence sat up straight, made a frown as if he had the most serious question of his life and I was the luckiest person in the world, or in Vietnam, that had the responsibility to answer him. He asked, "One more time for clarification. You're saying that the two of us aren't going out to sea and that we must dress like you?"

I was willing to answer him, but I didn't know if he was putting down the way I was dressed or that he was curious.

He continued before I could respond with, "You've been shot at?"

"Open your eyes man. Look around you. This is a war zone and all that," I answered.

As if I was a teacher and they were students trained to follow my every instruction, they both looked around. They seemed to realize that they were the only ones walking around in an all-white uniform in an area painted with greens and browns.

"Aren't we going onboard a ship? Ship, as in a big boat that needs deep water to float in?" Mickey asked most sincerely with a little fear in his voice.

Clarence added in, "Out to sea, we're going out to sea? Gray ships and blue water I was told. I signed on to do Navy stuff like tie knots and shoot the big guns. I want to visit exotic ports of call."

It looked to me as if these poor guys were going to start crying. I looked at the two of them and questioned, "You guys have no idea where your unit is, do you?"

Before they could answer me, and before they could ask another question, five military buses pulled up right in front of us. Two buses for the Navy, one for the Marines, and two for the Army. I looked at them and said, "Catch you guys later."

I got up, straightened my shirt, and continued with, "Hope you enjoy your first watch."

Nothing was said to me then, or it was that I didn't wait around long enough to get into another conversation. So, for now, I boarded the nearest Army bus. I looked back at the two of them and they were looking as if they didn't know whether to follow me or not.

As for the way I felt about them, I didn't need the competition in getting a room at the Army's BEQ. One looking for a room is good, two is okay, but a third person might create a hassle.

I took my seat, and naturally, it was an aisle seat. I looked back and could see that Mickey wanted to join me and that Clarence was deciding what it was that he wanted to do, or at the very least, review his options again.

To my surprise, Clarence walked towards my bus with Mickey in close tow. Just as they were about to board the bus, the driver yelled at them and said, "Army. This is an Army bus. Can't you Navy guys read?"

The two of them stopped right in their tracks and it appeared to me that they didn't know what to do next. The driver added some additional cuts, "Army. A R M Y. Not Navy. That's spelled N A V Y. Now get away from my bus."

Well, they did just that, lowered their heads, and headed away towards the Navy bus. At least, they didn't rat me out. They could have, but I was pleased that they didn't. What they did now was a little odd, but they were new and FNG's always seemed to mess up. They stopped between the other Army and Navy bus and didn't get on either one. As they stood there deciding on what to do, everyone came out of the airport terminal and headed toward their assigned buses. Now these two guys were in everyone's way and were pushed aside as some would make a nasty remark to them. They must have spent five or ten minutes deciding on what to do.

I just shook my head and said, "Damn, damn, damn. Those two guys won't last long in the military that's for sure. I didn't think they would make it long in The-Nam. Damn, these two won't last long in Saigon."

By the time they realized that they should have gotten onboard the Navy bus, the bus door closed and it started to back away. I could make out that Mickey was telling Clarence that they could still ride on the second Navy bus.

However, as the first bus pulled out, it was noted that this bus was really the second bus. Navy bus number one was already gone.

Quickly, they made their way back to my bus only to have the door closed in their faces. Now what we have here were two very unhappy, lost, and scared FNG's. For the most part, what did I care? I had a bus ride, a good seat, and hopefully a place to stay tonight. Screw those guys; I didn't know them and I would never see them again.

My bus slowly backed out. I was on the same-same route to the Army BEQ as before and the traffic was the same. Lots of noise, plenty of bikes mixed in along with some water buffaloes pulling carts. It wasn't long before we arrived safely and in one piece. I was one of the first ones off the bus and I made my way inside so as not to give a target for anyone to shoot at.

At the Army BEQ check-in process, I knew to wait at the end of the line. At least I remembered that if I didn't, that I would have been told to get at the end of the line anyway. When my turn came and after I explained my situation, I was informed that they did have an extra bed. I returned a smile to the sergeant because I knew that I had gotten away with this and I did it on my own.

The sergeant behind the desk sharply said to me, "We've had a problem here lately. It appears that some of you Navy guys, like yourself." He paused at this point and expressed, giving me a dirty look, "That you guys are checking in here in order to avoid standing watches."

I could only swallow hard and make an effort not to blush or look guilty. Before I could respond to his accusations, he asked loud enough for everyone in the lobby to hear, "So tell me Seaman, when was it that you were at the Navy BEQ? When was it that they told you about them being full?"

"Well Sergeant, it was yesterday when I was there. I stayed at my girl friends place last night," I responded, with that answer because if everyone were listening in on our conversation, at least everyone here would know that I had a girlfriend and that I was cool.

"That does it," he shouted at me. He said that with such passion and anger that I was more afraid of him than I was of the VC.

He continued with, "A girlfriend you say. I tell you this, take your little skinny white ass along with your crabs, Red Rose, and any other disease you have taken onboard from your, girlfriend, and go stay at the navy BEQ."

Well, this was not working out for me. My attempt to show that I had a girlfriend came back that I was living with a hooker. That was not what I meant and now, that was apparently, what it was.

Before I could come back with anything, the Sergeant questioned me with the statement, "You leaving now?"

I looked at him with my typical deer-in-the-headlights face, and could not open my mouth to say anything.

No problem, because he spoke for me. "Your response should be, 'yes Sergeant, I am leaving now. And I will never come back here again.'"

With my head held low, but trying to be prideful, I headed out. I knew the way to the Navy BEQ and that was a good thing. It would have been worse for me if I had to ask the sergeant for directions for a place that I supposedly just left.

After my short walk, I arrived at the front door at the Navy's BEQ at the exact same-same time, as did a taxi. Not that I should have been surprised, but out comes Mickey and Clarence. They were just a shocked to see me, as I was to see them.

# Chapter 13

Clarence looked at me, then at Mickey and said, "See, he's lost. He can't even tell the difference between an Army and the Navy BEQ."

I looked at Mickey after giving Clarence a dirty look, and said, "Lost hell. I've already been to the Army BEQ and it's full. This is my second stop and I still beat you guys here. Besides, the Annapolis BEQ has fine quarters"

Now that came out kind of cool. Mickey just looked at me and said, "Hi." It was apparent that he wanted nothing to do with his jerk-off sidekick.

Without warning, Clarence yelled out a yelp that sounded like someone just stepped on a dog's tail. Everyone nearby looked at him as if he was some kind of freak. Besides, a man, or even a boy, should never make a sound like that when startled. Even girls don't make sounds like that when they are caught off guard.

He pointed down at the sidewalk and said, "Oh my."

Well, it was not at all that big of a deal. It was another one of those fake, chalked out, dead body outline here on one of the few sidewalks in beautiful downtown Saigon. This one was complete with fake bloodstains near the head and who ever made this one up, did a very nice job. It almost looked real.

I said to Mickey, ignoring Clarence, and was overheard by a small group thought to be FNG's, "That's a good one. Kind of funny, don't you think?"

Well, as if I just shot the President of the United States, everyone there gave me a look as if I was the most insensitive person in the whole wide world. From this, I gathered that everyone was fully tricked by this fake chalking, or, to my misfortune, this was not a fake and that someone really did take a hit right there. I had no idea what to do about this. Should I tell them that I thought that it was a good fake, or just fade away and hoped that no one was armed and pissed at me?

Clarence tells Mickey, "See. I told you that this guy was not all there. He's Mr. Bullshit. I'm not going to be staying at the Navy BEQ."

Ignoring Clarence, and talking to Mickey, I explained, "The time that I was here last, there were two fake body outlines, just like this one, to scare away the locals."

Lucky for me, one of the guards guarding the front door had overheard us, well he spoke up in my support and said, "Welcome to The-Nam Newbies. The man is right. Take a walk around back and you'll see two more body outlines."

I gave the guard the thumbs up and said to Sissy Boy Clarence, "Next time you got to scream, try and scream like a man."

Well, Mickey broke up on that one and yelled out a howling laughter that was so loud, that it almost stopped traffic. With that, he and I were buddies and Clarence was the odd man out. He was definitely an odd man.

After I gave the dead body outline one last look, I made my way inside to check-in with Mickey and Clarence in close tow.

The check-in here was same-same as the Army's check-in. The process was quick and efficient. As each man approached the desk, a First Class Petty Officer took a copy of his orders and stamped the original. Next, each man was issued an orange pill along with a couple of meal tickets. The line moved right and another Petty Officer assigned each sailor a bed.

Another move right and I gave that Third Class Petty Officer my name, rank, and a copy of my orders along with my bunk number. He presented me with a copy of the Welcome to Vietnam pamphlet (APPENDIX H), an Annapolis Check-in sheet (APPENDIX I) with instructions to fill it out, and informed me that I was to keep an eye on the, 'Watch Board' that was behind him. That was where they would post the names, times, and places for those of us that were to be standing watches. He repeated the same-same to everyone as if he was a recording.

"You are responsible to review this board. I will not, I say again, I will not be out to remind you about your watch. I will not be around waking you up in the middle of the night for your watch. I will not make any changes to the board after your time is posted. Do you understand these instructions that I just gave you?"

"Yes," I responded, and I remembered not to sir him. Then I figured that while I was there, that I would do a look-see for my name. Irritated that I was doing that, and doing it right then, this legalistic Petty Officer shouted to me, "Ass hole. Did you expect to see your name there now?"

I gave him a look of, 'oops' and stepped away expecting him to drop it and snap at the next guy that was in line, which happened to be Clarence.

Well, the Petty Officer didn't say anymore to me, but he did say to Clarence, "Behind me is the Watch Board. There is where you will find your name, the time, and place for your watch. You are responsible to review this board. I will not, I say again, I will not be out to remind you about your watch. I will not be around waking you up in the middle of the night for your watch. I will not make any changes to the board after something is posted. Do not look at the board now for your name as your friend just did. I haven't had the time to post anyone's name that is checking in right now." After a short pause, "Do you understand these instructions that I just gave you?"

Would you believe that this excuse for a man that yelled like a little girl, who was afraid of his own shadow, spoke up in a deep, manly voice, and proudly announced, "I fully understand your instructions. They are not that hard to follow."

This little turd was starting to get on my bad side. Not a problem for now, I'll just make it a point to remember him at a later time, when the situation suits me.

I was going to return to the guy that controlled the watch schedule. I wanted to ask him about being issued a weapon, but decided against it. We weren't issued weapons probably because we were sailors and that they were going to issue us mops to swab this country clean instead.

Anyway, with my room number, I meant bunk number; I made my way upstairs to find my bed for tonight. The only difference between this room and the one that I stayed at before at the Army's expense was that here, there was a 100-watt light bulb in the ceiling fan. They even had the same-same type of bunks in just as small room. I had nothing to lock to my bedpost; I just wanted to see where it was. In addition, of course, I planned to find the correct place to take a shower, with hot water and a decent mirror.

Mickey was in the bunk next to mine and I suggested that he lock up his sea bag. He seemed puzzled at my idea but complied anyway. As he went through the motions, I filled him in on the reasoning behind it. He seemed pleased and asked in a joking way, "All I need now is a shoe shine and I'm set."

Of course, I came back with the details about the topless shoeshine shop. I just had to explain how entertaining it was. A few guys, FNG's to be exact, sort of hung around as I gave them the lay of the land.

With this newly forming little group, I told everyone about how that if you were to purchase anything from anybody, which you should bargain with them and try to end up at half the asking price. I made it a point to inform them about how smart the little kids were around here and how they should be on guard when approached.

One guy spoke up and asked, "I heard that there are some wild bars around here. You have any suggestions on where to go?"

I gave them the story where my assets were taken out and pulled around the bar and how painful and embarrassing that was. Gee, just thinking about all that I've been through would fill a book. A very interesting novel at that.

By default, I was appointed tour guide for tonight's activities. I enjoyed the new title and liked the idea of being in charge. Well, not as if I was an officer or anything, but in charge just the same.

Mickey asked, "So. What are you planning to do now?"

This was great. This had to be the cool feeling that Dan felt when I tagged along with him. I came back with, "Eat. I'm going to get something to eat. There was no telling or guarantees when or where our next meal would come from."

Everyone responded as if we were in a football huddle with, "Let's go. You the man." The only thing that we did not do was to clap hands or do any butt smacking. So for now, we were off to get something to eat. I had following me, Mickey, Clarence and four or five other FNG's. Right now, a handful of FNG's are following my every word because I'd 'knows the ropes.'

With everyone but me in his dress whites, it looked as if I had a parade behind me. It was still cool because I was in the lead. I didn't know if there was a supply of uniforms back at the barracks. Something that these guys could change into. However, I would check that out when I got back.

Lucky for me, we left by the back door and we did pass by one of the fake chalked, dead body outlines. Naturally, I had to make it a point to show everyone that, especially Clarence.

With my first direction at leadership, things were going smoothly for me, I felt as if I could have told everyone what to eat at the chow hall once we got there and that everyone would have followed those instructions.

We had gone less than a block when I heard some little kid shout out, "Joe. Joe. Remember me?"

Like everyone here, we all looked around to see who it was. I saw that it was a little kid selling something. I said to the group, "Be careful guys. Be cautious about what he's selling and for how much."

This damn little kid stepped between the group and me and said, "What you know Joe?"

I gave him a second look and he looked familiar. Of all the little kids in this ugly, little brown and green country, it was that same-same little turd of a kid that sold me the Christmas cards a few weeks ago. And of course, he would remember me. Now, how do I handle this? The last time I was with him, I wanted to shoot him and now, I wished that I had.

"Christmas cards. You want more. Same-same numba-one good deal Joe," he announced to me as he smiled back at everyone else.

I was hungry and wanted to eat. What I really wanted to do was to get away from this kid. With that, I suggested that we catch him on our way back. I must have said that with the voice of authority, because without question, everyone followed me away. Well, that was cool. Talk as if you have authority and they will follow.

Lunch was quick and lacked any kind of incident. Before long, we were back at the BEQ without having to cross paths with the little Christmas card salesmen. Naturally, it was most helpful that I went back using a different route with the excuse of giving them a little tour of the town.

# Chapter 14

Back at the BEQ, we all sort of ended up in the lounge area with a pool table, only there were no pool balls or pool sticks available. The pool table itself looked like a golf course. Cigarette ashes were neatly dumped in little piles like sand traps with beer stains snaked around like fine cut greens. Not able to play pool, Clarence, Mickey, and myself sat around and bullshitted about our lives back home. Each one of us had a story to out due the other. We bragged about how our girl friends had bigger boobs, longer legs and could scream louder than anyone else could during sex. Mickey even went as far as to say that when he had sex, it was so good that he would scream out his own name. We were just a bunch of good old boys talking/bragging about girls like fisherman brag about fishing and hunters brag about hunting.

Well, this went on for such a long while, that we realized that it was again time to eat. Dinner was what everyone wanted and maybe that could include a visit to a bar or two. After everyone made a head call, we were out and about. We wanted to find a nice place to eat and I secretly wanted to avoid the little shitty kids that would try to sell most anything. I didn't need any Christmas cards, watches, or small children with a wife to send home.

It didn't take long as we found a place just around the corner from where we were staying. It was a rather nice in that it had tablecloths. Not clean tablecloths, but tablecloths just the same.

Our waitress dropped off our menus and as we decided what to order, I noticed two girls that were standing nearby and that they were somewhat cute. I loved their American outfits of Go-Go boots and their little one-piece, short, very short skirts with lots of bright colors. Their hair was up in a beehive style cut instead of the typical long, straight, black, parted in the middle, oriental looking hairstyle.

They were wearing panty hose and it appeared that they were wearing them for the first time and that they were excessively way too big, as they would try repeatedly to keep them pulled up. The boots that they were wearing had three-inch soles along with six-inch heels.

With the combined issue of their panty hose falling down and their oversized boots, well, they were not going to be marching in any parade today as they were having plenty of trouble just standing up straight and not tipping over. They were having so much trouble standing in these boots, that it appeared to me as if they went from being barefoot all of their lives until today, and today, they had on monster boots.

A funny thing about these two was that most bar girls moved around, putting the, 'hit' on anyone with money to spend, and or money to lose. These two were contented just to stand in one spot and hope, because of their appearance, that guys would move in on them where they were standing.

It was hard not to miss their, 'panty hose pull,' activity of theirs because on every third or forth pull, they would simply reach up and under their dress and pull them up from the waistband. Not very attractive or sexy, but a few rednecks got excited over this. Hell, they could have been two dogs wearing panty hoses and they, the rednecks, would have gotten excited.

As you could imagine, when rednecks got excited, well they would simply make enough noise that it would catch the attention of everyone around them. They were making comments like, "You need an extra set of hands keeping those things up?" "How about you letting me pull them down for you," or the crude one of, "Check it out, they have that dang thing wrapped up in plastic."

I mentioned to Clarence and Mickey that they should turn around and check out these two girls. We watched these girls, with interest, their facial expressions as the different remarks were made at them. It looked to me that they would smile, a bigger smile, at the ones that appeared to have the most money. It didn't matter what they said or how they looked.

Still, it was odd that they would not move over to any of the tables. They would just stand there as if their boots were nailed to the floor, or that they were too heavy to move.

Just then, there was a very loud explosion right outside the front door of this establishment that scared the piss out of me, along with everyone else. It was hard to tell what happened. Was this a bomb that was dropped from an airplane, or did something else just blow up? Everyone had ducked under the tables for cover. Even the ones that were drunk, knew enough to hide beside, and or under whatever was near them.

It was just this one explosion and after the dust settled, everything was quiet, really quiet. Well, really quiet except for the two Go-Go girls, still standing in place, and they were crying uncontrollably.

My first concern was that maybe they were hurt, but from where I was hiding, I was unable to see any blood. Didn't mean to say that I was hiding, I was just taking cover and securing a defensive position until the dust settled.

One American service guy, army I think, made his way over to them to offer his assistance. I was expecting him to show compassion either to calm them down or to service their wounds, or both. However, he screamed out, "Gross, that's nasty man. You girls are nasty, nasty, nasty."

Well, this guy needed a lesson on how, what not to say, that will make an injured person not panic. Show a little sympathy will you, I thought.

He took a step back from them, pointed at their legs, and again shouted, "Gross, that's really nasty man."

Naturally, I could not help it, but I had to look more closely at them for myself and what I saw was gross, really gross. Yep, gross. They had apparently wet themselves and it was running down their legs, inside their panty hose, and into their boots. That explosion had literally scared the piss right out of them and it had started to puddle in their boots.

Everyone was staring at these two and they knew that they were now the center of attention, negative attention. In some ways, this was funny and only funny because no one else was hurt. No one else that we knew about for the moment.

Well, to add to this unusual humorous situation, as they made their way to the back of the room, it was made even more amusing as they would walk, 'Frankenstein' style, because of their oversize boots. Then, there were the sounds that were made by the pee in their boots, as it would squish out between their toes. And even with all that had just happened to them, they still had the frame of mind to keep their pantyhose pulled up.

As for the rednecks in the house, the issues created by the explosion and these two aqua girls overshadowed the caution of the possibility of a second explosion that we should have taken seriously. All they could do was to shout at each other as this one guy, the one with the most teeth, started to sing, "Splish Splash, I was takin' a bath, down near the DMZ. A rub-a-dub-dub, just relaxin' in the tub, thinkin' all I could do was pee."

Well, as for me, this singing was a little much and we decided to exit this place. Wow, only in the Nam would the unusual, be considered, not so unusual. Someday I'll get back home and as I try to tell this story, well, no one will believe me. Yet, I might get a believable audience, but he would most certainly be another Vietnam vet.

"I could use a drink after that little exercise. Let's find another place," suggested Mickey, and Clarence and I agreed.

It was too bad that we could not find a topless shoeshine place or visit the bar where the girls grab you at the door and greet you with a cold handshake. I was not in the mood to have my little Charlie and the twins towed around some bar. However, we did find a bar that looked promising but it appeared as if it served food.

As much as these two guys were following me around, I was very content to have them walk in first. Well, nothing happened walking in and I was a little disappointed. We past this one table with a few guys that must have been there all day as indicated by the number of empty beer bottles on the table. I guessed that this was a place that they would bring you a bottle of beer, but would not take any away.

We walked by another guy and he was putting a move on his girlfriend. Well, she might not have been his girlfriend, just a rental. Another way of saying this was to say, we walked by another guy and he was putting a move on his rental. Anyway, besides all that, we walked a little further and simply took a seat at the bar. Crap, it would have been fun to watch these two guys get towed around by there private parts. As for me, I would have guarded my jewels at all costs and informed the ladies to, 'back off, back away, and don't touch.'

Our bar was just like the one where Dan made that appalling remark to that old dancer about her stretch marks. It was not very funny when she jumped down on him and we found ourselves thrown out. Then again, it was so funny that I might be able to use it myself and have it turn out cool.

Mickey said that he would buy the first round and Clarence and I had no problem with that. With no explosions going on around us, no girls wetting themselves, no kids selling things that I didn't need, a round or two of free drinks would be just fine. All we need now was some good-looking girls dancing on the bar in front of us.

No girls came out to dance for us and we were now on our second round of drinks, courtesy of Clarence. It was now my turn to buy us a round and I asked the bar tender, "Dancers, you got dancers?"

"We got Dancers Joe. How many you want," he asked, as he gave us our drinks and collected the tab.

I looked at Mickey and Clarence and they just shrugged their shoulders. Okay, it was up to me to decide. "How many dancers you got?"

"One."

"One?"

"How many you want Joe," he asked, as if I had a choice.

This was turning out to be a strange conversation. "Okay, send out the one. Is she young?"

"How young you want," he asked, as he gave me my change. My change happened to be in MPC. Damn, this little country runs on American money.

"Does it matter if I only have one choice?"

"How young?"

Well, I had no desire to see a little kid dancing, nor did I aspire to see some old woman prancing around. Mickey smacked me on the shoulder and said, "Shit man, this is just a bar and any dancer we get, will be just a dancer."

"Okay Joe," chimed in the bar tender.

With no one on my side, I said, "Send her out."

Mickey, all smiles now, said, "If she is good looking, I will get us another round. However, if you picked out some ugly bitch, I am out of here."

"I didn't pick her out," I said defending myself.

Clarence stood up between us and said, trying to keep things cool, "Who cares? After a few more drinks, it really won't matter. You understand, the younger girls will get older and the old bitches will get younger the more we drink."

Well, Mickey and I just acknowledged that Clarence was probably right. I looked back at the little bar tender and said, "Bring her out."

He looked at me and said, "No can do. No girl here to dance."

The three of us looked at him as if we were going to drag him out from behind the bar and pounce on his face. He quickly came back with, "Joke Joe. Joke."

Clarence, apparently taking up for this creep, said, "Bring out the girl."

Well, that did change the focus from the little gook bar tender and Mickey said, "Get the girl and get us another round."

The gook was happy that we were buying more drinks and not giving him a hard time, as he yelled out, "Bring dancer. Bring me dancer now." This was followed with him placing our drinks on the bar and then taking away our half-filled drinks. Half filled, as in half finished. I didn't like that.

Just as I was about to say something to him, the lights dimmed, and the music started. It was show time. Out from behind the bar, comes a cute looking little gook girl. Well, I guessed that she was cute because she didn't have anything on, as in nude, completely nude. So much for her dancing a song or two before she would start taking if off, she was already naked. Maybe in this bar, you come out nude and as the songs play, you start to put your clothes back on. I hoped not, but this was The-Nam. This just might be the way that it always happens in this bar.

With the bar empty, the three of us had our own little show, right up close and personal. She was young, maybe late teens, and being that young, there were no stretch marks for me to count. It was just as well.

After a couple of songs, I had had about enough of this. Not saying that seeing a girl dance with nothing on wasn't cool, but she had no rhythm, little tits, and big feet. She did smile once and I could tell that she did have all of her front teeth. I mentioned to Mickey and Clarence that I wanted to head back and that seemed to tick Mickey off.

He snapped at me, "You are just leaving because it's your turn to buy. Or, maybe you are queer."

Clarence questioned, "You're queer?"

Wow, that caught me off guard. Not the part about not buying my fair share of rounds, but that he thought that I was a queer. Then again, maybe he was just drunk and I should just buy one more round for the two of them before I leave.

"Listen up Bud, I am no queer. Not today, not now, no way, no how. I will buy you guys a round, but I am out of here," I explained, as I reached into my wallet to pay the tab. "I am just tired, had enough of this place and I am simply ready to leave."

It might have been better if I would have just made fun of that little dancer and stayed for a few more round.

To make my life a little more interesting, well, this was The-Nam, and this dancer just simply jumped off the bar and wrapped her nude little self around me as if we were at sea and she was drowning.

"No go, no go," she shouted at me.

Damn, damn, damn. Why the hell was I so popular now? Crap, I just wanted to go home, or at least leave here, then go home tomorrow, and not be dragging around some little nude girl with me.

Okay, getting back to this monkey on my back, this girl was all over me like the one that was all over Dan when he made fun of her stretch marks a few days ago. At least she was not trying to hurt me, but by not letting me go, I could assume that before long, I would be a hurtin' for a certin'.

"Ride'm Charlie Boy, ride'm," shouted both Clarence and Mickey.

Go figure, that even with Clarence and Mickey enjoying my little adventure, the bar tender was not impressed. Just as quickly as she had jumped down from the bar, he was up and over the bar and now he was hanging onto me. Is this a bar that you cannot leave until it was closing time? Damn, I had paid my tab and hadn't broken anything.

"Okay, okay, okay, I'll stay," I shouted in an attempt to keep her off me and not to have the bar tender grab me or anything.

She did let go, got back on the bar, and went on her dancing as if nothing had just happened. The bar tender slowly made his way around the bar and resumed his bar duties of always wiping down the counter or cleaning beer glasses. It took a minute for me to mentally figure this out. It was clear to me that once you were here, you just can't leave until closing time, and my guess was that these bars never closed.

Well, after an unknown number of rounds along with the continuous dancing by Miss Nude Saigon, I had again, had enough. I said, "I'll get the next round, then I am, 'out of here.'"

Worried that my new drinking buddies were not ready to leave, I prepared myself with an excuse that I had an early flight to catch in the morning,

"Me too," said Mickey with Clarence looking like he had something very important to say.

Clarence said, "I am ready now." After downing his beer and slamming his empty glass down on the bar, he turned and started out without us.

With nothing exciting to report, we made it back to the BEQ. Bedtime was easy as the three of us just plopped down, face first in our racks. Just before I passed out, as if they had this timed out to show quality teamwork, both of them threw up. 'Team-Throw-Up' performed with all the sights, sounds and smells as if this was an Olympic event and that they just won the gold, with the Germans coming in second and Russians with third place.

As far as I was concerned, I was not going to A, clean it up, or even B, worry about it. Once I was asleep, I would no longer smell the smells. I did make it a point that in the morning, that I would get up on the far side of my bed avoiding stepping in barf in my bare feet.

With me almost asleep, Mickey tells Clarence that he should clean up his mess. Clarence tells Mickey that he wasn't doing shit and that if he had a problem with that, that he could clean it up himself. This went on for a few minutes with them repeating, "You clean it up. No, you clean it up."

I made it a point just to lay there, face down, and not look up at them. They would not stop arguing with each other and I was not able to fall asleep. Then I remembered, I was senior and could give them some orders. Orders as in, clean it up, or go to sleep.

Still, I did not want to get in between two drunks. Especially two sick drunk that were soon to be getting into a fight, but I did want to sleep. I said to get their attention, and I did so with authority as if I went to officer's school, "Boys."

Their bickering did stop and I assumed that they were looking my way as I kept my face in my pillow, "Clean it up in the morning. It'll be easier to clean. Now, good night."

I had said that so compelling, that even I believed that I was someone in authority and that my orders should be followed. Surprised, they said nothing more and it didn't take long before I heard one of them snoring. Snoring was better than fighting, and with that out of the way, I was soon sound asleep after saying to myself, "Only in The-Nam. Only in The-Nam."

# Chapter 15

I was the first one up and awake this morning. Today, I was headed home and I had an attitude. Don't nobody be a mess with me today, as I am a short, short-timer. With my head held high, I simply sashayed myself on down to take a shower. My last shower in The-Nam. As if the showers were primed especially for me, there was plenty of hot and cold running water. In no time at all, and after using all the hot water there was, I was clean as a whistle. My uniform needed some attention, but I was as clean as a whistle just the same and everything was hunky-dory for me this morning.

I didn't know what the opposite word would be for, 'Feeling Blue,' but for today, that would be me. Nothing blue for me today except for blue skies, a clear blue sky for my flight home.

I was too excited for breakfast and I just headed out for my final, as in, my last bus ride with the screened up windows and an armed escort trailing behind me. Well so far, things were going my way. I was the first one up, the first one to shower, and the first one on the first bus out for the ride to the airport. The only problem was that my bus didn't have a driver yet, but no sweat, I would just stay in place and if need be, I'd drive the bus to the airport myself or I'd even catch me a cab. Not the one with some guy running in front of me pulling me at a snails pace, but one that had a motor under the hood for a quick ride across town.

After only a few minutes, out came the driver along with a few passengers and one MP. As the driver went through the motions as if he was completing his check-off-list for take off, my smile grew and grew as if my face was going to explode. I was going home and thinking, as we pulled away from the curb, that life was good.

Minutes later, we pulled up to the terminal and we did this without any delay. No traffic problems, nothing broke down, and no one shot at us. Once the door opened, I was the first person off the bus and into the terminal. And, sorry to report, I was the first person that was approached by the guy that was selling those, Welcome to The Republic of Vietnam pamphlet, and the colorful and attractive, A Pocket Guide to Vietnam.

"I don't have time for this," I snapped at the sleazy salesman, allowing my attitude to show. In fact, as I walked by him, I almost knocked him down and that was a gutsy move for me.

I made my way to the information desk and found that Chief Petty Officer Fullam was on duty. It wasn't hard to miss his name, because Fullam was printed in very bold letters below the sign that read, "Information." He also had a large nametag on the right side of his shirt along with his name sewed above his left shirt pocket. Add to that, a nameplate on his desk in three-inch letters. He looked mean and grumpy as if he also had no intentions of answering any questions from me or anyone else. However, I had his name and I had a question. As far as I was concerned, Fullam's assigned task for today was to answer my questions, grumpy or not.

"Excuse me Chief Fullam," I said, showing respect and believing that I pronounced his name correctly.

I expected him to snap at me as my interruption had apparently caught him off guard. He seemed to be really surprised as well as shocked that someone had the nerve to butt in and boldly ask him a question.

I cringed a little and waited for the wrath of Fullam to take my head off. However, he didn't snap at me. In fact, I received a warm smile and he answered with, "Call me Gunny George. Or Gunny. How can I help you today young man?"

Wow! A Navy Chief and he be talking nice to a Seaman. Anyway, wanting to get some answers, I asked him about my flight. I was informed that my plane had landed and was preparing for the return flight back to the States. That it was on time and on schedule. I thanked him and figured that I had some time to take a seat and relax until my return to the real world. I found a row of empty seats and after making myself comfortable, I closed my eyes as I did not want to look at the wide open eyes of the in-coming FNG's and I especially did not want to make eye contact with the young guys, I meant old men. The old men that have served a year, a hard year, and that now were sporting the blood shot eyes of war.

I was only seated for a few minutes when I heard, "Your girlfriend is so fat."

"Shut up," was an expected reply. "She ain't no fatter that your girlfriend."

"She's so fat that when you get on top of her, your ears pop. A real SNAFU," came the unprovoked, and apparently, unwanted answer.

I thought that I was just day dreaming about this when I heard another voice say, "Oh yeah? Well your woman is so fat that when she has sex; she has to give directions."

Because this was so loud, I couldn't help but look over to checkout what I was missing and to see what this was all about. Unbelievably, what I saw was Anthony and Monroe going at it. I could not believe it. Not so much that I had once again met up with a couple of guys out of a million or so that were over here, just that they were still going at it. However, before I said anything to them, I was going to review some of my, self-imposed rules, on what to say, and more importantly, what not to say.

But, why should I review the rules or even need to review anything, I questioned myself. If I just kept quiet and didn't say anything, then, no way could I mess up. I decided that I was just going to sit here with my eyes closed and try to remember their jokes so I could use them later. Not just the jokes on colored guys, just on guys that date fat and/or ugly girls. As for me, I was not going to be dating any fat and/or ugly girls as I had finished high school and I had enough since to date girls that were thin, cute, and not colored.

It was Anthony this time, I believe, adding another comment about Monroe's fat girlfriend, "Yeah. And there be speed bumps all around her fat ass."

Monroe said in return, "No sweat nigger, no big thing. Now your fat thing is no better and when she goes to a restaurant . . ."

"Yeah," Anthony said, waiting for a response.

"She looks at the entire menu and says, Okay! Bring it on!"

I liked that one and that was one for me to remember. Anthony came back with, "Your girlfriend is so fat, that she had to go to Sea World to get baptized. And, before she went," he added before Monroe could respond. "Her drawers are so big, that she had to iron them in the driveway with a steamroller."

I snickered aloud on that one and I quickly recovered myself as if I was not paying them any attention. I turned my head away from them in the event they looked over and noticed me smiling.

"Your nigger girlfriend is so fat, that her senior picture for the year book had to be taken from an airplane flying overhead," Monroe continued without missing a beat, as if he had never heard that last comment about his own girlfriend.

"Oh yeah. Well my girlfriend doesn't need to use hula-hoops to hold up her socks," responded Anthony. That one was so funny that Monroe had to respond with some laughter of his own.

After giving that last remark some thought, Monroe smiled, and said under his breath, "Shit."

"No shit," Anthony added.

"Yeah, you shit for brains," Monroe shouted back.

Not a real shout, just a little louder than how they were talking earlier as this was the start of a different area of interest, other than their fat and ugly jokes and cuts about the women in their lives.

"Okay, I got shit for brains, but you always look shit-faced," returned a quick response from Anthony.

"At least I have my shit together," Monroe instructed.

"What little shit you have, it don't mean nothin', it don't mean shit, and it's just weird shit," Anthony explained.

Monroe questioned, "You been smoking some shit?"

"Eat shit," Anthony said in a, not so friendly tone.

It appeared now that Anthony and Monroe are in for some deep shit and heading up shits creek without a paddle.

"Your jokes are shitty," Monroe responded.

"I don't give a shit," informed Anthony.

"No shit, I thought that you gave a shit about my jokes because you use all of them, you shit head," Monroe bragged.

"You dumb shit, you use my jokes," defended Anthony.

Oh my, the shit was about to hit the fan.

"You can't tell the difference between good jokes and shitty jokes," Monroe responded, in his defense.

"Eat shit and die, you little shit," said Anthony, now a little upset.

"You chicken shit. Eat horse shit," Monroe said, putting a funny tone to his voice in an attempt to keep this shit from getting out of hand.

Joking back at Monroe, Anthony said, "No shit. What-do-ya say that we put this shit behind us and get ourselves something to eat? Maybe we can get some shit on a shingle?"

"Cool my man, no need for us brothers to act like dumb shits," Monroe said, as the two of them did their knuckle-knocking, finger-grabbing handshake thing.

"Nobody talks shit like us," Monroe boasted.

"No shit, shit head," Anthony fired back, and for some reason that was funny to me.

Well, so much for me able to hold back my laughter on that one. I cracked out a yell of laughter that caught the attention of everyone in the terminal. I had been caught now and what happened next was that the jokes were now directed to me.

Monroe said, "Hey white boy. You be Dan's little buddy?"

I acted as if I just woke up and was unaware of what was going on. "Hey man. What's up with you guys? You two still shootin' the shit?"

Anthony added, "Damn man. It be that dumb-ass, little white boy. He be that ugly white guy that looked like he been a bobbing for french fries."

Without clearly thinking this thing out, and believing that I was, in, with these guys, I came back with, "No sweat. You so ugly that in your high school year book, there is a picture of a paper bag with your name under it."

"Shit," said Monroe. "You be real funny for a white guy. You also be so ugly that if you look up the word, 'ugly' in the dictionary, it be your name."

"With his picture next to it," added Anthony.

This was great, because now we were pals. It felt groovy to be part of the group, even if it was with two colored guys. However, as quickly as I thought that I was included in with the jokes, I was just as quickly being ignored.

Anthony said to Monroe, "Your nigger girlfriend be so ugly, that her mother used to put rubber bands on her ears."

"Yeah man, and why is that?" Monroe asked. Even I was interested in why she had rubber bands on her ears.

"So people would think that your girlfriend was wearing a mask," Monroe explained, as he busted out with laugher that caught the attention of everyone around us.

"No way man. Shit, your nigger girlfriend be so ugly that she could scare a hungry wolf off a meat truck," Anthony quickly responded, and that was a hoot of a response.

"Damn, you niggers be funny," I said before I realized exactly what I had just said. Not only did these two guys give me a look as if they were about ready to kill me, but everyone else in the terminal had heard me. I looked around and it appeared to me that all the white guys that were here were now looking for a way out of the building. On the other side of the coin, all the colored guys who had overheard me were looking to circle around me. Why, why, why did I ever say that? Why, why, why did I ever say anything? Why, why, why did I ever say that to where they could have heard me? It was now the time for me to break out into a sweat, in this, very sweatable situation. I was going to die today, right here, and right now.

However, Anthony instead of standing up and crushing me down, which would have been the right thing to do, said to me,

"Well, my white, red neck, trailer trash friend. At least we have a girlfriend to talk about."

"You tell'em Monroe," Anthony added. Great, they were now a tag-team up against me

"You be so ugly that you can't even get an ugly girlfriend," Monroe said proudly, as if that was one hundred percent true.

Great, that was funny and it appeared that I was not going to die today. At least not right away. At least Monroe said that with a relaxed smile on his face and not one suggesting that he was going to kill me. Or was he?

My only response was for me to smile approval of his joke. For now, I should try and return to my nap, and with great determination; bite down on my tongue. If I was to keep my mouth shut until they left, I might survive this encounter. Anyway, I did just that. I closed my eyes, slouched down in my seat, and pretended to be sound asleep. Even if I did hear something funny, I was not going to respond. No way, no how, not today. I could do this because I had graduated high school, been shot at, shot back, been wounded, and was headed home after an honorable, but short tour of The-Nam. Having done all those things, I should be able to control my laughter and keep my mouth shut.

To my benefit, those two got right back into provoking each other. If I could ignore them for just a little while longer, I might live long enough to catch my flight out. Nice guys these two, but I would not put it past them to hurt me, especially if I was to call them any more disrespectful names.

If Dan could do it and get away with it, then it's just fine and dandy for Dan. Let him do the name-calling thing and I will just watch, look, and listen. Not, join in. So, for now and without me, the two of them continued at it for about an hour, a very long hour, before getting up to leave and go somewhere. I wasn't all that impressed that they continued for an hour, just that I was able to keep out of their conversation for that much time. I didn't hear any announcements about departing aircraft when they left, so I really didn't know why they departed when they did. Whatever, they were gone and I was still alive.

"Excuse me," a voice said from behind me.

I turned around and there was a young military guy, well, more like a kid, wanting my attention. He was in the air force, I believed, and he was looking rather sad. Sad looking as if he was a puppy dog, who had lost his owner or even a little kid that, had lost his puppy. This kid looked, as if he needed a hug. Anyway, he stood there staring at me with a pile of luggage at his feet. Seeing luggage piled at someone's feet at an airport normally was a very common sight; however, at a military airport, everyone would be sporting his or her military issue sea bag. Even officers had sea bags, nicer ones, but sea bags just the same.

Now this guy had two sea bags along with some extra luggage, and to me, that part was unusual. It looked as if he had purchased one of those group luggage package deals. You know, the ones that have six or eight pieces, that when empty, they all fit into each other making storing this kind of luggage simple. Nevertheless, this guy had them all filled. The two smallest ones could not hold more than three or four pair of socks each. They were more the size like makeup bags for girls.

Anyway, getting back to this guy, he held out his hand with something that he apparently wanted me to see, or buy. I quickly figured that I did not need anything from anyone, such as a pamphlet on Vietnam Phrases or another, A Pocket Guide to Vietnam booklet. I did not need another set of Christmas cards, or even some little kid to take home.

I looked down anyway, at what he had, and noticed that it was a plane ticket. A MAC, military plane ticket, and they were easy to spot because of their odd size and blue color. I instantaneously checked my pocket to see if I had dropped my ticket. To my relief, my ticket was there; however, why would he want to show me his ticket, I thought to myself and kept up my guard.

With consideration and curiosity, I asked him, "Do I know you?"

"No. You don't know me. I was wondering that if you had an aisle seat for the next flight out, and if you did, would you want to exchange it with my ticket. I have a window seat ticket?"

A window seat was something that I wanted, however, somehow there must be a scam working here that I needed to be aware. Besides, why would I care that he had a window seat and why would he care if I didn't. I would not think that riding in a plane was anything similar to riding on a bus in Saigon. Window seat or not, however, before I could think up something to say that would cause him to leave me alone, like, I already have a window seat, I could only muster up with, "Why do you want to change your seat?"

"My problem is that I must make frequent trips to the head, because of the medication that I'm on and having an aisle seat would make it easier for me. Not to mention anyone who is seating between the aisle and me. Know what I mean?"

He explained to me that this situation of his in a most sincere and convincing way as he pulled at his wedgies to, more clearly make his point. Well, so much for shaking his hand.

He explained this to me a second time, because I had not responded to him fast enough. Yet, I would like having a window seat and I could do a good thing for him at the same time, assuming that I was going to make this exchange with him. The only problem was that this still could be a scam and maybe he would scam me with a fake ticket. He could then sell my ticket and I would be out of luck and in trouble.

"No, I think that if you have this problem that the Master-Chief who assigned you your ticket should be the one to help you out," I said, as I finally answered his request.

I told him this trying not to sound too indifferent about his problem; I just did not want his problem, if that was what it was, to be a real problem for me.

"No way man, no can do. I tried asking that Chief back at the BEQ, but he would never listen to me. He kept on reading that cowboy book of his and he never would even look at my medical records or anything," he continued to explain; only now, it appeared that he was going to start crying. It was a pitiful sight to see him stand on one foot, then the other all the while wiping away the tears and scratching at his butt.

At this point, I started to feel for this guy. I knew about the Chief that he was talking about and completely understood his dilemma. So I thought to myself, how I could check this out for its validity, exchange the ticket to where we both would come out ahead. "Let me see your ticket," I instructed, as he eagerly handed over his ticket.

"Great. Thanks. No sweat. Check away," he answered, as If I did him the greatest favor in his lifetime by just taking the time to listen and check out his story.

He freely handed over his ticket to me and I compared it with my ticket. It was of the same material, printing looked real enough, and it did have today's date. Not that I could have spotted a counterfeit ticket, but even the signature was a dead on copy. Besides, it's the correct flight, 315 with a time of 230.

One more item to check I thought. "Can I see your ID?"

He did reach for his wallet and as he did, I could hear him say under his breath, "Shit man. I ain't trying to cash no check."

Well, I did a quick look-see to verify this and it was his name on the ID and his name on the ticket. With that, I figured that I could help this guy out. "Okay, here you go." And yet, I followed that up with, "If I'm getting screwed here, you have the Devil-to-Pay."

I handed him my ticket and he did everything but hug and kiss me because he was so excited. I believed that he was sincerely grateful and that made me feel good.

After we exchanged our tickets, he told me as he gathered up his suitcases, "I got to run to the head. My medical problem, you understand. See you on the flight. It leaves in about thirty minutes you know."

He left rather quickly and for a moment I thought that maybe, just maybe he did trick me. I saw that he went into the men's room and I knew that I had a few minutes to check on my ticket. I made my way up to the gate counter where I was to board my plane and asked the ticket collector, "Is my ticket correct? I got a window seat, right?"

It was my understanding that a ticket-collector person would be the one to know if my ticket was the real McCoy or not. If not, I would be able to catch up with the guy before he got away.

"Yes, this is a window seat, but your departing gate is the next one over and it will be boarding in a few minutes," he informed me, as he pointed to his left.

I answered, "Thank you. You've been very helpful."

I felt rather pleased with myself today. I had made someone happy, I had a window seat, and I was headed home for a couple of weeks. Not only that, my plane was even boarding a few minutes earlier. Not a bad day, not a bad day at all and I did this all without the help, correction, and or of any assistance from Dan. I was not the village idiot that he sometimes made me out to be.

I made my way over and took the last space in the other, correct line. In no time at all, a large number of people got in behind me. I gave my ticket a double check and saw that this was my flight and that I was boarding at the correct gate. Damn, I thought to myself, I believed initially that my flight left a little later than this. No sweat, I assured myself. It was just time to board the plane now so that it could depart on time.

The next announcement was that flag officers were to board first along with those that had medical disabilities. Well, I thought, that was a nice idea to help those who have been wounded. I looked for my new friend and I did not see him board. I guessed that he was still in the head doing whatever it was that he had to do. No sweat, that was not my problem, he'll make it because it should take a little time to load the plane and he was in an aisle seat. No reason for him to get on first just to get up again as someone would board that had an inside seat.

It did not take long and I was soon onboard. Strange feeling came over me as if I had a fake ticket. That someone would come over and ask me to leave. You know, as if I had their seat. Whatever, no one came for my seat and all seemed fine. Besides, what was my problem? I had a ticket, I had my seat, and I was onboard ready to head home.

The guy that sat next to me said, "Are you ready for this? This is going to be a great week of drinking, fun, drinking, women, and more drinking."

"Sounds good to me," I answered him. I wondered where he was from. He did not mention anything about family and friends, just that he had plans for lots of drinking.

He continued with, "I've never been down there before. Have you?"

Not knowing for sure what he was talking about, I assumed that he meant Mexico or Southern California. "Yep. I am ready for this and I have thirty days."

He looked at me oddly, apparently not wanting to talk to me any longer because I was staying home a few weeks longer than he was. He turned to the guy on his other side and asked him the same questions. I did not hear a response and I really did not care. I was just going to look out my window and enjoy my last view of Vietnam and with luck, never again to venture into a war zone. Or whatever it was that the military called it over here. I might as well call it a combat zone, because I did get combat pay for my time here.

With everyone seated and just before we taxied from the terminal, the stewardess placed herself in the front of the aircraft and gave the appearance that we should pay attention to her. She seemed serious as this was the standard, 'shut up and pay attention' presentation that we always had when flying.

"There may be 50 ways to leave your lover, 10 ways to kill someone with your bare hands, but there is only 4 ways to exit this aircraft," she explained, and it took me a moment before I realized that she was kidding.

After she pointed to the exits for our benefits and safety, she added, "And for you officers that are flying with us today, if you forget these instruction or that you are unable to comprehend what I just said, simply get in behind an enlisted man and follow him out of the aircraft."

Well that was cool and all of the enlisted personnel onboard had a good laugh at that. The younger officers laughed at her joke, but the senior officers just sat there showing disapproval. She knew that pissed them off and my guess was that she was once in the military and was just getting even with them.

It only took a matter of minutes after we took our seats before our plane taxied away from the terminal. I had heard that when a plane departed Nam and headed back to the States, that everyone would cheer as the plane nosed up and left the ground. Well, I was going to be part of this excitement and I was going to be the loudest and most animated person onboard.

I waited, and waited, and when we finally rotated, I gave out a very loud cheer only to realize that no one else yelled but me. I held my head down in confusion and shame as everyone looked at me as if I was the dumbest guy onboard.

Maybe I was mistaken and that the yelling would come when we left Vietnamese air space, some twelve miles out from the coast. I would just sit tight for now and wait until then. I then figured that I knew what might be the reason with the lack of enthusiasm onboard. Everyone here was coming back to do a second, third, or fourth tour and that leaving wasn't that big a deal to them anymore. Oh well, I muttered to myself, I was tired, and I might as well get a nap out of the way before we land at our first layover at Clark Air Force Base in the Philippines.

Taking a nap was easy for me and before we hit twelve miles out, I was already very much sound asleep.

A short time later, I felt sprinkles of water hit my face and that woke me from my nap. I hazily opened my eyes and was pleased not to see ceiling tiles going by. I slowly recalled that I was on an airplane flying five miles up. I thought to myself that if we had rain way up here, we were in serious trouble. Anyway, I looked up at the luggage compartment above my head searching for something that was dripping on me, like an AC duct or an open wine bottle. Without warning, I was sprinkled again. Only this time, it came at an angle. I looked over and a few seats away from me sat, Mr. Murph and Mr. Murph was just a smiling away at me.

"My man Murph. How you doing?" I said, and was very pleased to see that someone that I knew had made it out of The-Nam in one piece.

"I'm doing five by five my man," he answered, with a smile on his face and a little slobber down his cheek. "I thought that you were heading home," he questioned me.

"I am. I didn't think that you were heading home," I answered his question, with a question of my own.

"You live Down-Under," Murph asked.

I had never heard the expression, 'Down-Under.' Murph noticed my deer-in-the-headlights look and asked me again. "Do you live Down-Under?"

Others sitting around him picked up on his questioning of me as he was doing hand signals as if I was deaf. This would have been funny if it wasn't directed at me.

Figuring that he was just getting on my case, because he knew that I was from Baltimore, I simply accepted his jab. "Yeah, heading home to Baltimore."

Now, Murph had the deer-in-the-headlights look. He questioned, "Baltimore? As in Baltimore, Maryland. As in Baltimore, Maryland, U S of A?"

His confused look caused me to be even more confused. Wanting to take the lead here, I asked him, "So where do you think we are headed?"

Poor guy, I'd bet that he's on the wrong plane. How hard could it be to get on the correct flight? Flights out of Saigon were going back either to the states or on R&R runs. Hawaii, Bangkok, Australia for example. Oh shit, I then, with the beginning of a sick stomach, recall that Sydney Australia was often called the place, 'Down-Under.'

Then, trying to be cool, I reached in my pocket for my ticket. The ticket that I had exchanged earlier. I had to have a good ticket; I was allowed to board the aircraft. Then it hit me, what if I had a window seat, and this was a window seat, that was not going back to the states—as in the United States of America.

Naturally, Murph was not going to let this one go, as he asked, "So, based on your ticket, where are you headed?"

Giving my ticket a quick, look-see, I found that I was headed to Sydney, Australia. A nice place to visit, but I didn't want to head there now. Not now, I wanted to go home. However, wanting to get Murph off my case, I came back with, "I'm going to Sydney with you."

Okay, now what do I do. It wasn't as if I was on a bus or train and could just get off at the next stop. I was on this flight for the duration, shit.

Australia, well, that couldn't be all that bad. I'll just find an information desk and seek a return flight. Not that big of a deal. Then, on a lighter side, I might even be allowed to spend a day or two waiting for my flight. Hell, I had thirty days vacation a year and I could just use a few here. So for now, situation under control, I was going on R&R. Life was good, of course, unless this mistake could land me in the brig.

"Damn, damn, damn," I said to myself and that happened to have been heard by the guy next to me who was sleeping.

"What do you want," he asked, stretching out his arms above his head.

Here I go again, "Sorry, I was just talking to myself."

"I thought that you were talking to me." After a second to eye me up, he added, "My name is Sam."

"Charles."

"Well Charles, if you don't want to talk to me, then good night. Wake me up when we are Down-Under."

With that, I just looked out the window to avoid eye contact with Murph and my new friend, Sam. And, as usual, when I had nothing to do, I had always figured out that it was naptime. I didn't have anything to read, and I was not going to talk with Sam. Besides, Murph was too far away. So, in quick order, I was napping again and on my way to Australia.

I started dreaming about the TV show Wild Kingdom. It had to do something with gorillas as I could clearly hear growling sounds. Growling sounds as if the big male gorilla was horny and he had found a hot female ape that was in heat.

I could not get a visual on this dream, but the sounds were extremely real. However, I woke up from this dream as the growling sounds changed to, "What the fuck was that?"

Fully awake now and with sleep filled eyes, I could make out that something big was sitting a few rows up from me and on the other side of the aisle, in an aisle seat. As my eyes came into focus, I looked again and what I saw was a scary sight that astounded me.

Sitting over there was someone from my past. Sasquatch, Mountain Man, Big Foot was there, and he seemed as big and bad as I remembered.

He was looking up, down, and all around for something. Every time he would look my way, I was able to look down and cover from sight behind the seat between us. No way was I going to have him see me, remember me, and then kill me. Hell, I was going home, I meant, I was going to Australia.

After a few seconds that seemed like many minutes, I boldly ventured a look-see. I was careful enough only show my eyes. Now Big Foot was looking at the overhead and patting the top of his head. Then, out of the corner of my eyes, I could see that Murph was spitting water, beer, wine, or something wet at him.

This was great and I had a good seat to catch in all the action. Murph was able to get a good squirt, with plenty of volume, right on, and dead center on the top of Big Foots head. Big Foot's reaction was to respond in a very physical way by moving all around in his seat and bumping into the guy sitting next to him in the same way that he did when dancing.

"Jerk," I said aloud. Damn, damn, damn, I did not mean to say that and certainly not to say it aloud. Naturally and with my luck, Big Foot did hear me and I was able to duck down before he saw me. At least I believed that I got away with it.

As his growling got louder and his slapstick jesters grew, I looked over at Murph and he was laughing so hard that he had what appeared to be soda coming out of his nose. I guessed that it was soda; by the way it had fizzed up. This is funny stuff and will be hard to convince anyone that this really happened. This will go down in my history as something not to be repeated, as it will not be believed.

The guys sitting with Murph were encouraging him to stop. This encouragement happened after they saw how huge Big Foot was as he stood up in the aisle to get a better look at his surroundings. In a way, I wished that Murph had been caught because Big Foot was able to make eye contact with me. I did not think that he remembered me, but he did take a longer look at me than he did at anyone else. Oh well, we'll see.

As the flight stewardess made her way down the aisle with the soda and nuts cart, she was able to instruct Big Foot to take his seat. For now, maybe he will just relax with a soda and a bag of nuts, and then forget about little oh me. I was not going to look up at anything or anyone that walked by. I will just keep a low profile and also tune out all noises, just on the one in a million odds that Monroe, or Prez, along with his brothers John, Anthony, and Marvin are carrying on one of their typical conversation about fat and ugly women.

With self imposed direction and instructions, I closed my eyes and attempted to sleep until we land. If I had my way, no one on this flight will even know that I was onboard. Hell, I was not to be on this flight anyway. However, just as the soda and nut cart made it to my row, the stewardess said to the guy next to me, "Wake him, and see if he wants something."

Okay, I was awake now. I might as well enjoy my free soda and bag of nuts. No telling when I'll get some again and I do like free stuff.

While drinking my soda and wolfing down my bag of nuts, and, just as my mouth was full, I heard, "Charles. What's happening Charles?"

Before I looked up, I knew that it wasn't Murph, as Murph didn't sound like a girl. No way could it be Big Foot, as he was definitely not a girl. Oh my God, it was one of the girls from the beach—as in Denise, Betty, and or Rose. I was going to enjoy this flight and my time down-under.

I looked up with all kinds of smiles and there it was, it, as in, it was Louie-Louie. Damn, damn, damn, and shit, shit, shit. I'd rather be sitting between Big Foot with his growling and next to Murph as he spits and slobbers old beer down his cheek than to be talking with him. Anything was better than sitting with a queer.

I made it a point to drop my smile and to muster up an expression of, 'I really don't want to talk to you.'

By his response to my response, it was apparent that he had gotten the message. However, he was unable to move on because the soda and nut cart along with the stewardess had blocked his way. With this being one of those uncomfortable moments, I didn't have anything to say and the only thing that he could come up with was, "How about them tits at the shoeshine place."

"Good place to let it hang out, if you know what I mean," I quickly responded. Then I realized that I just opened up a conversation with him and I really didn't want to do that.

Luck was going my way as the Stewardess must have known about this place, as she did step aside to let Louie-Louie by. With that issue out of my life, I finished off my soda and nuts and went back into my nap.

Hours later, and as the plane started to descend, I was wakened by change in cabin pressure and the loudness of the passengers. We were almost there. Sydney, and how cool can that be?

Just as the plane touched down, everyone broke out in a roar. Happiness was everywhere. You would have thought that Johnny U. had just pulled another last second touchdown to win the game. The roar was odd in that I was the only one not roaring. It appeared to me that not everyone was all that impressed with the leaving of Vietnam as they were in arriving at Sydney. Wanting to join in and be apart of this, I yelled out a yell, only this time, I was yelling alone. I just can't believe that I was doing, dumb shit things like this on a regular basis.

Oh well, it didn't really matter and it don't mean nothin'. At least our landing was not straight down as was my landing in Saigon a few weeks ago. Our pilot just came in all normal like. The only thing not normal with our landing was what was going on with two of our flight stewardesses. As they made their way down the aisle, they were spraying something on us. I didn't think that it was Agent Orange. Hell, it could be room freshener or something similar for all I knew

In the process, the guy in front of me snapped back at the stewardesses and said something to the affect, "Don't spray that shit on me woman!"

Apparently, not wanting to take any shit from this guy, she came back with, "Sorry. It's the law down here mate. There is no way the doors are going to open until this is completed."

As if what she had said was enough, she continued on her way, still spraying. As the second stewardess came up the aisle, she made it a point to spray him a second time, for good measure. Not in a mean way, I assumed that she noticed how he was trying to wipe it off.

Under his breath, he said, "Damn foreigners."

At least no one else heard him and if so, that might have delayed our departure. Anyway, here I go again with another adventure and our departure was slow and orderly as if we were state side departing a commercial flight.

# Chapter 16

I made my way to the military information desk and informed the Air Force Sergeant there of my dilemma and how I wanted so badly to return to Saigon. He looked at me as if I had two heads. He asked, as he apparently tried very hard not to laugh, "You mean to tell me that even with you being here, in beautiful Sydney, Australia, that you want to cut your visit short?"

I could only look at him as if I just lost my puppy. I couldn't even muster up a deer-in-the-headlights look that I seemed to have mastered since I arrived in The-Nam.

"No one had ever requested that their time be cut short down here. If anything," he tried to explain with a straight face. "Everyone here wanted to have their time extended. Some have even agreed to re-enlist for years if they could have stayed a few more days."

I tried to put on a sad face and said, "I can understand that, but I am trying to get to Saigon to catch a flight home."

Just as it appeared that he understood my problem and was going to help me, he shouted to someone seated at a desk behind him, "Captain. Come check out this guy, sir. He just got here and already he wants to go back to Saigon."

Wouldn't you know it, everyone in the terminal heard that and as if on cue, they all turned and gave me a look. The look that gave me the impression that they were thinking that I was an idiot. Well, some were thinking that and others just knew that it had to be true.

Well, I had hoped that this ordeal of mine would end soon, but the Captain said to me as he approached the counter, "Young man. Would you follow me please?"

Before I could respond, as in, "Yes sir," or "do I have to," he had already turned around and was heading towards the office space behind the counter.

Looking at the situation, it wasn't all that bad. I mean, I was leaving an area where almost everyone was staring at me, but I really wanted to turn around and catch the flight out that I just got off because I believed that it was heading back for Saigon.

The Captain was kind enough to hold the door open for me as I entered. I sort of expected him to close it behind me and keep me locked up for seven days and six nights until my R&R time had completed. Well, he did close the door, but he did it from the inside of his little office, and for that, it was appreciated.

"Now Seaman, if you would kindly explain why you, or anyone for that matter, would want to leave this place early."

I gave the Captain my story and as I thought that I was home free with a ticket back to Saigon, he explained, "Sorry Seaman. The flights are set up for one seat in, seven days later, one seat out. Enjoy your stay."

Resolved to the fact that I was here for the week, I asked the Captain about the possibility of being paid, or at least, an advance. Finally, someone was helping me out here, because he picked up the telephone and made a call and worked it out for me to get an advance.

"Thank you sir," I said to him as he gave me directions to an office on the second floor of the terminal. Minutes later, I had a ticket for Saigon. A semi-blank ticket where the flight number, date and time were left blank. That not being good, but I did get an advance in pay. I was issued Australian money and that shot my idea of making a little money on the side with Greenbacks. Anyway, life had turned around for me and I was happy. Well, happy until I met back with the Captain. I was informed that my days here in beautiful Sydney, Australia, might be counted as vacation time and not as R&R time. R&R time does not go against my 30 days annual leave time, but that these days would.

I started to complain to the Captain, but I was cut off when he informed me that it would be counted as leave time, or that I would be considered AWOL. Well, not a problem, I could live with taking a little vacation time right about now. I'd rather go into the hole with leave time than to spend time in a cell.

Whatever, with that little detail cleared up, my next stop was outside in front of the terminal deciding on what to do next. It was not as if I was looking for the military buses heading off to the different BEQ's or anything, but there should have been something to give me a hint on what to do next.

Then I had an idea as I looked to my left and saw a bank of pay phones. I was filled with excitement until I realized that I did not have any change. Then again, no sweat, I would just call home collect.

Calling home from overseas was not as easy as it was back in the states. At least I was in luck and the operator spoke English. After telling her that it was a call to the United States and giving her the number, I was almost there. I was able to listen in as the operator made calls to other operators in order to complete my call. Next on the line was an operator from the Philippines followed by one from Hawaii. A third operator was one in Baltimore and I knew then that I was almost there.

A second later, I could hear my home telephone ringing and my excitement began to escalate. My Dad answered the telephone and when asked if she would accept a collect call from Sydney Australia, he said very clearly, "No. I don't know anyone in Australia," and before I could say something like, "Dad! Dad," he hung up.

Situation not good down-under. Just as the operator, the Australian operator, started to say something, I snapped in and said, "Please call again. Only this time, tell them it's from their son Charles."

She understood my situation and complied without a hassle.

A moment later, my telephone was again ringing. My Dad answered the telephone and as requested, the operator jumped in and said, "It's from your son, Charles. Will you accept the call?"

It was a long silence before he came back with, "Australia?"

"Yes," the operator answered. "Will you accept the charges?"

"Yes," was the answer that I expected and most wanted.

"Go ahead Charles," said the operator to me.

"Dad, it's me. I'm in Sydney, Australia," I shouted.

"You're not in Vietnam and did you know that it's 3 o'clock in the morning?" he snapped at me.

Before I could say anything, he was waking up my Mom as my little sister picked up the other telephone.

My sister asked my Dad, "Who is it Dad?" and, "What time is it?"

My Dad could not answer her right then because I could hear my Mom in the background asking, "Who's calling at this hour?"

My sister chirped right in and announced, "It's not one of my boyfriends. They know not to call here this late."

"Damn right, it best not be one of them," my Dad answered my sister as my Mom asked again, "What time is it?"

"3 AM," my Dad, shouted back to my Mom. He was not angry with her for asking, he was apparently mad at me for calling at this hour.

I had to break in and say something, "Everyone. It's me and I'm okay."

"We all thought that you were in Vietnam getting shot at. We didn't expect to hear that you were on leave in Australia," my sister snapped in as if I had lied to everyone. "You've only been gone a few weeks and already you are on vacation."

My Mom gets on the telephone and tells my sister, "I told you not to talk that way about your brother."

"But that's what he said," my sister responded, in her own self-defense.

My Dad in the background was shouting to my sister to, "Get off the telephone."

My Mom then yelled at my Dad not to be yelling in the house. It was my turn to yell because I yelled back with, "I'm okay everyone."

My Dad yelled back at my sister, "I told you to hang up."

In comes my sister yelling, "Why do I have to hang up?"

Mom yelled in, "Because your Father said so. Now go back to bed."

"I'm awake now. Even with him ten thousand miles away, he can still ruin my nights sleep," my sister yelled louder than my Dad did as she was trying to be heard.

"Don't back talk your Mother," Dad shouted back at her.

My sister added, "The neighbors are banging on my wall and yelling for me to keep it down."

Click, then silence.

That was it. The telephone was dead. My first guess was that my parent's neighbor had cut the telephone wire to get everyone to shut up. My second guess was that the telephone wires overheated with all the yelling on ten thousand miles of telephone line and underwater cable. Damn, not only did I not get a chance to speak with my parents; my Dad was going to be stuck with the telephone bill.

I could only look at the phone in confusion and discuss. When I did place it back to my ear, I could only hear, "Please deposit twenty-five cents and dial your number or dial zero for the operator."

Damn, damn, damn. With that telephone call over, I may never call home again. With that, I slammed the phone back into its cradle and kicked the bottom of the phone booth. I realized that I looked stupid doing that, but for a moment, it felt rather good.

"Lose your money mate?"

I turned around to see who was talking to me and found a cab driver looking at me as if I was a crazy man or someone that needed a cab. Well, I was not crazy and I could use a cab so I answered, "Just having trouble calling home."

Apparently not wanting to hear my sad story, he replied, "Where can I take you? You need a place to stay?"

Well, I did need a place to stay and a cab diver would know where to go. "Yeah. I need a hotel room that's close to the action. I need one for a few days."

"Hop in mate. I know just the place. It's right next to Hyde Park and Kings Crossing," he announced as he opened the door for me.

Oh well, I did need a room and a cab, and for now, I had them both. "Hyde Park, Kings Crossing," I questioned.

"Yes sir mate. You can meet the girls at Kings Crossing and then take them for a romantic walk in Hyde Park."

"Hotels," I questioned.

"Yes sir mate. All in the same area and all the girls down here have round eyes," he explained, as if he was more than a cab driver. He was also a local tour guide and he knew that I needed this information that, if he did this well, would cause me to give him a larger tip. With that, I believed it would be to my best interest to go with his suggestions.

Minutes later, he pulled over with the park on my left side with a hotel on my right. He was right for this being the place to be because I could see American type guys walking all around.

After collecting the fare, he gave me his card and pointed towards the hotel. Not being big on good byes, I took the card, said thanks, and got out. I did leave him a tip, not as much as he might have wanted and with luck, I won't need him again.

I walked into the lobby and before I made my way to the front desk, I did turn around and looked for the bellhops, girl type bellhops. To my disappointment, there was none. I was thinking to; at least, see some hookers that had round eyes. Then again, what for? I was not going to do anything with them anyway.

Then again, maybe it would not be as bad if there were a chief standing nearby handing out those old, army issue, olive green, rubbers. The ones with the instruction printed on them. Then again, maybe not.

Getting back to the check-in process, it was quick and easy. I paid the clerk, got my key, and found my room. The first thing I looked for was the TV. I was disappointed not to find a set of vice grips for a channel changer, but most happy that I had more than one station to select. Only three stations, two, eleven, and thirteen, but they were in English and I did have three choices.

My next move was to checkout the toilet. I heard that the water down here during a flush circulates right to left rather than left to right. On the other hand, was it left to right rather than right to left? So with that, I flushed and watched. But wait, what was I doing? I was on vacation, from a combat zone, during a time of war, in Sydney Australia, and I was checking on the status of toilet flushes. The only thing positive about this stupid moment in my life, was that I did not tell anyone what I was doing and Dan was not here to read my mind and call me an idiot.

As I was about to regain normal control of my mind, there was a knock at the door. A smile came over my face as I imagined that a set of Welcome Wagon girls were here to see me. Quickly, very quickly, I made my way to the door and opened it with all smiles only to be disappointed with the front desk clerk that was here to visit me.

"Can I help you," I asked sadly.

"Towels. I have some bath towels," he explained, as he made his way to the head, I meant bathroom.

"Thanks."

After he hung my towels, he looked at me and smiled. He pointed at the toilet, which had just now filled, and said, "Checking the spin on the water, are we now mate?"

What else could I do but to give him my, deer-in-the-headlights look. He came back with, "You Americans. You Americans always do that. If it wasn't for you Americans, my water bill would be half as much."

I could not tell if he was joking with me or being serious. I could only respond with the shrugging of my shoulders. He apparently took the hint that I did not care what he thought one way or another and he just left. To be a smart-ass, I went and flushed it again and I did not bother to look to see which way it flowed.

For now, I wanted to go out and check out the town.

# Chapter 17

I showered and shaved, as I needed to freshen up. For an outfit, I took off my shirt and wore my t-shirt. I was not pretty, but this was all that I had for now and out the door I went. I did not know which way to go, but because I was downtown, it should not really matter. I would just decide when I get outside.

As I passed through the lobby, the lady behind the front desk suggested that I head right. I looked at her and at first; I thought that she was talking to someone else. Nope, she was looking right at me.

I looked at her expecting an explanation, which she easily volunteered, "You're looking for a good time, right?"

With my shoulders up, and trying to look as if I knew what I was doing and where I was going, I said, "Sure."

"Turn right, walk two blocks. That's Kings Crossing and that's where all you Americans want to hang out."

If she would have been halfway good looking and about 100 pounds lighter, I might have wanted to stop and attempt to put a hit on her since she got it started. Nevertheless, this was a big city with lots of women. Then again, if it was last call and I was alone, then maybe. Then looking at all that weight and her body folds, no way.

"Thank you for your suggestion. I'll head that way and check it out," I informed her and out the door, I went, quickly. I wasn't running, but a fast walk just incase she wanted to say something else.

The weather was nice and the sun was shining. I was able to see that there were more girls here than anywhere else in the world. Not to mention that all of them had round eyes and there were no VC nearby with me in their cross hairs.

I couldn't help but notice this one particular, very large sign in a storefront window. Not that seeing a sign in a window of a storefront would have been very unusual, but it was what it said that caught my eye. 'Need a date for tonight?'

I didn't know why, but I thought this was an interesting way to advertise for hookers. Of course, I didn't want a hooker, but the sign was an eye catcher and I did stop to read the small print. Just maybe these kind dates were grown in the desert. Nah, I can't be that stupid to think that.

Now, before I could read the small print, an extremely attractive, older woman standing nearby in the doorway, said to me, "It's not a Cat House. If you're looking for a prostitute, you'll need to continue down for six or seven blocks that way."

She pointed to my left and continued with, "You'll know when you are there because that part is easy. You will see lots of ugly women sitting on the door steps."

See seemed friendly enough; however, I didn't see the difference between the two. Other than here, she had a nice sign and that she was a pretty woman.

I smiled at her and responded, remembering to be polite, because I should always be polite to older women and I was a visitor in her country. "Thank you. I was just window-shopping. Not ready to buy right now."

Damn, damn, damn, I thought. Window-shopping. Now that was a stupid thing to say. She must now think that I was really looking for a hooker.

She looked at me as if I was some redneck; fresh off the farm, and that this was my first night in the big city without my parents. She came back with, "If you're thinking that my establishment is a whore house, well young man, you are grossly mistaken."

Her friendly smile suggested that she was telling me the truth. Maybe she was really selling dates, one of those fruit things.

She added, "Let me guess. You are here on your R&R and you have seven days and six nights to enjoy yourself before you head back to the fighting."

I looked at her with a little more interest this time. It wasn't too hard to figure out that I was in the military and that was why I was here. However, I figured that I might as well entertain myself with her, because I had nothing else planned for tonight. Hell, I didn't have anything planned for the rest of the week. Hell, I shouldn't even be here.

"So what do you sell that's different from the place that you said is down the street six or seven blocks?" I asked, believing this to be a limited question and I was kind of hoping for a straight answer.

"We do dates. Just as the sign says, dates. We have lots of young, single, attractive girls that are available here for the purpose of dating," she explained as I enjoyed her Australian accent.

Still wanting to be polite, I continued my conversation with, "You're not talking about an escort service, and you're running a, blind date, dating service."

"Yes, you are correct. Why don't you come in see what we have to offer? It doesn't cost you a thing to look." As she said this to me, she gently grabbed my arm and escorted me inside. At least she didn't grab me and drag me inside with my 'pride' sticking out.

Once inside, she led me towards an empty desk and graciously seated me. For a madam, she had style that I wasn't accustomed too. She moved around, seated herself, and just smiled a most reassuring smile as if everything was going to be okay. It was at this point that I started to figure out that she wasn't a madam and just maybe, she was doing just that, providing a dating service. Anyway, I didn't see any bar girls and I did look up to see if there was a balcony going around the room leading to a row of doors. Somehow, I imagined this kind of view because of watching plenty of western movies that took place in bars with dancing girls like the TV shows Gunsmoke, Have Gun, Will Travel, Bonanza, and Raw Hide.

I looked around the office and saw about a dozen desks. Six or so other guys were there going through the process the same as me. I looked back at this lady and returned a smile. This all seemed simple enough and just maybe this was some kind of scam. Too bad Dan wasn't around to encourage or warn me about what I was doing.

She placed a brown three-ring binder in front of me and opened it to the first of many 8x11 photographs. I looked down and saw a very attractive girl posing in front of a tree in the middle of some park. The photo seemed normal and that almost caught me off guard. I was sort of expecting to see a naked girl lying on a bearskin rug in front of a fireplace, or some rough looking girl in an odd position that was supposed to excite me.

I turned to the next page and looked at the next two photos. Again, same-same, nothing nude, rude, or crude about these two photographs of these very attractive, yet very ordinary young girls. Both of them were fully clothed, dressed very stylish, and were probably about my age.

Turning to the next two photos, I saw again, two very attractive, fully dressed girls. Only this time, they appeared to be a little older, maybe 20-22 or 23 years old.

"Find anything you like," she asked very politely, as if not trying to force an answer from me, which I found to be most disarming.

"I like them all so far," I answered, however I was still cautious with what I was saying and no way was I going to purchase anything. I did decide to make a joke, and I asked, "Can I get a group rate if I like them all?"

She apparently didn't like that remark and I could tell that much by her posture. Now before she could respond, I added, "Just joking."

Her smile returned and I felt that all was cool again.

I continued for another dozen or so pages and it only got better. I could not believe that one city would have that many beautiful girls. Much less, that many that would be looking for dates. Back home, every one of them would have a dozen or so guys competing for a date. I would gladly take any of them home to meet my parents.

She must have picked up that these photos had my full attention, because she asked me, "Do you want to hear about our program?"

Before I could respond, she was already up and out of her seat, as she asked, "Want a cup of tea?"

"No thank you," I answered.

"I'll be right back. Keep looking," she instructed.

Well, I figured that I might as well listen in to see what the punch line was. My initial thought was that no matter whom I chose, that young lady would not be available, but that she had someone of similar appearance and age that would make a fine substitute.

"Yes," I answered as she returned with a cup of tea for herself. She came back with an even more attractive and disarming smile that now had me totally at ease. I questioned myself, where was the punch line. How much will this cost me and how much will I lose. If Dan were here, he would have an answer.

"We have a one time cost of thirty dollars, Australian. We do not accept American money or MPC," she replied softly. This was quickly followed with, "And you have nothing to lose."

"Okay," I answered. "How does your program work?" I might as well check it out.

"You make your selection from our booklet and give me a time that you would like to meet with her. We will then give her a call and if she's available, she'll give us a time that she can meet you here. Naturally, after we go over a few rules and run an identity check on you."

After a short pause, she turned from being extremely friendly, with a nice smile of course, and faced me dead on to explain; "This is for the protection of our girls. And in a small degree, for your protection also."

Normally, this would have turned me right off; however, just maybe this might be a legitimate place of business. Before I could comment on the, identity check issue, she continued with, "We will supply you with a coupon booklet valued at over two hundred Australian dollars."

Before I could ask about the coupons, because I loved to use coupons, she placed a booklet in front of me. I browsed it and saw coupons for discounted taxi service, a number of buy-one-get-one meals with a selection of theater tickets for movies and plays. Same-same, buy-one-get-one. Overall, it appeared that this booklet was created expressly for anyone wanting to go out on a date. I was about to ask a question for the locations of all these places where I could use the coupons when she placed an open map of downtown Sydney in front of me for my viewing.

Looking at the map, it must have been made with the coupon booklet in mind because; every restaurant, theater, nightclub, museum, and taxi stands were listed and highlighted along with the local bus services.

"Is this map helpful young man?" She said, as she moved her well-manicured hand across the map indicating to me exactly where we were. The map was of downtown Sydney with cartoon characters being used that would indicate different places of business. I started to get the impression that maybe this wasn't a whorehouse after all. I turned back to the book filled with photos and worked my way towards the end. This just might be a good deal after all.

She placed her hand on mine and asked, "Do you have any questions that I could help you with?"

Well, I did have questions, but I was enjoying myself just checking out the photos of all these lovely ladies. After a few weeks of seeing only oriental women, and most of them bar girls or hookers, this was a real pleasure. However, I did have a few questions and I might as well ask them. "Yes mam. You are saying that I simply select one of these ladies, pay the fee, and receive the coupon booklet valued at seven times what my fee is."

"That is correct then, if she is available when you are. You might want a date for tonight or maybe tomorrow. Why don't you decide which one of our girls you find attractive and I will tell you a little about her. See if you two have some common interest."

"Let's say I select one for tonight and we want to go out again tomorrow. Assuming that she is available, is there another charge for tomorrow?"

"No. Once you two get together, anything after that is between the two of you. You can see her every night while you are here, at no additional cost. If you want, you could even come in at another time and make another selection. Of course, there would be the additional charge for your second, third, or fourth first dates. You understand, don't you?"

"Of course," I answered, thinking that this wasn't a bad deal after all. None of these ladies looked like hookers, as if I knew what a real hooker looked like anyway.

"Let me help you with your selection. First, find one that you find attractive and I'll tell you about her."

"Okay," I answered, and I continued with my viewing. After just flicking over one more page, I asked, "Are there any other costs that I should be aware of? You know, taxes, carrying charges, deposits."

"No. Just the one time cost and the two of you are on your own. We are simply, and basically, a blind date service and after that, it's totally up to you and your date. If it works out for the two of you, then it works out. If for some reason you two do not hit it off, then you part ways as you would any blind date."

Wanting to be funny, I asked in jest, "Do you have any, buy one, get one dates?"

Well, her friendly smile turned quickly and completely into anger and it was directed totally at me. I felt as if she took my joke as an insult directed directly at her and this organization. If it weren't for the desk between the two of us, she would have been in my face like an angry officer that I have experienced in the past. Immediately, I responded with, "No, I was just joking. I'm not that way at all."

The anger in her face softened a little as she responded with, "I see that with you, we'll need to do a full cavity search along with fingerprinting and photos."

Wow, that caught me off guard. I really pissed her off. Damn, damn, damn, and here I thought it was going along so well.

She busted out into an uncontrollable laugh and said, "Relax young man. I have a sense of humor also."

I was relieved at what she said and found myself totally at ease with her. This might be fun after all, I assumed. Besides, I didn't have any place to go and nothing to do anyway tonight. I might as well give this a try and see how it turns out. I would only be losing thirty dollars and I would still end up with a coupon book complete with good deals that I could use for the rest of the time that I was here. I still had a full week to go and now I would at least have a map to navigate myself around town.

With nothing else to say and while she was catching her breath from her outburst of laughter; I turned to the next page. There I found this strikingly beautiful girl that did everything but reach out, grab me, and say, 'pick me, pick me.' Short dark hair, eyes that were bright blue and clear, and skin that was as smooth as a baby's butt. Hold on that one, I didn't recall ever feeling a babies butt before so I would just leave that description out. Anyway, her smile was most captivating with bright teeth that were straight as an arrow. No way could she be a hooker and look that good. However, if she was, then just maybe I need to reconsider my views on hookers. She had a smile that would give competition to a cocker spaniel puppy.

The lady from behind the desk said to me, "Excellent choice. Dietz is her name and she's a nursing student in her last year at St Elizabeth hospital just around the corner from here."

"She's very attractive. I would find it hard to believe that she would be available," I responded sadly. She, Dietz, must be a ringer and I would bet that she was not available. Someone else would be a close match. Probably with long hair and crooked teeth with a smile like an alligator. Add to that, skin like the bottom of my shoes. With those assets, I might even get a good deal with her. Half-off, two dates for the price of one, or some other incentives just to get her out the door with a promise not to bring her back.

"Do you want to hear about her first before I see if she's available?"

"Yeah, sure," I answered, as I patiently waited for the bad news. The girl that I would probably get could beat me in an arm wrestling match for beers and was able to braid the hair under her arms. Body odor that could be seen as well as tasted from a distance.

She, I wish I knew her name; she opened another book and searched for this selection of mine. "She's five foot seven," she started out. "123 pounds and loves to see movies and plays along with inexpensive dinners; such as hamburger and french fries. Expensive dinners are nice, but would rather spend the time walking around checking out the sights than waiting for a well-done steak to be served," she read from the informational sheet.

"Sounds good so far," I answered, still waiting for the bad news. For now, I saw her as a cheap date. Thirty dollars so far. I could even afford to have cheese on our hamburgers and not use a coupon. Nah, I'll still use a coupon.

"Should I give her a call," she questioned.

"Yes. That would be great. What are the odds that she's available?"

"We will not know until I give her a call. What time would you like to meet her?"

"Now is good. We could meet for lunch, talk a little, and walk around for a while. She could show me the sights."

She smiled approval and I added. "Then later on, she can make the selection for a show or a play for this evening."

"Let me give her a call, and if the timing is acceptable, we can workout the details."

I smiled at her and she must have taken that as a yes, because she got up and walked into another room apparently to make the call.

I looked around the room and noticed that there were a few other guys, like me, doing the same-same. I hoped that I was doing the right thing here. I will still keep my guard up just in case there are some strings attached. I was a little concerned about the ID check that she mentioned earlier. However, I shouldn't worry about that, I am who I say I am, and I was not someone that had a questionable background.

A moment later, she returned. "How about an hour from now? Is that a good time for you to meet with her here?"

"Yes," I responded most excitingly, "You mean she's available for me, for now?"

"You must have been thinking that maybe we were tricking you or something. Giving you the run around, not giving you your selection, scamming you?"

"Well, yes mam. That thought did cross my mind," I answered, a little ashamed of myself. Then it hit me, maybe the photo was of Dietz, but this was a 'before' photo. Before she gained a hundred pounds, lost a few teeth, or of her fifteen or twenty years earlier.

Before I could ask those questions, my new lady friend indicated that it was time to do my ID check. She explained, "Not a big deal. I need to make a copy of your military ID card, driver's license, and any other items that may have your name on them. Next, we'll do a quick photo and take your finger prints."

I was about to tell her that I was not here to cash a check, or apply for a loan, but figured it best that I go along with the flow for now. It did make sense; however, that these precautions were for the safety of the girls.

"No sweat. Not a problem with me. Do I get a photograph of her?" I asked, only cracking a joke to take the nervousness off me.

The look I received from her was not a pleasant one. I quickly responded with, "Just joking."

Her smile returned and everything seemed normal again.

Fingerprinting, photographing, and making copies of my ID only took about thirty seconds and it was obvious that they had it worked out to a system. Lucky for her, I mean lucky for me, I had the thirty dollars available and was excited about my blind date.

I had to sign a few forms, check a few yes and no blocks, and that only took about fifteen minutes. She told me, "You may have a seat out in the lobby. Seat number eight is available."

What a strange rule they had down here. Not only did she tell me to take a seat in the lobby; I had to take an assigned seat. Number eight to be exact.

I sat down on the seat marked eight and noticed that it faced the window. It was my guess that a girl would at least have the first option to back out of this engagement. She would simply look in the window at seat number eight and review her rent-a-date ahead of time. Then, if she wanted, she could just keep on walking.

Therefore, I figured that I could do the same thing. I would just sit here, look out the window, and see who was looking in for the same-same reasons that I was a looking out. If my date showed up looking nothing as I imagined, well, I was out of here and she could keep my thirty dollars. It would be worth it to save my young butt from being embarrassed by taking out some old, over weight, toothless date out on the town. Coupon booklet or not.

I was only seated for about five minutes when a tall, dark hair, very attractive girl walked by and looked in at me. She was nothing as I thought she would be like and if this were she, I would most graciously accept her as my thirty-dollar door prize.

I kept my eye on her as she entered the room and noticed that she had the walk of a professional runway model. I got up as she approached me; as I wanted to introduce myself, only to have her say; "Excuse me," as she walked passed me. She walked right around me and met up with some guy that was three seats down from where I was seated. He was a weird-kind-of-looking guy; but tonight, he would be a weird-kind-of-looking guy dating a beauty queen.

Because I was already up and standing, I did not want to sit right down and look like an idiot. With that in mind, I walked over to the soda machine that was near the door and made it appear that I was doing just that, only getting up to get a soda. My luck continued because I didn't have any Australian coins for the soda machine. With that, my idiot self moseyed on over and took my seat again.

A few minutes go by, and I get this tap on my shoulder. Damn, I missed her walking by. Anyway, I turned around and to my surprise, there was a tall, colored girl standing behind me smiling. Damn, damn, damn, I done go and rented me a colored girl. This was not going to work out. I had no problems with colored girls; I just didn't want to date any colored girls. Twenty thousand miles from home or not, no way was I going to date a colored girl.

"Miss," I said, as I got up and made myself as pleasant and polite as possible. "There has been a mistake."

I felt like a creep telling her this and in some ways, I thought that she would have understood. No way did I want to hurt her feelings. Before I said anything else, I looked the room over for the odd chance of seeing Dan there making fun of me.

With a cute smile, dark bedroom eyes, and showing off her dimples on both cheeks, see proceeded to tell me, "Yes. There has been a mistake."

Damn, damn, damn. What was this? She was turning me down. Me? How could she turn me down? I paid my thirty dollars and if she was going to turn me down, I wanted my thirty dollars back. Damn, how could she do this, I was an okay sort of guy. Now my feelings were hurt. Damn, she really turned me down. I'm not a bad looking guy. I did have all my teeth and I shaved today. Damn, I already had a hooker turn me down once and now it was a paid date that was turning me away. I can't even rent a rental date.

"Mr. Edwards. Relax; the mistake is that you are in the wrong seat. My name is Tracy and I work here as the Marketing and Sales Promotion Manager. Please Mr. Edwards, your seat is number eight and your date, Dietz, will be here shortly. She's a nice girl and you two will have a great time. And, she is very, very white."

My response to her was a smile. "White," I finally said, and that did not come out right. "I did not mean white as in, your colored, and she's white." Boy oh boy, the more I spoke, the dumber I sounded.

Even with her pretty face, I still got a deer-in-the-headlights look out of her. She apparently felt sorry for me as she added; "Dietz is so white, that maybe you could take her to the beach for a little sun."

"Okay, can do."

With the return of her smile, Tracy lightly touched my shoulder with her right hand and indicated to me my seat, with her left hand. Feeling like an idiot, I calmly and sheepishly took my seat and said nothing more.

I could hear the others in the room chuckling at me for the way I acted. I should just ease my way on out the door and cut my losses. I could still tour all of the downtown area and bypass this street with no problem.

I was about to do just that, when I got another tap on my shoulder. I turned and before I even saw whom it was, I started out by saying, "Sorry. This was a mistake on my part. You can keep the thirty dollars and I'll just be on my way."

"You mean our date is cancelled?" Came a sexy voice that relaxed every muscle in my body, except one, and I was ever so grateful that I was wearing jockey shorts instead of my military issue boxers.

Damn, it was she. She, as in my date, and she were more attractive and taller than her photo indicated. I went from being a loser to a winner in just a blink of an eye.

"Hi. I'm Dietz. You must be Charles, she questioned in a voice that was most captivating to hear. It had the mixing of the Australian accent along with the Queen's English. She was very Australian looking and had everything but a pet koala bear in her arms.

I couldn't say anything. I had apparently said too much earlier, because I was all out of words. I love looking into her eyes. They were so lovely and I found myself fascinated by them.

Dietz, apparently having had this type of reaction before from other blind dates, knew to grab my hand and say, "What do you say we head out and have a bite to eat? We can get to know each other over lunch."

I could only smile at her with my deer-in-the-headlights look and follow her lead. She led me out the door and I followed like a little kid being dragged around by his mother while she was shopping.

Then it hit me, what was my problem? I was nineteen years old, I had graduated high school, seen combat, been wounded in action. I could certainly handle this date. Even a good-looking date. Hell, I've had good-looking dates before; this was not, 'new ground' for me to cover.

No sweat, I would just speak right up and create some small talk. However, I couldn't think of anything to say. My mind went blank just trying to create small talk. This was going to be a long date. At least I will get my money's worth. It would have been better if she and I didn't speak the same language. At least that way, it wouldn't be so awkward.

"Where are you from Charles?"

Great, she broke the silence for me. "I'm from Baltimore, Maryland. I'm from America. Where are you from?"

"Here, born and raised here in Sydney," she responded.

All seemed to be going well so far, I thought.

"How long have you been here," I asked, trying to keep the conversation going.

She responded jokingly, "All my life, I was born and raised here in Sydney."

Her smile after my repeated question relaxed me a little and I said to her, "I'm a little nervous. I don't know the rules here for blind dates."

I didn't mean to say it that way, but it came out that way anyhow.

"I see, so there are rules here? What are these rules?" She questioned me.

I wanted to head away in any direction other than the way we were going. I came back with, "I don't know anything about any rules. It was a statement that just came out. I'm sorry. Give me a break."

"I should give you a break, why?"

Before I could answer, she came back with, "I was joking with you Charles. You seem like a nice guy."

I answered her with, "Thanks. What do you say we start over and try this conversation again?"

"Good idea," she agreed.

A second later and with a smile that showed off her straight white teeth, she pointed to a little restaurant across the street and said, "We can have a bite over there. It's a nice place and they make good hamburgers. Do you like kangaroo?"

"I've never eaten one. What does it taste like?"

"No. Not to eat. I just made that up. I was just trying some small talk because you seem so up tight. Are you okay?" She questioned me, and it seemed that she was sincere.

I came back with a smile and nodded yes, as I opened the door for her. Inside was a pleasant enough little restaurant. Not unlike our small sub shops back in the states. I led her over towards a group of small tables by the window.

After taking her seat, she handed me one of the menus stuck between the mustard and catsup holders. Even without those little pictures next to each meal item, I was still able to make my own selection, as even down-under here, English, the Queen's English, was easy to read and understand.

She suggested, "Fish and fries are good here and that's what I'm having."

I went back of forth on what to order. I didn't want to say simply, 'I'll have the same," and I didn't want to take a chance or ordering something that I would not like. However, fish and fries seemed like something that I would have ordered anyway. "Fish and fries for me also," I announced as if I really did study the entire menu.

In no time at all, our meal came and it was good and hot. No ice for our sodas though, but it was a little cold just the same.

"Do you like plays?" Dietz questioned me, after she had taken a few bites.

I answered, "Yes," because I knew that I had some coupons for a theater near by. I didn't remember what plays were playing, but I figured that she would know and would suggest something good.

As if she knew what I was thinking about, she suggested that I checkout my coupon booklet to see what was available. Only four pages in, I came across a coupon for the play Hair. Thinking that would be a cool thing to do for tonight, I tore the page out and said, "What do you say we check out the play Hair? It says here that it just came out this week."

With that comment, I felt like I did a good thing. Any date would have enjoyed seeing that play. However, she came back with, "Good idea Charles, assuming that I haven't already seen it."

Damn, damn, damn, I thought to myself. She must be thinking that I was a cheapskate by picking the first coupon that I came across. I must have looked rather pitiful because she quickly came back with, "Relax Charles."

"I should have known that as beautiful as you are that you would have been on many dates and have probably seen all the plays in town," I complimented her.

"Thank you for that flattering remark, but just the opposite."

"You don't like plays," I asked.

"No, not to brag, but I am a pretty girl and pretty girls don't get asked out that much."

"No?"

"No. Lots of guys coming in look at the photos and believe that I must be a ringer and that they would just end up with someone else. So, they don't bother to pick me. But you did," she ended that with a smile and added, "I have an idea."

Anything that she would bring up would be an acceptable idea to me. "What do you have in mind?"

"Have you seen Hair?"

"No, but that would be great. It's playing at the new Opera House down at the harbor. I'd love to go and catch a show there."

"No. We cannot go there. It's not open yet and it'll be another year before it's completed," she sadly explained. She must have believed that my feelings were hurt, because she added, "But where we are going is much better."

With a smile that would make me want to see any show, anywhere, she continued with, "You'll like this place, promise."

Not wanting to make her feel as if I was disappointed, I answered, "No sweat. I think that what you have is a great idea. When are we going? Same show, Hair?"

"Yes, we can still go and see Hair. And, we're in luck; it's playing right over there. Look," she said, as she pointed across the street.

Sure enough, there was the theater, all lit up, and the marquee that display Hair.

"All we need now is tickets," she said with a sinuous smile that made me think that we would end up in the back row kissing away and never even see the show.

Well, it must had been my, our destiny, because we were able to purchase tickets for the show that was to start in only thirty minutes.

Instead of going inside for the next half hour or so, we spent the time standing on the corner talking about our families and the difference between America and here, down-under. We had a lot in common, and other than her accent, we could have been on any street corner in America. Well, maybe not on any corner in New York City.

Moments later, we had good seats about ten rows from the front on the aisle. I thought it was a movie but soon found out that this was a play, which I was enjoying very much, even though we were not in the back row making out.

Everything was going fine with the play, until we get to the part where everyone on stage ended up without his or her clothes on. Now this part I liked. However, as I was checking out all the girls on the stage, the police came in. The house lights came on as several policemen made their way down both aisles instructing those without their clothes on, to get dressed.

This Dietz thought to be funny. Instead of showing fear that we were in trouble, she was enjoying this.

One policemen, he must had been the one in charge, made his way on stage with a bullhorn and informed us that we were all under arrest. We were to proceed to the exits and to board the waiting paddy wagons.

Damn, damn, damn. My first day here and I was to spend the rest of my time in jail. I could not believe it. I was in a country that I did not belong, and now I was going to be locked up in a jail for something that I did not know was wrong. Nor, was I apart of any of this, other than purchasing our tickets for this strip show.

With all this going on around us, Dietz finally let loose with a roar of laughter that she had been holding back. "This was not funny," I explained to her. "Once the Navy finds this out, they'll turn around and lock me up again."

"Relax. It's part of the show," she explained between laughing at me and catching her breath.

Again, my face fell, into my familiar deer-in-the-headlights look. She came back with, "Like all you Americans boys say, "Don't sweat it. Don't sweat the small stuff, it don't mean nothin. Am I right?"

Okay, I got it now. With that little detail out of the way, I went back to enjoying the girls on stage without any clothes. I had never seen so many boobs at one time in my whole life. Hell, even if I was to add them all up, never have I seen so many. Damn, damn, damn, this was cool.

The ones that were on the stage, still without their clothes, well, before long, they were soon undressing the police. Now everyone was nude but us here in the audience. Wanting to check on my limit with Dietz, I suggested, "Let's you and I follow the cast's example."

This produced a smile and I assumed that I was on my way to something cool, when to my dismay, she informed me, "In your dreams Sailor boy. In your dreams."

My inside smile dropped yet I was able to made my outside 'happy face,' smile believable. Oh well, I gave it a try and now this play was starting to turn out kind of crummy. I did not care how it turned out; I was still going to be disappointed. All those boobs were just a tease as everyone stayed dress the rest of the show.

Before long, the play was over and the night was still young. I kind of wanted to keep doing something with my date, but I didn't have anything but a book of coupons to help me make a decision of what to do.

Dietz said to me, as I was about to say something, "Want to go dancing?"

I responded quickly with, "Yes, oh yes. I love to dance."

"Then follow me. King's Crossing is just around the corner and it is open 24 hours a day and seven days a week."

"Are all the clubs down here like that," I asked, as I never heard of anything like that back home.

"Oh yes, as long as you Americans keep coming here for R&R with only seven days and lots of money to spend, they will be open all the time," she explained.

At first, I didn't know how to respond to that. Were I and all the other Americans that came here for R&R, only good for our money? Then if so, so what? I only have a few days here and I might as well party. I could always catch up on my rest on my flight home.

Okay, for now, the two of us, holding hands, made the short walk to King's Crossing for some dancing. Just as I was about to cross the street from the middle of the block, she pulled hard on my arm and said, "Hang on mate."

I looked at her and figured that I was looking the wrong way before crossing, but I wasn't. "Okay," I questioned.

"We must cross at the cross walk. Can't you see the sign?"

I looked to my left and as I watched a double-decker bus passed by; I noticed a round yellow sign for crosswalks. "Sorry about that. I guess I owe you my life."

I sure had had a problem with crossing streets ever since I traveled overseas. Back home, living in Baltimore, I crossed the streets everyday and never had any problems. Damn, it sure would be a shame if I were to be killed by a bus while on R&R. I could see my poor parents now explaining how their son was killed while serving in Vietnam and was killed by a bus. Oh well, I should drop that negative thought for now and put a positive focus on my date. For real, I had a date and she is beautiful. Now, if only Dan could see me now.

At the door, we had to pay a cover charge and as I was getting some cash out of my wallet, I got a whisper in my ear of, "You have a coupon for this place."

Trying to act cool, I smiled a smile of thanks and paid the few dollars with my coupon. Instead of giving us a ticket, or to stamp our hands, we were both given a little basket of fish and fries. I thought this was odd but figured that free food was free food.

On our little walk down a long dark hallway to the dance floor, Dietz mentioned that our fish and fries were high in salt and that would make us drink even more while we are here.

We took a seat near the dance floor and ordered our first round of beers. The band was rather good considering their appearance. What we had here were six midgets dressed in clown outfits complete with make-up, orange hair, and everyone had a big red nose. Another odd thing about this band was that their equipment, drums, and guitars, were the normal size and that made the midgets appear even smaller. I asked Dietz, "Do all the bands down here dress like this?"

She chuckled at my question and answered, "No. Not hardly. The bands down here dress regular like. However; this, band came from the United States. California, I think."

I figured that it just had to come from California and that there was no place else in the world would create a band like this one.

She asked, "Do all the bands in California dress like that?"

That question caught me off guard, because I didn't know. Just how many bands did she think that I saw in my young life and I had never been dancing in California? I could only respond with a smile as I shrugged my shoulders indicating that I didn't know.

"It's just that I never seen anyone dressed that way on Dick Clark's American Bandstand," she explained.

I came back with, "This band seems to have its own thing going for it with these clown outfits. The red noses are a nice touch."

Right then, I felt some water dripping down from the ceiling. I looked up as Dietz asked, "Anything wrong?"

"Nah, just felt a little water dripping down from the ceiling," I answered.

It happened again, only this time it came from an angle. I looked over and they're looking at me about ready to burst out laughing, was Murph. "My man Murph. How's it hanging?"

He walked over, ignored me, and introduced himself to my date by saying, "Well good evening. I know that a fine looking woman like you could in no way be with Charles here. Would you like to dance? Dance with me?"

Damn, damn, damn, some friend he was. Before I could respond to make it clear that she was my date, Dietz spoke right up and said, "Sorry Murph. I'm spending my time with Charles. But feel free to look around."

Murph was caught off guard, and I like that.

Dietz continued, "I'm sure that there are other girls here that would love to go out with a guy that spends his time spitting on people."

I loved the way she put him down. However, I did feel a little dejected by how she took control and saved me. I came quickly back with, "So Murph, you don't have a date?"

I did not bring that up in order to tell him about how I got my date, just to make him feel bad that I had one and that he didn't. It apparently worked, because he came right back with, "Later. I have a date later on tonight. I was just looking for a quickie to fill in until then."

He looked over and told Dietz, "And she likes me because I can and do spit on little people, like Charles here."

Once again and before I could respond, Dietz jumped right back and slammed dunked him with, "Well, I bet that she's a nice girl and that her mother would be very proud to meet you."

That was funny and she's quick. I liked that. I could only hope that she wasn't that quick to put me down. With nothing more said between us and with Murph not having an answer, he headed on back to his table all the while spitting beer on people that he passed.

Murph gone, our beers came, we tapped glasses, and I took a small swig to be polite. Dietz on the other hand, took a smaller swig like a lady. She treated her beer as if it was a fine glass of wine and that it would take her all night to finish off just one beer. I asked her, "You ready to dance?"

To my surprise, she picked up her 'fine' glass of beer, and downed the entire drink with one swig. She then slammed down her empty glass hard on the table and followed that with a sizeable burp, "Yes, I'm ready, let's do it."

I assumed that now that I had to down my entire beer with one swig as she did. Not only to stay current with her drinking; but to keep her from showing me up, again.

Well, I tried. It took me two swigs and one cough to get it down, but I did it. At least she didn't see me take the two tries as she was already out on the dance floor waiting for me.

Our first dance was a slow dance and we did pretty well in getting our rhythm to match up with each other along with the music. At the precise moment that I felt the most comfortable with her, we got bumped, big time bump, by some one, or something very large behind us. I turned to see whom it was and damn, it was Big Foot, and he was still doing his bump and shove thing. Lucky for me, he had his back to me and I was able to move Dietz and myself out of his vision of sight, and reach.

I was thinking how it was a damn shame that one person could ruin someone's good time. Especially, with Dietz and me starting out having some fun together. Anyway, with little trouble, we did move to the other side of the dance floor and out of his range, both from his sight and his bumping.

Dietz said to me softly after we resumed our dancing, "Nice move. Thanks for getting him away from us."

"I've seen him before," I answered, tenderly in her ear and holding her a little closer. Feeling bold, I added, "If he gets anywhere near the chains that cordons off the dance floor, I will show you a great trick."

"I would like that," she replied, holding me a little closer.

Oh well, this is getting good and with a hold like that, I best do something if I wanted to impress her even more. Hell, if I did a good enough job with Big Foot, I might get some more time with her and not have to pay an additional thirty dollars for another date. But wait! If I get lucky with Big Foot, then I might get lucky with her.

Anyway, we danced a few more dances and were having a great time. We took our seats for a couple of songs and downed a few more drinks. I thought she had forgotten about Big Foot as it might have been to my advantage, however, she leaned over to me, and asked, "So what's this cool trick that you want to play on the big guy? You remember, the one doing all the bumping."

I answered with, "Oh yeah. I almost forgot." Damn, now what was I to do?

Dietz said, as she pointed to the dance floor, "See. He's doing it again."

Okay, I got to do something now. I came back with; "Here's the deal. When I say that we must leave, believe me, we must leave. As in, we might have to run out the door and not stop running for a couple of blocks."

"Is this going to be fun?" She asked, in apparent anticipation of having a swell time with me.

"Yes," I answered. "As long as I don't get caught."

"I'm with you," she replied and then gave me a kiss on the cheek. I thought to myself, this was great. Another girl that I found most attractive and exciting and after a few days, I will never see her again. This military life could be most disappointing. At least, she thinks I was cool. All I have to do now was to impress her with Big Foot and not get myself killed.

At this point, I gave Dietz a little background on what I was about to do. She gave me another kiss on the cheek and this time, it lasted a little longer. I could not tell if that kiss was because she liked me a little; or that it was my last kiss before I got myself killed.

The only thing that I could think about now was the strong feeling that I might get lucky tonight and of course, the wrong head was giving me directions. Then again, Big Foot could always catch and kill me. Either way, I should get screwed tonight. Apparently, I'll get lucky. In addition, with more luck, I'll get screwed to death.

Anyway, getting back to the situation at hand, I got up and made my way over to the chains that separated the dance floor from the tables. It didn't take long for big foot to work his way over in my direction. It was still no problem for him to knock people over to get where he wanted to go. As if timing was on my side, the music stopped and Big Foot was only inches away and facing the band. Quickly, I unhooked the chain from the pole and made a feeble attempt to attach the chain up with his belt loop.

Well, I missed and almost caught as he turned around. Damn, I said softly to myself. It would be my luck that he would turn around and not only catch me, but also remember me. Then he'll have a couple of additional reasons to hurt me. However, it was dark in here, and he just might not see me.

Big foot had moved over and he was now standing just a few inches too far away for me to reach him. As I waited for him to back up, he tapped the top of his head and looked up. Without any reason that I could tell, he looked forward and took one step towards the band. Before I could figure out what that was all about, it happened again. He tapped the top of his head and looked up at the ceiling. With that, he then took two steps back and was right where I wanted him to be.

Quickly, I was able to attach the chain to his belt loop and all seemed just fine. However, I felt a lot of water dripping down on me. I tapped my head with my hand at the same time that Big Foot tapped his head. As if on cue, we both looked up at the ceiling. As for me, I was looking to see what was dripping when it hit me that it smelt like beer. I turned around and could see Murph doing his beer-spitting trick. It was a good deal for me because it had caused Big Foot to move within range. Murph, along with a big smile, gave me the thumbs up. Wow, I got some help from an unexpected source. Appreciated, but unexpected just the same. I thanked him with a smile and gave him the thumbs up in return.

With the connection made, I turned around to head back to my table; I ran into our waitress and caused a small commotion as a few empty beer glasses fell off her tray and crashed onto the floor. Of course, it was louder than the music and it got everyone's attention.

The next sound I heard was a growl from behind me. Sure enough, Big Foot was checking-out my situation and apparently, his laugh was a growl. He backed up a step to avoid standing in the spilled beer that was now creeping towards him. Of course, his backing up caused the chain to tighten and then to bring down one of the poles.

With everything being quiet, as everyone checked-out the confusion from the broken glass and spilled beer, the sounds of the pole hitting the dance floor was louder than expected. Once Big Foot noticed the chain attached to his belt loop, he immediately figured out that it was me.

Anyway, it was time for me to disappear. He reached out in an attempt to grab me and the only thing he could do was to fall down from slipping in the spilt beer. At least that gave me some extra time for my escape. I meant, our escape. No need for me to lose Dietz now. I had scored some major points for myself and I want to cash them in.

Everyone in the place was laughing now at the confusion. Yet, I could hear over all the laughter, a most powerful growl and I knew that it was directed solely at me. Whatever, he was on the deck and attached to the chain and those details should give me a little extra time for our get away. With Dietz laughing and pointing at Big Foot, I grabbed her hand in an attempt to lead her away.

It was at this point that I noticed that my plan wasn't going well. When Dan did it, the crowd knew to step aside and let him escape. However, for my escape, there was no escape route. It appeared to me that everyone was standing between the door and us. I could only yell, "Excuse us. We got to go now. Make a hole."

Halfway to the door, I felt this grab on my shoulder. I looked back thinking it was Dietz, however, it was Big Foot, and he had me before we made it to the door. He pulled me back and as he was going to hit me, and all of a sudden, he tapped his head. As he took his free hand, the hand that was folded up into a fist and designated for my face, to checkout his head, I was able to break lose from his grip. With this new freedom, I was again making it to the door, with Dietz in close tow.

I could only assume that Murph was coming to my aid. I didn't have time now to thank him, but I must remember to do so when I see him again.

We made it to the lobby and as I turned to exit out the front door, I crashed right into the arms of an MP. It was easy to spot because the bright black and white arm ban was very obvious.

Before I could explain anything to justify my running out like I was, I saw that it was Jersey Joe. No way was I goings to give much thought about how or why I was meeting up with Joe again, or even how or why he was down here as an MP. Almost out of breath, I said, "Joe, there is this big guy chasing me. Please hold him up so I can escape."

He gave me a look as if suggesting, okay, how about telling me what this was all about.

Not giving him time to ask and not allowing me the time to explain, I said, "Will explain later. Gots to go now."

Before he could ask anything, we turned towards the sounds of growling coming up behind us with the additional sounds of poles being dragged with some chains attached to them.

Big Foot and I made eye contact at the exact moment that he realized that he was still attached to the chains. Because of his size, he was unable to reach behind and undo himself by yanking at the chain and pulling them lose from his belt loop.

I knew at this precise moment, that it was time for me to leave. However, I could not move fast enough and was still in range of Big Foot's reach. He had unhooked his chain from the other poles and was standing there with one hand on my shirt and the other holding onto the chain. Quickly, for such a big and drunk guy, he easily attached the chain to my belt loop. Now I was a dead man.

Damn, damn, damn. I was in for a world of shit. This man was going to kill me and there was not a thing that I could do about it. However, just in the, 'nick' of time, Dietz was there to unhook me and away we went. Naturally, Big Foot was right behind us and still no one was making it easy for us to escape. It appeared that everyone wanted to see what was going on and to do so; they had to stand right in our way.

On reaching the sidewalk outside, we ran right into some other MP's. Their hands went up, ordering us to stop. I bent over and as I caught my breath with my hands on my knees, I said, "You got to let us go. Some big guy is in there and he's after us."

"How big," snapped a question from one of the MP's.

"How big my ass," I said, as I stood up projecting a bad attitude.

The one MP looked at me as if it was time for, 'night stick' practice and I was the dummy. Feeling uneasy with this fellow, I turned to the other MP and saw that behind him, that Jersey Joe had caught up with us. Well, that certainly made me feel better, but now was not the time for small talk. Besides, I did not care at this time, what Jersey Joe had planned for himself after the war; I only cared about the safety of my new lady friend and me.

"Joe. We got to get out of here. Please, no time for questions. Just let us pass and hold up the big guy that will be coming out here looking for us," I said as quickly and clearly as I could. No need to repeat myself right now.

Well, Joe did step aside and said, "You may pass."

With that, together, Dietz and I thanked him and ran on past, not looking back. We ran on down the street laughing all the way. We were holding hands and skipping as if we were eight years old.

"Wow," I said. "I'm having a great time with you."

"You are kind of cool, for a foreigner," she added, with a big smile that once again showed me her straight white teeth that turned me on.

I was about to give her a kiss on the cheek when out of nowhere we heard this sound. A sound like a bear that was in heat, or in a great deal of pain as if he stepped in a bear trap. We both turned at the same time and could see nothing else but Big Foot running down the street towards us. Talk about a real turn off, this was it. I had no idea what to do now. It appeared to me that I was going to get killed today as the girl that I was having a good time with, watched on.

To my surprise, Dietz grabbed my hand and yelled, "Follow me."

Well, I didn't need to be told twice. As long as she had a plan and it was heading away from that giant, I would follow. What she did was to jump onto one of those double-decker buses that happened to be going past us, slow enough for us to jump on. She jumped on the back step of the bus and worked her way up the spiral stairs to the top level. No sooner than when I placed one foot on the bottom step that the bus picked up a little speed, thus leaving Big Foot unable to catch-up. I quickly ran up the stairs only to bang my head on the low ceiling.

Anyway, I lost my balance, rolled all the way down the steps, and fell back out onto the street. Luckily, for me, the bus had slowed down some and was not going very fast. I lucked out again in that I only rolled a few times. I quickly got up and in front of me, was the bus that was leaving without me. To my rear, Big Foot saw what had happened and was now making his way towards me at full trot. I did not have much of a choice of which direction to go, so I took off and I did catch up with the bus. Only this time, I took more care in going up the stairs and I used caution once I made it to the top.

Once upstairs, I was out of breath, away from Big Foot and into the waiting arms of my new girlfriend. The only thing that could mess up this moment was for me to belch right in her face, which I did. For my ill manners, I did get a smile from her and a chance for a second kiss.

"You are a funny guy," she informed me with a smile on her face, which made me tingle all over. Life was good and I love this town, and she was the best thirty dollars that I had ever spent.

She had moved over towards me in order to get a little closer. This was good and I liked that she had done that. Hell, I like the fact that she was sitting close, good looking, had a great smile, and Big Foot was unable to catch up with me. No need to get my ass whipped in front of her or anyone else for that matter.

Out of nowhere, I was on the receiving end of a, 'welcome back—my hero,' kiss.

I might as well see where this takes me. I boldly said, "I have a place that's not to far from here."

"It's getting late," she said with another kiss on my cheek, and effectively cutting me off.

I could not tell if that was a, 'take me to your place,' kiss, because it was late and she wanted her way with me, or that this was a, 'no way, not with me tonight,' kind of a kiss, because it was getting late and you should have started in on me earlier.

Damn, damn, damn, now what do I do? It was getting late, I was on a bus, and I had no idea where it would be going, or even exactly, where I was. I would like to find out now what my status was for the rest of the night. Do I get bold and ask her to stop over at my place? If she says 'yes,' then I will get lucky. If she says 'no,' then I messed up and I will be most unlucky. Yet, I could just take her home to her place and hope that I would get a second chance to take her out tomorrow, and then, only if she was available, and if she wanted to spend time with me, will I have a second chance.

Decisions, decisions, decisions. And, speaking of decision, what would Dan do in a spot like this? I'd bet that he would just go ahead and ask her straight out, 'do you want to fool around?' Besides, what do I have to lose? If she said, 'yes,' then that will be wonderful. If she was to say, 'no,' well, there was always tomorrow and I would just have to shell out another thirty dollars and take my chances with my second choice.

"I have an idea," I said, looking into her eyes trying real hard to be romantic.

She looked back at me, with of all things, the deer-in-the-headlights look. Crap, and damn, damn, damn, this was not starting out well and I had another decision to make. Well, I was just going to wimp out on this and give this a shot for tomorrow night. "I would like to take you out again tomorrow, and I would like and make it a whole day, if possible."

The deer-in-the-headlights look faded away and that was replaced with a warm, sexy, smile. So far, this was starting out wonderful. She tells me, in my ear, "I can't tomorrow night, I have to work."

I was almost in tears, but was able to hold them back. Then, just as I was about to say something, she placed her fingers over my lips and added, "I am off tomorrow in the day and I would like to go to the beach."

Bingo, I had a date and just as I was about to ask her about the details, she stood up and announced, "This is my stop."

I stood up beside her and she placed her hand on my shoulder and said, "No. You stay on and get off in four stops. You'll be right across the street from your hotel."

I did as suggested because I would do anything she said right now to see her again tomorrow. "What time and when?"

"I'll call you in the morning."

"You don't have my number. Hell, I don't even have my number," I explained knowing that this would be the last time that I would see her. Shit, I hate this military stuff where you make friends and then lose them.

"I have your number," she explained with that same sexy smile. "Your number was listed on your application, remember?"

Cool, I had a date and she was going to be the one calling on me. I like this town. No real reason to hurry back to The-Nam now.

Because the bus was only going to stop for a minute, she got right off and waved bye. Then before I could really see which way she headed to go home, my bus pulled off and away I went.

Okay, she said to take the bus four stops before getting off. Did this last stop count as one of the four, or was that stop not to be counted. Most importantly, I didn't know what stops there were. I could only count them if someone got on or off my bus. If the driver skipped a stop because no one was getting on or off, it would not be counted.

No problem really, as I would simply walk up to the driver and ask about my stop. However, before I decided to approach the driver, I'd just assume that her stop didn't count as one of the four stops. Anyway, I'd only be off a block one way or the other.

Okay, I held on for four blocks, assuming there'd be a stop on every block, and as I got off, luck was in my favor because, there on the corner, was my hotel. I danced my way across the street recalling what a wonderful night I just had. I found a gorgeous girl, a girl that wanted to see me again. A nice meal, a good play, a little dancing, an excellent escape from Big Foot, and a little kiss good night that made it all worthwhile.

However, shit, shit, shit, I was not prepared for tomorrow. In didn't have an extra set of clothes, no swimwear, or even a towel to lie on today. Fresh out of suntan lotion and now I realized that tomorrow was going to be a failure as far as dating goes, maybe.

Any way, there was my hotel. At least I have a place to say tonight and no one will be trying to blow me up.

Once I made my way into the lobby, I found it to be a very happening place. With the way that the guys were dressed, it was apparent that they were all in the military. For example, nothing that they wore matched up and what they were wearing, well, nothing that they wore fitted very well. It looked at if everyone had gained some weight after eating three square meals a day in the military.

As for me, I hadn't been in the military long enough for my clothes, which I purchased before boot camp, not to fit me.

For this late at night, I would have thought that everyone would be in his or her rooms sound asleep. However, like Dietz had mentioned earlier, this city will always be awake as long as Americans spend their R&R time down here, I meant, down-under. With only seven days and six nights of R&R, no reason to spend it sleeping.

I noticed that off to one side of the lobby, was a rental store. Not to rent cars, moving trucks, or equipment for lawn work, but for clothes and the like. As you could imagine, I made my way inside and found that I was able to rent almost anything. I figured, what the hell, I would rent all the items that I would need for tomorrow. With little trouble, I had a nice summer shirt, shorts, and swim trunks. I was even able to rent a pair of sandals and all this was rather inexpensive, if I did the money exchange calculation correctly. Naturally, I hoped that everything that I rented was in style and that this was not a Goodwill store outlet.

On a positive note, how great this was that I could rent a young lady, and the clothing to wear out on my date. However, I did not inquire about renting a jock strap or toothbrush.

Okay, I was outfitted for tomorrow. I would just take a few hotel towels with me and with additional good fortune; Dietz will have a blanket for us to lie on. It would be nice if she had a little blanket so we could lie close together.

Just outside the rental store, I came across a row of telephones with little stools for each phone and it dawned on me that I could call home. I would just try again and see what happens.

I took a seat, picked up the phone, and a sexy voice, an Australian female sexy voice, came on the line. She asked, "Number please."

"Yes, I wish to make a collect call home," I replied.

"Very well, I can help you. Where is home?"

"Baltimore."

"Baltimore," she questioned.

"Baltimore Maryland."

"What country?"

Crap, I had forgotten just where I was. "I would like to make a collect call to the United States of America. Baltimore Maryland to be exact."

"Number please."

"Hopkins 8-0414," I said this clearly, so that she would get it right the first time.

"Your name."

"Seaman Edwards, no wait, Charlie. Tell them Charlie."

Okay, she had the information and soon I would be talking with my parents. I just need an open line, someone home, and not to be hung up on.

On the line, I could hear the different operators talking to each other. I could hear my first operator talking to someone that sounded oriental. Next, I could hear the oriental operator talking to what appeared to be an American-speaking operator.

The American operator mentioned that she was in Hawaii and that she was making the call to the mainland. After a few more minutes, I could hear that the next operator had said something about Chicago. This had been going on now for almost fifteen minutes and I was about to fall asleep. Just as I was about to nod off waiting for my connection, I heard my little sister answer the phone.

At first, I wanted to give her instructions about saying 'over,' at the end of her talking when one of the operators asked, "Will you accept a collect call from Charles?"

My sister answered, "Where is he calling from?"

"This call is originating from Sydney Australia, will you accept the charges?"

"No. My brother is in Vietnam and not in Australia. Besides, he would not call again this late at night."

With that said, she hung up the phone.

Okay, another tried and failed attempt to call home. My next call just might be from the airport in Baltimore asking for a ride home. But, no sweat, it don't mean nothin and tomorrow I will be at the beach with a girl, and a cute girl at that. I'll just have to take care of my little sister when I get home.

All right, life moves on and I was excited that I had plans for tomorrow. With all that, I was not all that tired, but I knew that tomorrow would be a long day and that I wanted to be rested. In the likely event, that it becomes a long day and an even longer night. In no time at all, I was in bed and with the volume on the TV turned down low. It didn't take long and I was soon asleep dreaming about the next day.

# Chapter 18

Ring, ring, ring. Ring, ring, ring. Ring, ring, ring. I was half awakened by this ringing in my head, which I initially took as an SOS distress signal. It did it again, ring, ring, ring, and that was followed with ring, ring, ring, short pause then, ring, ring, ring.

I started to process the SOS signal and realized that it was not correct. What I had here was three short, followed by three short, then three more short rings. SOS is three short, three long, then three short rings.

I surmised that who ever was in trouble was also having trouble with his SOS'ing. Being that I knew about all this, I would volunteer myself to help this poor guy out for making such a major mistake.

Ring, ring, ring. Ring, ring, ring. Ring, ring, ring. There, he did it again. Someone is stupid, stupid, stupid.

I finally got around to opening my eyes as I looked in the direction of the ringing and I realized that I was the one that was stupid, stupid, stupid. It was the telephone ringing, not a distress call. I had spent so much time listening to the ring, that I almost forgot to answer it. Now that would have been a serious mistake on my part as the call must be from my girlfriend, Dietz.

Well, I did take too much time and I did miss the call. By the time that I took a deep breath, grabbed the phone and attempted to answer as if I was cool, there was no one on the line. Damn, damn, damn and shit, shit, shit, along with stupid, stupid, stupid. I done messed up and missed my call.

However, before I could feel even worse than I already was, my phone perked up and the down-under ring, rang again. Ring, ring, ring, and it must be Dietz.

Well, thank you God, my new girl friend was on the phone, and she was on the phone for little old me. Cool, little old me. "Hello, hi, good morning!"

I must have been happy sounding as Dietz asked, "You sound in high spirits this morning mate."

"Yes, yes, yes," I answered, not willing to explain myself.

Then, before she could view my happiness as if this was my first date ever, I came back with, "I am just happy to be going to the beach. And, a little excited that I get to go with you."

A short pause for effect, I continued with, "I thought at first that I might have missed your call."

It worked as she thanked me for saying such a nice thing. Great, I had apparently scored this time and with luck, I will score tonight. And, let me not forget that today's date won't cost me an additional thirty Australian dollars.

It's not that I was cheap, I only had a little bit of cash, and it would be another thirty days before I get paid again. At least, if I could make it home on what I had, I could always hit my parents up for an advance.

Oops, almost forgot, "Dietz, when and where?"

"Okay mate. Write this down," she instructed.

"Wait one. I need to find pen and paper."

I found pen and paper right next to the Bible. "Shoot," I shouted and remembered that was not the correct phrase to use. I quickly came back with, "Directions please."

"At noon, catch the bus in front of your hotel. You will be looking for the R-2 heading towards Center City. You will need fifty cents for the ride to town."

"Got it. Romeo 2. Which way will I be going?"

"Romeo?"

Crap, I wasn't talking on the radio, giving my location. "Sorry, R-2, which way?"

"Which way," she questioned, as I was making my simple note taking routine, very difficult. Damn, I could send and receive successfully military information on the locations of friendly and non-friendly forces and yet, I was unable to write down correctly one simple bus boarding transaction. After just a few weeks in the military, was I turning into a lifer?

Getting back to what I was doing, I asked while trying not to sound stupid, "Am I getting onboard on this side of the street, or do I cross over from the hotel."

"Cross over, R-2 Center City. Okay," she repeated. "It will say 'R-2 Center City' on the sign above the front windshield and again above the little window next to the bus door."

"No sweat. Just tell me where to get off. At the beach?"

"No, not the beach, you will do that later," she said, and with luck, I would be correct in what she meant by that. I was going to get lucky tonight. Now if I could just avoid getting sunburn. No need to be romping around in the sack with a sunburn.

"Ask the driver to let you know when you get to Market Street. You will want to catch the R-1 to the airport," her instructions continued.

"Okay, the R-1 to the airport. Are you sending me back home," I asked, hoping to add in a little humor.

"Oh no. I don't want to send you home. That is not where I want to you to get off," Dietz answered, and I had inserted a little romance in her tone. For sure now, I didn't want to get sunburned.

"Got it. What's next?"

"Tell the driver that you want to get off at the beach. There is only one stop for the beach."

"This is great. What should I bring?"

"My friends and I will have everything we need. Except for your swim trunks," she explained.

"Friends?"

"Just a couple or two. Two of my friends have dates and they will join us. You don't mind, do you?"

"Of course not, as long as you and I are together," I answered, and I did not want to give her the impression that I was jealous. Well, I was a little, but had no reason to be.

"Okay then. I will see you when you get off the bus," she ended our conversation in a cheerful manner as if she was happy that I was able to make our date.

"Should I bring anything?"

"No. Just come expecting to have a good time. I promise that you will have a good time mate."

With instructions in hand, our phone time was over. I ended with, "I'll keep you to your promise, over."

"Over?"

"Never mind. See you soon," I said, and ended again our conversation.

Wow, was I one lucky guy. I was not getting shot at today, being chased by officers in the United States Navy. One, the captain of my ship, another one with a missing leg along with a third officer, that I keep running into. I will not be standing any watches and doubling as a target for the VC in Saigon. Girls, well, I will not be running into Big-Ass Bertha with those two girls that Dan knew at her birthday party, Jackie and/or Gail and her friend.

No way will I run into Crapper, Louie-Louie, Murph, or anyone else that had given me a new appreciation and understanding of mankind. It was just going to be me with my date Dietz, along with a few of her friends, and with luck, this will be a topless beach.

After just a little while watching TV, to kill time, and I enjoyed it as it was in English, a shit, shave, and shower was next on my list of things to do today.

With precise military timing, I was at the bus stop with time to spare. With this little extra time, I took an inventory of my gear. No need to show up unprepared. My swim trunks were on and under my shorts. Two hotel towels were rolled up and I was as prepared as could be. Then, of all things to think about, I recalled the one time in The-Nam that before heading to town, we were all handed rubbers. Military issue rubbers, but rubbers just the same. Great, I might get lucky and instead of getting it off, I might get something on, like crabs or the clap. I was not sure what the clap was, but I knew that it was bad. So, according to my inventory, I was short a rubber. If I were lucky, I'd be short two or more rubbers. Well, I would not call that being lucky. Naturally, it would have to be before she leaves for work, then if she still must go to work.

Before I allowed this negative thought cloud my mind, I made it an issue to think positive. Positive as this date didn't cost me anything and if needed, I could find a rubber someplace.

Standing there, heavy in thought, I failed to notice that a bus had just pulled up and with the door open, the driver yelled at me, "Getting on mate?"

I was about to answer him, 'No, I was just thinking about how and when I was going to get it off,' when I simply smiled and jumped onboard. I dropped a fifty-cent piece into the coin collection thing-a-ma-jig and asked him, "Can you let me know when we get to Market Street so that I can catch the R-1 to the airport. Please."

"Young man, it will be the first stop after we cross the Sydney Harbor Bridge. The R-1 will pick you up where I leave you off."

After he closed the bus door and before he pulled off, he snapped at me, "Have a seat please."

I thought that he was just another unhappy person with his job. How hard could it be? You just drive a planned route, if someone wants off, her or she would just pull the string to sound the buzzer, and if someone wanted on, they would simply stand at the bus stop. You don't even need to decide where to go, as your route is the same-same, every day.

"If you sit upstairs, you will have a lovely view of our city," he said, in a very friendly tone.

"You will not see that much sitting behind me," he added, and pointed towards the stairs. Either he was being nice to me or that he didn't want to be bothered by me.

Oh well, I would just assume that he was a nice guy and that the view from the second level was a better view. Naturally, I would take my time going up the stairs so that I would not fall out again and miss out on getting off at Market Street, off at the beach and with luck, I will be getting off later on tonight.

Once seated, he was most correct. The view was much better being up top, here, down-under. One point of interest was the way that some of the local stores advertised. Where there was a row of sidewalk shops that had an awning or roof above the sidewalks, you would find store signs right there at the end of the awning or roof. Naturally, it was right at the window of the second level of the bus. In fact, these signs were close and big enough, that you could not miss them, or see another store.

Looking around, it was obvious and not hard to miss out on how clean this city was. If this had been New York City, these signs would have been complete with graffiti and gang trivia. Along with the normal notes like, 'Sam loves Pat' spray-painted on in bright brilliant colors in unusual and artistic fonts

In addition, it was sure nice to be in a country where I could read and understand all the signs and I really did not expect to see one that displayed, 'Topless Shoe Shine.'

This was a pleasant ride and I especially enjoyed not having my window screened in. There was no jeeps riding shotgun behind us and the traffic down-under was tranquil and orderly. Everyone seemed to be following the rules of the road with no one blowing their horns at everything and everyone. I also did not miss having rednecks yelling out at all the pretty girls. It was too bad as there were pretty girls on almost every street corner.

This was one bus ride that I enjoyed and was not looking forward to getting off, well, not really, as I remembered why I was on this bus. I had a date, a good-looking date and I was going to the beach. Today I was cool and Dan will never know about this.

Just then, right in the middle of my daydreaming, the bus driver yelled out, "Yankee. You just missed your stop."

Being that I was the only person on the second level, I assumed that he was yelling at me. Well, I de-de-maled myself right down the steps and in my haste, I fell right into the street. Shit, I've done this before. So, for right now, I was not cool and was glad that Dan did not see this. More importantly, I was very glad that Dietz was not around to catch my clumsiness.

I stood up and made it a point not to appear as if I was dazed. The driver chuckled at me and pointed to the bus stand on the other corner. "Over there mate. The R-1 to the airport will be by in a few minutes. Be careful getting on and off."

With that, he laughed out loud, closed the door before he moved on. To make a long story short, the R-1 came, I got onboard heading to the airport, I meant, the beach, and I did so without falling on or off the bus.

I made my way to the second level and noticed that there were a lot of other folks heading to the beach. It was easy to tell as they had on their beach attire along with blankets, towels, and coolers filled with beer.

No need to ask the driver where to get off as Dietz informed me that there was only one stop for the beach. With everyone onboard, here going to the beach, I would just get off when they did thus making this a, no sweat situation. With that, I would just relax, enjoy the view and will try not to fall asleep, and or fall off and out of the bus.

Apparently, a few minutes from the beach, a couple of little kids that were on the bus started to get excited. Their excitement worked on me and I found myself getting excited with them. They were going to get down in the water and play around and I was going to get down with Dietz and play around. Only I'd be doing some adult type playing around. Life was cool for me right now, really cool for someone who just turned nineteen from Baltimore, Maryland. And here I thought that I would had just stayed in the city and never ventured out into the world. Wow, going to the beach in Sydney Australia with a beautiful girl.

For a normal person, this might not be that big of a deal, but just the other day, I was in a war zone and people were trying to kill me. And in some small way, they almost succeeded. I mean, I was injured and I had received the Purple Heart.

These kids, these very excited little kids, all made their way towards the stairs in anticipation of getting off. Well, not wanting to miss my stop, I did same-same. I gathered my things and got in behind them. My excitement was soon quenched as the parents told them to sit back down because we were not there yet.

Even down-under, the tallest of the little kids questioned, "Are we there yet?"

And naturally, the father answered with, "Almost. Sit down."

The shoulders and smiles dropped on these little kids as they sat back down in their seats. Crap, what was I going to do now? I was not getting off here. So, I made my way around the kids then down to the first level and took a seat behind the driver. I figured that when I could hear and see the kids stampede their way off the bus, that I would follow. Naturally, only and if their parents were in close tow behind them.

This bus ride seemed as if it was never going to end. I started to get worried as I could see up ahead of me planes taking off and landing. I assumed that the beach came before the airport, as the airport was the last stop for the R-1. Then, before I could get all upset about the possibility of missing my stop, the kids came running down the stairs and got in line, ready to jump off and into the fun time of being at the beach.

Again, their excitement got me excited. I looked ahead at the bus stop and my excitement just doubled, as there she was, Dietz. Damn, damn, damn, boy oh boy does she look good. She was still strikingly beautiful. Short dark hair, eyes that were bright blue and clear. Skin that was as smooth as a baby's butt. Her smile was most captivating with bright teeth that were straight as an arrow. The smile on her face made me feel as if she was just as excited to see me, as I was to see, and to be with her.

With my excitement building, I went into a military mode, a military mode in a war zone and I wanted to be the first one off the bus. I had apparently been trained to exit buses this way and with her waiting for me, I had good reasons to be first one off the bus. I got up and just as I was about to kick these little turd kids out of my way, I remembered the things that my parents taught me about being polite and waiting your turn. Besides, no need for Dietz to witness me being rude to little kids. With that, I humbly backed up and waited my turn. However, these little turds took their time getting off and as I was about to get in behind them, their parents moved in on me. Crap, I was never going to get off this bus and into the waiting arms of my date.

It was hard not to look irritated with the time it took for all these kids, followed by six or so parents dragging, pushing, and pulling beach gear, to get off the bus. Then, before long, it was my turn and in taking my turn, I made it such a point not to fall of the bus, that I did slip a little.

This caused Dietz to snicker at me and I responded to that with, "I am so excited to see you, that I almost broke my neck getting off the bus."

That earned me a hug, a kiss on my cheek, and that was followed by a warm smile. I could even mess up a little and still look cool. I was thinking, as Dietz grabbed my hand, that this was most definitely a most enjoyable way to start a date. Down here, down-under, and right now.

This was a beautiful beach. White sand, clean white sand and not the beer can littered beaches like at Ocean City, Maryland. Not really crowded, just enough to make it difficult to walk in a straight line. I didn't find this a bad thing in that at times, when walking behind Dietz; I could see that she had a nice ass and long legs. She needed a tan though, but that was okay as she could use a couple layers of suntan lotion applied to her hot body, and naturally, that would be me, the hot handed, hot tan lotion sort of guy.

We came up to a large yellow blanket and Dietz took a seat. She patted her hand gently down on the blanked indicating where I was to sit. I had no problem in taking orders from her as long as I was to sit close. It was and I plopped myself right down close to her.

"I see that you rented some clothes for today," she said.

At first, I must have given her a look as if I was just insulted with that comment. She quickly came back with, "Don't be offended, I think that it was sweet of you to take the time to look nice for me."

Still, I did not know how to respond. Dietz, seeing that I felt uneasy, added, "No sweat GI. It don't mean nothin'. What you are wearing is same-same for everyone that comes down here."

After she gave me another kiss on the cheek, I felt much better. At least she was giving me a compliment, in military terms, but a compliment just the same. Wanting to return the favor, I said, "You look nice, really nice. I love your little outfit."

"It's the best I could do with the laws that they have down here," she answered, looking at her breast, which gave me the chance to stare at them also without being noticed.

You could dress like clowns down here but you had laws how to dress at the beach. "Laws?"

She pulled at the waist of her bathing suit and said, "There must be a least one inch of material going around your waist. Anything less than that, the beach police will make you leave or put on something else."

I found this to be strange, but at least this gave me another good reason to stare at her outfit and not worry about getting caught. However, I must remember not to over do it. At least I had a reason to stare at other girls as they walked by, you know, just to see if they were breaking the law.

"I have a few friends coming over later," she informed me.

"No sweat. Are they as pretty as you?"

"Why? You want someone else," she asked, as if I just insulted her.

Oh my, I just broke some sort of down-under rule. I was always breaking rules at the beach, first with the girls in Cam-Ranh Bay, and now here.

"No way, I am very excited to be with you today. It was just a comment. Nothing more than that," I explained, and hoped that I scored well enough to get a free pass.

A little smile, but not enough to break even as I came back with, "I just find you to be most beautiful and would find it hard to visualize anyone being more attractive."

Well, that scored a passing grade and this time; I got a kiss on the lips. No tongue, just a lip kiss that did last more than a few seconds. Great, I was still cool, getting hot, but still cool.

I laid down and looked up into the sky. Nice dark blue sky with no clouds in sight. I didn't know why, but I commented, "Being that we are here, down-under, should we not just fall off the bottom of the earth?"

That caused her a deep belly laugh and she asked, "I'd bet that you watched as your toilet water corkscrewed down backwards after a flush."

Decisions, decisions, decisions. Do I tell her a lie, or do I tell her the truth and look like an idiot, and/or, be honest and make a joke out of it. Well, because she knows military slang, then she may know how we think. Okay, I decided to be honest.

"Sure did and I found it to be most exciting. Not something that I would write home about, but exciting just the same," I told her trying to project that I was just an average guy, but not too average.

By her smile and little chuckle, I scored again as she informed me, "If I ever get the chance to venture north of the equator, I will be doing the same thing. I've never given that much thought until you Americans found it so entertaining and amusing."

To keep this going, I added, "Except for the American Red-Necks. You know, they don't have anything to flush back home."

Okay, we were having fun and my last comment got her to thinking. I hoped that she was not aware of what I was talking about because she had never dated any Rednecks. "Nothing to flush," she questioned.

Great, she didn't know. "Oh yeah," I answered. "Red-Necks don't have much, but they do have a pot to piss in. Pots don't flush."

Before I could continue on a role with my toilet humor, one that would be on an even keel with Anthony, Monroe, and the boys, Dietz's friends showed up.

Dietz introduced them as Sam and his girlfriend, Susie. They looked like a nice couple and another couple, Justin and Stephanie, followed them.

Okay, this was cool. Six of us and I had the prettiest girl of them all. After our introductions and following the proper placement of everyone's towels and blankets, it was time for Susie to change her clothes. She had mentioned that she was not wearing her swimwear, as the others and that she needed a place to change.

As she looked around for a changing area, like a rest room, well, do I have a great idea and one hell-of-a funny thing to do to her. It happened to me and everyone had the best laugh of all times at my expense, and this was payback for me. Besides, I might even get to see where the sun does not shine on this cute little girl from down-under.

"Susie, we could all hold up our towels and blankets for you and you can change right here," I offered this cool suggestion of mine, that was received with some apprehension and appreciation.

"Out in the open like this," she questioned, as Stephanie looked at me for an answer.

Dietz didn't seem to care one way or another as she said, "Just do something soon so we can all get in the water."

Susie, at this point, seemed to be under some pressure. Again, with apprehension and appreciation, she accepted my suggestion. "What do we do," she questioned me.

"Simple," I said, as I passed out a towel to each of us.

Everyone seemed to get the gist of the idea and a small circle was soon formed around Susie. Susie didn't waste any time, as she was soon half-undressed before we had everything in order. Okay, now I just had to wait for the most favorable time to complete my trick. It didn't take long and now that I figured that she had her pants down to her ankles, I dropped my towel and turned around. I shouted, "Surprise!"

Well, I was very pleased with my view and Sam and Justin were equally as thrilled. However, Dietz was not thrilled along with Stephanie, as they were alarmed at what had just happened to their friend. Their negative and shocked reactions were nothing compared to Susie. Susie was fit to kill me, and I do mean to really kill me.

Down she goes along with a towel thrown in by Dietz and Stephanie. Well, the towels were small and she only had two towels and three things to hide. Once she realized that she needed more and bigger towels, her yelling was soon heard by everyone on the beach. Damn, damn, damn, I was again the center of attention and it was negative attention.

A moment ago, I would have thought that I was about ready to get a, 'well done,' from Dietz and some high fives from Sam and Justin. At least a smile and kiss on the cheek from Dietz acknowledging that what I did was cool. However, things looked bad for me right now and if I was lucky, that I would be able to stay with the group, and not be expelled from the country.

Susie was able to recover without too much difficulty, but her dirty looks were enough to turn the world upside down thus making Australia on the top of the world. That would make a mess of American history books.

Whatever, I did my best to apologize to Susie and the group. Mentioned that it had happened to me and figured that little side note would score points in my favor. However, and with little surprise, it didn't. Stephanie said, "Did you like it when it happened to you?"

"Of course not," I quickly responded, and made it a point to be sincere.

"Apparently not," was the response from Susie, just after she had straightened herself up. At least in the confusion, she was able to change into her swimwear and we had that little matter out of the way. On a sad note, she had sand everywhere stuck to her skin.

I made a feeble effort to wipe it off, but I had my hands smacked.

Even though I did not get a high-five from Sam or Justin, Sam did give me the thumbs up and I got a wink from Justin with a smile. Just as I started to feel okay with Sam and Justin, my new friends, Dietz whispered in my ear, "Not a good move."

Oh well, I scored fifty percent and it was with the wrong fifty percent. Crap and damn, damn, damn. Maybe one of us would get struck by lightning or something and my little prank would be forgotten with the excitement a good lightning strike could create.

"Sorry guys," I said in an honest tone, with a facial expression that I hoped would be believable and acceptable. "It seemed like a good idea at the time."

Stephanie was not impressed, but Susie seemed to have gotten over it. If I could only get Dietz to give me a little slack, I could live with that. Then, out of the blue, Dietz grabbed my hand and said, "Come on mate. Let's get wet."

I assumed that it meant just for the two to jump in the ocean for a little, 'wet and wild.' For now, I would be happy just to get the two of us alone. Then for the next hour or so, we were alone as the other couples stayed on the blanket and got some sun.

We just talked about our homes and families. Nothing was asked about the war. For me, that was just as well as I was only in-country for a few weeks. No way would I consider myself a war hero kind of a vet. Even with my newly awarded Purple Heart, because there were a lot of guys that had suffered a lot more and worse than I had. Even if they were not wounded, they still had duty that would easily give them the title of a real war veteran.

One thing we discussed was about how we celebrated Christmas as their seasons were opposite from ours. Even if it did snow here, down-under, it would only snow in July and August. I asked about how Santa would come to town, as in what sort of sled he would be driving. Was jokingly told that Santa would arrive wearing a bathing suit with a large bag of toys over his shoulder. Instead of a sled guided by reindeer, their jolly old guy would come in on the perfect wave riding a surfboard.

So for now, my life was wonderful. Pretty girl with me at the ocean and my only drawback was that in a few days, I'd be gone, never to see her again. This part of the military really sucks. It must be great having a girl in every port, but if you were never to return to any ports more than once, what good would it be?

As for me, I'd rather have one girl in one port that I see all the time, than to have a dozen girls in a dozen ports. Then again, having a dozen girls in a dozen ports would mean that I had just that, a dozen girls. Hell, a dozen girls, not a bad count for someone that just turned nineteen.

Well, no reason to dwell on the sadness of my current situation, or even to daydream the thoughts of having a dozen girls. I might as well enjoy the moment and this was a moment to enjoy. For the rest of the day, we spent time in and out of the water with little interaction with her friends. No need for me to spend time with them as I might end up saying something about Stephanie's stretch marks that looked like a map of the Mekong Delta. Susie didn't like me anyway for my, 'drop the towel trick.'

Before long, I knew that this day had to end as my suntan, or sunburn, was now giving me the hint that I had spent enough time in the sun.

Dietz's friends were getting ready to leave. First, it was Justin and Stephanie to head out. Sam left a few minutes later. He shook my hand as he told me good-bye, but Susie walked away without saying anything to me, obviously still mad.

No sweat and good riddance, I thought to myself, as Dietz and I laid back down to enjoy a few more moments of sun. Without thinking about the timing, I said, "Nice beach. I like it down here," as I made an, more than obvious gawk, at a hot chick that happened to prance her stuff right in front of us wearing a very small, bright two piece.

"You like her, the beach, or me," questioned Dietz.

Okay, big evaluation time here. How to respond as I knew that she saw me give this girl the once over, well, maybe more than a little once over. It was a, 'big all over' look. You know, the one that starts at the face, and then travels down, with a short pause at the tits. The bigger the tits, the longer the pause. The look then continues down for a long view at her bottom as she passes by, just to see how it moves as she walks. The legs will get a, 'down and up' review with a return to her butt.

"I was just thinking about how her swimwear would look much better on you. You have the body and grace to properly show off something like that," I said this so convincingly, that even I was convinced.

Oh my, what I got in return was most gratifying, wanted, needed, and greatly appreciated. Not only was this a kiss, but also a kiss on the lips with a little tongue added in.

Our kiss didn't last long enough for me, as I was okay with that because I felt that she might be in a hurry to get back to my place. You know, for a little show and tell of how she felt with my lovely, thoughtful, and generous comment. I was going to get laid tonight.

"That was sweet. Thank you," she said, as I could pick up that I had just placed her in heat. As in, she wanted me.

Dietz looked deep into my eyes as if she was about to beg for it right here on the beach, and said, "It's time to go."

"I'm ready," I expressed, and maybe I expressed that a little too expressively.

Before I could say anything else, like, 'my place, or yours,' she placed her finger over my lips and sadly explained, "Remember, I must work tonight. I cannot miss work. You understand mate?"

Looking and feeling like all my Christmas toys were just destroyed in a house fire, I asked, "For real? I mean, really for real, for real?"

"Sorry. Yes. For real," she explained, as my woody became— wood putty.

"What time must you be there," I asked, hoping that we at least had time for a quickie.

"I will have just enough time to get back if I leave now. We can do something tomorrow. Maybe you can show me your place."

Okay, again, decision time. I could look pissed that our day was over, or, look pleased that we get to go out again. It was a quick decision and wanting to put a positive spin on this, I came back with, "Tomorrow will be great, even wonderful. Besides, I'm a little sunburned right now and might not be as much fun."

Not being pushy with this, and taking some of the edge off my/our disappointment, this earned me another kiss. A longer kiss this time with a little more tongue.

Wanting to change the subject and get this over with, I asked, "How are you getting home?"

I did not know if I was just being polite, so that she would not be late for work, or that I was thinking that the sooner I get back and changed, the sooner I could go out tonight. Being on vacation/R&R, there was nothing on TV that I wanted to see while here.

"Susie is coming back to get me after she drops off Sam."

I was about to ask if she had a suggestion for my ride back to my hotel, as if I could bum a ride with them when she added, "We can't give you a ride because we are going the other way from your place."

"Not to mention that she is not thrilled with me," I suggested.

"True, she is not thrilled with you, but I am," Dietz said, as that was followed with another kiss.

For now, strike one, but I was still up to bat and capable of hitting a homerun on the next pitch.

"For me, just catch the same buses back," I asked.

"Yes mate, hope you don't mind."

"Can do and how do we work out tomorrow?"

Before Dietz could answer, Susie showed up and didn't seem all that happy that I was still around. She probably thought that I needed a ride and she was unwilling to help.

"I know you have to go now. I'll be okay getting back. All I need is a, 'see-you-later' kiss to hold me over until tomorrow."

I got just that, a kiss that most definitely would hold me over until tomorrow. "Will you call me?"

"Yes," she promised with another kiss.

"What time?"

"Noon."

"Noon it is," I agreed, and this time, I gave her a kiss. Not a long one because I didn't want to hold Susie up and give her another reason to be pissed at me and end up talking Dietz out of seeing me tomorrow. Tomorrow at noon that is.

With the pleasantries out of the way, the girls were soon out of site and I was at my bus stop. Nothing special happened on my bus ride back to the hotel. If I had given this too much thought,

I would have missed my stop and never gotten back to my room to shit, shower, shave, before heading out on the town.

I've spent enough time traveling around in The-Nam on military vehicles, boats, and aircraft of all types that this was a simple bus ride back to my hotel with only one transfer. I could handle this.

A short time later, I was back in my hotel without incident. A little surprised though, as I thought that I might have missed my stop, at the least, transferred to the wrong bus, or gotten the right bus, just the wrong way.

When I got back to my room, it was still early and I decided to take a short nap before I readied myself for a night on the town. As I decided on what time to get up, I fell asleep.

# Chapter 19

There was a knock at my door. "Room service," was shouted from the hallway and I knew that I was not onboard a naval ship and that I was not checked into a, 'one star' hotel or better yet, I was not in Vietnam. Even being startled by the banging at my door, it was much more acceptable than, 'Reveille, Reveille,' et cetera, et cetera, blasted at me from a speaker that was only inches from my face.

Maybe this nice thing was happening to me, as it could be a set of, 'Welcome Wagon,' girls bringing me a basket of goodies and coupons. Then again, it could be a set of young hookers with breaths that smelled like a mixture of beer and whisky with the addition of potato chips wedged between their teeth and cheese balls stuck in their hair.

"No thank you. Not now," was all that I could say, as I was not even in the mood to see anyone of them face to face.

Oops, I was not in Vietnam, I was in Sydney Australia, and the only really negative thing about waking up in a hotel, in Sydney Australia, in a country where the women outnumber the men by 3.5 to 1, was that I was waking up alone. Then again, maybe this was a good thing. I just won't tell anyone that I was here and that I did not have someone to sleep with. Well, not the first night anyway. There was always tonight with Dietz and I'll know for sure when she calls me at noon today.

Again, the knock at my door, "Room service."

Damn, damn, damn, I'd best see who that was before they break down the door or that they leave, and I would miss out on whatever the room service was. I cracked open my door, just a little, and just as she said, it was room service. I was supplied with a continental breakfast and the morning newspaper.

Feeling like a king, as this was my first time that I'd had ever enjoyed room service, I welcomed her in and watched with great interest as she unwrapped my breakfast items and even opened the newspaper for me. I enjoyed this and it was greatly appreciated. She completed her duties and before she turned to leave, she held out her hand. Not that this was a big deal, but wanting to shake my hand was rather odd in the way that she held out her hand. This was certainly not the beginning of the knuckle-knocking, finger-grabbing handshake, handshake.

Just maybe, it was just another way of giving someone the high-five. With her palms up, and with this being, 'down-under,' then my guess was that they did it backwards. So, immediately and with a smile, I returned her, 'high-five.' Well, that was not what she had in mind as her friendly smile was replaced with a look of, 'I am pissed.'

Then it dawned on me, she was asking for a tip. So, with that new piece of knowledge, I did the right thing and gave her the smallest bill that I had in my wallet. I would have given her something bigger, but she only removed the aluminum foil from my breakfast items and opened my newspaper for me and that was not that big of a deal. Well, not a big deal for me if I must pay for it.

Okay, my small tip created a small smile and away she goes. With that detail out of the way, I enjoyed my breakfast and watched TV for a few minutes. Australian TV was in English and I had four stations to select. And I could do so with a normal channel changer.

After that, I was soon showered, shaved, and out the door as I had some time to kill until noon. At least getting ready was easy as I was not sunburned too seriously. Outside and directly across the street from my hotel was, of all things, a KFC, as in Kentucky Fried Chicken, American style.

Being that I was still hungry and had learned to eat whenever I had the opportunity with the anticipation that I might miss a meal, it was a simple move for me to get something else to eat.

Right now, for me, life was good. Fried chicken, french fries, and a Coke was now on my itinerary for lunch today. However, running across a wide street was not as easy as it may sound. First, I ran to the curb, looked left, and took off for the medium strip. Then after safely making it to the medium, I looked right and darted for the other side. The next sound that I heard was the screeching of tires from about four or five cars and maybe a truck or two.

I had forgotten that the cars down-under here travel in opposite directions as back home and that I had been looking the wrong direction both times. I almost got myself killed today over a chicken dinner with fries and a small coke. With my little scare out of the way and no damage to any of the cars, I figured, no sweat, it don't mean nothin and I had lunch.

To my surprise, there was nothing special about this meal. I ordered chicken, fries, and two rolls and that was exactly what I got. Four pieces of chicken, fries, and two rolls and that also came with a soda, and it was of all things, Coke. I guessed that I was kind of expecting kangaroo chicken or something.

After my American, down-under meal, and remembering how to correctly cross the street, I walked the few blocks to get downtown to checkout the sights. After only a few blocks, a car screeched to a stop right next to me. That really caught me off guard for a few reasons. I was not crossing the street the wrong way, and that a screech that close and coming towards me, could not be a good thing. Plus, it frightened the crap out of me.

I looked down at the car that had stopped only a few inches from me and I did not know whether I should step away or to step up and look to see who was driving. However, before I decided what to do, I noticed that the driver's side window was darkened and that I would not have been able to tell who was driving anyway. Slowly, the back seat, driver's side window, was rolled down. It was being rolled down so slow that I almost wanted to reach over and shove it the rest of the way down. The suspense was killing me.

Then from inside the car, a cheerful voice chirped up and asked, "Charles. How's it hanging my man? Want to party with me and my friends?"

I still could not see who was doing the talking, but it did seem familiar and with that, I stepped closer and lowered my head down to peek into the back seat. And oh my God, what a sight this was. In the back seat was Louie-Louie and he did not have a shirt on. I stepped back because I did not want to see if he was not wearing his pants. I could only muster up a response of, "Louie. Good to see you again."

I hoped that he did not misunderstand what I meant by, 'good to see you again.' I believed that I was seeing more of him than I ever wanted to.

He responded, "Yeah. Yeah. Yeah," and giggled like a girl. Guys should not giggle like a girl. Even queers should not giggle.

Still not wanting to step any closer to the car, I asked, "What party are you talking about?"

"My party. It started late last night we are out to get some breakfast," he shouted at me, as the other people in the car laughed in apparent agreement.

A party sounded like a good idea right about now, especially with me having a little time to kill. With that reasoning, I asked, "So where was this party?"

I would not mind going to a party with him; I just did not want to go to a party with him as his date. Especially now that he already had his shirt off.

"Right here in the back seat," he answered, as the window finally made it all the way down.

Without thinking, I bent down again and peeked inside to see who was all there with him. Oh my God, another surprise. In the back seat with him were two guys dressed-up like girls. With their five o'clock shadow a couple of hours old, these women/guys were very . . . very . . . very, hell, I did not know what they were or what to say about it.

This was just not my type of party and I would be better off in the arms of Bertha Butt and Juicy Lucy at the same time. Now why did I even consider asking him about a party? I was not going to go to a party with him and his little friends anyway. I politely responded, "No thanks. I have someplace to be right about now."

"Okay, this will be your loss," he explained.

"Need a ride," asked the guy/girl sitting to the right of Louie, as the queer sitting on his left was giving me the eye that made the hair on the back of my neck stand straight-out.

"No. I'm okay. You guys enjoy each other," I responded, as I stepped away from the car to allow for some space between us, just for fear that, one of them might decide to grab me, and then the car would pull away.

The queer sitting on his right leaned over and yelled out at me, "We heard about your topless shoeshine place. You go there often?"

"Just the one time," I answered, and realized that I did not want to continue this conversation, with him, his pal, or with Louie-Louie. With that, I smartly turned away and said, "Later," as I headed on down the street wanting nothing more than to put a lot of distance between us. Those guys were in heat and I did not want to be involved. Quickly, but not quick enough, the car filled with queers sped off and was soon out of site and with little trouble, out of mind.

A few blocks later after working my way across the street, without incident, I noticed a very large park that was full of people. Not that a park, full of people was an odd thing; it was how they were assembled in little groups that made it odd. Each assembled group encircled one person who was either standing on a chair, stool, or some boxes. I found this rather odd, so I made my way to the nearest group. Apparently, what we had here was a place to state your opinions to a group of people that would gather around you.

At the group that I mingled with, well, this guy spoke about some new legislation that was before their parliament. I thought that this format was a cool thing. Anyone that had something to say, at least over here, had a place to go and say it.

I found it fascinating that not everyone agreed with the speaker. It appeared that half the crowd agreed with him and showed that by their applause. The ones that were undecided, or just taking a look-see, as I was; only clapped a little to be polite. Others that had decided against the speaker, well they had clearly and in all ways and manner, displayed their disapproval. In some cases, empty beer cans were thrown at the speaker.

I moved on to another group and he was speaking out against the war in Vietnam. I had seen Australian soldiers while I was in-country, but I did not know if they played an active part in the war or not. What I meant was, I did not know if they were involved in any combat operations. I stayed there for a little while just to hear what he had to say. His accent was so strong that it was hard to follow.

Looking at my watch, I noticed that it was time to head back for my call from my new girlfriend. Yet, in some ways, I was a little scared that she might not call back. If she didn't, I had a backup plan.

My backup plan was to make a second trip to the dating service and invest in my second choice. Naturally, being sure not to mix it up with the hooker/whore house that was located a few blocks from there. Then, out of curiosity, I wondered what the price would be for a hooker. Not that I wanted to fool with any of them.

At least getting back to my hotel was easy and I made it back well before noon. I even had time to try to call home and as my other attempts had failed, this one failed too. It didn't fail as in not getting through or that my sister hung up on me, it failed because I hung up before the call completed, so that I could make it back to my room before noon.

Back at my room, my phone was ringing. I almost broke my neck getting to the phone figuring that an early call from Dietz meant that she wanted me, and wanted me soon. Hell, she could even come here now and we could get started early for a little, 'noon-time nookie' or some 'afternoon delight.'

Life was good here down-under, and I was going to get down-under-and all over her.

Ring, ring, ring, and I answered, "What's happening beautiful? Can't wait to see you. How soon before we get together?"

The phone went quiet, an uncomfortable kind of quite. Almost as if, no one was there. I could not have missed her because it had only rung two times. Well, six times with two times three short.

"Edwards. Seaman Charles Edwards," questioned a man's voice.

Okay, this was the boyfriend or parent of Dietz. Not a good way to start a conversation with me experiencing some fear.

Afraid to say anything, and even more afraid to hang up, I sheeplessly kept silent and waited until I was asked again, and again I was asked, "Edwards. Seaman Charles Edwards."

"What," was the only response that I could muster up right now.

"Are you Edwards? It's a simple question young man. Either you are or you are not Edwards."

"Yes, I am Edwards."

"Yes, you are Edwards, what," he snapped at me.

Okay, I may not be the smartest guy around, but I do know that this was not Dietz and that he was most certainly a military person, and to top it off, he was a military person that happened to be an officer.

"Yes sir, I am Seaman Edwards, sir," I replied, rather pleased that we were not face to face as to save me the embarrassment of having an officer stare me down as they do.

"You are hereby directed to report to the Military Information Desk at Sydney International Airport by fourteen hundred-fourteen hundred today. You copy?"

"Ah shit," I quickly responded, then remember that I was talking with an officer, as I added, "Ah shit sir."

"Can do sailor?"

"Yes sir, can do, but tomorrow would be better sir," I pleaded.

"Don't care Seaman, fourteen hundred today. Copy that mister?"

"Sir, yes sir, copied that. Fourteen hundred today, Military Information Desk at the Sydney International airport."

"Any questions Seaman?"

"Yes sir. Am I heading back," I asked, as I made a face, squeezing my eyes together as if doing that created a favorable answer for me and that I was not going back today. I had too much going on right now.

"Fourteen hundred, Military Information Desk, Sydney International Airport."

"Sir, yes sir," I was just able to say before he hung up and the line went dead.

Before I could hurl the telephone across the room, ring, ring, ring. I looked at the telephone and hoped that it was one of Dietz's friends playing a trick on me. A good trick, but a mean one. Then again, it was just as bad as me dropping the towel on Susie.

"Hello."

"Can't wait to see you. How soon can I come over? I have some great plans for us today," Dietz explained in a most joyful way. Hell, I got excited about her by just hearing her voice, and a little excited about thinking how she would look nude across my bed saying, "Make like a kangaroo, and hop on this."

All this excitement was on hold until; I asked her, "Did one of her friends just call me?"

She didn't answer right away and I could not tell if she was thinking on how to tell me, 'yes, and wasn't it funny.' Or, 'no, what are you talking about?'

"If it wasn't you, then I am heading back this afternoon," I explained and really, really hoped that she would butt in and tell me that it was a joke.

Her silence was about ready to make me cry. I was getting screwed today, but not by Dietz.

I spoke up and sadly expressed, "Got my orders to head back. This will ruin my day, as I was all excited about spending time with you. Then, to add salt to my wound, I can't even see you to tell you good bye."

Still silence on the line, At first, I thought that she was just waiting as she only wanted to see how long she could string me out.

"I did not and would not pull a joke on you Are you pulling one on me?" she asked, and I felt that she was genuine.

For the second time today, I was about to fling my phone across the room. Why could I have not missed that first call?

"For real, I would not joke about not wanting to see you," I said all the while holding back tears and trying not to sound like I was holding back tears.

"What if you don't show up? You know, tell them that you thought that it was a crank call or something," Dietz suggested, and her suggestion sounded like a grand idea.

"No can do. Must do. As much as I want to see you today, I just can't."

"You are an honorable man Charlie."

Not wanting to drag this out, I asked for her mailing address before I told her good-bye. That didn't take long and I was soon packed and checking out at the checkout counter.

After I paid for my room and as I turned to walk away, the hotel clerk called me back. I returned to the counter as he explained, "One moment mate. You have a letter."

"A letter," I questioned.

I watched as he turned and pulled from one of the mail cubbyholes, my mail cubbyhole, and a folded sheet of paper.

How about that, I finally got myself a hotel note. Now this would be really cool if I was checking-in and not checking-out. With curiosity and wonderment, I read my hotel note. It was a note from Dietz. She must have called it in last night after our date. It reads, 'Had a lovely time. Can't wait until I see you again.'

Fuck, not cool, not cool at all. Damn, damn, damn, and shit, shit, shit. I wanted to tear it up and throw it away and I wanted to save it forever. Oh well, I have a plane to catch and my love note made its way into my wallet.

Setting that aside for the moment, I headed to the bus stop. Because I knew how to get to the airport, it was a simple matter to board the R-2 and then transfer to the R-1 like before.

After my transfer to the R-1, I realized that I was assuming that I was headed to the correct airport. Luck was with me, or not with me, as this was the correct airport and I was without a good reason for not showing up.

The Military Information counter was easy to find, again, and in no time at all, I had a ticket back to Saigon and was even provided with a military escort. An escort as if I was not going to board my flight. No sweat on that issue, as I was going back.

I liked the idea of having this escort, an Army Private, as this gave me someone to talk to, and I didn't have to worry about catching the incorrect flight. However, I didn't care much for the fact that he was an MP with a very large MP armband that could be seen from anywhere in the terminal.

Then again, it wasn't as bad as he was and I took a seat by the gate and waited for my flight, which was going to depart in about two hours. With the way we were talking about home, our duty stations, and how we don't much like the military, it gave the impression that we were buddies and that I was not his detainee.

Well, it gave that impression until two Marine MP's showed up with three prisoners. I had hoped that the prisoners would sit across from us with the two Marines on either side, away from me, but, nope. The three prisoners were left in my MP's care. It got ugly, ugly for me, when my MP got up and allowed the prisoners to sit next to me. One on my right, and the other two on my left.

Okay, here I was. My time in Sydney, down-under, Australia, and the only way that I got screwed was to be kicked out of the country and spending my last few minutes before I leave with convicts.

At least with all this help with me catching my flight out, no way was I going to miss it or catch the wrong flight. Damn, this was nothing to call home about, only this time, I'd get through.

Before long, we boarded our flight and were soon on our way. At least I was not sitting with the jailbirds and I had a window seat. I looked around the aircraft and picked up that everyone was recovering from a weeklong party. Some were sleeping it off as others did what they could not to throw up. Now I know how we got the term, 'red-eye' for the red-eye flight. With no VC to kill and only having time to kill, as usual, it was sleep time and sleep I did.

# Chapter 20

I was waken by a sudden change in cabin pressure and noticed that we were headed almost straight down. Looking around the aircraft, I expected to see major panic, however, it was apparent that everyone had done this before, before as in landing in The-Nam, thus creating a, 'no sweat' situation. I then recalled my first landing in Saigon where the pilots did same-same. Level and straight across the Pacific, then straight down for a controlled crashed landing.

Given this a little more thought, I came up another reason for our, 'controlled crash.' The VC would not shoot us down if they thought that we were already headed for a crash. I started to realize that being in the military has given my thought process a different outlook on life in general. Life and death situations happened to be the first thing that I think about lately. Hopefully, this kind of thinking goes away while I am on leave.

Not only was our descent quick, but also our trip to the terminal was even faster. Our wheels touched down and before you could unbuckle your seat belt, we were at the gate and the door was opened. This happened so fast that you would have thought that we landed on the taxi way rather than the runway.

Only this time, instead of a few guys running off the plane as if we were in a marathon, everyone seemed to know this. It was a fast, but a very orderly exit out and off the aircraft. All you really had to do was to keep up, stay in the flow, and not stop to look back. If you wanted to return to your seat to retrieve something that you had forgotten, forget it. You would just have to come back after it later.

Once inside the terminal and after I made my money exchange back to MPC, I decided to see about getting a ticket home. It was easy to find the Information Desk because I'd been there before. And as before, there was Gunny George and he was still reading a letter from his girlfriend back home.

Letters from home from girlfriends and wives, well, they all looked same-same. They all had a fragrance that had the smell of love and they were never written on everyday, regular white paper. Light pink, blue, and some light reds seemed to be the color of choice. Maybe after I return back home and if I find a girlfriend, I will get a love letter or two.

Getting back to Gunny George, he still looked mean until he looked up to answer my question.

I explained the circumstances of my dilemma and he didn't seem to care. It was more like I was creating additional paper work for him and that was not a part of his job description.

"You just got back for R&R and you want to go home already," he answered, and his friendly smile changed to one of, 'you got to be shitting me.'

"I got to pass this stupid issue to my boss. Have a seat over there," Gunny instructed me as he pointed to a row of chairs across the terminal. "I'll call you in a minute."

"Thanks Chief," I answered, and I did just that, headed across the terminal, and settled in as I figured that I was going to be there for a while. I did make it a point to be facing Gunny to make it easier for him to spot me and harder for him to forget about me.

After only a few minutes, an officer came over to him and as they spoke, Gunny pointed to me a few times. I didn't know why, but it didn't feel right. Damn, damn, damn, I didn't screw up lately. I only want to get out of this ugly little country and to try and figure out if this Navy routine was a good career move for me or not.

This time when I looked up at Gunny, he motioned me to join the two of them. Oh crap, I would just have to see what was in store for me this time. I could not complain as it was me that approached him for help.

I quickly joined up with Gunny George and this First Lieutenant. The First Lieutenant asked me for my orders and ID. I didn't say anything to him; I simply gave him what he wanted. I did stand at attention all the while he looked over my stuff and when he noticed that, he said to me, "Relax Seaman, I will have the Gunny here cut you new a set orders and issue you a ticket stateside."

"Thank you sir."

"No, thank you Seaman. You served your country well and in the process, you were wounded. Orders stateside for thirty days medical leave while you wait for your next assignment, was the least we can do."

Feeling a little guilty for what he just said, as I was not all that worthy for his praise, I knew enough to keep my mouth shut. Yet, however, there are and will be plenty more guys that are really, really hurt from this little nasty war we have going on here.

All the while, the First Lieutenant and I were talking, Gunny was busy looking in his three ring binders and making a phone call, and I assumed that he was getting me a flight. As it happened, that was exactly what he was doing.

The Lieutenant looked over at Gunny just as he hung up the phone, they spoke for a few minutes, and after the Lieutenant gave a positive nod to Gunny, Gunny proceeded to issue me my ticket home.

The Lieutenant looked at me and held out his hand as if he wanted to shake my hand. Well, he did and because I had not yet mastered the DAP, I did not return his handshake with the knuckle-knocking, and finger-grabbing things. After we did shake hands, and before I could salute, he was already turned and headed away. This seemed odd and I knew with Dan not around, that I would not ask anything about that.

Gunny had apparently taken notice that I looked confused as he said, "He ain't much into the military stuff. He would just as well shake your hand than to return your salute."

Again, without Dan, I would not ask a question and like Dan, I would just act as if that was the norm. Whatever, Gunny handed me my blue MAC ticket and said, "Your flight is scheduled for tomorrow afternoon at 1500. Your flight number is 1500 and that is simple enough for even a Navy Seaman not to mess up."

"Thank you Chief," I said, trying not to appear too humble.

"Report here tomorrow, here at my desk, three hours before your flight and I will make sure that you board the correct flight, at the correct gate, and at the correct time."

I thought, 'crap you old fart, I didn't mess up all that bad before.' Yet, he was being nice to me and I did get what I wanted, my ticket home.

I collected my ticket, my orders, along with my ID, and after thanking him, I headed out. I knew where to go until tomorrow, the Army BEQ.

Finding the bus stop was not an issue, but finding a bus was. There was just one bus and it was Navy. I took a seat on the bench next to another Seaman, dressed in greens. He looked over at me and said, "If you are waiting for an Air Force bus, there are none. If you are waiting for an Army bus, you just missed the last one."

"Guess I am out of luck."

"Nope, I am the driver to the last bus for today, and today, I am making the last run to the Navy BEQ. You need a ride?"

Not having a choice, I said, "I must be your last passenger for today."

He gave me a smile as if because of me, his day was almost over. With that, we boarded the bus. After he took his seat behind the wheel, he said aloud to himself, "There is always one lone strangler after each flight. Did you have a problem changing your money or figuring out where you are to go?"

I ignored him and took my seat up front, across from the driver. My issue was not his concern. He was just a bus driver and he should just drive the bus. Normally, I would talk with the driver, but my attitude had hardened a little in the last few weeks. I hope that being in the military does not take away my sense of humor.

The ride to town was uneventful, quite, and I was soon at the check-in counter. The First Class Petty Officer behind the desk asked me, "What happened Seaman? No more room at the Army BEQ and you are stuck with us?"

His question caught me off guard, but I should not have been surprised as I remembered him from before. I answered, "Nope," remembering not to 'sir' him. "These accommodations are fine with me. I am Navy and I should not mix it up with those Army guys."

Wow, that sounded kind of cool to me. I answered his crude remark with a little humor, which I still have, and with luck; he will find it funny also and not assign me to a 24-hour watch.

After I received my bunk assignment, I did what I had gotten into the habit of doing when I had time to kill, I plopped myself down for a nap in anticipation to rest up before going out tonight.

However, before I could make myself comfortable, the Master-At-Arms came up to me, and asked, "You Edwards?"

Knowing not to sir him, I simply answered, "Yeah Chief. What can I do for you?"

He didn't have a clipboard with him, so I knew that a working party was not in my near future. "You haven't been on guard duty and we have an open slot for you to fill," he said, as he walked away and suggested with a hand motion that I was to follow him.

He was right and I almost got away with not standing any watches. Therefore, I decided that it was best that I follow him. No need to tick him off and made to stand an extra watch or two. I followed him back to the front lobby where he announced to the Petty Officer on duty behind the desk, "Here's your watch replacement, Mr. Edwards. Make sure that he has a good rifle and plenty of ammo. He'll be in Tower 6."

I was pleased that he asked for some extra ammo for me, however, I wasn't too excited that I might have to use it all. Was there something I didn't know about Tower 6? Oh well, he was a chief and I was just a little enlisted guy and what he said, goes.

The Petty Officer behind the desk handed me an M-16. He then reached under the desk for a large pouch of ammo. At least I had the tools for war. Now if I could only mark up my face with camouflage grease, I would at least look good and it would make me feel like John Wayne in the movie, The Green Berets.

With rifle and ammo in hand, the Master-At-Arms told me, "Out front, turn right, second guard stand on your right."

I asked, "Am I to replace anyone?"

The Petty Officer behind the desk said, apparently without thinking, "He's not there. He was wounded and taken away. He'll live and be available for duty tomorrow. Nothing to worry about."

I looked at him with a facial expression of, 'what,' and that was followed by me repeating damn, three times softly to myself. Before I neither said anything that could be heard, I figured that I was not scared nor was I a scare die cat. I could do this guard duty thing. It would be all right and no way would I tell my parents what I was doing today.

I looked at my new gift, the M-16, and made sure that the safety was on. It was and as I readied myself to head out, I asked the Master-At-Arms, "When will I get relieved?"

"It depends," butted in the Petty Officer from behind his throne, I meant desk. He acted as if he was a king by the way he sat back there and could look down on everyone.

The Master-At-Arms asked him, "On what? That depends on what?" Then he apparently remembered something and told the Petty Officer, "Never mind. I know."

Hell, I wanted to hear about this. I didn't want to spend all day out there and not get relieved. I looked at the Petty Officer and asked him, "What? What about getting relieved?"

The Petty Officer, reluctant to respond, spoke up and answered with, "You'll be there for at least four hours. Unless of course, you are wounded in the meantime. Then, we'll relieve you early."

"In that case, four hours is not all that long then," I said, trying to give the appearance that I was not scared. "This will be the first time that I didn't want to be relieved early," I added to create a little humor and to make myself feel a little better.

"You'll do just fine Seaman," the Chief said, in a reassuring way that he must have hoped would calm me down. Well, it didn't. Damn, the guy I was relieving was shot and I have extra ammo. This was not a good sign.

I responded with, "No sweat. I can do this." Great, now I was lying to a Chief. I wondered if he could tell that I was lying to him? Whatever, it don't mean nothin'. I was going to be on guard duty whether he thought I was scared or not.

With that said, I turned to walk away when the Petty Officer snapped a question at me, and asked, "You have everything you need, John Wayne?"

At first, I thought he was saying something to someone named John Wayne. I soon figured it out when I realized that there were only the three of us here. I turned and politely asked, "What? Did I forget anything?"

The Petty Officer responded, and explained, "You need to take a flack jacket and helmet with you. No need to make it easy for them to shoot you."

The Master-At-Arms laughed at that one and they both did the hand jive, knuckle knocking, hand shaking over the counter. I was so pleased that I had made their day. Now, if no one would shoot me while I was on guard duty, well, that would make my day. It was odd to think that just to make my day; I had to think about not being shot at by a sniper.

Oddly enough and on top of what just happened, I found myself presently engrossed in a little daydreaming. I was recalling my first day here when the one sailor from my flight to Saigon, The-Nam, in where he was shot while he was on guard duty. I could only hope that my, Tower Six, was not the same guard tower where he was shot.

Well, moving on with my life and out of my woolgathering trance, I returned to the present time and with the pleasantries out of the way, I could only answer with, "Later gentlemen. I got some guarding to do." With that said, I turned and headed out.

I made the right turn, passed the first tower, and made it down to the second guard tower. No one was there. I was most pleased that this was not the same-same guard tower from my last visit to Saigon. The one where a guy took a bullet a few weeks ago. I worked my way up the ladder and looked suspiciously around for blood. I didn't see any and decided to believe that the two of them were just joking with me. At least I didn't panic and embarrass myself.

I stepped in, sat down, and made myself comfortable. I took the safety off my rifle and made sure that it was loaded. I should have seen if it was loaded first before I released the safety. But damn, lucky for me, it didn't go off. Also lucky for me, I had had some experience with the M-16. I found it odd that between the Chief and the Petty Officer behind the desk, that neither one of them asked me if I knew how this damn thing worked. No sweat, I guessed that I looked like I could do the job, I was already dressed like I could do the job as I was in a military uniform, and what the hell, I was in the military, and I was in a war zone. I guessed it was assumed that I could shoot.

I decided to checkout my pouch to see how much ammo I had. Doing so, I found that I had ten clips and a manual. Hopefully, by the time I used up, my ten clips, the Calvary should be here to help me out with reinforcements and more ammo.

Scoping out my area, especially across the street, I could see that there were too many open windows. All those windows sort of reminded me of Daily Plaza where Kennedy was shot. Damn, there were a lot of windows here.

To add in a little more fear, everyone that passed below me smiled directly at me. I could not tell if they were smiling because they were happy to see me and to show their appreciation that I was there to protect them. Or that maybe they were the VC and their mission for today was going to use me as a target later.

My thoughts of smiling friends/VC were interrupted with, "Hello."

I looked up and down the street to see, who it was. I did not see anyone and assumed that I did not really hear anything. I went back to checking-out my area when I again heard, "Hellooooo."

I knew that I heard something that time. I looked up and then down the street, no one. I looked up at the rooftops thinking that they were on the roof. Nothing.

Someone was playing a trick on me and it was making me nervous. Here I was on guard duty and I could not even find whoever it was that was yelling at me. Well, maybe they were not yelling at me. Then I figured, that if this were a trick. Definitely something Dan would do, I would not give him the pleasure of showing him how gullible I was. I would just ignore it for now, and still look around to see whom it really was.

"Hello. Can you hear me?"

There it was again. This time, I focused on all the windows across the street from me. This was not funny now. Being a little scared at this shit, I looked down to double check that the safety was off my rifle. I didn't know why, but I positioned my finger on the trigger and at that same instance, I was hit with a roll of toilet paper. Well, go figure; my jolt caused my rifle to fire. The recoil then banged the hell out of my arm. The next sound that I heard happened to be, "Are you crazy man. What's wrong with you? You trying to kill me?"

Now that came back loud and clear, and I was able to trace its location, and it was across the street. In fact, it was directly across from me. I didn't know how I missed him before, but there was another guy on guard duty right across from me. It might even have been Tower 5 or Tower 7. Before I could say anything, like, sorry or I didn't mean it. The guy that I almost killed yelled again, "Now send it back."

Back, what was he talking about? Back. I looked over and saw that it was Cleve, Crapper, Randy, or one of those damn names. Everyone has too many names over here like Billy-Bob-Joe-Jim. Anyway, after a closer look, I saw that it was the toilet paper hoarder, Crapper. Damn, I almost killed a guy that poops all day.

"Sorry," I yelled over at him, after we made eye contact.

"Damn right you are sorry. You are one sorry bastard," he screamed. He held up a roll of toilet paper that appeared to have been torn to shreds. With a closer look, I realized that I had shot a hole in his toilet paper. He added, "Look what you did ass-hole!"

"Sorry," was still the only response I could give.

"That's my last roll that you have. Let me have it back, un-damaged. Can you do that for me?"

The only thing that was more surprising than being hit with a roll of toilet paper, or almost killing somebody, was that my shot didn't cause any alarm. No one came out and asked about what happened. Even the people on the street walked on by as if nothing happened, oh well.

Crapper was more concerned about his toilet paper than the fact that I almost killed him. Because he gave that little attention, then so would I. I simply stood up and hurled the roll back over to him and, of course; I threw it the wrong way, as it unrolled in flight. I didn't know if I should have thrown it counter clockwise or just plain clockwise, but it unrolled all the way across the street. It reminded me of one of my high school football games where throwing toilet paper down on the playing field was a cool thing to do.

Well, it was not a cool thing to do today. Anyway, Crapper was able to catch what was left of the roll and he started to reel in what had reeled out. If it weren't for the traffic, reeling the toilet paper in would have been easy, but not today though. By the time a few cycles, four dump trucks, and a dozen or so taxies ran by, well, there was toilet paper everywhere like a ticker-tape parade in New York City.

I thought this was an interesting sight until Crapper reminded me that he was going to kill me for what I just did. What could I say? I had some guarding to do and I figured that I would get back to my assigned task. Besides, he must have squirreled away enough toilet paper to wipe all the asses of all the U.S. forces here in, The-Nam.

In only a few minutes, Crapper had gathered up all the toilet paper that he could. Most of it had blown its way down Main Street, Saigon, Vietnam. He maintained an, 'evil-eye' on me and here I was again getting another shitty deal.

I kept my eye on him also, as I looked around at all the windows above him. Not that he could tell that I was staring at him, just enough to see if he planned to shoot or attack me with another roll of toilet paper. However, for the next five minutes or so, instead of looking at me, or even around the area, as he should have, he spent his time trying to repair the roll that I shot to pieces. From what I could see, it appeared that it was a regular roll with two holes instead of one. He'll get over it. Damn, I can't tell anyone about this because no one would believe me. I would just chalk this up as yet, another in The-Nam experiences.

When Crapper did look over at me, he said nothing, but he did give me the finger. I did not like getting the finger, but that was much better than being shot.

I was giving some thought about whether to return him the finger or not when I heard another voice, "Mr. Charles. Mr. Charles. How you doing?"

Who was that, I questioned myself. Someone knew my name and was calling me, Mister. I looked down, and of all the people in Vietnam, there was Billy-Bob. Billy-Bob was all smiles and he had a girl with him, a very attractive Vietnamese girl. In fact, she was so attractive, that I would not mind taking her out myself. Yet, I did not have any cigarettes to pay for her and her time. I smiled back and said, "Billy-Bob. How's it hanging?"

"Right now, pretty low. Later, it'll be straight up," he replied, with a child like grin that reminded me of a kid holding back a secret from his parents.

She looked at me and only smiled. I did not think that she understood what he meant by that remark, or maybe she did not speak any English. "What are you guys up to," I asked.

"Nothing much. We have a date for tonight and I'll be heading back tomorrow. What's up with you," Billy-Bob asked, as he held his girl a little closer to him as if I didn't notice that she was there and with him. It appeared to me that he wanted me to notice that he and she was an item. Or, he was just rubbing it in. For whatever reason, he had a date and I was here stuck on guard duty.

"Just doing my guard duty thing, nothing else going on here with me," I answered, trying to sound positive about my current situation and not to let it show how ticked I was that he had a date and that I didn't. Even if she was a rental date, he still had one, and I didn't. And, she was good looking.

With a smart-ass snicker, he asked, "How did you get stuck on guard duty? Didn't Dan teach you anything about how not to do shit like that? You know that you should never stand guard duty in Saigon."

He was right and I did not need him to tell me all this, especially in front of his girlfriend. Billy-Bob looked over at his girlfriend and said, "He no bright. He little slow on up take. Numba ten brains."

She only smiled back at him and maybe she did understand. Anyway, Billy-Bob continued with, "He's the guy that fell for the blanket trick down on the beach a few weeks ago just before I came over to your house."

She finally spoke up and asked, "He Joe with shit on pants?"

I could only hold my head down as they both broke out in laughter. Well, they had better be careful now, because I had a loaded M-16 in my lap and I knew how to use it. Now, what was I thinking? That thought sounded like something Dan would say.

Then, as if Billy-Bob just remembered the most importing thing in the world, he reached into his front pocket and pulled out a photo. "Next time you see Dan; would you give him his picture back for me?"

I responded with, "Sure. Pass it up."

Billy-Bob did that just after he showed it to his girl. She came back with a little giggle that sounded kind of cute. Damn, I noticed again just how nice looking she was. Damn, damn, damn, she was great looking for him. Hell, I'd still go out with her.

Anyway, he passed the photo up to me and of all the pictures ever taken over here, in The-Nam; it was the one that Dan had taken of himself at the beach with Billy-Bob's camera. Shit, I did not need to be carrying around this photo. It was the one that Dan took looking down his pants. Damn, damn, damn, I didn't need to be carrying around this photo or anyone's photo looking down anyone else's pants.

I handed it back down to Billy-Bob and said, "No way man. You will see him before I do. You can give it to him."

Billy-Bob did not take it back and now I was stuck with this damn photo. Then I figured that I would try and give it to his girlfriend. Why not? She wasn't all that nice of a girl if she was with him and she was probably just a rental. Maybe, she might even have similar photos of her own of Billy-Bob.

I pleaded, "Would you take these please?"

Well, did I ever get a wake-up call on this move. She glared at me as if I was passing out used baby diapers and Billy-Bob here was no longer my friend. He snapped at me and asked, "What kind of girl do you think she is?"

Oh great. I had done it again. In quick fashion, I came back with, "Joking. Just joking my man. It's just that I don't want this picture of Dan no more than you do. What was I going to do with it?"

"You think that I wanted to keep it," snapped Billy-Bob, with his girlfriend in strong agreement to what he just said.

Wanting to defuse this as quickly as possible, I held up the photo and tore it into many small pieces. And with one smooth move, I threw them up into the air and the little breeze that we did have, took away the photo. Hopefully, and with luck in my favor, this would save me from being on Billy-Bob's hate list. If not, I would be on the lookout for the VC and an angry Billy-Bob.

The only response I got from the two of them was a smile. Not a big smile, but a smile as if I was going to survive this incident and that my course of action was most correct.

Apparently, they had somewhere to go and, Billy-Bob then said, "Catch you on the flip side. We have some time to spend together before I head back."

And with that, the two of them just moseyed their way on down the road as if they were going to see the Wizard of Oz.

Reviewing this situation, disappointedly I thought, here I was doing guard duty when I should not be guard duty. Mr. Retard there was off on a date and his date was beautiful. Any way, getting back to my current situation, I had a city block to guard. Looking back out at all those windows was still not a comfortable feeling. I adjusted my flak jacket to cover most of me to where only face was showing. My helmet was heavy and hot but I felt safe with it on my head.

I watched as the two lovebirds walked hand in hand, on down the street and soon out of sight. For a retard, he seemed to have it more together than I did. Hell, he had a girl and I was on watch being used as target practice for the VC. Something is wrong here with this picture. At least it wasn't a picture of Dan's Little Dan and the twins.

So for now, I would let that one go. At the same time that I was trying to think of positive things, I heard someone say, "Edwards. Aren't you Edwards?"

It didn't sound like Billy-Bob, Louie-Louie, or the girls that I missed earlier. I turned to my right and came face to face with the officer that had been trying to speak with me ever since I stowed away on the chopper. This time he had me cornered. The only thing that I could think about right now was to try and do something that Dan would do if he were in this spot. Then it hit me. Before I could respond with anything, good, or bad, he snapped, "I know you now. You were on the chopper a few weeks ago and you pulled that escape act on me."

Oh well, here goes. "Sir. No sir. Not me."

Before he could respond, I quickly jumped back with, "Sir, I can't talk right now. I'm on guard duty and I will be glad to speak with you when I'm off guard duty, sir."

Because I was being bold here, and the fact that he didn't respond back, I figured that I would scan the surrounding area as if I was serious about my guard duty and that I didn't know he was even there. The funny thing was, that it worked. He did huff and puff a little, but he eventually walked away leaving me here alone on guard duty.

I felt so proud of myself for making him leave when I realized that if he had stayed, then he would have been the target of choice and not me. Damn, damn, damn. Maybe that wasn't such a good move on my part after all. I meant, I was going to be chewed out eventually anyway and now would have been as good a time as any. Whatever, he was gone now and I was going to get my ass chewed out when I got off watch. I might end up getting lucky and get myself shot in the meantime. Either way, my ass is grass.

My excitement/disappointment soon left because he returned. He asked me, "You staying at the BEQ?"

"Sir, yes sir," I responded quickly, still not making eye contact.

"See you then," he said with a smile that made me feel as if I was cornered with no way out.

"Yes sir."

The officer turned and again headed away. Now I was not looking towards getting off watch. Then I figured that it wouldn't be all that bad. It was much better to get my ass chewed out by this officer than to get it shot up by the VC. Whatever, I was just going to make this a no sweat situation for now. It don't mean nothin'. Besides, what was the worst thing that could happen to me? I was already going home.

Whatever, anyone would have thought that a parade was going by my location by the way everyone would stop by to speak to me. Next in line to greet me, was Louie-Louie. I saw him heading my way and I decided to avoid making eye contact with him. I just could not stand to have that little queer talking with me. The fact that he looked and acted like a queer, anyone that walked by would see that and then think that I was the same-same way.

However, as my luck would have it, he saw me and made it a point to stop and talk. But wait; this could work out to my benefit. With him standing there near me, well, my odds of being shot have just been cut in half. Apparently, now that I was thinking like Dan, he just might save my life.

"How's the weather up there?" He asked, and even that came out sounding queer like.

Oh well, no reason to be rude to him. "Not bad. At least I have a good view."

"Didn't Dan ever explain to you how you can avoid standing watches while you're in Saigon?"

I did not want him to think that I was too stupid to avoid watches, even after I knew how to get away with it, I responded with, "No. He didn't tell me anything like that."

He replied with an attitude that I was not Dan's friend and that he was. He excitingly said, "That's a shame. He told everybody. Even me?"

Well, that made me feel good.

Louie-Louie spoke for only a few minutes and in that short time, he suggested that I go with him for a shoeshine later after I get off watch. Naturally, I declined his offer. Besides, I would get excited over the girls and he would get excited over the old man with only two teeth. And, if the old guy were to ask him, "How are they hanging," Louie-Louie would not think that he was asking about tits.

Crap, no need to give this situation any more attention. With that, I said, "Can't hold a conversation right now, I'm on duty don't you know."

Looking a little ticked, the little queer gave me his little queer smile, and away he sashayed on down the street. Then, not meaning to stare at him as he walked away, I did think that his walk would be a plus on a hot chick. I then remembered that he had that same sort of walk after he had those shots in the butt my first week here. Maybe he got that shot again.

At that moment, Louie-Louie turned and caught me staring at his butt. At this point, his little queer smile became a, 'big queer smile.' Damn, damn, damn, and crap, crap, crap.

"I just wanted to thank you for suggesting to me the other day that I checkout the shoeshine place. I like going there. I might want to get a place like that started back in the states. I believe that it will be a real money maker," he explained.

I didn't mean to smile back at him, but that would be a grand idea of a little business. That would do well at New Orleans during Mardi Gras and on Baltimore Street in downtown Baltimore at a place called, the Block.

Not wanting him to come back and hang around, I just said, "Cool." I then looked the other way as if I was fulfilling my guard duties. It apparently worked as he turned and continued on his way.

Anyway, I resumed my duties of guarding whatever it was that I was guarding. I made another scan of all those windows across from me and didn't see anything suspicious. As if I knew, what was suspicious and what wasn't suspicious. I figured that by the time I saw something, or anything suspicious, that it would have been too late for me to respond anyway. So, for now, I planed to look as if I knew what I was doing.

A couple of hours went by and I waited with anticipation for my relief to show up soon. I hoped that I had not been forgotten about out here. And if I were, would I be allowed to leave my post to check on that? At that moment, I felt something on my face. I wiped it off thinking that it was bird shit or rain. To my surprise, it was water. I looked up and did not see a cloud in the sky. I then looked directly over my head expecting to see on open window above me, or a rainspout that spouted a leak. Nothing of the kind. I ignored it and it happened again. I looked to my right and a little ways from me was Murph. My man Murph was spitting on me.

Murph walked up to me and said, "Some guarding you're doing."

"What do you mean," I questioned. I didn't think that I had missed anything. There were no shots fired or anything.

"You're supposed to be on guard duty and I was able to get close enough to spit on you. You didn't even see me coming."

He was right and I was apparently doing a bad job. My only response was to say, "No sweat. What-do-ya' say that I just shoot you in the ass and we can call it even?"

"You're a funny man Charlie Brown," he told me, and I assumed that he took it as a joke.

Charlie Brown he called me. My name was not Charlie Brown. Was he joking with me, or should I tell him that my name was Charles Edwards, and that he could call me Charlie. Nah, I would just drop it for now.

We both then just looked at each other expecting the other to say something. I could not think of anything to say and he apparently couldn't either. Finally, he spoke up with; "You couldn't get out of guard duty?"

"Well, I," I tried to respond, but Murph quickly came back with, "I thought that you and Dan were buddies."

"We are, but I haven't seen him for a few days," I answered.

"He didn't tell you anything about how to avoid guard duty while in Saigon? Hell, he brags that to everyone."

"He did explain that to me and I got guard duty anyway. Besides, it's only fair," I said in defense of myself, and if I ever stand guard duty again, I hoped that it would be in another country far away from Dan and anyone that knew him.

"Fair shit!" He explained, "You screwed up and got caught. As for me," he continued, "I've never been on guard duty. Not in Saigon anyway. Damn man; especially ever never do guard duty in Saigon. You can get killed standing guard duty in Saigon. Here, you are just target practice for the local VC."

I was thinking, well good for you and thanks for the information. Now why not just go away. However, I came back with, "No sweat. It's only for a couple of hours. After this, I'm heading home," I bragged hoping that I ruined his day as he ruined mine.

Well, it did ruin his day, because he said, "Yeah, okay. Got to go. See you later." And off he went on his way spiting on young and old gooks alike.

I went back to my guarding duties thinking on whom might come by next. For the next few hours or so, no one came by. I had spent most of those two hours checking-out and counting all those windows that I felt were a threat to me. Damn, eighty-six windows in all and all those windows, as in ALL of them were opened. No way would I want to be on duty here at night. There could be a whole company of VC in all those windows.

Another hour or so goes by and I was most anxious to be relieved. I wanted to make a head call and get something to drink. My helmet was extremely hot and heavy and getting hotter and heavier. I had stopped sweating because I had run out of body sweat. I was getting the feeling that I was due for a heat stroke or something. Even though I had no idea what a heat stroke was, I just knew that I didn't feel well and that I should get out of the sun.

"Edwards," was a shout that appeared to be from someone of authority. I looked over and down and saw that the Master-At-Arms was on his was to see me.

"Yes Chief," I answered with a smile because I was very happy that he was here to relieve me. Yet, there was no one with him and I knew that Chief's never stood watches like the kind of watch I was standing right now. There was no place for him to place his coffee cup.

With some compassion, he informed me, "Your relief will be here soon. You've had enough time in the sun for one day?"

"Yes Chief. One a day is enough for anyone. Glad to have helped out."

The Chief just huffed and puffed, turned and headed away. I wanted to yell something at him but I figure it best to keep quiet. If he said that I was going to be relieved soon, then soon it would be. I would just keep an eye out for my relief so when he does get here, I could leave quickly for the safety of the BEQ. It does not bother me that someone else would be a target for the next four or five hours. And I certainly would not be available later on tonight if the Chief needed another slot for me to fill.

A little voice from below me spoke up and asked, "You feel lucky Joe?"

I didn't respond right away, because whoever it was, he, or she, was looking for Joe. Again, the little voice spoke up and repeated, "You feel lucky Joe?"

I looked down and below me was a little kid. I had hoped that it was my relief, but it was not. This kid, well he was not carrying anything so I could assume that he didn't have anything to sell me.

Wanting to be funny, I asked him, "You VC?"

"Fuck you. I no VC," he responded, and it was extremely apparent that he was serious, or that maybe he was a good actor. The kids I've seen so far over here, well, they all seemed to be good little actors.

I came back with, "Okay. What you want me?"

Even with him not holding onto anything, there must be a scam coming or he has something that was small to sell.

"Listen up Joe. You lucky Joe?"

He seemed pretty instance and I might as well answer him. "If I was lucky, I wouldn't be here in your little country and I wouldn't be on guard duty."

"I thought so," he replied, as he turned from the appearance of a little kid to the stance and mannerism of a used car salesman. The only thing that he was missing was a pair of white shoes and a worn out white belt. He went on with, "Because you no lucky Joe, you need life insurance."

"Life insurance?" I answered him totally surprised at what he was asking me. Life insurance?

"Damn Joe. You no lucky Joe and you no can hear. You need life insurance," he announced in a very grown up way that easily caused me to want to pay attention. Not to buy anything from him, but this would kill some time and I didn't think that the VC would shoot me if I were talking to a little kid.

I asked him, "How much? Life insurance, how much?"

In one swift move, he whipped out from his right back pocket some papers, folded papers like one of the maps you keep in your car. He unfolded the papers that he had, read over a few items, and asked me. "Joe. You thirty year old or older."

"A lot younger than thirty," I shot back quickly. The little shit; he knew that I was not that old.

I would have thought that he was going to make a come back with an apology, however, he answered as if he didn't hear me with, "Okay Joe. You need insurance much. You look old. Buy insurance before you die of old age."

The only response that I could come back with was, "No need death insurance. How about car insurance?" I might as well have fun with this.

However, this little kid instead of getting the hint and leaving because I was playing with him, reached into his left back, pant pocket and pulled out another brochure. To my astonishment, he appeared to have been prepared for me. Damn, this little turd might be working for Lloyds of London.

"What you drive Joe? You drive American Jeep. You got jeep?" He questioned me expecting an honest answer and preparing for a sale.

Wow, this guy was serious. Just what I needed, car insurance and I didn't even own a car. It might be to my advantage that I break this off now. No need to waste his time and anger him. He just might be angry enough to take a seat in one of those many windows across the street and take me out. If that were to happen, I would be sorry that I didn't purchase the life insurance. "No thank you. My car back home. No can drive until I go home. Get car insurance then."

On top of that, I thought to myself that my buddy Murph would be selling insurance and I could just get it from him. He might spit on me, but I should get a good deal.

Looking disappointed, he informed me in a nasty tone, "You be sorry Joe. No good town, Saigon. You think again. I come back later."

I was about to apologize to him for wasting his time, but before I could, he was already heading on down the road. I watched him for a few minutes and he did stop and start up a conversation with the next American service guy that the saw.

Good, I thought. The longer he spent time talking to someone, the closer it was getting for me to get off duty and I'll miss him on his return trip.

As I was making my last check on the windows across from me, I heard this growl from below me. Ah, shit. It was Big-Foot and he had a rifle with him. He was looking at me as if I was his target for today. By his expression and mannerism, he most definitely remembered me. This was not a good thing for me. And, to add to that, he was able to sneak up on me. Kind of reminded me of Godzilla taking over Tokyo. Now I could see how that could happen.

I said to him, "You my relief?"

He did not answer me. He just used a hand and head movement combination to instruct me that I should just get on down. Immediately, I did just that. I did not know what else to do; I was not about to stand around and hold a conversation with him or anything.

As I started to walk away, he snapped at me and said, "See you after I get off of watch."

I looked back and tried not to look scared, I responded with, "No sweat. See you then."

I took off quickly because I did not want to hear anything else that he had to say to me. Whatever it was, it was not going to be nice.

At least I completed my watch and I didn't get hurt, however, I might get hurt when Bigfoot gets off watch. With that little TAD, temporary assigned duty, I was heading back to turn in my weapon.

# Chapter 21

Half way back to the BEQ to turn in my weapon from being on watch, I heard my name being called out, "Charlie." Damn, for being a new guy in this little country, a lot of people sure knew me.

"Charlie! I thought you were dead," questioned a voice that I recognized and it sounded like it was coming from behind me. I looked around and there was Benny E. Lee. Not Cherry, Benny E. Lee, but the Stud Man, Benny E. Lee.

"How's it hanging my man? How's the love of your life?" I asked, and then remembered his nightmare experience with that Juicy-Lucy, Mountain Woman. I probably just shouldn't had said anything about her; it just Hara-kiri came out that way. My questioning might work him back into flashbacks and he could commit or something.

"We are doing fine," he answered, as if he knew that I was talking about his, first love of his life. Was he joking about that or was he serious? I was not sure even if I wanted to know about that or not.

"We who? You have a girl friend, Stud Man?" I asked, because I just could not let that one go. And besides, it couldn't be Juicy-Lucy. It might be that old woman we had for our waitress. Better yet, that old dog that the chickens kept picking at.

"Juicy-Lucy. My girlfriend. You didn't know?"

I was unable to answer him. This must be a joke I thought.

Benny E. jumped right in and added, "She's Chinese you know. Chinese like me. I go by and see her every chance I get."

Another, in The-Nam surprise I thought, and I would definitely remember this one.

I asked him, "You are dating Juicy-Lucy?"

I didn't think that anyone would date her. Not in public anyway. I would have thought that she would just need to be taken for a walk every now and then. A simple scratch behind her ears or a good rub on her head could probably turn her on.

"Yes and no," he answered hesitantly, as if he said too much already.

"Yes you are, or no, you are not?" I asked, and then remembered that maybe I didn't want to know.

As if he did not want to answer me, and I could understand that coming from anyone that admittedly was dating a hooker, an ugly hooker at that, but a hooker just the same, Benny E. lowered his head and said, "We are checking with our parents about dating. We notified them by mail. We are still waiting for their response."

"What have your parents got to do with this?" This has got be a good answer, I questioned. Maybe Benny E. needed a few shots and she needed rabies shots before they could go out with each other.

He didn't answer right away, so I asked a second question. "Is your girl pregnant?"

Holding back a smile, because I thought that if she did give birth, that it would be a litter of four or five.

"No. She is not pregnant," he responded quickly, as if I was out of line with my question. I was probably out of line with that question, but then again, why else would he go out with her. Then I thought to myself how that was a good thing that she wasn't pregnant. She was dirt-ugly and could only produce dirt-ugly children.

Benny E. slowly let out a sigh, and then finally said, "We got to talking one day at the bar, and we think that we might be related. That's why we are waiting to hear from our parents. We need to check on that before we do the wild thing again."

Damn, damn, damn. I didn't know what was worse. Dating your cousin, going out a second time with Juicy-Lucy, or both. My immediate thought for Benny E. was that he needed to be sent home and soon. A date with her would certainly earn him the Combat Action medal, a Good Samaritan medal, and some kind of award from a Wildlife Foundation.

Benny E. must have realized that I was viewing his girlfriend as a hooker. He added, "We are good friends and if you want to call us boy friend and girlfriend, that's okay with me. We are not having sex or anything like that."

Well, that's good news. If she was to hurt him during sex, I wondered if they would award him a Purple Heart. Anyway, Benny E. continued with, "We can sit for hours on end just talking about things and more things. We have a lot in common."

In some ways, I wanted to hear more, and in another way, I could do without the details, but I didn't want to hurt his feelings, so I figured that I would be polite and listen. As long as he leaves out all the sex stuff. Anyway, I asked, "What do you guys talk about?"

"She's really smart. She had a few classes in college and has been to France twice," he started out. "She knows a great deal about America and wants to go there. We even talked about her staying with my parents."

"That's nice," I commented. If she came to America to visit me, I would ask her to take a room at the Baltimore Zoo and not the Holiday Inn, and no way at my house. My parents already had a dog.

After about five minutes of this crap of hearing how wonderful she was and how much important stuff she knew, I thought that I had heard enough for one day. I wished him luck and headed away. I felt bad doing that to him, but that was just a little more than I wanted to know about his Jungle Woman. I might even get nightmares about the two of them. I could not get the picture of him out of my mind that day Dan and I did our rescue and saw him there in the bed, with only his T-shirt and socks on. Not a very pretty sight then and not a pretty memory.

Benny E. did make one last comment that I failed to acknowledge, "If everything turns out, would you come to the wedding?"

Oh, shit. No way would I go to his wedding. I had always heard that a woman looks great in a wedding dress, but not in this case. That was one wedding veil that I would not lift up, especially if I must give her a kiss. If I were him, I would make her wear it for the rest of her life. However, I didn't want to be rude, so I yelled back, "No sweat. I'd love to go."

He asked, "Did I tell you about the photograph?"

Well, he didn't and I was not sure if I wanted to know about it or not. Oh God, I was sure that I did not want to see any photographs of her. Fully dressed or not, no way, no how. Yet, after giving this some thought, it might be interesting. I might be able to talk him into selling them to National Geographic or Playboy. I answered, "No. I didn't. What photo?"

With that, I walked back to him as he pulled a photo out of his shirt pocket. I braced myself, took it from him, and held my breath. And to my, yet another in The-Nam surprises, I saw that it was a picture looking down a guys pants at his manhood. I closed my eyes and handed it back to him. My worst fears came true; it was Juicy-Lucy she, or he, was a man with boobs. I could only respond with, "You can't marry her, I mean him. Him, She-it is a man woman!"

"No. No. No. You don't understand," Benny E. responded quickly, as he grabbed my arm anticipating that I was about to run away. "It's not her."

Well, that sounded better, but I surely did not want to see a picture looking down his pants. Yet, Louie-Louie might want a copy, but no way did I even want to look back at that photo again.

"It's Dan. He's pulled that trick on me once before with my camera. Would you give it back to him for me?"

I wanted to do him a favor. However, this was twice now in one-day that a photo of Dan showed up. No way would I be caught carrying around a picture like that. It would be my luck that I would be killed with those pictures in my possession. Then the Navy would send the picture to my parents with my other personal effects. Now that would really get them upset. "Sorry Benny. You should give it to Dan yourself. He'd appreciated it more coming from you than from me."

Before he could answer back, I had turned around, headed away, and yelled back, "Let me know about the wedding. Later my man."

Anyhow, away I went and hoped that he had nothing else to show me. Damn, that was awful. I did not know which was worse, seeing that photo twice in one day or knowing that Juicy-Lucy and Benny E. might mate and produce little ugly Chinese babies.

I made my way back to the desk to return my rifle. The same Petty Officer from before was still behind the desk. He asked me, "You have anything for me to put in the log?"

I was getting rather good at my, deer-in-the-headlights look, because I did it again. With little patience, he snapped back with, "I need to log in anything out of the ordinary that might have happened while you were on watch?"

He then looked down at a logbook and with pen in hand, waited for me to fill him in with, anything out of the ordinary. Well, as far as I was concerned, that was an ordinary day for me. I did my ordinary reaction with my fellow military brothers. Most of them wanted to kick my butt in one way or another. I answered the Petty Officer, "No. Nothing out of the ordinary on my watch."

Not wanting to hang around to explain anything, and most importantly, not wanting to be added to another watch, I walked away and planned to act as if I could not hear anything if he was to say something else.

I turned so quickly, that I ran into a guy that was coming out of the men's room, I meant head. It was Crapper and he had three or four rolls of toilet paper in his arms. We bumped and the rolls bounced on the deck and rolled in all different directions. The Petty Officer behind the desk yelled, "Crapper! Put them back. Put them back now!"

I helped Crapper retrieve the rolls and for my appreciation, he gave me a mean stare. After collecting all the rolls of toilet paper, and with a huff and a puff, Crapper returned to the men's room with his stolen inventory. He came out a moment later empty handed and continued with his dirty look that was directed at me.

I could only stare back as if he did not scare me. Maybe that was a dumb move on my part, but I was leaving the country soon anyway. Oddly enough, Crapper walked down the hallway backwards and I thought this was to continue with his stare until the Petty Officer behind the desk snapped, "Crapper! What do you have behind you? Turn around. Let me see your hands."

Damn, the man was hiding a roll of toilet paper behind him and by walking backwards; he almost got away with it.

With an even louder huff and puff, he stamped his feet back to the head and he did not come right out. I assumed that this was a good time for me to exit the area. No need to hang around here any longer.

I need to find a place where I will be left alone. It was not as if I could get in my car and go for a drive or catch a movie. My only safe place around here would be in my bunk. Now, if Dan happened to be in this situation, what would he do? He'd do just that, hide out. Yet, somehow, I believe that he would do something extra. Something extra like place a note nearby, letting anyone that came by, that I was on guard duty all night and that I needed my sleep.

Excellent idea. Now, if I could just get some paper and a pen, I will camouflage myself right here in the middle of the barracks.

Luck was in my favor as there was this big guy sitting in the bunk next to mine. He just happened to be writing a letter, and a fellow brother in arms, should have no problem in sparing a single piece of paper for a good cause.

I got his attention and said, "Hi. My name is Charles."

"I'm John," he answered, and he didn't seem very nice, as I must have interrupted his writing.

Oh well, here goes. "Could I borrow a sheet of paper?"

"You gonna give it back?"

Crap, this simple task was not going my way. I continued, "How about letting me have a single sheet. I need to leave a note on my bunk so that no one will disturb me."

"You are disturbing me. I am writing a letter to my woman, Tina. Would you have left me alone if I had a note stapled on my forehead?"

Okay, time to step up to the plate and take care of this issue. ""John, sorry to have disturbed you, but I've been on guard duty for most of the day and I am going back on duty in a few hours. I really need the rest and I will not bother you again."

His angry look soon turned to that of compassion. Great, I just fooled him and I thanked him as he tore off a sheet, a single sheet for me.

Wonderful, I have my notepaper, but I don't have a pen or pencil. It would have been a simple task just to ask to borrow his pen for a moment, but he was already back into writing to his woman, Tina. I didn't like the idea of going down to the desk to borrow a pen. So, now was major decision time for me. But hell, this John guy was right here and what could I lose?

I interrupted him and said, "John, may I borrow your pen for a moment?"

"You gonna give it back?"

"Yeah. I just want to write, 'DO NOT DISTURB,' on the sheet of paper you gave me. Please, do you mine?"

"Okay, my Tina can wait." And with that, he handed me his pen.

Just after I printed DO NOT and before I wrote DISTURB, I realized that I did not know the correct spelling for disturb. Well, no way was I gonna bother John again. Hell, if I was to do that, I might get an angry letter from this Tina girl on how much time I took from his writing to her.

Crap, and double crap. Looking for a quick solution for this, I turned the sheet over and spelled out, 'LEAVE ME ALONE—BEEN ON WATCH ALL DAY.'

Immediately, I handed John his pen back and placed the note at the head of my bunk. I quickly undressed and dove under the covers. I made it a point to cover my head with the covers so to make it impossible to tell it was me.

After closing my eyes, I recalled that this was going to be my last night in Vietnam. Would I be considered a real Vietnam Veteran with less than a month in-country? Does my Purple Heart give me extra credit? If I wanted, could I request another tour or two like Dan? Is that something that I would want to do? Would my parents be happy with me being home so soon and how would they feel if I were to come back?

All this thinking was starting to give me a headache and I should be thinking of pleasant thoughts instead. Then, as I kept thinking, I thought, why do I need to be thinking of anything right now anyway? And so, with that final thought, my mind went blank, which was easy, and I was soon asleep.

# Chapter 22

I was not sure how much time went by from when I hid under the covers, but I could hear a couple of guys holding a rather loud conversation. Oh well, it must be time to get up as I could not sleep anyway. Besides, I was hungry.

I got up from my bunk and the tallest of the three guys that were sitting on the floor playing cards asked me as I walked by them, "Where are you going?"

I found this a little odd because I didn't know these guys and I was not accountable to them. Anyway, I responded in a way as if asking them, why are you asking. "Going to get a bite to eat."

The guy sitting next to the tall one that asked the first question, "Can we tag along?"

"Yeah, no sweat," I responded, not knowing for sure what I was getting into.

I did look around for John, but didn't see him. I looked over at his bunk and there he was, under the covers and with my note at the head of his bed. I should have taken my note back but decided against it. He did me a favor and no need for me to be rude. In a way, it was kind of funny.

As they packed up the deck of cards they that they were playing with, the third guy, he was the one wearing glasses, said to me with his hand out for a normal handshake, "I'm Bob. We haven't eaten all day because we didn't know where to go."

Well, lucky for me. It was a sad state of affairs that when you are hungry, that you would rather play cards than to ask around if anyone knew where the chow hall was.

He added, "We were going to ask the guy in the bunk next to yours, but we saw his note and decided not to bother him. We assumed that you two were on watch together, so we left you both alone."

"I appreciate that," I answered him, after giving him a confused look.

Bob must have picked up my uneasiness as he added, "We heard that the chow hall here was closed for repairs. Something about a rocket or mortar attack."

"Okay," was my initial response. I came back with, "I noticed a place a block or two from here. I was going to try it myself. You guys are most welcome to join me."

After I said that, they all seemed to share the biggest smile that I had ever seen. I didn't know if they were happy because they were going to get something to eat, or that they thought that I was treating. So, wanting to get off on the correct foot, I made a small joke by saying, "But I'm not buying."

They seemed to appreciate a little humor and I, wanting to keep this, 'good will' thing moving along, I started out with my introduction. "I'm Charles, Charles Edwards from Baltimore Maryland."

Regular handshakes went out between us. Everyone introduced each other, to each other. Apparently, they had not done this before.

"I'm Triple-T," said the tall guy. "From the little home state of Delaware." ·

"My name is Mike Mick. I'm from Mount Holly, New Jersey. My friends call me Mick, not Mickey. Glad to meet you."

And the last guy added in his introduction, "Bob Scott. My name is Bob Scott. You can call me Bob, or you can call me Scott. Don't care, don't care at all."

"All right. Now that we have the pleasantries out of the way, let's eat," I announced as if I had appointed myself in charge.

Moreover, why not? I'd been here the longest in-country. I knew where to go, they were all only E-2's, and I was an E-3. I was senior in rank to them and they apparently knew that, as they formed a single line behind me and out we went for a bite to eat.

With no trouble at all, we quickly made the two block walk to the restaurant that I remembered when I came in before. As we approached this little, truly out of the way restaurant, there were two little kids hanging around out front. Now, seeing two little kids standing on a street corner should not had been that big of a deal, but it was the way that they had positioned themselves in front of the restaurant door. If they would have been much older than say, seven or eight for the little girl and 13 or 14 for the little boy, they could had been standing there as bouncers for a nightclub. They both stared at us as we walked towards them and I almost expected the boy to speak out and ask us for our ID.

As we got near them, I commented to Triple-T, Mick, and Bob. "Watch out guys. These little kids are going to sell us something that we don't need."

"We won't buy it then," Mick spoke out, suggesting that he was not an easy mark.

I interrupted Mick before he could explain any more to us and said, "I don't trust gook kids. Especially, the little cute ones."

My last comment got the three of them thinking. They looked so confused as if it was difficult for them to walk, talk, and think about this, all at the same time.

"They have a way to make you feel bad if you don't buy it from them right then and there," I ended, trying to sound like someone that had first hand knowledge of their sales tactics. Which I did, but I was not going to go into any of the details for them.

My comment got a few chuckles from the Pep Boys, Manny, Moe, and Jack, but not as if they believed me. I picked up the impression that they felt that in no way, could these cute little kids do anything but sell Girl Scout Cookies or candy bars, and that their parents were standing near by keeping a close eye on them. They were both clean little kids, not the dirt-poor kids that generally bugged the hell out of us wanting money and cigarettes, or worse, the selling of their little brothers and sisters. And I do remember this one kid selling his mother and trying to convince us that she was a virgin.

The little girl was very cute and had long, straight, black hair with brown eyes. Well, there was nothing unusual here, being that she was Vietnamese, and that all Vietnamese girls had long, straight, black hair with brown eyes. She was not wearing any shoes and had on a white top with blue shorts. Her older friend, or maybe he was her older brother, was wearing a white top with torn brown or tan pants. He seemed rather normal looking except for this huge mold on his neck that after closer examination, it looked like President Richard Nixon or even maybe George Washington.

Triple-T interrupted my daydreaming/examination and asked, "Come on Charles. What's up with these kids? They are adorable and look adoptable, if you were to ask me."

With this lack of trust that seemed to have developed with my new set of friends here, I must step-up to the plate and say something, or at the very least, set Triple-T straight before he goes and orders one of these kids to ship home.

"Okay my friends, lets see what we have here," I announced as we stopped in front of this little pair of kids. Then again, it was not all that difficult, as they stood right in the doorway, sort of blocking our way in.

Everyone was now looking at me as if I was to entertain them with my knowledge of Vietnamese children. Oh well, I tried with, "My guess is that they have an item to sell. Something that we must have while here in-country or something really valuable and unique for us to send home to our girlfriends."

For now, the boy stared at me as if he had something to say. This little girl smiled at all of us as if she had nothing to say. I continued, "The little girl, well, her name will be something like Cau Duc, Long Qin, or Bin Trang. The boy, well, he is the one in charge here and he'll do all the talking as she stands next to him. She'll do all the smiling for the both of them."

"And his name," questioned Triple-T.

"It'll be a manly name, nothing too strange. Something like Wo Dun, Xlyn Sun, or Min Trang," I answered, as if I really knew what I was talking about, well; at least I sounded as if I knew what I was talking about this time.

"You know how to talk to them," returned another question from Triple-T. "Do you know their language?"

Speaking with authority now, I came back and said, "Everyone over here seem to want to learn and speak English. When speaking to them, just leave out a few words. You know, instead of asking, 'where are you going,' ask, 'where you go.'"

Triple-T then reached into his pocket and pulled out a handful of those little Pocket Guides to Vietnam pamphlet along with the Vietnamese Phrase pamphlet, and said, "I got these free at the airport. Is this okay to use?"

He paused for a moment and shared them with Mick and Scott, I meant Bob. Mick asked, "How much are they?"

His response to Mick irritated to me. Not by the way, he said it, just the fact that Triple-T was going to announce again that they were free. He answered, "Like I said, they were free. No one should pay for these things. I have a couple of extra ones for each of you all. Who all wants one?"

As he passed them out, he added, "Some creep at the airport was selling them for a dollar a piece. Can you imagine that? A dollar for this?"

Well, he had enough to go around for everyone and he even had one left over for me, which I declined to take. I explained that I already had a couple of copies as I stopped in front of the oldest of the two kids and asked him, "So little man, what is your name and what are you selling today that my girlfriend back home needs?"

All he did was to smile at me as if he had no idea what I had just asked him. The little girl quickly moved over and stood between he and I. She looked up at me and said, in very clear English and using complete sentences, "My brother does not say very much. His name is Austin and he does not have anything for you to purchase for your girlfriend. Assuming that you even have a girlfriend back home, sailor boy."

Well, this was off to a bad start I surmised as everyone circled around us to listen in as if she was the quarterback giving us the next play and that it was third and long.

"And what name you," I asked, and then realized that I sounded stupid talking that way.

"You are a very stupid Joe. It appears to me that the way you are speaking, that you did not complete high school," she said, creating laughter all around with everyone, everyone except for me. I did not find this amusing at all.

Before I could respond to this, not so cute any more, little girl, she was already back at me with, "We are not selling anything for your pretend girlfriends back home. In fact Joe, we are only selling information. Information that you might find useful."

For now, I will just go along with her to see what transpires. She already had one up on me and I was not going to let her get in any more digs. I asked, "What kind of information? You VC? You know some VC?"

Triple-T butted in and asked, "What's you name little girl? How old are you?"

The way that she was asked for her name and age, well, that placed a smile on her face. You would have thought that she was the Queen of England and that he was giving her, her due respect.

"My name is Abigail and I am seven years old."

Wanting to put an end to this, 'social hour,' I asked her again, "What kind of information do you have for us today?"

Putting her hands on her hips as if she was about to punish me verbally for being bad, she answered while pointing to her left, "I will count the dogs and cats that are in that yard next door." Then with a serious look, as if the following information was most important, she said, "And that Joe, will only cost you and your friends one American dollar."

Well, I was not impressed that this little turd for a kid could count and I certainly was not willing to pay her a dollar for that information. I asked her, "That's all? Nothing more for a dollar? Big deal, so you can count."

Triple-T, Mick and Bob were silent now waiting for whoever would respond next. Crap, I believed that I was about to be made a fool of by this little seven year old.

"Oh no stupid Joe. In addition, I will also give you a count of the cats and dogs when you leave this fine establishment."

Triple-T, let's remember that he's an FNG, spoke up and said, "How cute. This little lady can count. What a way to make a living."

"And why is that worth a dollar," I asked, wanting to put an end to this and get something to eat.

Taking one hand off her hip and pointing her finger right at my face, she proudly blared out, "If my count shows that there are fewer cats and dogs when you come out, then you will know what you had for dinner."

Well, Mick threw up his breakfast, and went into a gagging routine, which was soon followed with the dry-heaves. Bob, who was standing next to him and had some barf blown on his shoes, started making those sound that dogs usually make just before they throw up.

After Mick regained his composure and wiped the barf off his chin, he looked a little embarrassed. Embarrassed and having lost his appetite, he turned and walked away back to the barracks. It was funny to watch him walk away as he would take a few steps, gag a little, and then walk a few more steps, then gag again.

At any rate and no matter what they may think of me, I was vindicated with these kids. I knew that they were little con artists and it had been played out for my benefit. Wanting to show that I was in charge and that things were under control, I gave the little girl a dollar and asked for a current, 'cat and dog count.'

Looking at me as if I just took away her brand new Barbie doll, "I said that it was going to cost you one American dollar. All you have is MPC?"

"Yes, that's all that I have. Cash is cash," I answered, just as Triple-T spoke up and told me, "I have plenty of green backs with me. You only need one?"

"Yeah," I responded.

"You can pay me back later," Triple-T explained.

Triple-T then tells Bob and me, "When I was the airport and picked up on how badly they wanted my green back, well my man." He then stopped for effect and to look around to make sure that we were paying attention to what he was about to tell us. "I felt that I should keep some in reserve. If they wanted it that bad, so would others."

Great I thought, he's an FNG and he had a whole wad of green backs. Maybe I can buy some from him, but for now, I'll just move this along. "Yeah, I'll take it," I said with my hand out. I gave her the one-dollar; one American green back dollar that I just got from Triple-T and we waited for her count.

"Four cats and five dogs, sailor boy," she explained with a smile, after taking my dollar.

For now, the five of us just stood there with no one wanting to make the next move. With nothing more to discuss now that she had the money and we had the count, I made my way inside the restaurant with Triple-T and Bob in close tow and leaving those kids outside.

Triple-T mentioned to me, "Damn man. Did you see all those sick animals?"

Wanting to be funny, I answered, "Yep. They are so thin that they might only be used as appetizers."

I got an open mouth expression from Triple-T of, 'Oh my God.'

Continuing to talk, as if I knew everything in order to survive The-Nam, I added, "That's nothing. Wait until you see a real sick or dead water buffalo lying next to the kitchen door. Now that's something to see."

"That's healthy? What about health inspectors," he questioned with much concern.

"No, not really," I responded.

"Won't a dead animal attract flies?"

"Flies just might be a positive, good sign on a dead animal. It shows freshness," I said, as we looked for a table.

With fear in his voice, Bob spoke up and questioned, "You sure?"

I explained to these guys as we sat down at a table in the corner, away from any windows and doorways, "This country spends all their money on helping people in the south, kill people in the north. The people in the north are also trying to kill the people in the south so more money is spent on protecting the people in the south from the people from the North. Health inspectors are a luxury item and not a priority looking at the big picture."

"That makes sense," they both responded, at the same time as if they believed me a hundred percent.

"In addition," I continued, "the body count for those dying by food poisoning is not that important to worry about when you look at those that are dying by bombs and bullets. Know what I mean?"

Well, that subject was dropped for now as we were handed our menus. I watched, as they looked over the menu in total confusion. Before I opened up my menu, I said, "If you can't read the menu, when she comes back, just point to the picture of what you want."

Still, there was confusion and I didn't understand why or how hard could it be to point to a picture of a hamburger and coke. Then I realized the problem as I opened up my menu and to my surprise, there were no pictures. Just funny looking words with squiggly marks on them.

This should not be fun, I thought to myself as Bob and Triple-T looked to me for help. Damn, I wished Dan were here. But then again, I could handle this.

"What are you getting," asked Bob with Triple-T looking on.

Before I could answer, our waitress came back with her pad and pencil at the ready. I didn't know why, but she looked right at me. "Do you speak English," I asked.

She looked mean, very mean. She came back with, "You order. You order now."

Okay, this was good. She spoke English. Well, kind of I found out as I ordered, "Hamburger, fries, and a coke. Hold the dog."

This got a chuckle from my two friends but nothing from our waitress. She repeated, "You order. You order now."

Crap, she only knew two sentences. I responded, "H a m b u r g e r, f r i e s, a n d a s m a l l c o k e."

No luck with her and to boot, I was getting no help from my friends. Not that I expected help from any FNG's right now. Wanting to be funny, as this was something that Dan would probably do, I said with wild jesters, "Moo," trying to help her visualize a cow.

With that, she smiled at me as I added in the motions of eating a hamburger. That was followed with me pretending to pick at some french fries and drinking a coke.

She returned a pleasant smile and said something in Vietnamese. Assuming that she understood what I said, Triple-T and Bob closed their menus and pointed to me indicating that they wanted what I ordered. Bob then gestured to her something to the effect that he did not want a coke. With his 'Moo-ing' and hand motions of milking a cow, I picked up that he wanted a glass of milk instead.

Right now, everyone was happy. She had our orders and was off to get it started.

The three of us looked around the room and we agreed that this was a very clean place. Because of how clean this placed looked, we all agreed that there was no way would they consider serving dogs or cats.

After about five minutes of small talk about where everyone was from and where they went to high school, our meals came.

Surprised looks were everywhere. Surprised looks from us because of what was on our plates. A surprise look came from our waitress because she noticed the surprised look that was on our faces. This was not going well as I did not like surprises at mealtime. Before any of us could complain or ask any questions about our food, she smartly turned and quickly headed away towards the kitchen. I was not sure, but I could swear that I heard her laughing.

In our plates, our surprise special, were little strips of meat along with a glass of milk for Bob.

Triple-T asked, "Okay. I have a question. Do you think that my milk is fresh?"

"You can count on it," I answered, as I took my fork and moved the meat strips around for a closer inspection. I was not sure what I was looking for and hoped that I did not find any dog hairs or a flea collar.

Bob, after spitting his milk on the floor, said as more milk oozed from his mouth and nose, "My milk is hot. It tastes like shit."

As Triple-T looked at him, all the while holding back from throwing-up, Bob instructed, "Here, you taste it."

Triple-T, not being the smartest guy in Vietnam right now, reached out and did just that. He took a swig from Bob's glass and that was quickly followed by him spitting it out on the floor. Dinner was not going well today.

Before any of us could recover from this, or before Bob and Triple-T could start cleaning up their mess, our waitress returned yelling for us to clean up our mess. Thinking as if I was Dan, I sat back and did nothing. Hell, it was not my mess and no way was I going to clean up anything that was not my mess unless an officer told me to do so.

Triple-T and Bob did oblige the old lady and the two of them started to clean up. I looked at her and said, "Coke. I want a Coke."

"Okay Joe. One Coke for you. You no spit on floor. Okay?"

Now before long, I had my Coke, a cold Coke, and they still had their luke-warm milk to clean up and finish off.

"Why didn't you say something," they both asked at the same time.

"What was I to say?"

"Something," Triple-T explained, as he moved back into his chair.

"Where did you think that milk came from over here? Did you think that they would stop by a 7/11 for a loaf of bread and fresh milk?"

Bob, after taking his seat, asked, "What do you put in your cereal over here?"

"Cereal," I questioned with a little laughter added to be cool. "This isn't Howard Johnson. You are in a second rate, third world country where everything they eat over here has rice in it. Milk does not go well with rice."

Our little waitress came back and gave them a look as if they were her children, and that she was very pissed at them. Bob and Triple-T both chimed in and sounded off, "Coke. We want Coke."

"Okay Joe. You get coke. No milk today," she answered.

Just as the two of them showed an expression that they were going to be happy with a coke, she added, "You get coke now. You pay for milk. You pay for coke."

I added, "No sweat. We pay."

"Why did you step in and say that," Triple-T snapped at me, as if he was not going to pay for anything that was spilled.

Taking a history lesson from Dan, I boldly answered, "Then go ahead my friend. Piss her off, then she tells the cook and see what you get for a meal. I would think that eating a cat or dog right now would be more of a concern than the price of a single glass of milk."

Pausing for effect, I added, "That you ordered, I might add."

Both of them were now looking at me as if I was the smartest person in the world. Well, maybe the smartest person in The-Nam, or maybe, the smartest person in this lovely one star luncheonette.

Anyway, their cokes came and with our drinks taken care of, we ventured into unknown territory as we individually examined our meals for any tale tail signs of dog or cat. Now they were looking at the outside of their burger strips. As for me, I had to cut one of those bad boys in half. If I were to find a flea collar or a dog license, it would be inside my burger.

Okay, our meal was what we ordered. A hamburger with fries. Nothing fancy, just a hamburger and fries. Then, after a more detailed closer look at our hamburger paddies/strips, questions did arise. Even I had a few questions after looking at my hunks of little strips of meat.

Bob asked with much skepticism, "Is your hamburger paddy in little strips too?"

I answered Bob with, "Yeah. What about you Triple-T?"

"Don't know yet. I was first checking to see if any part of my meal was still moving."

Any other time, and with someone else's meal, this would have been funny. But not today, not with my food.

Our waitress came over and asked, "Okay? You okay Joe?"

As each of us waited for the other to say something, nothing was said. Our waitress must have assumed that everything was all right, because she turned and walked away laughing. That kind of laugh was not a good sign, not at mealtime. Not at my mealtime.

Triple-T, being the big deal that he was, dove right into his burger. He did this as if this was an expensive meal and that he was not about to let it go to waste, or that he was starving. Not wanting to have him show me up, I did the same and after a few bites, my burger was gone.

Bob, on the other hand, and apparently using wisdom, waited before eating his burger by finishing off his fries first.

I asked Bob, "You going to eat your burger?"

Bob, apparently not wanting to eat his burger, and not wanting to give it away, picked up his burger and explained, "Just waiting till it cooled down. I like hot fries and cold burgers."

Just then, Triple-T swallowed his last bite and this was followed by a facial expression as if his burger was on its way back up. Not wanting to be sitting directly across from him if he was to explode, I moved my seat a little to the left.

Bob, now having believed that he made a good decision by not eating his burger, decided to have some fun with us as he finished off his fries. He jokingly asked Triple-T and me, "So, if I was to rub your tummy, would your foot jump up and down?"

Before I could muster up something smart to say in return, Triple-T answered him quickly with, "Go ahead ass-hole. Rub my stomach and I'll pounce up and down on your face with my fist and then I will bite you."

Looking to really have his face punched out, he came back with a smart remark of, "Bad dog. Bad dog."

Wanting to get in on this, 'little dinner time irritations,' I added in my two cents with, "Yeah, as he's pounding you a new face, I'll come around and pee on your leg."

Now it was two against one and I liked those odds. Bob calmed down some with his insults, as Triple-T acted as if he was starting to get pissed.

Our waitress came over and asked, "Okay?"

This time, still no response from us. As if we did say something, she said, "Okay, okay. You pay now. You pay me now."

Triple-T and I were ready to pay up and leave. This was not the kind of meal that one would light up a smoke; enjoy one more cup of coffee. Then relax and take in the ambiance. Well, maybe it was if I was a local.

Bob spoke up and said, "I'm not finished yet."

"Well my friend, finish up so we can pay up. I'm ready to go," I said, and reached for my wallet to pay my share of our meal.

Triple-T did the same as Bob slowly finished off his burger just to hold us up. However, by the way we looked at him; it did encourage him to eat a little faster. Moments later, he was finished and we each threw in a couple of MPC dollars and left the table. I threw in a five spot and took back some of the ones. I figured that if Triple-T didn't ask, I was not going to give him his one-dollar back. I would just consider that my tip for showing them such a fine place to eat.

Just outside, I looked around for Austin and Abigail, especially Abigail, and they were nowhere to be found. I said under by breath as not to be detected by Bob or Triple-T, "Damn, damn, damn. I was taken by the little shit, Abigail and her silent partner in crime, Austin."

Well, Triple-T had heard what I said. To make it worse, he spoke up with, "You were right Charles. They were con artists and you my man, got taken."

Laughing a little too loud for this joke, Triple-T added, "You were taken, you knew that you were going to be taken, and you still got taken."

Responding quickly in self-defense, I said, "We both did. Remember, it was your dollar."

"Kind of," laughed Triple-T. "I only let you borrow my dollar. You now owe me a dollar."

"Yep, I got taken and I still owe you a dollar," I said sadly. Then, to my rescue and surprise, Abigail showed up and asked, "Joe. How was your meal?"

Trying to put on a proud, 'see I did not get screwed,' look, I said to her, "Delicious meal. Almost like home cooking and I even enjoyed my cold soda."

Triple-T just had to add in his two cents, as he said, "Yeah, just like home. Of course, if home was India."

Bob looked at him and then me as if suggesting that one of us should fill him in on what Triple-T meant by that.

I took it upon myself to help Bob out, and said to him, "India. As in a place where they do not eat hamburgers made from cow, but do eat hamburgers made from dogs and cats. You get it?"

"It be cool," he responded, and gave us the facial expression as if he knew that all along.

Tired of being ignored, and again, with her little hands on the hip look, Abigail announced to me so that everyone could hear, "Now Joe, would you and your friends like to know the count?"

"Yes we do," I responded, and again trying to make my mannerism show that I was not to be taken advantage of by this little girl, not again anyway. She had been paid and now I expected her to give me the totals, I thought, as that was my understanding.

"One American dollar," she announced with her hand out.

A little pissed at her boldness, I explained to her, "I already gave you a dollar for the count."

"Yes stupid Joe, you did, but that dollar was for the count before you GI's had dinner. This dollar is for the current count," she explained, and I felt that she was just too damn smart for anyone that young.

"Shit, shit, shit," I said, only this time, everyone heard me. I'd bet that Dan had heard me all the way back at the ship, and for sure; anyone that I knew back in the states. This was the same-same type of deal that I got taken advantage of on the Christmas cards a few weeks ago. You would have thought that by now, that I would have learned my lesson or at the very least, known better.

Triple-T spoke up and said, "No problem my man Charles. That one-dollar that you owes me, well, give it to her. As for me, I want to know the count. If what I had was a bow-wow or a meow-meow burger, I wants to know."

If this guy wanted to give up another dollar for that, that was just fine with me.

Abigail, with her hand still held out, only now she was facing Triple-T, moved it around to get his attention. He took notice of her persistence and said pointing to me, "He has your money honey. See him."

Reluctantly, I paid up because I did make a bet and I lost. She examined my MPC dollar as if it was counterfeit before stuffing it in her pocket. She turned back towards Triple-T and smiled. He then tells her, "Okay sweetie, give me the count."

Her friend Austin displayed a smirk look towards her that I picked up that he knew that we just got screwed for two dollars.

Here we go with the count, Abigail looked at us and said with authority, too much authority for such a little girl, "Gentlemen, four cats and five dogs were alive and well before dinner."

"Your first count may be accurate little girl, but no way were those animals all that healthy," I said to be truthful and funny. However, Bob and Triple-T were not impressed as I assumed that they assumed that their meal came from healthy animals.

Ignoring what I said, Abigail turned toward the other two guys and said, "There are still four cats, but now there is only four dogs."

After a little snicker, she added, "Only the four healthiest dogs are left."

Well, I thought that was funny and enjoyed the solved mystery of my meal. Because the dogs were small, even the healthy ones, and that they were not big enough for a single burger, I didn't know if I myself had a buffalo burger or that it was dog. If it was the dog, then only one of us got the doggie meal.

Then I figured, what the hell, it was well done and it came with plenty of mayo and that it was only one in three that I had the dog.

Triple-T looked at me as he started to turn green. "Suck it up sissy," I told him. Bob on the other hand apparently had heard about enough of this and he was already on his way back to the barracks. So, for now, it was just Triple-T, the two little con artists, and me left in front of this little place.

A moment later, as if the two brats had had enough of us, they approached two other army guys that were headed our way, apparently going to execute their little scam on them.

I looked over at Triple-T and suggested that we head on back. Then I noticed that he was half bent over and making an awful noise. It looked to me as if he was going to explode. His body went into convolutions and it looked as if he was a German Sheppard about ready to barf up his lunch or pounce on a female dog and do the wild thing.

I stood back and moved over right beside him. Not real close and not in front of him. Triple-T was a big guy and I could see him throwing up his entire lunch in one swift move. Then, he looked as if he stopped breathing. Well, no way was he going to get mouth-to-mouth from me. Not today, not after what he had for lunch. This was not going to be a pretty sight.

This little turd Abigail had heard his gagging, and came back over. Thinking that she was a compassionate little girl, I refreshed my opinion about her. With him all bent over like he was, she was able to yell right in his ear from only inches away from his head. "Don't puke here on the street Joe."

He looked at her as if saying by his facial expression, 'Okay little girl. Where would you suggest that I puke up my guts?'

"Over here," she shouted at him as she moved over and pointed to the pin where the dog and cats were. When Triple-T didn't move, she came back and guided him towards the fence. Well, her timing was good because Triple-T did cut loose with a few pounds of his lunch into a neat little pile that the dogs ran over and devoured completely in no time at all. There he was, frozen in place, all bent over at the fence as one dog, the smallest, and apparently the hungriest, jumped up towards his face trying to lick off the little bit that was dripping from his mouth.

Watching this, I was thinking how these were some nasty dogs. Not the kind of dogs that you would want licking your face. Face nothing; I would not want one of these animals licking my hand. Then again, they could lick the face of a VC.

Triple-T was not finished yet. The way he was gagging and standing on one foot, then the other, I was expecting to see his breakfast come up next. This additional gagging got the dogs more excited as if they were expecting additional treats.

As this went on and between his gagging and the dogs barking, well, this entertainment started to draw a crowd. Now all the dogs were jumping up and down trying to be the first to get what comes out next. As a little slobber would drip down from his face, this would get the dogs even more excited and into a shark feeding kind of frenzy.

With his eyes closed, Triple-T did not notice the dogs pouncing near his face. Because this was so cool to watch, I did not want to see it come to an end and one marine guy that was in the crowd started to cheer for the dogs.

Damn, damn, damn, I thought. I must get me a camera. No one will ever believe that this really happened. I was not very good in English in school, but it would be worth taking a few classes in writing so I could write a book about my time in The-Nam and especially now.

The two little kids that got all this started with their counts, were having a ball laughing it up with others that were standing near them. Any minute now, the local police will be needed here to direct traffic and to maintain crowd control.

Just when I thought that things could not get any better, well, they did. Triple-T opened his eyes just after his breakfast came up and saw all those dogs jumping up at his face. He did jump back and in doing so, forgot to let go of the fence. As expected with him being such a big guy, as he went back, so did the fence and both came crashing down on the payment.

With his screaming, the dogs barking, everyone laughing, and the gooks talking in their gook language, well, what I needed now was to have an 8-track tape recorder, or at least a super-8 movie camera to make a movie out of this material. My God, this was fun and unbelievable.

As Triple-T attempted to crawl out from under the fence and to get up and away from the dogs, before he could compose himself and wipe his face clean, the owner of the restaurant was out screaming at him.

The owner started out just yelling at him and pointing at the torn fence and at the same time, the dogs realized that this was their time to escape, and escape they did. The owner then moved his anger and attention to the escaping dogs, or his escaping inventory.

The two little con artists must have seen that this was yet another opportunity to make money in helping the owner recapture his inventory as they started to round up what cats and dogs they could.

As far as the cats go, well, cats were cats and they didn't do anything except squat there looking around and licking themselves. Okay, enough about stupid cats, getting back to Triple-T and normally, in a situation like this, everyone, if not, at least one person would have stepped over and helped with getting the fence off of him. However, the dogs wanted one last lick before they skipped town and were fighting each other to get the closest to his mouth and that last dripping of barf slobber on his chin.

It was more fun watching than helping, which was what I was doing. I got to write a book about this and it just might be a hard sell because this kind of happenings can't be made up. It might even be hard to tell this story to a group of friends. No matter, it don't mean nothin.

By the time Triple-T was up and had composed himself, it was hard not to notice that his face was licked clean. Nothing goes to waste in a third world country. Even 'people barf' was food for the animals over here and this gave new meaning to recycling.

Triple-T then brushed off his uniform that was layered with dirt and dog hairs, along with a few wet slobber spots from him and the dogs. He tucked in his shirt and straightened his cap as he made a face and stood in a stance as if suggesting that he wanted things to turn out the way they did.

Well, because he was so tall and mean looking, none of us were willing to say anything to him in fear of getting our butts whipped. Hell, even a hug from him was most undesirable right now. As if this was a, 'no sweat' situation, we simply upped and walked away and we soon caught up with Bob as he had heard the confusion and had turned back.

Nothing was said about what had just happened and as we rounded the next corner, and out of sight from the restaurant, Bob and Triple-T then pulled out menus that they had all taken from the restaurant. Damn, damn, damn, everyone had taken a menu and all of them had gotten away with it. Well, I wanted one but was unwilling to go back now. I asked the group, "Anybody willing to give up a menu? I forgot to get me one. I'll pay a dollar for one."

Bob laughed at me and explained, "Shit man. It ain't no big deal stealing one. Get your own the next time you eat out my man. This is my third one in just two days."

After a silly smile, Bob added, "It ain't no big deal to steal a worthless piece of paper. How hard can it be?"

Triple-T looked at me, and questioned, "You've been here in-country how long, and you never took one?"

"Nope never thought about it until now," I answered. No way was I going to say anything smart in return to Triple-T. Maybe he was smiling on the outside, but I'd bet he was still pissed on the inside.

In a few minutes, we were back and I headed right for my bunk to take a nap. We found Mick playing cards by himself.

Bob sat back down on the floor and started playing cards again with him. Triple-T announced that he was going to take a shower and change his uniform. So for now, I was able to relax in my bunk and kill some time.

Just as I was about to close my eyes, two guys walking by my bunk carrying a couple of bottles in three or four bags, bumped into my bed, almost knocking me out and onto the floor/deck. I looked up, expecting an apology, but didn't get one. After a closer look at these two, obviously drunken sailors, I believed that I had met these two guys before. I did not know from where, but as they slowly fell to the ground, being careful not to break any of the bottles, it came to me.

The one guy, a Second Class Petty Officer with the name Bruder, sewed above his right shirt pocket, well, he was a fellow crewmember from the Summit. As he composed himself, he said to the guy with him, "Hawk. You okay buddy? You didn't break anything did you?"

Hawk, being more concerned about having broken any of his bottles, ignored his own personal condition after hitting the deck very hard, opened one of his bags, and smiled. "Nope. Didn't spill a drop. Hell, I am so practiced at falling down, that I can fall down a flight of stairs and not spill a drop."

I remember now, Bruder and his buddy Hawk, they were the two guys that were giving away Acadoma Rice Wine and San Miguel beer at the striptease show a few days ago. As I remembered more about that time, this striptease show was going on below me, a loaded M-60 machine gun was behind me, and the two of them were passing around free booze to all of us. Getting everyone drunk, even the one on guard duty manning the M-60.

Bruder looked me square in the eyes; well maybe a little crossed eyed, and said, "I know you."

That was quickly followed by a burp and two farts. His friend Hawk said, after waving away the fart smell, "I know you also. You're the same guy that he knows."

"We both know who you are," said Bruder as he tried to stand up, but was unable to do so.

I could only smile back at the two of them. I really wanted to burst out laughing but I didn't know how that would affect them. As in, would they laugh back with me or get angry and bang me over the head with a cheap bottle of Acadoma Rice Wine.

"How you guys going," I asked, to break the silence.

Bruder, now sitting up straight and tall, said, "We had a good day and as always, it didn't cost us a cent and we walked away with a couple of bottles of free booze."

Hawk sat up beside Bruder and said the exact same thing. "We had a good day and as always, it didn't cost us a cent and we walked away with a couple of bottles of free booze."

Mick and Bob, after hearing the words, 'free booze,' came over and joined in with us as if they were already a part of this little meeting.

Mick smoothly asked, as he showed a very friendly smile, "You guys have a free booze deal going on here in town?"

Bruder and Hawk looked at them as if this duo of Mick and Bob were trying to mussel in on half of their business. Hawk looked at Bruder and Bruder returned a shit-eaten grin as if suggesting to them that he could work out their own deal for free booze, elsewhere and in another town.

"Go away," said Hawk as Bruder motioned with his hand for them to leave the three of us alone. Well, they did just that; they moved back over and sat next to Triple-T. Even though they were a few feet away, they still had an ear out for our conversation. This Bob Scott character looked to be a wheeler-dealer.

I questioned Hawk, "I see that you made some good trades today with your C-rats by the amount of wine that you guys have."

"Shit man, we didn't do no trade for no C-rats for no wine," Hawk announced, and he did so with much pride.

I questioned, "Wasn't that what you told me before?"

Bruder leaned over towards me and said, in a whisper, "That's what we tell everyone. If we told them the truth, then they'd go and do what we do and we will soon be out of business."

Even with talking to two drunks, I could still provide them with my deer-in-the-headlights look. It must have worked because they seemed anxious to tell me their little secret.

Hawk said, after raising his leg to fart, "You can tell him."

"Why, then he will move in on our business," answered Bruder sounding not very happy with Hawk's request.

"It don't mean nothin telling someone that be heading home. Remember, he's going back to the real world. He don't belong here no more."

There was nothing more amusing than to see a drunk trying to remember something and then come to an agreement with another drunk. I didn't think that he remembered anything about me being shipped home; I believed that Bruder just said that so that he could just move along this conversation, and to put a halt to his thinking.

Bruder's response was cool, "You can tell him. I need to take an inventory of what's in my brain."

And with that, Bruder closed his eyes and didn't say anything as Hawk explained. "It's a simple plan really. My father did it in World War II and my uncle did it in Korea."

Hawk paused for a minute as if gathering his thoughts, but he was soon asleep or passed out.

Bruder didn't open his eyes, but he did step in and took over where Hawk left off. "It's a simple plan really. His father did it in World War II and his uncle did it in Korea."

This was followed with Bruder passing out. Crap, I guessed that I would never find out what the scam was here. But then Hawk opened one eye and said, "My buddy and I have it all worked out."

"All worked out," added Bruder, as if they were a comedy team.

Hawk, ignoring Bruder, said, "Every time we are in a new town, my man here and me try, and visit all the bars."

"All the bars," Bruder added as if the two of them had this conversation planned out earlier.

Wanting to get to the end of, this story and fit in a nap, and all of this in the same-same day here, I said to the both of then, and trying not to offend either one, "Okay, you are in a new town and hitting all the bars. Isn't that a little expensive?"

"Shit," added in Bruder after a burp that produced a spray of old beer.

"Like the man said," Hawk now speaking with both eyes open, "We tell the bar owner that we are checking out places to hold a party for our unit."

Bruder then said, "For about 25 to 30 guys."

I was not sure where this was heading, but for now, I would just listen and hoped that we all stayed awake until the end of the story.

Bruder, now with his eyes opened also, said, "We tell the bar owners about a party that we are planning and in the process, he gives us a few free drinks to create a little favor towards his establishment."

"Okay," I questioned, "How does that explain your bags of booze?"

"Simple," they both said at the same time.

Bruder took over and explained in more detail, "We describe to the owner that we would like a sample bottle to take back with us. We convince him that our buddies want to test what his establishment has to offer."

Hawk, as if it this was his turn to talk, added, "Without a problem, we get a free bottle to take back with us."

"For the cheap stuff that we get," Bruder explained. "We sell that to the FNG's and tell them that it's a fine French wine."

"We drink the good stuff and a few bottles make it to a few selected officers," Hawk added.

Bruder then said, with a drunken smile, "Lately, because we have visited so many places, we have a large inventory and sales have been very, very good."

As if on cue, now that they have told me everything, the two of them fell asleep right where they were sitting. Between the two of them snoring and farting, taking a nap might not be all that easy with them right next to my bunk. However, that was quickly resolved. The two of them woke right up as they heard Mick and Bob making plans with Triple-T to take a walk to town and to pull off the same scam with a visit to a few bars.

No sooner than when the three of them headed out on their new mission, did Hawk and Bruder stumble up and were in hot pursuit. I wanted to nap more than I wanted to see what would happen when Hawk and Bruder caught up with them. I did just that; I laid down and closed my eyes to enjoy the peace and quiet. I enjoyed the peace and quiet along with the fresh air now that the two fart generators are gone.

I started to daydream about what it was back home that I missed the most and just after I covered my parents, dating, school, and driving around, I fell asleep.

# Chapter 23

Just a few minutes later, I got banged on the bottom of my boot with a stick or something. I looked up, wanting to yell at whomever it was, and there stood the Master-At-Arms. It was a good thing for me that I did not wake up yelling and screaming at him. Anyway, if one of us was to be doing any yelling, it was not going to be me at him, but the other way around. He was yelling something at me about being in my bunk with my clothes on, and wearing my boots.

Damn, damn, damn. I could even get myself into trouble while simply taking a nap. Oh well, I just simply sat up, placed both feet on the deck, apologized saying that I was sorry and that I didn't know any better. As he was only a Chief Petty Officer, I made it a point not to 'sir' him so not to give him any additional ammunition to use on me. Apparently, he had enough just covering the fact that I was napping with my clothes on.

In my little mind, I was thinking that it might be a good to be dressed just in case we are under attack. No need to spend time finding and getting dressed when my timely response could be helpful.

He viciously and relentlessly continued with, "Didn't you get a copy of the Welcome to The Republic of Vietnam pamphlet? Everyone gets one that gets assigned a bed here. It tells you about keeping your boots off the bed. Where's yours?"

"My boots?" Now why did he ask me that? Isn't that why he woke me up because he saw that my boots were on the bed?

"Seaman. Your pamphlet. Where is your pamphlet? I know where your damn boots are," he answered back quickly, as if he had been given that smart-ass remark before and that it was not appreciated.

"Sorry Chief. I have a copy in my bag," I said looking around for my bag, which I did not have.

The Master-At-Arms came back with, "How many bags do you have?"

"Just one Chief. Just one. I had most all of my things shipped home already. Sorry Chief. My pamphlet must have been shipped home with my things."

So much for him accepting my apology. He just stared at me with an angry stare that only officers and Chief's knew how to give with great effectiveness, producing fear in anyone nearby, especially me.

I believed that he liked to push his weight around, as some Chief's do, and that he was looking for a way to vent. Well, it happened to be my turn to give him a reason to vent and venting he did.

"Sorry Chief. It won't happen again," I said, as that was about the only thing that I could think up to say. Beside, what's the big deal anyway?

He responded only with a huff and a puff before he turned and walked away. I was so glad that I did not work for him on a daily basis. He seemed to be the kind of person that always stayed pissed at everyone for anything. Maybe he served in-country for one tour too many. I wondered if Dan would turn out that way if he kept returning for additional tours. Even with additional tours only being six months long, that was still six months too long in a very bad place.

With the Chief out of sight and with things quieted down some, I did what I had been doing a lot of, trying to take a nap. Then, after giving this some thought, maybe this was not such a good idea. Why not take a walk as I will have a long flight home and could nap all the way across the Pacific.

Besides, with me being up and awake, along with this my last night in this part of the world, I might as well do the tourist thing. So, out the front door I go, and I go at it alone. Maybe not a good idea being by myself, but I believed that if I stayed away from trouble, I would be okay.

After a nice long walk, I easily found a little eating-place that was almost empty with only one other table occupied. I simply took the first table I came up to for myself. Not a nice table, as in fancy tablecloths, expensive candleholders or real silverware, but a nice table, that was away from the windows. Even away from the doors that were next to the kitchen or bathrooms. Also far away from any tables filled with loud drunks or hookers doing their thing while I feasted on my buffalo burger. It was just simply, a nice table. Nothing special, but I would be alone and not distracted by anyone or loud explosions. I could grab a bite to eat and no one would be grabbing at me. I did not wish to play tug-of-war with my little Eddie and the twins with some hooker or enterprising waitress. For Louie-Louie, it would be tug-of-war with a waiter.

With little difficulty, I successfully ordered my burger and coke. Wasn't sure if I would be getting fries or not, but didn't really care. A simple task of getting my food ordered was an accomplishment all by itself and I did it without looking at the menu. I took it off the table and placed it in my pocket. This way, she would think that the last customer took it and not suspect me.

My food came, with fries, and just as I was about to chomp down with my first bite, three little gook kids came up to me, and the taller of the two asked, "You know me Joe?"

Well, the first thought that came to mind that was that I hadn't had sex with anyone in this little ugly country, which left out the possibility of me being his father. I didn't owe them any money and they were way too young to be the VC.

Trying to be cool and firm, and at the same time, take a bite of my burger, because it was still hot, I answered, "No. Don't know you and you don't know me. Besides, my name is not Joe."

With his hands on his hip, as if what he had to say next was most important, he explained, "We did you trick. You said you pay. You no pay."

"What trick," I asked, as this was apparently a case of mistaken identity. Didn't we all look alike to them anyway?

"We do trick. Jump in water. You pay. You pay soda. You throw soda in water. Soda sink, we no get paid."

This little turd was pissed and pissed at me for all the wrong reasons. Tricks, sodas, what was he talking about.

Realizing that I didn't know for real, or that I was pretending that I didn't know, he came back with, "We jump over each other. We land in water. You pay soda. We no get soda. You bad Joe."

Now I remembered. This was the time that Dan didn't want to pay-up for our little entertainment on the pier one day a week or so ago. These little kids were jumping over each other and landing in the river. Dan did mess with them and now it was pay back time. Damn, and now I was the only one here. Dan tricked them, and then it should be Dan here comforting them and not me.

Before I could say something positive or offer an apology, this little, ticked-off, gook kid said in a mean and ugly tone, "We tell VC. VC come, kill you. What say you now Joe?"

Damn, damn, damn, I said in my mind. I could not believe that I might get myself killed in this little shitty place by a couple of little kids my last night in-country as I feasted on my buffalo burger and fries.

How would they notify my parents about this? 'Mr. and Mrs. Edwards, you son was killed over the price of a few sodas today. He was not killed in combat action, but killed for the non-combat action of his dear friend Dan, over the price of a few sodas. He was not killed by the VC, or even friendly fire, but by little kids.'

As I was about to offer them some money to cover the damages, another kid came over to join the party, and he added, "I know this Joe. He okay. Numba one, okay."

The angry kids came back with, "Numba ten, he numba ten."

I didn't remember this kid either, but he was on my side and for now, that was a good thing.

Seeing my, deer-in-the-headlights look, and picking up on the fact that I was in trouble, the kid on my side said to them, "His friend give money me. I go school. You know, my parents dead. VC killed my mother and father."

Okay, I got this one already. Dan gave this kid money to go to school when the VC killed his parents. I would be thrilled to send all his little cousins to school if he could save me from this assignation squad right about now.

As the three kids argued back and forth, I thought it would be a good idea to remain calm. And because I was hungry, I had a few more bites of my burger along with a few fries. Any other time and place, eating anything while all this was going on would normally be out of the question. But, this was The-Nam and I was hungry.

This went on for a few minutes more and before I knew it, I had eaten my burger and fries. As if I was not a part of this conversation, I finished off my soda and quietly attempted to remove myself from the area.

As I made my way to the door, I passed my waitress and paid my bill. Of course, I had the menu in my pocket for a souvenir, and, most importantly, I got away with it. Not only did I get away with my menu, but also the one little kid kept the other three busy allowing me to make my escape. Maybe this was not all that big of a deal to mention, but it could have been a mess with these three mess-ies and me as the, one mess-er, getting messed up.

Okay now, it was time to head back, only, I did not know which way was back. Well, this was a no sweat situation. I would simply hail a taxi and inform him where I wanted to go.

Luck was in my favor as just across the street from where I was, was a whole swarm of taxies of all types and sizes. It was a simple choice of picking one.

As I crossed the street, every driver must have known why I was headed his way. All at once, each one of them took one step towards me and started shouting. Not sure just what they were shouting, but I did pick up that they were not angry with me. I've never seen so many slanted eyes and white teeth at one time in my life.

Then, there was this one driver, he ended up taking two steps towards me instead of one, and he had the biggest smile of them all. Well, that made my decision for me.

I made my way towards him and after he opened the door for me, I fell into this little toy size taxi. He jumped in the front and after pulling away, he asked, "Okay Joe. We go."

It took him a block or two before he asked, "Best way? What best way? You say, okay."

Damn, I didn't know. If I knew, I wouldn't have gotten a cab. I asked him, "You know the way."

"Best way? What best way? You tell best way."

"Navy BEQ. Your way, best way," I said back at him, all the while hoping that we were at least headed in the right direction.

Again, he snapped back at me, "Best way. What best way?"

"Navy BEQ," I repeated. "You know. Navy hotel."

He must have known what and where I was talking about as he kept going. Then, after another block or two, he said again, "Navy BEQ. Best way. You say, best way. Okay."

Well, this was going to be entertaining. Hell, and damn, damn, damn, I didn't know best way. No way did I know any which way. Okay or no okay. Shit, now what do I do, I questioned myself.

"No way you say," popped another question from my driver.

"Stop here. I get out," I instructed. Damn, I could not even get back to the safety of my own barracks.

He did pull over, held out his hand, and said, "Two dollar. You pay two dollar."

I answered back with, "No pay two dollar you." I was starting to sound like them now. I rephrased and said again, "Sorry, no BEQ, no two dollar."

He made an angry face at me, with his hand out for his two dollars, that was a little scary and using good judgment, along with being scared, I paid the man his two dollars. I did this in MPC and he just had to settle with that.

At least I was able to get myself completely out of the cab before he pulled away at full speed, kicking up lots of dust and plenty of stones on me.

At this time, it really didn't matter to me if the two dollars I just lost was the correct amount for such a short ride or not. Well, maybe it wasn't such a short ride if I must now walk back to square one to start over.

I looked around before I started to walk back, just to make a look-see to see if anything nearby seemed familiar. Well, of all things, something did look familiar, very, very familiar. Not only familiar in sights, but also familiar with some sounds. The sound of dogs barking made my look-see, a hear-see.

There it was, the little restaurant where we got our dog and cat count earlier. I looked for Abigail and her little friend, but they were nowhere to be found. I did take a step towards to newly repaired fence and noticed that there were four cats and five dogs. It appeared to be the same-same, the very same-same, four cats, and five dogs from before.

Damn, we were taken, as they never did serve us any cat or dog. Naturally, I was not going to tell those guys anything about that. At least this way, they had a good story to tell when they returned home. A good story that no one would believe.

Okay, back to my original situation, getting back to the BEQ. Now that I had my bearings straight, it was a simple task of walking a block or two, and with little trouble, I found my accommodations for tonight.

Finding my room may sound like a simple task, a simple task to most people in normal circumstances, however, you must remember that I must first past the check-in desk and avoid being picked for a watch. Also, I must avoid the Master-At-Arms for the very same-same reason. Not to mention a few other people that would like to yell a few choice words at me.

In my room, or dorm, or a better word for it, barracks, there were already a few guys in bed and with the way they were snoring; you would have thought that the Three Stooges were in here. One would inhale though the nose; another would exhale and sounded as if he was a waterfalls next to a freight train. Then, add in another guy that was talking in his sleep. Not to say that talking in your sleep was a bad thing; it was that he would fart every now and then just to add an explanation point to his point.

This all looked as if it was planned, because they each made their own noise separately. This was going to be a long night, but not that long as this would be my last night.

Shortly after I adjusted to the noises, I was soon asleep.

# Chapter 24

For the first time in many weeks, since I first showed up in-country, I woke up on my own. No one was getting me up for a watch that I was not standing. The loud speaker shouting, "Reveille, reveille, all hands reveille. Sweepers man your brooms. The smoking lamp is lit. All hands must turn too. Reveille, reveille," was not going off inches from my face. Mr. Circumcised man was not pointing at me, nor was there a one legged officer looking for me.

This was a positive start and I must make it a point not to speak or make eye contact with anyone. There was not a single reason, or situation, that I could come up with to even consider playing a trick on anyone with the shower routine. I would clean up real nice like with my shit, shower, and shave and find me a bus going to the airport. Catching a flight to the Real World on the Freedom Bird would be my mission for today. Not trips to any foreign port of call. I was homeward bound.

In very short order, I was the first person on the bus that was parked out front. It was the only bus out front and the motor was running. No driver, but this just had to be the correct bus. Not a problem as I would most assuredly ask him when he arrived if this was going to the airport. Then, thinking like Dan, I best make sure that we were going to MY airport. No need to end up somewhere else and going to another somewhere else place.

Before the driver arrived, a few guys boarded and asked me where this bus was headed. I quickly responded with, "Don't know for sure. Hope it's going to Tan San Nut Air Force Base."

That seemed like a reasonable answer to me, however, they chuckled at that and made a few comments among themselves as if I was the village idiot. You know, being on a bus for a ride and not knowing for sure where it was going.

They are just ass-holes. With that in mind, I came back with, as they sat down, "Yeah, like you guys are real smart."

The shortest of the three, a little Napoleon kind of guy, looked at me as if he was looking for a good argument, responded, "What?"

Crap, just thinking about Dan had caused me to start talking like him. Oh well, here goes, besides, what was the worst that could happen to me? I could not get myself sent to hell, as I was already there, as in this little hellhole for a country, The-Nam.

"Look bud, this bus just might be going to the airport, and maybe not. You don't know any more about that than me. When the driver gets back, we'll both know. Now turn around and shut up."

Oh shit, I said all that.

He came back with, "I should come back there and kick your ass."

Without thinking this out, I responded with, "No sweat little man. Come on back right now as I won't have any time to waste when we get to the airport."

Wow, that sounded really bad. Bad, as in I was a person not to mess with. Even with there being three of them and only one little old me.

With luck in my favor, his two friends suggested to him that he just drop it. It was most apparent that I had made a stand that stood. Wow, it felt great to be a bad ass. It felt even better than they did not put me to the 'test,' on how bad they thought I was.

Before any of us could say anything else, our driver boarded the bus and announced, "Tan San Nut Air Force Base, next stop."

Looking back at what just transpired, what was it that made me respond that way? I could not blame the military, only been in a few months. I could not blame being in combat; I had only seen combat a few times. I was not a bad ass, just didn't like someone making fun of me. Whatever the reason, being a combat vet bad ass, seemed kind of cool. Kind of cool until someone decides not to take any crap from me and kicks my butt. Especially when they find out that, my combat experience was little or nothing. Being wounded was really not that big of a deal and I now had a little more respect for the one legged officer from the other day.

Right then, our driver grounded the gears so bad that it made our faces contort a little as he pulled, or jumped, from the curb. Everyone onboard was eyes-front, as they/we wanted to see what our driver would do next. It would not surprise me if he hit the curb and ran over a few bikes in the process, but he didn't. Anyway, so much for a little excitement at the start of our ride to the airport.

Yet, it didn't take very long for a little excitement to start up again to take place on the bus. What I had in front of me were two guys, two nerd white guys, that back in the states would have those plastic pocket protectors in their shirt pocket filled with pens, pencils and a slide rule. Not to forget the white medical tape keeping their coke bottle thick glasses together.

These two guys were the white equivalent to Monroe, John, Anthony, and or Marvin in their conversations. They weren't making fun of each other's girlfriend repeatedly or anything like that; they just kept talking about dumb shit.

Even with what they were saying was stupid; it was difficult not to listen in. The one guy with curly red hair, made comments like, 'what is another word for thesaurus,' 'is there another word for synonym,' 'I used to be indecisive, now I'm not sure,' and 'what if there were no hypothetical questions.'

His buddy, still wearing his hat, made similar comments, but from another angle. Statements like, 'they told me I was gullible, and I believed them,' 'my weight is perfect for my height—which varies,' 'I had amnesia once, or was it twice,' and 'is it possible to be totally partial."

Then, as if they needed to rethink what they were going to say next, the two of them took a deep breath and started back up. Only this time, they took turns trying to out do each other.

'What is a free gift, aren't all gifts free,' 'if swimming is good for your figure, then explain why we have whales,' and 'can two can live as cheaply as one, if so, only for half as long maybe.'

It was at this point that I had had about enough of them and turned my focus and attention to everything else around me but them. There was little traffic today and maybe this was because it was Sunday. The only problem with that was that I had no idea what day of the week this was. I had even forgotten the month. Crap, I could not even remember the current date. Then, I figured no sweat, as it didn't really matter. I got my ticket yesterday and I was told to report today. With that logic, I had my bases covered. If not, how would I recover from this issue? I could only act stupid a couple of times, and get away with it, not to act stupid all the time and expect to get away with it some of the time. Wow, thinking all that gave me a headache.

Well, before I could give this any additional negative thoughts, we pulled up to the terminal. For now, I was a little step closer to getting myself out of this little shitty country.

I didn't exit the bus, as quickly as before, I wanted the three guys that got on last, especially this little one, to get off first. Then no matter which direction they went, I was going to go the other. I had a little time to kill before my flight left; however, I must exchange my MPC to green backs.

Just outside the terminal, there were a couple of guys standing around with money in their hands fanned out like a deck of cards for all to see. The way they had themselves positioned out in front of the main doors to the terminal, I almost felt that I was back in Baltimore at Memorial stadium trying to get some tickets from the local ticket-scalpers to see the Colts or the Orioles play. Anytime that Johnny U called the plays, it would be a sell out crowd and the only way to get in to see the game was to get tickets from scalpers.

As I approached the one guy that was the closest, I decided not to do anything. It would most assuredly, be my luck that it would be a sting, and I'd be stung. Then I'd be thrown in the brig and end up serving my one-year, in-country tour behind bars.

I made a slight turn to by-pass this guy and as I did that, that must had caught his attention as he approached me, and said, "Come on man. You got some money. Let's do some business."

Crap and damn, damn, damn. "Nothing to trade my man. I have nothing for you. I spent it all. So be cool."

I had hoped that what I said had been enough, and naturally, it was not. He made it a point to stand in front of me, blocking my way to the terminal. Not wanting to cause a scene, and yet, wanting to get past him, I raised my voice some and said, "No way, no how, and not now."

Just as I was surprised from how I spoke earlier on the bus, I was equally surprised on how I reacted this time. And, to my astonishment, he did step aside and didn't say anything more. The other scalpers near by that had overheard me went as far as to turn away, not even wanting to make eye contact with me.

Wow, I was really pushing my luck today. Maybe it was the uniform. Yet, I must make it a point to tone down my attitude before someone tones it down for me.

Once inside the terminal, the first thing or person that I noticed was the same-same guy from before selling those free booklets. Maybe, I could tone down my attitude after I dumped on this guy, as I felt so strongly that he would deserve it. Then again, I just knew that this would be a mistake on my part and I decided to give him a free pass. I'd would surely cause a scene and by the time things got cleared up with the MP's; I'd be looking for another flight out and or I'd maybe never get to leave this place.

For now, I needed to find the information desk, not a problem to find, and I had hoped that Gunny, what's his name, would be there. He wasn't but, there was a very attractive airman, or airwoman or whatever you call a girl that was in the Air Force, at the counter. She was probably my age and she had the biggest smile that I'd ever seen on anyone. Her nametag said that her name was Patty and this Patty was most definitely someone that I could and would ask out on a date. She was hot and maybe she was so hot that some guys would come back and do a second tour just to see her again. For now, she had made my day and she had not even noticed me.

She did have a lot of hair, red hair. So much red hair, that if someone had gotten a hold of her with sheep sheers, they could make an extra large sweater from the cuttings.

She had to be the first choice for someone to man an information desk. You know, attractive, bright smile, and naturally, you would assume the skills to do her job. At least, my visit to the information desk would be a pleasurable one this time.

"Hello," I said, with a smile to match hers.

She ignored me and that caught me off guard. Naturally, I'd been ignored before and the last time that that comes to mind, was the one time that a hooker that I wanted to talk to on the corner overlooked me.

"Excuse me," I said, only this time, a little louder than my first, 'hello.'

Well, she turned and gave me a mean look that would have scared a pack of hungry wolves off a meat truck. Her smile completely disappeared off the face of the earth and I was in fear for my life of what she was going to say to me.

"What, you lost little boy," she snapped at me.

Damn, damn, damn. What the hell did I do to piss her off just now? Then, thinking quickly, I realized that I hadn't done anything in error to her, nor did I break any military rules or regulations.

I stood up straight and tall, displaying that I did not fear her, and answered, "Just checking on my flight. I need to verify that flight 1500 is still departing at 1500 today."

"Give me your fucking ticket," she snapped again at me.

This was not going well, but I was not going to back down on this one.

She looked over my ticket for a little bit, as if this was the first time that she'd ever seen one of these blue MAC tickets.

She looked at me, and asked, "Your name."

"Edwards," I answered, and decided not to say any more than that, in fear that whatever I said, that it would be the wrong thing.

"And the name on your shirt belongs to," she asked, and in doing so, she was giving me a dirty look as if no matter what I answered, it would again be the wrong thing.

However, before I could answer her, I realized that I didn't know whose name was on my shirt. Hell, this was not even my shirt and as I looked down, I was unable to read it upside down and backwards. Naturally, it was not going to be a simple name like Smith or Jones.

"Your name," she asked, again. Even with this being hard to believe, she looked even meaner than before.

Okay, not a time to panic. This was a non-sweatable situation. I came back with, "Edwards, and this is not my shirt. I got this issued to me at the Annapolis BEQ."

Well, this eased her mean looks off a little. Not much, just a little.

"Okay," she said, as she again reviewed my ticket.

"And what day is this for," she asked, and this time, it looked as if she was going to burst out with laughter, and that it would be directed at me.

This must be a trick question and I best think about this one before I answer. Well, I had thought about it too long as she asked me again, "What day is this for?"

"Today, flight 1500 at 1500," I answered, as I added in the flight number and time to save her the time of asking me anything else.

She reviewed my ticket some more. Now, this just could not be a fake ticket. No way as I got it from here, at this very desk, just yesterday.

Now her pretty smile was returning. Well, not really pretty, as it looked more, pretty-evil than a pretty-pretty.

"Right time, right flight, right place, but my man, not the right date,"

My face fell right into my, deer-in-the-headlights position.
This happened so many times to me that my face just might get
stuck in that posture.

Okay, what do I do? For one thing, I could not tell her that
she was in error because she would jump the counter and beat
the crap out of me. I could act stupid, but that would not solve
my issue. What would Dan do? Dan would be clever, but how
should I act clever?

"Well," she questioned, and was starting to look irritated.

"I was informed that my flight would be for today. This is why
I am here. If I had been given bad orders, is there a way you can
place me on a flight today?"

I made it a point to look like a person that anyone would
want to help. Not too sad looking as if I was a lost, wet, ugly dog
that needed a home. Just enough for her to show a little
compassion to a fellow comrade in arms, if you know what I mean.

"Why? Here you are with the wrong date and your name
doesn't match your shirt."

"Yes. Good point and I certainly understand why you are
thinking that way." A little pause and I added, "Like I said, I got
this shirt at the Annapolis BEQ because my uniform was bloodied
up from my injuries. As you can understand, I would be out of
uniform if I was dressed that way traveling home for my medical
leave."

Compassion slowly came over her. I was on a roll now and
the next thing I said was, "I'm in a hurry to get home to be with
my Mom before she gets notified that I was wounded. She's very
old and ill. Something like this could push her over the edge."

Damn, that sounded cool, believable, and downright, Dan-
issum.

Looking as if she was about to cry, she told me, "Let me see
what I can do."

In return, I gave her a smile that was one degree from me
tearing up.

She left her post behind the Information desk and walked a
few steps to an office door. She was only gone a few minutes.

When she returned, she informed me, "Good news Seaman. I was able to switch you to a flight that is leaving today."

"Thank you very much. And my mother thanks you," I responded, remembering not to over do it.

For the next few minutes, she spent time making notations on my ticket and in some logbook that was on her desk. I didn't really care what she was doing, just grateful that it looked to be going my way. Just give me my ticket with a flight out today and I promise that I will never return.

She finished up with what she was doing and handed me my ticket. I thanked her and thought it best not to hang around in case she decided to make a change.

After just a step or two, she called me. "Your flight leaves in a few minutes. You need to get onboard now."

She pointed to her left and explained, "You need to go that way. Hurry, you just have enough time to get onboard."

I took her advice and followed her instructions. She was most correct, as I just did make it onboard my flight before the door was closed.

I easily and quickly found my seat. It was the only open seat onboard and no sooner than I buckled up, the stewardess started in with the flight instructions.

Excitement started to build as the engines started, next stop, Clark Air force Base in the Philippines.

It just happened that we had this one guy onboard, I assumed that he was an airplane mechanic or something, as he would announce, as each engine would start.

"Engine number one is starting up," he would shout at first. Then, just after he announced, 'engine number two is starting up,' everyone was starting to pay attention and he didn't have to shout.

"Engine number three is starting up," he said, and this time, everyone that had a window seat was looking out the window as if the engines were being started by a hand crank or something, and that it would be something worth witnessing.

After much anticipation, he announced, "Engine number four is starting."

This created much cheer and excitement from everyone onboard.

With all this going on, it was not hard to be caught up in the moment. For me, I found myself looking out at the engines on my side of the aircraft eagerly expecting to see smoke exiting the engines as they start. I was a little disappointed not to see that along with an occasional backfire from the engines. You know, like there was for the bombers getting ready to bomb the shit out of Germany in WWII.

With all four engines up and running, conversations between everyone increased. Everyone except for me, as I was just excited to be going home after only a few weeks. I did not feel comfortable in letting it out that I was headed home after such a short tour. Even with me going home under medical orders, it just did not seem fair.

As I mentioned earlier, it was very easy to see the combat experience in someone's eyes. It was not the look as if they were on drugs or drunk, just the look as if they had seen Hell up close and personal like, a look commonly called "The Thousand Yard Stare." This was not a place for anyone to visit twice and God should grant special privileges to anyone that had been in combat in service of their country.

Okay, getting back now to my flight on the Freedom Bird for my ride back to the real World. We backed up away from the terminal and we backed up a long ways. I was not sure about the distance, but we moved back enough for some to make comments about it. Comments like, 'Not that way,' and, 'at this speed, I'd get credit for a second tour.'

Anyway, we did stop and after we were unhooked from the tractor and as we started forward, excitement increased ten-fold. Voices rose up and a party atmosphere was generated, as this was a little different from my last flight out of country. Naturally, my last flight out of country was not heading home and everyone onboard knew that except for me. Well, this time, I was sure that we were headed back to the states and along with everyone; I joined in with the excitement.

Moments later, we were flying down the runway and as we rotated and lifted off, the following feeling overwhelmed everyone. Feelings in one degree or another were; joy, laughter, delight, happiness, pleasure, enjoyment, elation, glee, gladness, satisfaction, cheerfulness, amusement, euphoria and much jubilation. And lets not forget the feeling of a, 'job well done.' Just the pure fact of going home after whatever time you spent in-country and that you were going home alive and by sitting in coach and not as cargo in a body bag. Well, maybe not in a body bag in the cargo hold, but in a coffin. In reality, I had no idea on how my fallen comrades were sent home.

That was such a sad thought that it almost took away the excitement of the moment. Not that I wanted to be selfish, but I was going home you know.

Conversations continued for the next few minutes until the pilot came on the intercom and announced that we were twelve miles out and no longer in Vietnam airspace. Again, the feelings in all degrees this time were of joy, laughter, delight, happiness, pleasure, enjoyment, elation, glee, gladness, satisfaction, cheerfulness, amusement, euphoria, and even much more jubilation.

I, we, were heading home. Even with home still being a few days off, I was on my way.

As time passed, so did the conversations. Some guys got into small, low volume conversations and others, simply went out like a light. Some slept so soundly that you would have thought that they were awake for their 365 days while here in-country. With nothing to talk about with anyone, I spent the next few hours or so reading the magazines that came with the aircraft. Not a very impressive magazine to review/read, just lots of little ads about things that I'd never buy and maps of the Pacific Ocean showing their routes.

Reading myself to sleep was easy as the next thing that caught my attention was what came in over the intercom.

"If everyone would please take his or her seat. We are starting our descent to Clark Air Force Base." After a second or two, "Please buckle up," was added in.

A second or two passed, we then got our final message, which was, "For those officers that need assistance in finding your seat, or on how to buckle up, please seek help from the nearest enlisted personnel."

As you can imagine, this got a round of laughter from everyone, well, almost everyone. It didn't seem very funny to the two officers that had not yet found their seats. It wasn't as if they were lost or anything, they just took their time in getting back to their seats and that gave the impression that they were lost.

To continue with their embarrassment, a few guys yelled out, "Need any help sir?"

This received even more laughter. It appeared to me that the two or so guys that were mocking these two officers, were short-timers. My guess was either that they were out of the military or that they were just about to get out as soon as they reported home or to their duty station.

Now that I was awake and alert, I hoped that something would develop with these two officers and their tormentors. However, nothing did happen and moments later, we were down and starting to exit the aircraft.

# Chapter 25

"One hour and thirty minutes. If you decide to exit the aircraft, you must be in your assigned seat in one hour and thirty minutes," explained our flight stewardess.

The way everyone stood at that exact same-same moment, you would have thought that we were at the Naval Academy preparing to sit down for a meal, or that we were members of a military drill team. So much for how good we looked, everyone still had to get out and stretch his legs. We were kind of crammed in rather tight and the only difference between this and a cattle car was that this cattle car had wings.

"One hour and thirty minutes is when we depart. We will not be taking a head count," she shouted. As for me, I will be back in just sixty minutes. No way was I going to mess this up and miss my flight out. I had enough trouble just getting this far.

Other than making a head call and splashing a little cold water on my face, there was little else to do here at Clark Air Force Base. Walking back to the plane, I noticed a long line snaking into the duty free shop.

I asked the last guy in line, "Something on sale in there?"

"You might say that," he answered without turning around. Hell, if I had answered a question like that to someone, without having first turned around to see who it was, it would have been an officer that I had forgotten to 'sir.' And of course, I would be in trouble again.

Getting back to the line that I was in, I figured that if there were a sale going on, I might want to take advantage of this. However, I did not want to be in line for something stupid. "What's the attraction," I asked.

Looking around at me as if I should have known this, he responded, "Booze. Five bottles of booze is going for just ten dollars. It's a Duty Free shop."

He quickly turned back around as if either I bored him or that he did not want to miss out if the line moved up.

Okay, I thought, I could use five bottles of booze for ten dollars, besides, who wouldn't. Then again, it would be my luck that the extra added weight of the five bottles of booze per passenger, could easily cause the plane to be much too heavy to take off. Of course, it would end up being me and my five bottles that would be ordered to get off the plane and ordered to catch the next flight.

It was not as if they would shift everyone around and have us sit in the middle of the aircraft to better place the weight for take off. As if I had nothing else to think about, I figured that if I was not removed from the flight, after being classified as 'extra weight,' I did not think that I had enough room to store the five bottles under my seat, or in the overhead compartment. No way did I want to have five bottles of booze sitting in my lap all the way across the Pacific Ocean.

The line moved up and I had to decide weather to say in line or get out. Dan would have stayed in line and taken advantage of this good deal and even Billy-Bob, would have gotten himself a few bottles. Hell, even Cherry Benny E. Lee would not pass us this great deal. Okay, I just talked myself into staying in line and getting myself some liquor.

The line did not move very fast and now I had time to have some second thoughts to my latest adventure. A good deal, yes. Did I really need that much liquor, no, I did not. Should I stay in line . . . yes and no.

Lets see how many reasons I could come up with not to purchase the booze. Storage, was there enough storage space for my booze on the plane? Need, do I really need this stuff. Hell, I was only nineteen and I was a beer drinker. Legally, would I be allowed to transport this stuff around? The drinking age in Maryland was 21 and if a cop were to stop and question me, he'd take it from me. Damn, I might not even get past customs with all this booze. I could have stayed in this line for a long time, spent ten dollars, and had miserable seating accommodations on a 12-hour flight just to hand it off to some law official.

The longer I took to decide my fate, the closer I got to the counter. By the time I had decided not to get the booze, I had already purchased my five bottles.

"Ten dollars," the sales lady said as she boxed my five bottles. I had one bottle of Jamison, one bottle of VO, two bottles of Seagram 7, and a bottle of Canadian Club. I assumed that I got a good deal, but then again, I did not know for sure. This was the first time that I had ever legally paid for booze as I reminded myself that I was only nineteen years old.

My bottles were boxed up neatly and securely into a cardboard box that was not very big, and I believed that it would fit under my seat. I was pleased with the way they were boxed and very happy that I was not carded.

In no time at all, we were airborne and on our way to Hawaii and my box of booze did fit nicely under my seat.

I could hear a couple of guys in front of me talking about this being their R&R and that they were meeting their wives or girlfriends in Hawaii. This seemed sort of odd to be in combat one day, travel the next day just to meet up with your love one on the third day. Not very much time to adjust from one life style to the other. Then, seven days and six nights later, you have one travel day then you were back in combat. I wondered how many people this procedure screwed up?

About half way across the Pacific to Hawaii, two guys across from me had opened their boxes and had started to sample their selection. They were clandestine at first. You know, sneaking a little swallow every now and then while trying not to have the flight stewardess catch them in the act.

Three guys behind me ordered some 7Up and asked that the cups be only half-full. I was not much of a whiskey drinker, but I could tell where this was going. As if an order was given, almost everyone on my flight at the same time started to sample his booze and order 7Up. At first, guys would look around as if what they were doing was wrong. However, after a few drinks go by, they apparently did not care.

I did over hear one guy say, "What? What are they going to do? Send me to Vietnam. I've already been to Vietnam. Hell, it don't mean nothin. Don't mean nothin anymore."

For that statement, what he got was total agreement from everyone around him. Even the few officers that were onboard agreed with him. They had also started to sample some of their own booze. It was at this point that bottles were being switched around. They were sold, bartered for, promises made with IOU's as collateral, and heavy duty trading with some bottles of vodka going for two and three bottles of something else. Then as the bottles started to run dry, the requests on certain bands of booze were in even higher demand.

My only concern right now was that the pilots were not in this same-same frame of mind and that they were not drinking. Hell, someone had to be sober and fly the plane. As for me, I kept my five bottles closed. They might even be more valuable after we leave Hawaii for the final leg to Travis AFB in California.

Well, things calmed down after a little while as the passengers ran out of booze, passed out, or simply took naps or passed out. Speaking of naps, that was just what I did.

An unknown time later, I was awakened by the sounds of everyone cheering and shouting. It was hard to tell immediately if they were cheering because we had taken off from Saigon, landed stateside, or that we were about to crash. Better yet, there were naked girls running up and down the aisle and that I should join in with this celebration.

Disappointed that there were no nude women running around, I then looked out the window to see if I could find the horizon, and if it was vertical or horizontal. If the horizon was vertical and we were going down fast, then we were going to die soon. However, it was horizontal, as in straight and level, then that was cool.

I was under the impression that life was good because as we were not going to crash, until I noticed that I could see Diamond Head off in the distance and fading away. Damn, damn, damn. I had gone and slept through the landing and take off from Hawaii.

Damn, damn, damn. I had been denied the hula girl routine once again. If I was to write a book about my time overseas, I will most certainly leave this part out. With that note, I decided not to ask anyone if there were any hula girls giving out lei's. There was no need to have it rubbed in, as I felt bad enough as it was.

Instead of asking about that, I simply looked around the aircraft to try and pick up on why everyone was so happy, my initial guess was because we had taken off and that our next stop was California. Now this seemed like a good scenario until I noticed that everyone, as in everyone but me, had a lei. Even the flight stewards had one on. Hell, I'd bet that the pilot, co-pilot, and the flight engineer had one on also. Damn, everyone but me had one and everyone was happy, except for me.

How will I ever explain this to my mother that I had passed through Hawaii, twice, and didn't get a lei. No problem, I just won't mention it and with luck, no one will ask me.

Before I could feel bad for myself, the guy sitting next to me asked for the time. It was a simple enough request, I looked at my watch and said, "6:15."

"AM or PM," he asked.

Hell, I did not know. "Don't know," I responded.

"Is this Wednesday or Thursday," he asked this time.

"Wednesday," I responded, and believed that I was right. We've only been gone a dozen or so hours and no way did I sleep and miss a whole day. A whole layover at Hawaii maybe, but not a whole day.

He chuckled and said, "You had slept through a couple of time changes and even the International Time Zone. The captain would tell us every time that we passed through a time zone, but

I failed to keep up. I thought that maybe you knew the current time and date."

"Sorry. I am just going to wait for the announcement at the end of our flight," I said, and getting in return, the deer-in-the-headlights look from him.

"Come on guy," I started to explain, because I knew about this part. "You know, the one where the captain would announce the time and weather conditions of the city where we are landing?"

The guy sitting on the aisle seat that had heard our conversation, well, he quickly added, "Announcements. How would you know anything about no announcements?"

We looked at him as if relaying our thoughts of, 'what are you talking about?'

In his defense, he quickly answered back to the guy next to me, as he ignored me, and he said, "Don't you remember? Didn't your buddy miss out on the landing in Hawaii and the take off? Didn't he miss out on all the previous time zone announcements? And you still want to ask him the time?"

Crap I thought. I didn't know that it was all that hard to explain to someone that I didn't have the correct time and date. What I would like to have right now was that little kid that had watches up both his arms. Ladies and men's watches and I would bet that all of them had a different time so that everyone would be happy.

So, as those two made little rude comments between themselves, I closed my eyes and got comfortable. Giving the suggestion that I would rather take a nap and not listen in on what all they had to say to each other.

I must have fallen asleep again as I was wakened by the two guys that were sitting next to me. The one next to me had leaned over me looking out the window. I must have missed something because I asked, "What did I miss?"

"An aircraft carrier, we just passed over an aircraft carrier," explained the guy sitting next to me.

"It was cool, we even passed over a whole fleet of other ships," added in the guy that was in the aisle seat. "I saw it also."

The guy sitting next to me then said, "The captain came on the intercom and said that we could see a whole mess of boats just below us. I wish he would turn around and go by them again."

Damn, damn, damn. The only way that I was ever going to see an aircraft carrier was for me to go out, buy a model kit, and build me one. I can't believe that I missed it.

I asked the two guys, "Do you know which carrier that was?" I really wanted to know.

They both shook their heads as the guy on the aisle seat said, "It didn't matter. A carrier was a carrier. Shit man, you missed it."

Crap, if I ever do write a book, I would leave this part out, as I was a little embarrassed to tell anyone about this. And, add to that thought, if I was to leave out half of this stuff that I wanted to leave out, and then there would be nothing left to write about. And, to add to the added, if I was to write a book, this would be the last chapter. Well, maybe, next to the last chapter. I still must land in the U. S. of A. and make it home. I didn't believe that I would ever have this much excitement at any other duty station to which I may get assigned.

Still with sometime to kill, taking a nap was the easiest thing to do. I did not have anything to read and talking with these two would not be very entertaining at all. Well, maybe a little entertaining, and I would be the entertainment. Without delay, I was soon into something like a coma.

Before long, there was more screaming. Screaming as I had never heard before. As I rubbed my eyes, I asked the guy sitting next to me, "What did I miss this time?"

"The announcement," he answered, leaving out the most important part, the announcement.

His buddy, the guy sitting next to the aisle piped in and said, "It was announced, that Travis Air Force Base was only thirty minutes away."

Well, I could not help myself, I yelled out a yell that was rather loud. It was louder than normal, especially with me being the only one yelling. Now this time, instead of me checking out everyone that was on the plane, everyone on the plane was checking me out. They must have been thinking that I was not someone to share a cab.

Didn't care, didn't care at all. I was on my way home. And then I remembered that they too were on their way home and I'd bet that almost all of them had already put in a complete tour, if not, then a couple of tours like Dan.

I was now awake for the announcements that followed every five minutes. It was kind of cool with the pilot giving us a countdown. Each time he said something, we all cheered, at least this time, I was current with what was going on. On his, 'ten minute,' announcement, he did announce the date and time with the weather forecast.

"Tuesday, the 13th. 12:35 pm, local time and it was a cool 84 degrees with sunny skies."

Our plane landed at Travis Air Force Base in California and there was nothing but yelling, screaming, high fives, knuckle-knocking, and finger-grabbing between everyone. Well, the knuckle-knocking and finger-grabbing was only between the colored guys. If I was going to stay in the military, I must learn how to do that.

I looked outside my window to take in the beauty of the good old U. S. of A. The only thing that I noticed right away over anything else, was that everything wasn't all brown and green. Hell, I was just thrilled to be back on American soil and all that, but I just could not get it out of my mind that the only thing I noticed was all the colors. There were plenty of blues, reds, and yellows. Along with some colors that only girls knew how to pronounce. This exciting view reminded me about the time that my parents got their first color TV. Before then, everything was black and gray. All shades of black and gray, but black and gray just the same.

Anyway, I was home and I was delighted, excited, wound-up, and keyed-up. More words came to mind like overjoyed, pleased, tickled, elated, thrilled, jubilant, and very energized. If I had thought up of any more words, I would have gladly added some more pages to this book.

Getting off the plane was smooth, orderly, and very military like. The flag officers got off first and that was followed by the junior officers with us enlisted personnel taking up the rear. This was nothing like the aircraft departure that I experienced when I arrived in Saigon.

The only thing that held up the line exiting the aircraft was that most everyone had to stop and kiss the tarmac. As for me, I didn't feel like bending over to kiss anything unless it was a beautiful girl. So for now, I just worked my way back to the rear of the aircraft as I figured that I might as well be the first one to retrieve my bag as the luggage gets thrown off the plane. As I waited, I noticed that I was the only one back here waiting for our bags. I thought to myself, checkout all the idiots. They'll be back here soon to get their things. As for me, I was cool because I had my act together. It's cool being cool and I liked being cool.

I heard a noise behind me and as I turned, I saw that it was a military police jeep. The one guard was looking at me, giving me the 'evil-eye,' as if I was about to do something wrong. Before I could respond to his 'evil-eye' on me, he said, "You'll get your bags inside the terminal, like everyone else. No special treatment just because you were in Nam."

Then in a low voice, apparently he was just talking to himself in a whisper and could not do it like me, I heard him say, "Dumb ass marine. Not even enough common sense to know how to get their own luggage. What an idiot."

That was not exactly the welcome home treatment from the war that I expected, especially from a military brother at arms. I could only respond with, "I didn't know. No sweat."

So, for now, I headed on towards the terminal. Only this time, instead of being at the head of the line, I was at the end. Not the way to start things out.

At the luggage carrousel, I realized that I didn't have any luggage to pick up. I walked away and trying not to be noticed that I didn't any luggage. If anyone were to ask, I'd just explain that I decided to mail my sea bag home instead of carrying it around across half the world.

I headed out to see if there were any buses heading towards the San Francisco Airport. With luck finally on my side, there was a bus waiting for us and it was going to the airport. I climbed onboard and headed for a window seat. This time, I wanted a window seat that was not barred up with screen mesh. I wasn't expecting anyone to be throwing anything onto the bus now that I was back in the states. There was no war going on here. This was America, the land of the free, home of the brave, and no VC to worry about.

However, after settling into my seat, I looked out my window and could not believe that the windows were indeed barred. This cannot be. I had to reach out and grab at the screen just to touch it and make sure that I wasn't seeing things. Damn, it was real.

At first, I was going to give this a lot of thought; however, now that I was back in the states, I should spend my time thinking about dating, driving fast, and getting drunk. Whether the bus had screens or not should be of little concern to me. Yet, I did look behind the bus to see if there was a jeep giving us an armed escort and saw that there wasn't. The only thing behind my bus was a second and third bus. However, after closer examination, I did see four guys in a dark sedan as if they were our bodyguards parked behind the third bus. I didn't know why, but there they were.

So for now, I was just going to sit back and close my eyes. I was almost home and I might as well be rested up before I go partying. Once the bus was loaded, it pulled away moments later and we soon were stopped at the main gate. We were unable to exit the base because of all the demonstrators blocking our path. This was not good and I wondered what they were demonstrating against, or for today. Everyone looked too young to be unhappy union workers on strike for whatever reason union workers go on strike for.

Right then, a head of lettuce smashed into the screen across from me sending shredded lettuce throughout the bus. Lucky for me, I was not in the path of the lettuce spray. Okay, I understand now why we have the screens, but why the demonstrators? Are these unhappy farmers or something?

I leaned a little closer to the window on the other side of the bus because I wanted to hear what they were chanting. To my surprise, they were pointing and calling everyone on the bus a baby killer. Damn, damn, damn, this was not the welcome home celebration that I was expecting. With this welcome home treatment, you would of have thought that I pulled the sneak attack on Pearl Harbor or shot both Lincoln and Kennedy. But, no sweat, my parents will be glad to see me and proud that I did my part.

After a few minutes, the military police did clear us a path and we were on our way. I looked back at the demonstrators as we passed them and I still could not believe my eyes. They were mad at me?

For the next few miles, instead of looking around and enjoying the beautiful California countryside, most everyone onboard the bus had something to say about the demonstrators. Then, the conversations turned to the war and who did what, while they were there. For example, sitting in front of me were two guys slowly getting into an argument about which military service was the most capable during a military emergency. If you were to add in some name calling, negative comments about someone's girlfriend or mother, along with calling each other a nigger, it could have been Monroe, or Prez, along with his brothers John, Anthony, and Marvin carrying on one of their typical conversation.

The one guy, sitting in front of me, right hand side, said, "The Air Force has the most intelligent enlisted personnel of all the armed forces."

He said this with much enthusiasm, and he made it most apparent that he was in the Air Force and very proud of it. The guy sitting next to him that he was having this conversation with, was an army guy, and he responded with, "What makes you think that the Army doesn't have any smart guys."

"Okay, let's take the Army, for instance," the Air Force guy said after he turned to face the Army guy. "When the shit hits the fan, you Army guys get wakened up by your Sergeant. You then grab a set of BDUs out of your foot locker, you get dressed, run down to the chow-hall for a breakfast on the run, then jump in your tank. A minute later, your Sergeant gives you a big salute, and says, 'Give'm Hell. Go Army.'"

Before the Army guy could respond, a guy that was sitting in front of them turned around and stated, "I'm a marine. Your Air Force guys are in no way, smarter than a marine is. What about me? I'm a smart Marine."

Even with a mean look from this Marine, and apparently not fearing for his life, this Air Force dude jumped right back on this Marine and added, "Now, for you marines, when the shit hits the fan, you Marines are kicked out of your beds by your own Sergeant. You then put on a muddy set of BDUs because you just got back in from the field three hours before. You get no breakfast, but instead you run out and form up with your rifle. A little while later, your Platoon Leader comes out and says, 'Give'm Hell Marines!'"

Well, now there are two guys pissed at this Air Force Jerk. I might as well join in to make it three against one. Besides, I like those odds and with everyone white, I won't have to worry about messing up and saying the wrong thing.

I tapped this Air Force dude on his shoulder and said, with boldness, because I had graduated high school and had survived The-Nam, "What about us Navy guys? You think that all you Air Force dudes are special?"

"Navy," he answered, all the while looking down and shaking his head from side to side as if it was disgusting for him just to say, 'Navy.'

"Navy guys," he continued, "when the shit hits the fan, you Sailor boys are probably eating breakfast in the mess hall. You get up and walk the 20 or so feet to your battle station, carrying with you extra pastries that you stuck in your pocket as you left. So there you sit, in the middle of the ocean, with nowhere to run. Your Captain comes on the 1MC and says, 'Give'm Hell!'"

Damn, I did not have a comeback for this guy. Now, the Marine sitting in front of him spoke up and said, "Okay Mr. Air Force. Are you saying that you Air Force guys have it so great that shit for you guys never hits the fan?"

Sitting back, crossing his leg, and holding his chin up with his left hand, Mr. Air Force spoke up and said, "We have a fan, and at times, the shit does hit our fan. But, as I will explain, it ain't that big a deal."

"Just tell us already," I snapped at him, as a parent would to a child that was not forthcoming with an answer.

"When the shit hits the fan," Mr. Air Force started, "we handle it a little different."

"And," I said, only this time, I made a face suggesting that he move along with this story. He was taking too much time with this and this was not a very long bus ride.

The Marine spoke up with his two cents, "This guy has nothing to add. Nothing worth listening to anyway."

Right behind this comment, the Army guy stepped in and inserted, "Are there any Air Force guys stationed in The-Nam? Don't these guys live in Guam and Thailand?"

Now it was my turn to add in one more item, because of the four of us, he was the only one not from The-Nam. I figured that out because he was not wearing a Nam issue type uniform and that he did not have a tan. You see, everyone coming home from The-Nam had a tan. Hell, it was summer there all year long and there was no way you did not get a tan after a yearlong summer.

"It starts off with a phone call from the duty officer to me at my off-base housing," he continued with his, better than thou attitude. "I get up, shower, shave, and put on a fresh uniform that I just picked up from the cleaners the day before. I jump into my car, and make a stop at Howard Johnson for breakfast. Once I arrive at work, I sign in on the duty roster and proceed to my F-4 Phantom. After thirty minutes of pre-flight, I sign off on a few forms. Pretty soon, the pilot arrives, gets in, straps into his plane, and starts the engines. I stand at attention, salute the pilot and I tell him, 'Give'm Hell, Sir!'"

"Let me guess," the Marine said to the Air Force jerk after he looked at the Army guy and me. "You've never been to The-Nam have you?"

"No need to. I know plenty of guys that have been there and back," he answered, giving us the impression that a tour in Nam isn't all that bad.

The Army guy spoke up and asked the Marine, "I notice that when you boarded the bus, that you had a limp. You got hurt in The-Nam?"

"Yes," the Marine replied as he sucked in his stomach and stuck out his chest. In a way, it seemed odd for someone who had been wounded to be so proud, but he was a Marine and Marines are very proud to be a Marine.

"Me too," the Army guy added as he turned toward me. "I was wounded twice."

Before the Air Force guy could respond to our unity, I added in my present medical condition. "Me too. In fact, I'm on my way home now for thirty days medical leave."

Well now, this Air Force guy had started out joking with us with the intention of starting in on the teasing that goes on between all the military services and he came up short because, three out of the four of us have been wounded. Not to mention that we had served in The-Nam.

Wanting to ease things out between us, and to save face, the Air Force guy said, with a believable mannerism of sadness, "Just trying to razz you guys. Didn't know that you guys just came back from Vietnam."

For the next few moments, it was very uncomfortable for the four of us. In one way, I wanted to jump in this guys face for putting us down and then again, maybe he did make an honest mistake.

Well, the Marine was not going to show any mercy, he informed him, "Listen up ass-hole. When the shit hits the fan, Marines are there. Of course, it's the Navy that gets us there and then it's the Army that comes in to replace us after we kick ass."

Getting in on this, the Army guy added in, "And, when you Air Force guys need a target to hit, it's the U.S. Army that points it out to you."

The Air Force guy looked at the Army guy as he continued with, "And you know that when we point out a target for you guys at ten thousand feet, we are there, down on the ground with our face in the dirt."

Wanting to join in with the ribbing, I added, "The reason that the Navy takes the Marines to where they must go is because they'd get lost without us."

The Marine appeared to have enjoyed that remark; however, I guessed that he had heard that one before.

For now, the Air Force guy appeared to have relaxed a little as the Marine and I made a few jabs at each other. All in fun, as for me, not to get him ticked off. So, at least for now, he, the Air Force guy, wasn't the center of negative attention or the avenue of any frustrations that he may have created among us. Then, as if he had this timed for himself, two blonds pulled up beside our bus that caught everyone's attention. They were riding in a bright red GTO. A bright red GTO convertible. A bright red GTO convertible with the top down. Wow, welcome home I thought.

As you could imagine, there were all kinds of comments from the guys on the bus to these girls. Moreover, to make it more entertaining, the girls seemed to enjoy the attention as they maintain pace with the bus. In just a manner of a few seconds, everyone on the bus was on the port side.

Listen to me, 'port side.' Damn Charles, you're on a bus and not some riverboat going down the Mekong Delta looking for VC. Okay, everyone had moved over to the driver's side of the bus. With no officers onboard and the driver just an E3, no one was in charge and it was every man for himself to get a good window view anticipating that the girl riding shotgun would lift up her shirt and show us her boobs. At least, that was what some of the guys were yelling for her to do.

All kinds of comments were yelled at these two girls and it was not important if they were good looking or not. Just the fact that they were girls, round eyed girls, and maybe, just maybe the thought that we might see a little skin had given them the total attention from everyone onboard. Even the driver had a difficult time keeping in his lane as he was spending more time looking in his side mirror as not to miss out on anything.

Some of the remarks, facial expressions, and hand jesters were not very appropriate. Even to where some of them were down right nasty. Yet, no one said anything to anyone to curb or tone-down on what was being said. I was just happy that my little sister was not in the car. Then I would have said something.

It was very apparent that these girls seemed to enjoy the attention and that just egged the guys on even more. As for me, I was pleased with watching the way everyone was acting. From my observations, it looked as if the married guys were just looking and not making any comments. The guys that had girlfriends back home were making remarks that were not too bad. The sort of things that you would not mind them yelling at your sister. However, then you had the Rednecks slash White Trash group of guys.

I then remembered what Dan had said about Rednecks the first time that they were away from home. He said, 'this most assuredly may be the first time that they have seen girls that they were not related to.' That just might explain why they seemed so excited and that excitement grew as these two girls gave them the attention they wanted.

It was also apparent to me that the way and what all they were yelling at these two girls, well, they did not know how to pick up girls. At least, not the kind of girls that you would want to pick up anyway. Unless, of course, you were a Redneck the first time away from home and that you wanted to bring home a girl that you weren't related to just to add something new to the gene pool in your trailer park.

This one Redneck, tall, skinny, with one upper tooth, two lower with one rotten on the one side along with a crappy mustache, well, he was yelling at the girl-riding shotgun as if he was a prized bull or something. Comments like, 'My sex is so good that I sometimes yell out my own name,' and my favorite, 'Yeah girl, I do smoke after sex, I smoke for about two days until the fire goes out.'

These two girls were not impressed with him, or with what he had to say. If my little sister even considered dating something like that, I would have to step in and have her locked up. Then again, if they dated and then got married, he would probably want livestock for a wedding gift. Now there was a gross thought as Rednecks probably had sex with their livestock. Then, not wanting not to injure themselves, they would paint a big 'X' on the backsides of the ones that kicked.

Damn, I needed to stop thinking about these guy as I was getting a little carried away with them and their activities behind their house trailers at night. I was starting to sound like Dan. Not a good thing.

Anyway, this went on for a little while longer before the girls became bored, speeded up, and continued on their way. As they pulled away, the yells, facial expressions, and hand signals became extremely rude and in many ways, more disgusting. The screens on this bus apparently had another purpose, to keep the Rednecks onboard and away from the general public like wild animals at a zoo. Yet, this little show that the Rednecks had performed with no class what so ever, was about to continue as each of them tried to out do the other with their wild stories of lovemaking behind the many barns and sheds on their farms back home.

Anyway, forty-five minutes later, we arrived at the San Francisco Airport and a few demonstrators were waiting for us. They seemed ready and prepared to greet us before we arrived. One would have thought that they had someone up on the roof to announce our arrival. You know, "Here comes the green military bus filled with baby killers."

As we pulled up, we could hear them yelling almost the same things that they yelled at us at Travis. At least they didn't throw anything at us or block the road this time. Not yet anyway, and I was very happy that my parents were not here to greet me and see all this stuff. Wow, my fellow Americans were acting this way and here I was, doing my patriotic duty for God and country.

If I had my way, I'd pack them all on this bus and ship them all to North Vietnam. Let them try and do a peaceful demonstration in the capital city of Hanoi and block the arrival of new American

POW's being locked up in the Hanoi Hilton to be tortured for years to come.

At the terminal as we got off the bus, the crowd approached us and they seemed to single out anyone that was dressed in utility greens, like myself and were ignoring the ones in their dress uniforms. I assumed that they knew that the ones in their dress uniforms had not just arrived from Vietnam.

A couple of guys held up their fists to me as other just gave me the finger. I did not know why, but I was giving them a dirty look trying to suggest that I was not someone to mess with. Naturally, it was helpful that I was tall and my boot gave me another inch or two in height to 6-4 or 6-5.

For the first time in my life, I had an urge to, kick-ass, anyone that got to close to me. With the crowd being half girls and half guys, I hoped that it would be a guy and not a girl that got in my face. I was mad enough to hit a girl, but had enough sense not to and wished that I was not put in that situation. Another reason that I was pleased that my parents were not here.

There were no demonstrators inside the terminal and I only had to focus my time on looking around for where I was to go next. Right then, I heard someone call out my name. "Edwards. You Edwards?" Damn, I would have loved it if that had been the voice of a few young ladies yelling out my name. But nope, just some Navy Lieutenant.

"Yes sir," I replied, thinking that maybe I was going to get another medal for coming home or from surviving the bus ride from Travis Air Force Base.

"Your orders," he said, as he handed me a large envelope and pointed to something for me to sign on his clipboard.

"Me," I questioned.

Looking at me as if I was giving him a hard time on purpose, he answered, "If you are Edwards, then sign here. Is there a problem with that Seaman Edwards?"

"No sir. No problem sir," I answered, and I quickly grabbed the clipboard. I signed on the dotted line after placing my orders under my arm.

Before I could ask the Lieutenant anything, or even verify that I was the Edwards that he wanted, he retrieved the clipboard and quickly turned and headed away. It was so quick in fact, that I thought that maybe he had bad news for me. Bad news, as if he did not want to be around to answer any of my questions. Hell, if I would have been a civilian, it could be said that I was just 'served.'

I stepped aside and stood next to the wall to get out of everyone's way that entered the terminal behind me. I took a deep breath and opened my orders. With a second deep breath, I read my orders.

"Oh my," I thought to myself, "Can this be true?"

# GLOSSARY

| | |
|---|---|
| A TEAMS | 12-man Green Beret unit. |
| AFB | Air Force Base. |
| AFT | directional—in, at, toward, or close to the back or STERN of a BOAT or SHIP. |
| AFTERDECK | the STERN or AFT open area of a SHIP, also called the FANTAIL. |
| AGENT ORANGE | one of several defoliants (herbicides) containing trace amounts of a toxic contaminant, TCDD (dioxin). Defoliants were used to kill vast areas of jungle growth. |
| AHC | Assault Helicopter Company (HUEYS). |
| AHOY | traditional greeting for hailing other vessels, originally a Viking battle cry. |
| AK-47 | basic infantry weapon of the NVA and VC |
| ALPHA BOAT | Assault Support Patrol Boat (ASBP). A light, fast, shallow draft boat designed specifically to provide close support to Riverine infantry. Armament consisted of machine guns (M-60 and .50 cal.), plus whatever the boat crew could scrounge. |
| AMF | literally, "Adios, Mother Fucker." |
| AMMO | ammunition. |

| | |
|---|---|
| AMNESTY BOX | a bright blue box made of solid steel shaped like a freestanding US Postal box but about half again as high, twice as deep, and maybe four times as wide. It stood in front of the customs line so you could dump any contraband (drugs, weapons, porno magazines, whatever) no questions asked, before going through customs. |
| AO DAI | traditional slit skirt and trousers worn by Vietnamese women. |
| ARL | Repair Ship Light. |
| ARVN | Army of the Republic of Vietnam. |
| ASAP | (A-sap) As Soon As Possible. |
| ASBP | Assault Support Patrol Boat—see ALPHA BOAT. |
| ATC | Armored Troop Carrier—see TANGO BOAT. |
| ATCH | Armored Troop Carrier Helicopter—see TANGO BOAT. |
| AWOL | Absent Without Official Leave. |
| BAHT | Thai unit of currency. |
| BEQ | Bachelor Enlisted Quarters. In Saigon, everyone stayed at the Annapolis BEQ. |
| BID BOAT | any boat patrolling around an anchored ship on the rivers. |
| BILGES | the rounded portion of a ship's hull, forming a transition between the bottom and the sides. The lowest inner part of a ship's hull. |
| BITTS | tie-down points on a SHIP or BOAT that provide places for mooring lines to attach the SHIP or BOAT to the pier. |
| BLUE LINE | a river on a map. |
| BOAT | a relatively small; usually open craft of a size that might be carried aboard a ship. An inland vessel of any size. |

| | |
|---|---|
| BOAT CAPTAIN | usually a First Class or Chief Petty Officer in command of a BOAT. i.e. TANGO or ALPHA BOATS, etc. |
| BOATSWAIN | an enlisted rating, running from Boatswain's striker (E-2) through Master Chief and then into Warrant Officers. A deck crewmember. |
| BODY BAGS | plastic bags used for retrieval of bodies on the battlefield. |
| BODY COUNT | number of enemy killed, wounded, or captured during an operation. Used by Saigon and Washington as a means of measuring progress of the war. |
| BOHICA | short for "Bend Over, Here It Comes Again." Usually describing another undesirable assignment. |
| BOOBY TRAP | explosive charge hidden in a harmless object, which explodes on contact. |
| BOOKOO | Vietnamese/French term for "many," or "lots of . . ." |
| BOOM-BOOM | term used by Vietnamese prostitutes in selling their product. |
| BOONDOCKS | expression for the jungle, or any remote area away from a base camp or city, sometimes used to refer to any area in Vietnam. Also knows as BOONIES and BRUSH |
| BOONDOGGLE | any military operation that has not been completely thought out. An operation that is considered ridiculous. |
| BOONIES | expression for the jungle, or any remote area away from a base camp or city, sometimes used to refer to any area in Vietnam. Also knows as BOONDOCKS and BRUSH. |
| BOOT | negative common name for anyone recently out of BOOT CAMP. |

| | |
|---|---|
| BOOT CAMP | initial training for anyone in the military. |
| BOQ | Bachelor Officer's Quarters. |
| BOUNCING BETTY | explosive propelled upward about four feet into the air and then detonates. |
| BOW | directional—in, at, toward, or close to the front of a BOAT or SHIP. |
| BREAK SQUELCH | to send a "click-hiss" signal on a radio by depressing the push-to-talk button without speaking. |
| BRUSH | expression for the jungle, or any remote area away from a base camp or city, sometimes used to refer to any area in Vietnam. Also knows as BOONIES and BOONDOCKS. |
| BUAER | Bureau of Aeronautics. |
| BULKHEAD | one of the upright partitions dividing a ship into compartments and serving to add structural rigidity and to prevent the spread of leakage or fire. A partition or wall serving a similar purpose in a vehicle, such as an aircraft or spacecraft. |
| BUNAV | Bureau of Navigation. |
| BUNO | Bureau of Numbers. |
| BUOY | a floating object moored to the bottom, to mark a channel or to point out the position of something beneath the water, as an anchor, shoal, rock, etc. |
| BUPERS | Bureau of Naval Personnel in Washington, DC. |
| BUWEPS | Bureau of Naval Weapons. |
| C-130's C-130 | Lockheed Hercules 4 engine, high wing cargo plane with a rear loading door. |
| CAO BOIS (COWBOYS) | term referred to criminals of SAIGON who rode motorcycles. |
| CAPTAIN'S MAST | military trial usually tried on naval ships by the CO. |

| | |
|---|---|
| CCB | Command & Control Boat. A converted landing craft of the MONITOR class Riverine boat, packed with radios, designed for forward command and communications. |
| CHARLIE | Vietcong—short for the phonetic representation Victor Charlie. |
| CHARLIE BOAT | see CCB. |
| CHECK-IT-OUT | a common slang as ubiquitous as "okay," meaning to have a close look at something or someone. |
| CHERRY | a new troop replacement. Someone fresh out of BOOT CAMP. |
| CHERRY BOY | term given to anybody still a virgin. |
| CHEWING THE FAT | "God made the vittles, but the devil made the cook," was a popular saying used by seafaring men in the 19th century when salted beef was staple diet aboard ship. This tough cured beef, suitable only for long voyages when nothing else was cheap or would keep as well (remember, there was no refrigeration), required prolonged chewing to make it edible. Men often chewed one chunk for hours, just as it were chewing gum and referred to this practice as "chewing the fat." |
| CHICKEN PLATE | chest protector (body armor) worn by helicopter gunners. |
| CHIEF | Chief Petty Office in the Navy. E7, E8, and E9. An enlisted rank that is above Petty Officer First Class. |
| CHINOOK | the CH-47 cargo helicopter, also called "SHIT-HOOK." |
| CHIT | a signed voucher, short letter, note; a written message or memorandum; a certificate given as a pass, permission, or the like. |

| | |
|---|---|
| CHOKE | peanut butter. |
| CHOPPER | helicopter. |
| CHURCH KEY | bottle opener. |
| CIB | Combat Infantry Badge is awarded for actual time in combat. |
| CINC | Commander in Chief |
| CINCLANTFLT | Commander in Chief, U.S. Atlantic Fleet |
| CLAYMORE | a popular fan-shaped antipersonnel land mine. An unorthodox use—the explosive burned with intense heat, and a small amount of explosive could quickly heat a can of C-RATIONS. The method became one of the most popular field stoves in the war. |
| CNO | Chief of Navy Operations. |
| CO | Commanding Officer. |
| COASTIES | nickname used to identify the US Coast Guard servicemen. |
| COBRA | the AH-1G "attack helicopter." Nicknamed by some the "Shark" or "Snake." Most of the COBRAS were painted with eyes and big, scary teeth like a shark for psychological impact. |
| CO-CONG | female Vietcong. |
| COMIC BOOKS | military maps or COMIC BOOKS. |
| COMM | Communications. |
| COMNAVFORV | Commander Naval Forced Vietnam |
| CONCUSSION GRENADE—an explosive device thrown in the water to keep away swimmer or SAPPERS. Attachment W. | |
| CONTACT | condition of being in CONTACT with the enemy, a FIREFIGHT, also "IN THE SHIT." |
| CONUS | continental US |
| COOK-OFF | a situation where an automatic weapon has fired so many rounds that the heat |

has built up enough in the weapon to set off the remaining rounds without using the trigger mechanism.

COXSWAIN     generally a BOATSWAIN'S MATE in charge of steering and/or directing the crew of a BOAT. A boat is defined as a vessel smaller than a SHIP.

CP     Command Post.

C-RATIONS     canned meals used in military operations. Also, know as C-RATS.

CREW CHIEF     crewmember that maintains an aircraft.

CUP OF JOE     Josephus Daniels was appointed Secretary of the Navy by President Woodrow Wilson in 1913. Among his reforms of the Navy was the abolishment of the officers' wine mess. From that time on, the strongest drink aboard Navy ships could only be coffee and over the years, a cup of coffee became known as "a CUP OF JOE."

CYA     Cover Your Ass.

CYCLICAL RATE     in machine guns, the number of rounds fired in one minute.

CYCLO     a three-wheel passenger vehicle powered by a human on a bicycle.

DAP     a stylized, ritualized manner of shaking hands, started by colored American troops consisting of knuckle-knocking and finger-grabbing.

DCNO     Deputy Chief of Naval Operations.

DEEP-SHIT     the worst possible position, such as being nearly overrun. See SHIT.

DEROS     Date Eligible for Return from OverSeas, a person's tour was to end.

DEVIL TO PAY     today the expression "DEVIL TO PAY" was used primarily to describe having an unpleasant result from some action that has been taken, as in someone has done something they should not have, and, as a result, "there will be the DEVIL TO PAY." Originally, this expression described one of the unpleasant tasks aboard a wooden ship. The "devil" was the wooden ship's longest seam in the hull. Caulking was done with "pay" or pitch (a kind of tar). The task of "paying the devil" (caulking the longest seam) by squatting in the BILGES was despised by every seaman.

DI-DI-MAU    move quickly, also shortened to just "DI-DI."

DINGLE BERRY    a piece of dried feces caught in the hair around the anus. An incompetent, foolish, or stupid person.

DINKY-DAU    Vietnamese term for "crazy" or "You're crazy."

DIVINING ROD    a forked branch or stick that is believed to indicate subterranean water or minerals by bending downward when held over a source.

DMZ    demilitarized zone. An area from which military forces, operations, and installations are prohibited

DOC    affectionate title for enlisted medical aidman/corpsmen.

DOD    Department of Defense.

DON'T MEAN NOTHIN'—term meaning nothing to worry or SWEAT about.

DONUT DOLLY    American Red Cross volunteer—female.

DOUBTFULS    indigenous personnel who cannot be categorized as either VC or civil offenders. It also can mean suspect personnel spotted from ground or aircraft.

| | |
|---|---|
| DRESS WHITES | summer uniform. |
| DUFFEL BAG | oblong, unwieldy bag that troops stored all their gear. See SEA BAG. |
| DUSTOFF | nickname for medical evacuation helicopter or mission. See MEDEVAC. |
| E & E | Escape & Evasion. |
| E1, E2, ETC | enlisted men's grades, E1-Seaman Recruit, E2-Seaman Apprentice, E3-Seaman, E4-3$^{rd}$ Class Petty Officer, E5 2$^{nd}$ Class Petty Officer, etc. |
| EIGHT BELLS | aboard Navy ships, bells are struck to designate the hours of being on watch. Each watch is four hours. One bell is struck after the first half-hour has passed, two bells after one hour has passed, three bells after an hour and a half, four bells after two hours, and so forth up to EIGHT BELLS are struck at the completion of the four hours. Completing a watch with no incidents to report was "EIGHT BELLS and all is well." The practice of using bells stems from the days of the sailing ships. Sailors could not afford to have their own timepieces and relied on the ship's bells to tell time. The ship's boy kept time by using a half-hour glass. Each time the sand ran out, he would turn the glass over and ring the appropriate number of bells. |
| ELEPHANT GRASS | tall, sharp-edge grass |
| EM | Enlisted Man. |
| EM CLUB | Military club for enlisted personnel only. Officers and Chief Petty Officers are not allowed. |
| ENIFF | Enemy initiated firefight |
| ENSIGN | entry-level officer (US Navy). |

EQUAL TURNING POINT—a point determined by the "HOW GOES IT CURVE" beyond which it would not be possible for an aircraft to return to the point of origin. A plot of speed, distance, engine settings, remaining fuel, etc., that assisted the crews in determining the crucial, "POINT OF NO RETURN."

ET     Electronics Technicians.

EVAC     see MEDEVAC.

F-4 PHANTOM     a twin-engine, all weather, tactical fighter-jet.

FAM     Federal Air Marshal.

FANTAIL     the STERN or AFT open area of a ship, also called the AFTERDECK.

FAST MOVER     usually a jet

FATIGUES     standard combat uniform, green in color. Sometimes called GREENS.

FEELING BLUE     if you are sad and describe yourself as "FEELING BLUE," you are using a phrase coined from a custom among many old deepwater sailing ships. If the ship lost the captain or any of the officers during its voyage, she would fly blue flags and have a blue band painted along her entire hull when returning to homeport.

FIELD OF FIRE     area that a weapon or group of weapons can cover effectively with fire from a given position.

FIGMO     state of blissful abandon, achieved after receiving orders out of Vietnam. Literally "Fuck it, I Got My Orders."

FIREFIGHT     exchange of small arms fire between opposing units.

FLACK JACKET     heavy fiberglass-filled vest worn for protection from shrapnel.

| | |
|---|---|
| FLAG OFFICERS | an officer in the navy or coast guard holding a rank higher than captain, such as rear admiral, vice admiral, or admiral. |
| FLARE | illumination projectile. |
| FNG | most common name for newly arriving person in Vietnam. It was literally translated as "Fucking New Guy." |
| FOM (short) | French River Patrol Boat. |
| FORWARD | directional—in, at, toward, or near the BOW of a SHIP or BOAT. |
| FREE FIRE ZONE | any area in which permission was not required to fire on targets. |
| FREEDOM BIRD | name given to any aircraft that took troops out of Vietnam. Usually the commercial jet flight that took men back to the WORLD. |
| FREQ | radio Frequency. |
| FRIENDLIES US | troops, allies, or anyone not on the other side. |
| FRIENDLY FIRE | a euphemism used to describe air, artillery, or small-arms fire from American forces mistakenly directed at American positions. |
| FUBAR | "Fucked Up Beyond All Repair" or "Recognition." Impossible situations, equipment, or persons as in, "It is (or they are) totally FUBAR!" |
| FUNNY BOOKS | military maps or COMIC BOOKS. |
| GALLEY | the kitchen of the ship. The best explanation as to its origin is that it is a corruption of "GALLEY." Ancient sailors cooked their meals on a brick or stone gallery laid amidships. |
| GANGPLANK | a board or ramp used as a removable footway between a ship and a pier. Also called gangway. |

| | |
|---|---|
| GCT | Greenwich Civil Time |
| GERONIMO | an expression used when doing something exciting in combat. |
| GOOKS | slang expression brought to Vietnam by Korean War Veterans. The term refers to anyone of Asian origin. |
| GQ GENERAL QUARTERS—battle stations where military personnel are assigned to go ASAP when alarm sounds. | |
| GREENS | same as FATIGUES, standard combat uniform, green in color. |
| GREEN BACKS | term used to describe American money. |
| GREEN BERETS | members of the Special Forces of the U.S. Army. Awarded the Green Beret headgear as a mark of distinction. |
| GREENWICH MEAN TIME—zero degrees of longitude runs through Greenwich; time is measured relative to GREENWICH MEAN TIME. It is used in airplane and ship navigation, where it also sometimes known by the military name, "ZULU TIME." "ZULU" in the phonetic alphabet stands for "Z" which stands for longitude zero. | |
| GROSSCHECK | everyone checks everyone else for things that are lose, make noise, light up, smell bad, etc. |
| GRUNT | a popular nickname for an infantryman in Vietnam, supposedly derived from the sound one made from lifting up heavy items. |
| GSW-TTH | casualty report term meaning "gunshot wound, thru and thru." |
| GUARD THE RADIO | term meaning to stand by and listen for messages. |
| GUERRILLA | soldiers of a resistance movement, organized on a military or paramilitary |

basic. GUERRILLA warfare military operations conducted in enemy-held or hostile territory by irregular, predominantly indigenous force.

GUN SALUTE guns were first fired as an act of good faith. In the days when it took so long to reload a gun, it was a proof of friendly intention when the ship's cannon were discharged upon entering port.

GUNG HO very enthusiastic and committed.

GVN Government of South Vietnam.

HANOI HANNA Propaganda radio announcer representing North Vietnam. She was known for having "good music, but lousy commercials."

HANOI HILTON nickname American prisoners of war used to describe the Hoa-Loa Prison in Hanoi.

HATCH another name for doorway onboard ships.

HE KNOWS THE ROPES—in the very early days, this phrase was written on a seaman's discharge to indicate that he was still a novice. All he knew about being a sailor was just the names and uses of the principal ropes (lines). Today, this same phrase means the opposite and that the person fully knows and understands the operation (usually of the organization).

HEAD a bathroom aboard Navy ships. Term comes from the days of sailing ships when the place for the crew to relieve themselves was all the way forward on either side of the bowsprit, the integral part of the hull to which the figurehead was fastened.

| | |
|---|---|
| HOOTCH | house or living quarters or a native hut. |
| HOT | dangerous, such as HOT LZ. |
| HOW GOES IT CURVE—see EQUAL TURNING POINT. | |
| HUEY | nickname for the UH-series utility helicopter. |
| HUNKY-DORY | everything is "O.K." was coined from a street named "Honki-Dori" in Yokohama, Japan. Since the inhabitants of this street catered to the pleasures of sailors, it is easy to understand why the street's name became synonymous for anything that is enjoyable or at least satisfactory and, the logical follow-on is "Okey-dokey." |
| INCOMING | receiving enemy mortar or rocket fire. |
| IN-COUNTRY | term used to refer to American troops operating in South Vietnam. They were all IN-COUNTRY. |
| IN THE SHIT | see SHIT. |
| JCS | Joint Chiefs of Staff. |
| JESUS NUT | main rotor retaining nut that holds the main rotor onto the rest of the helicopter. If it came off, only JESUS could help you. |
| JOHN WAYNE | can opener for canned C-RATIONS, also called the P-38. |
| KA-BAR | type of military combat knife. |
| KIA | Killed In Action. |
| KLICK | short for kilometer. |
| KP | Kitchen Patrol or kitchen duty. |
| LAUGH A MINUTE | translated as a "Walk in the Park," but it meant going up a river. |
| LAY-CHILLY | lie motionless. |
| LBGB | little bitty gook boat, (small watercraft for one or two people). |
| LCM | Landing Craft Mechanized. |
| LCPL | Landing Craft, Personnel (Large). |

| LIBERTY | permission given to a sailor to go ashore. |
| LIFER | career sailor. |
| LOGBOOK | in the early days of sailing ships, the ship's records were written on shingles cut from logs. These shingles were hinged and opened like a book. The record was called the "LOG BOOK." Later on, when paper was readily available and bound into books, the record maintained it name. |
| LSIL | Infantry Landing ship (Large). |
| LST | Landing Ship, Tank. |
| LT | Lieutenant, US Navy (O-3). |
| LT | (JG) Lieutenant (junior grade) US Navy (O-2). |
| LURPS | lightweight food packet consisting of a dehydrated meal and named after the soldiers it was most often issued. |
| LZ | Landing Zone. |
| MAA | see Master-At-Arms. |
| MAAD | MINUTE concentrated fire of all weapons for a brief period. |
| MAC | Military Air Command |
| MAGS | magazines where ammunition kept/stored until placed in a weapon. |
| HOLE | term spoken, "Make a HOLE," when you want people to move out of the way. |
| MAIL BUOY | fictitious location for collecting the mail. This trick is same-same as sending someone Snipe hunting. |
| MAMA-SAN | mature Vietnamese woman. |
| MARKET TIME | Coastal patrol operations off the coast of South Vietnam, 1968-71. |
| MARS | Military Affiliate Radio System. Licensed ham radio operators (sometimes known as radio geeks) in civilian life, were given |

civilian amateur radio equipment and told to use their ham radio skills to run phone patches, or telephone calls home for their fellow Marines. Their counterparts in the United States placed collect telephone calls to the families and friends of the Marines in the field and patched the calls through on frequencies near the ham bands.

MASTER-AT-ARMS usually a senior Navy Chief Petty Officer on a navy ship. The MAA holds the position of police officer or sheriff onboard naval ships.

MAYDAY the internationally recognized voice radio signal for ships and people in serious trouble at sea. Made official in 1948, it is an anglicizing of the French m'aidez, "help me."

MEDEVAC medical evacuation by HUEY, also called an EVAC or DUSTOFF.

MIA Missing In Action.

MONITOR BOAT A converted landing craft packed with radios, designed for forward command and communications. See CCB.

MOO-MOO DRESS one-piece dress worn by Vietnamese woman.

MP Military Police.

MPC Military Payment Certificate, used instead of US dollars (Green Backs), was also used to replace US coins.

MRF Mobile Riverine Force.

MSB Minesweeping Boat.

MSM Minesweeper (medium).

MUC Meritorious Unit Commendation.

MUZZLE VELOCITY The speed at which a projectile leaves the muzzle of a weapon, generally measured in feet per second.

| | |
|---|---|
| MWOK | Married With Out Kids. |
| M-16 | nickname, the widow-maker, the standard American rifle used after 1966. |
| M-60 | American-made machine-gun. |
| NDSM | National Defense Service Medal. Awarded to US military personnel who enlisted in peacetime. |
| NEWBIE | any person with less time in Vietnam than the speaker. |
| NEXT | person who had been in Vietnam for nearly a year and who would be rotated back to the WORLD soon. When the DEROS was the shortest in the unit, this person was said to be NEXT. |
| NO SWEAT | can do—easily done or accomplished— nothing to worry about. |
| NON-LA | conical hat, part of traditional Vietnamese costume. |
| NUC | Naval Unit Commendation. |
| NUMBA | slang for number. |
| NUMBA-ONE | good. |
| NUMBA-TEN | bad. |
| NUMBA-TEN-THOUSAND—very bad. | |
| OCS | Officer Candidate School. |
| OJT | On the Job Training. |
| OOD | Officer of the Day. |
| OPNAV | Office of the Chief of Naval Operations. |
| OSD | Office of the Secretary of Defense. |
| P-38 | can opener for canned C-RATS, also called JOHN WAYNE. Attachment W. |
| PACV | Patrol Air Cushion Vehicle. |
| PAPA-SAN | elderly Vietnamese man. |
| PBR | Patrol Boat River. Another name for Pabst Blue Ribbon beer, the only beer a PBR sailor would drink. |
| PCF | Patrol Craft Fast—Swift boat. |

PCF MK1 — Patrol Craft, Inshore—Swift boat.

PEA COAT — sailors who have to endure pea-soup weather often don their pea coats but the coat's name is not derived from the weather. The heavy topcoat worn in cold, miserable weather by seafaring men was once tailored from pilot cloth and a heavy, course, stout kind of twilled blue cloth with the nap on one side. The cloth was sometimes called P-cloth for the initial letter of "pilot" and the garment made from it was called a p-jacket and later, a pea coat. The term used since 1723 to denote coats made from that cloth.

PETER PILOT — the less experienced co-PILOT in a HUEY

PETTY OFFICER — U.S. Navy enlisted personnel, higher than SEAMAN. E-4 and above.

PFC — Private First Class (US ARMY).

PGM — Patrol Motor Gunboat.

PH — Purple Heart. Medal issued to anyone wounded.

POD — Plan of the Day. Daily newsletter published onboard U.S. Navy ships. Will list watch schedules and ships schedule.

POINT OF NO RETURN—see EQUAL TURNING POINT.

POP SMOKE — to mark a target, or Landing Zone (LZ) with a smoke grenade.

PORT — directional—left side of the ship or boat when facing forward.

PORTHOLES — originated during the reign of Henry VI of England (1485). King Henry insisted on mounting guns too large for his ship and the traditional methods of securing these weapons on the forecastle and aft castle could not be used. A French shipbuilder named James Baker was commissioned to solve the problem. He put small doors in the side of the ship and mounted the cannon inside the ship. These doors protected the cannon from weather and were opened when the cannons were to be used. The French word for "door" is "porte" which was later Anglicized to "port" and later went on to mean any opening in the ship's side, whether for cannon or not.

POW — Prisoner Of War. Also known as Petty Officer of the Watch.

PRC — River Patrol Craft.

PRC-25 — nicknamed PRICK, lightweight infantry field radio.

PRESSURE WAVE — Damage inflicted by ordnance dropped into the water next to a ship. Transmission of explosive force is conducted through hydraulic effect to crush the hull of the target.

PRICK — lightweight infantry field radio, PRC-25.

PUC — Presidential Unit Citation.

PUCKER FACTOR — assessment of the "fear factor," as in the difficulty/risk of an upcoming mission.

PULL-START — a negative name given to anyone wearing a turban. The PULL-START signifies the starting of a small motor. For example, where you would grab a part of the turban and pull in the same manner as in stating up a lawn mower. See PUSH-START and RAG-HEAD.

PUSH-START — a negative name given to anyone wearing a turban. The PUSH-START signifies the starting of a small motor. For example, where you would push the dot on the forehead of the person wearing the turban to start a motor. See PULL-START and RAG-HEAD.

R & R — Rest & Recreation. One-week of free-leave awarded to military personnel serving In-Country during a one-year tour of duty. Married personnel would mostly select Hawaii where they would meet up with their spouses. Single personnel usually selected Tokyo, Hong Kong, Sydney Austria, or Bangkok Thailand.

RAG — Vietnamese River Assault Group boat.

RAG-HEAD — a negative name given to anyone wearing a turban. See PULL-START and PUSH-START.

RECON — reconnaissance.

REVETMENTS — A barricade against explosives.

ROACH COACH — something like the lunch wagons found around construction sites.

ROCK 'N' ROLL — to put an M16 on full automatic fire.

RON — Remain OverNight.

ROUND EYE — slang term to describe Americans.

RTO — Radio/Telephone Operator who carried the PRC-25.

RVN — Republic of Vietnam (South Vietnam).

SAIGON TEA — high-cost drink that one would buy the bargirls that would have little or no alcohol content.

SAME-SAME — same as.

SAPPERS — North Vietnamese Army or Vietcong demolition commandos.

SAR — Search And Rescue.

SCUTTLEBUTT — a nautical parlance for a rumor. Comes from a combination of, "scuttle" and to make a hole in the ship's hull, thereby causing her to sink. And "butt" and a cask or hogshead used in the days of wooden ships to hold drinking water. The cask from which the ship's crew took their drinking water, like a water fountain, and was the "SCUTTLEBUTT." Even in today's Navy, a drinking fountain is referred to as such. But, since the crew used to congregate around the "SCUTTLEBUTT," that is where the rumors about the ship or voyage would begin. Thus, then and now, rumors are talk from the "SCUTTLEBUTT" or just "SCUTTLEBUTT."

| | |
|---|---|
| SEA BAG | oblong, unwieldy bag that sailors stored all their gear. See DUFFEL BAG |
| SEAL | Navy special-warfare force members—Seal Air Land team. |
| SEAMAN | Low ranking U.S. navy enlisted personnel. |
| SECDEF | Secretary of Defense. |
| SECNAV | Secretary of the Navy. |
| SERETTE | little disposable needles with morphine. |
| SHAKEN-BAKE | an officer straight out of OCS without any combat experience. |
| SHIP | a vessel of considerable size for deep-water navigation. |
| SHIT | a catchall multipurpose term, i.e., a FIREFIGHT was "IN THE SHIT," a bad situation was "DEEP SHIT," to be well prepared and alert was to have your "SHIT WIRED TIGHT." |
| SHIT-HOOK | name applied to Chinook helicopter because of all the "SHIT" stirred up by its massive rotors. |
| SHIT WIRED TIGHT | see SHIT. |
| SHORT | someone whose tour IN-COUNTRY was ending. Also called SHORT-TIMER. |

| | |
|---|---|
| SHORT-TIMER | see SHORT. |
| SHOTGUN | armed guard on or in a vehicle who watches for enemy activity and returns fire if attacked. A door gunner on a helicopter. |
| SICK BAY | mini hospital onboard ship. |
| SIT-REP | situation report. |
| SIX | from aviation jargon, 'My 6 o'clock.' Directly behind me, hence my back— cover my back or rear of operation. |
| SKATE | goof off. |
| SKY PILOT | another name for the Chaplain. |
| SLOPE | a derogatory term used to refer to any Asian. |
| SMALL STUFF | not a big deal, nothing to worry about. |
| SNAFU | Situation Normal—All Fucked Up. |
| SOP | Standard Operating Procedure. |
| SOS | "Shit On A Shingle." Creamed meat on toast. |
| S.O.S. | contrary to popular notion, the letters S.O.S. do not stand for "Save Our Ship" or "Save Our Souls." They were selected to indicate a distress because, in Morse code, these letters and their combination create an unmistakable sound pattern. Three short, three long, three short. |
| SPORKS | combination of a spoon and fork. |
| STAB BOAT SEAL | Team Strike Assault Boat. |
| STAND DOWN | term used to indicate that a naval ship, squadron, or other military unit will stop all operations and do a safety review. Also, period of rest and refitting in which all-operational activities except for security is stopped. |
| STARBOARD | the Vikings called the side of their ship its board, and they placed the steering |

oar, the "star" on the right side of the ship, thus that side became known as the "star board." It's been that way ever since. Moreover, because the oar was in the right side, the ship was tied to the dock at the left side. This was known as the loading side or "larboard." Later, it was decided that "larboard" and "starboard" were too similar, especially when trying to be heard over the roar of a heavy sea, so the phrase became the "side at which you tied up to in port" or the "port" side.

| | |
|---|---|
| STARLIGHT | Scope. Light amplifying telescope, used to see at night. |
| STEEL POT | standard US Army helmet. The outer metal cover. |
| STERN the | AFTERDECK or aft open area of a ship, also FANTAIL. |
| SWIFT BOAT U.S. | Navy patrol boat, designated PCF (Patrol Craft Fast). |
| SYNCHRONIZED FIRE—firing through the propeller an airplane that coupled the machine gun sear mechanism with a cam on the engine crankshaft. Shots were timed to miss the propeller. | |
| TAD | Temporary Additional Duty. |
| TAKEN ABACK | One hazards faced in days of sailing ships is incorporated into English to describe someone who has been jolted by unpleasant news. We say that person has been "TAKEN ABACK." The person is at a momentary loss, unable to act or even to speak. A danger faced by sailing ships was for a sudden shift in wind to come up (from a sudden squall), blowing |

the sails back against the masts, putting the ship in grave danger of having the masts break off and rendering the ship totally helpless. The ship was TAKEN ABACK.

TANGO BOAT     Armored Troop Carrier. Nine seats for troops and a canvas top. Each tango could carry a fully equipped rifle platoon.

TDY     Temporary Duty.

TEE-TEE     Vietnamese term for, "A little bit."

TET     Vietnamese Lunar New Year holiday period.

TF     Task Force

TG     Task Group

THE-NAM     slang term for Vietnam.

THREE-MILE LIMIT     a recognized distance from a nation's shore over which that nation had jurisdiction. This border of inter-national waters or the "high seas" was established because, at the time this international law was established, 3 miles was the longest range of any nation's most powerful guns and there-fore the limit from shore batteries at which they could enforce their laws. International law and the 1988 Territorial Sea Proclamation established the "high seas" border at 12-miles.

THREE SHEETS TO THE WIND—describes someone who has too much to drink. As such, they are often bedraggled with perhaps shirttails out, clothes a mess. The reference is to a sailing ship in disarray, that is with sheets (lines, not "ropes" that adjust the angle at which a sail is set in relation to the wind) flapping loosely in the breeze.

THUMPER (THUMP-GUN): M-79 grenade launcher.

| | |
|---|---|
| TIGER BALM | foul-smelling oil used by many Vietnamese to ward off evil spirits. |
| TOUR | a one year tour was equal to 365 days. |
| TRIP-WIRE | thin wire used by both sides strung across an area where someone may walk through. Usually attached to a mine, flare, or booby-trap. |
| TURRET | On ships, a rotatable armored enclosure-protecting heavy rifled ordnance. |
| UA | Unauthorized Absence. |
| USO | United Service Organization. |
| USS | United States Ship. |
| VC VIETCONG, | called Victor Charlie (phonetic alphabet) or just CHARLIE |
| VCNO | Vice Chief of Naval Operations. |
| VERY | the name of the inventor of an extensive production series of bright flares for illumination at night, either dropped from the air or fired from a hand-held pistol. |
| VIETCONG | communist forces fighting the South Vietnamese Government. |
| VN | VIETNAM. |
| VNSM | Vietnam Service Medal. |
| WAKE-UP | term to indicate that being in THE-NAM was a bad dream, a nightmare, and that when you leave; you will WAKE-UP from your nightmare. |
| WAKEY | the last day in country before going home. |
| WATCHES | traditionally, a 24-hour day is divided into seven watches. These are: midnight to 4 a.m. [0000-0400], the mid-watch; 4 to 8 a.m. [0400-0800], morning watch; 8 a.m. to noon [0800-1200], forenoon watch; noon to 4 p.m. [1200-1600], afternoon |

watch; 4 to 6 p.m. [1600-1800] first dog watch; 6 to 8 p.m. [1800-2000], second dog watch; and, 8 p.m. to midnight [2000-2400], evening watch. The half-hours of the watch are marked by the striking the bell an appropriate number of times.

WATER-COOLED — water circulating within a jacket surrounding a machine-gun barrel that transfers heat away from the surface of the metal.

WHITE MICE — South Vietnamese police. The nickname came from their uniform white helmets and gloves.

WIA — Wounded In Action.

WORLD — the WORLD, the United States.

XO — Executive Officer onboard Navy ships, second in command.

YANKEE STATION — operational staging area at 16N-110E in the South China Sea off the coast of Vietnam.

ZIPPO — flame-thrower. Also refers to the popular cigarette lighter.

ZIPPO BOAT LCMs — with flame-throwers.

ZULU — TIME SAME-SAME as GREENWICH MEAN TIME. It is used in airplane and ship navigation. Zero degrees of longitude runs through Greenwich; time is measured relative to GREENWICH MEAN TIME. "ZULU" in the phonetic alphabet stands for "Z" which stands for longitude zero.

1-MC PA — system onboard Navy ships.

365 — the actual number of days in a one year tour. See TOUR.

# Appendix A

## PLAN OF THE DAY (POD)

USS SUMMIT (ARR23)
FPO San Francisco 96601

NOT TO BE REMOVED FROM THE SHIP

PLAN OF THE DAY FOR SATURDAY

<u>SHIP'S ROUTINE</u>.

0630-Reveille. Breakfast.
0745-Quarters for muster.
0800-Turn to.
1130-Knock off ship's work.
1200-Dinner for the crew.
1300-Turn to.
1600-Knock off ship's work.

<u>ANNOUNCEMENTS</u>.

1.  Movie clean-up—R-3.

2. BID ALERTNESS

Last night while on Bid of the Patrol to the East MRF, crew of ATC-17 RAD 131 sighted suspicious debris in water. Debris was taken under fire with small arms resulting in explosion and 70 ft waterspout.

The alertness of crew of T-17 may well have thwarted the mining of a major unit of the MRF. To the crew of T-17, WELL DONE.

3. Liberty in Can Tho

Liberty will be granted in Can Tho to expire on the Vietnamese Police Landing at 1800.

NOTES ON LIBERTY IN CAN THO

1. SAPPER Activity is high in this area. Several incidents have occurred resulting in US Servicemen being killed or wounded. DO NOT stay in groups of more than 3 or 4. If waiting for a Bus SPREAD out. Large Groups of US Personnel make excellent targets for SAPPERS.

2. Use the "buddy system" and do not stray alone down back streets.

3. In Bars and on the street watch your wallet and Wristwatch. They can ride by on a motorbike and steal your watch especially those with expansion bands. The BAR GIRLS are excellent thieves whether you are drinking with them or in bed with them. Mama-son might relieve you of your wallet while you are busy relieving something else.

4. OFF LIMITS AREAS. All modes of transportation including Vietnamese Taxis and Pedal-cabs are off limits. Only military transportation is authorized. Military buses do run thru out Can Tho. There is a bus stop in front of the MP Compound downtown.

A. All bars not having an <u>ON LIMITS</u> sign displayed are off limits. Get out immediately if this sign is not visible. There are approximately 50 Bars that are on limits.

B. Only the following establishments are inspected by the US Army and found sanitary for food consumption.

(1) SUONGS

(2) OLGAS

(3) HOLLYWOOD GRILL (good-looking girls)

(4) INTERNATIONAL HOTEL (Expensive)

Don't expose yourself to HEPATITIS or worse at these places.

5. <u>MONEY</u>. No MPC will be used in CAN THO. Money exchanges are located at the USO and CORDS Compound in CAN THO. Money may also be exchanged in BINH-THUY.

6. <u>CONDUCT</u>. CAN THO is not the place to become so drunk you do not have control of yourself. Your life may depend on it. There will be several other areas, such as Drugs, Black Market, and VD, which have been of no concern before, except possible VD. Just "Be Prepared" if you engage in the latter. Avoid any association or contact with drugs or the Black Market. Both may result in servers Disciplinary Action.

7. Same rules apply concerning liberty cancellation for CAN THO as for BINH-THUY.

8. <u>UNIFORM</u>. Greens are authorized for all personnel on board. Either Greens or Dungarees will be worn. Uniforms will not

be mixed. When Dungarees shirts are worn both on liberty and on the ship, they will be buttoned and tucked in. "T" shirts may be sworn on the ship.

9. <u>LIBERTY UNIFORM</u>:

    (1)   Greens with green hat, or
    (2)   Dungarees with white hat.

P. L REA
Executive Officer

# Appendix B

## NOTICE OF RETURN

This declaration is issued as a solemn warning this _____ day of
_____,19 _____ to the friends, neighbors, relatives, loved ones,
and fellow countrymen of one sailor named _____ who
has last been seen when leaving your presence on the _____.day
of_____, 19_____ has been absent from family circles and former
haunts since that day.

In the very near future, the above named man will once again
be in your midst. De-Americanized, demoralized, and
dehydrated, combat ready sailor to take his place once more
as a human being in a society of freedom and justice for all.
To engage in life, liberty, and the somewhat delayed pursuit
of happiness.

In making your joyous preparations to welcome him back to a
civilized society you might make certain precautions to make
allowances for the crude environment in which he has suffered
for the past _____ months. In other words, he may be a little
Asiatic, suffering from advance stages of Viet-congitis, too much
Ba-Muio-Ba (Beer); and Saigon Tea, as well as all sorts of rare
tropical diseases.

Therefore: Show no alarm if everyday he looks for a little bottle of little white pills, and every Monday frantically searches the medicine cabinet for a bottle of much bigger orange pills, or wakes up in the middle of the night for a Mid-Watch. Pretend you don't worry when he take his bread and closely examines it for bugs. Don't worry if, when you serve Roast Beef, he excuses himself and goes to the bathroom and vomits. Take it in stride if on a Friday morning he salutes you and says, "standing ready for inspection." Be sympathetic if he buttons his shirt up all the way to his throat, tucks his trousers into his socks, roll down his sleeves, and grabs a pot for a helmet every time the doorbell rings. Above all, keep faith if you don't hear any water running when he says he's taking a shower. If you overhear him utter the words "Di Di Mau" with an irritated look on his face, simply leave quickly and quietly, for it means none less than "Get the Hell out of Here."

Never ask why he didn't make rate as fast as the other guys did, and by no means mention the terms "Extend" or "Re-enlist." Do not ask at any time if he tried to save any money while in Nam. This may put him in a state of shock in which he may mumble something about Craps, Poker, Blackjack, Cribbage, Pinochle, or donations to the Red Cross, Navy Relief Society, or Going on R&R.

His intentions will be sincere, although dishonorable. Keep in mind that beneath his tanned and rugged exterior, there beats a heart of pure gold, crying for love, and understanding. Treasure this, for it is the only thing of value that he has left. Treat him with kindness, Tolerance, Love, and an occasional Fifth of Good Bourbon, and you may be able to rehabilitate what once was a proud, happy-go-lucky, nature loving human being, and who is now one-hell-of a disillusioned member of the human race.

Last but not least, send no more mail to the U.S.S. SUMMIT (ARR-23), FPO San Francisco, 96601. Just fill the reefer with Beer and Whiskey, get out the Civvies, fill the car with gas, and get the women and kids off the Street, because . . . .

The Swabbee is Coming Home . . .

Soon!!!

# Appendix C

## WARNING LETTER

From:   Commander, US Forces, Vietnam
Subj:   Indoctrination for return to Zone of America
To:     All Military Personnel Returning Home

1.  In compliance with current problems for rotation of Armed Forces Overseas, it is directed that in order to maintain the highest standards of character of the American Sailor and to prevent any dishonor to reflect upon the uniform. All individuals are eligible for return to the United States under current directions will undergo a somewhat change and before a sailor is allowed to return to the USS SUMMIT (ARR 23), he will have to be stationed in the U.S. for a period of two (2) years with all the comforts of home.

2.  The following points will be emphasized in this course:

    a.  In America, there will be a number of beautiful girls. These young girls have not been liberated and many are painfully employed as stenographers, salesgirls, beauty operators, and welders. Contrary to popular belief, and current practice, they should not be approached with "How Much." A proper greeting is, "Isn't it a lovely day?"

b. A guest in a private home is usually awakened in the morning by a light tapping on his door and the invitation to join the host at breakfast. It is a proper thing to say, "I'll be there shortly." So, do not say, "Blow it out your ass."

c. A typical breakfast in America consists of such strange foods as cantaloupe, fresh eggs, milk, ham or bacon, etc. These foods are highly palatable, and though strange in appearance are extremely tasty. If you wish the butter, turn to the person nearest it, and quietly ask, "Please pass the butter." Do not say, "Throw me the damn grease."

d. Very natural urges are apt to occur in a crowd, if it is necessary to defecate, one does not grab a shovel in one hand, paper in the other and make a mad dash for the garden. At lease ninety per cent of the American homes have one room, which contains a bathtub, washbasin, medicine cabinet, and a toilet. It is the latter that you use in the case. Instructors should be sure that all personnel are taught operation of the said toilet, especially the lever that prepares it for further use.

e. In the event that a helmet is retained by the individual, he will refrain from using it as a chair, washbasin, and footbath, as all the things are furnished in the average American home. It is not considered proper form to squat Indian fashion in the corner of the room in case all the chairs are occupied. The host will provide suitable seats.

f. American dinners, in most cases are served in separate dishes. The common practice of mixing various items, such as corn beef, pudding of lima beans and peaches to make them more palatable will be refrained upon. In time, the separate dish system will become enjoyable.

g.  Belching or passing wind in company is strictly frowned upon. Should you forget however, and you belched or passed wind in the presence of others, a proper phrase is, "Excuse me." Do not say, "It must be that louse chow we have been having lately."

h.  Americans have a strange taste for stimulants. The drink in common usage in the Aleutians, such as under ripe wine, GI alcohol, grape fruit juice of gasoline, and bitter water, commonly know by the French as Cognac, are not ordinary acceptable in civilian circles. These drinks should be served only to those who are classified in the inner circle of friends. A suitable use for these drinks is the serving of ones landlord in order to break the lease.

i.  The returning Sailor is apt to find that his opinions and ideas are entirely different from those of his civilian companions and friends. One should call upon his reserve of educate and correct his acquaintance with remarks such as, "I believe you have made a mistake." Or, "I am afraid that you are in error on that." Do not say, "Brother you are really fucked up."

j.  Upon leaving a friend's home after a visit, one may find his hat misplaced. Most frequently, it has been place in a closet. One should turn to one's host and say, "I don't seem to have my hat. Will you help me find it?" Do not say, "Don't anyone leave this room. Some son of a bitch has stolen my hat."

k.  When traveling in the U.S., particularly in a strange city, it is often necessary to spend the night. Hotels are provided for this purpose and one can get directions to the nearest hotel from anyone. Here one can spend the night. The present practice of entering the nearest home, throwing the occupants into the yard, and taking over the premises will cease.

l.  Whiskey, an American drink, may be offered to the Sailor on various social occasions. It is considered a reflection on the uniform to snatch the bottle from the hostess and drain it, cork and all. All individuals are cautioned to use extreme control at all times.

m.  In motion pictures theaters, seats are provided. It is not considered good form to whistle every time a female from eight to eight passes the screen. If vision is impaired by the person in front of you, there are many empty seats to which you can move. Do not hit across the back of the head and say, "Move your head, jerk. I can't see a damn thing."

n.  It is not proper to go around hitting everyone of Draft Age in civilian clothes. He might have been discharge from the service for medical reasons. Ask for his credentials, and if then he cannot show any, go ahead, and slug the bastard.

o.  Natural function will continue, as it may be necessary to urinate. Do not walk behind the nearest tree, building, or vehicle to accomplish this. Toilets, (see D above) are proved in all public buildings for this purpose. Sign on some doors will read 'Ladies,' which literally means, "Off limits."

# APPENDIX D

### Surrender Pass

**HỒI CHÁNH RẤT DỄ DÀNG !**

HÃY GIẤU VŨ KHÍ CỦA CÁC BẠN ĐỂ ĐƯỢC LÃNH THƯỞNG SAU NÀY.

ĐẾN TRÌNH DIỆN TẠI MỘT TRUNG TÂM CHIÊU HỒI, CHÁNH QUYỀN XÃ HOẶC GIỚI CHỨC QUÂN SỰ CHÁNH PHỦ HOẶC ĐỒNG MINH

CÁC BẠN KHÔNG CẦN PHẢI CÓ MỘT THÔNG HÀNH QUI HÀNG HOẶC TRUYỀN ĐƠN ĐỂ HỒI CHÁNH NHƯNG NẾU CÓ, BẠN NÊN DÙNG ĐỂ TRỞ VỀ, CHÁNH PHỦ QUỐC GIA ĐANG CẦN ĐẾN TẤT CẢ NHỮNG NGƯỜI CON CỦA ĐẤT NƯỚC.

—————————— **CHIÊU HỒI** ——————————

**CÙNG CÁC BINH SĨ, SĨ QUAN VÀ CÁN BỘ ĐANG CHIẾN ĐẤU CHỐNG LẠI CHÍNH PHỦ QUỐC GIA**

ĐÂY LÀ LỜI KÊU GỌI CỦA CHÍNH PHỦ VIỆT-NAM CỘNG HÒA

CÁC BẠN HÃY TRỞ VỀ VỚI CHÍNH NGHĨA QUỐC GIA QUA CHÍNH SÁCH CHIÊU HỒI

CÁC BẠN SẼ ĐƯỢC TIẾP ĐÓN NỒNG HẬU VÀ SẼ KHÔNG BỊ HÃM HẠI

HỒI CHÁNH ĐỂ GIA ĐÌNH ĐƯỢC ĐOÀN TỤ VÀ NÂNG ĐỠ

HỒI CHÁNH VIÊN ĐƯỢC LÃNH TIỀN THƯỞNG VỀ NHỮNG VŨ KHÍ MANG VỀ.

—————————— **CHIÊU HỒI** ——————————

### Safe Pass

GIẤY THÔNG-HÀNH

SAFE CONDUCT PASS TO BE HONORED BY ALL VIETNAMESE GOVERNMENT AGENCIES AND ALLIED FORCES

# Appendix E

## VIETNAMESE MONEY

# Appendix F

## POCKET GUIDE TO VIETNAM

# Appendix G

## LOTTERY TICKET

# Appendix H

## ALL HANDS INFORMATION
## WELCOME TO NAM

WELCOME TO

THE REPUBLIC OF VIETNAM

and the

ANNAPOLIS BOQ/BEQ

'Saigon's Innkeeper'

A COMPONENT OF

NAVAL SUPPORT ACTIVITY SAIGON

# ALL HANDS INFORMATION
# WELCOME TO NAM

Welcome aboard the Annapolis BOQ/BEQ and the Republic of Vietnam. Depending upon which unit you are assigned to, you can expect to remain here approximately three days. During that time, with the exception of shipboard, HAL-3, VAL-4, RIVFLOT ONE, and TAD personnel, you will participate in an administrative briefing at which time you will complete your travel claims, Dislocation Allowance/Family Separation Allowance, Postal Locator forms, Ration Card, and Currency Control Card applications. Enlisted members will be counseled on their duty preferences for their next tour (VEY Interview). One of the members of the Master-at-Arms force will conduct an in-country security briefing and marijuana lecture to be attended by all new arrivals. Later, depending upon your assignment, you will draw either a weapon or field gear, or both. Finally, you are required to take part in the Personal Response Discussion, conducted in Saigon.

While you are at the Annapolis, you are under the command of COMNAVSUPPACT, Saigon. In addition, there are a few rules, which must be adhered to as well as some pertinent items important to you, namely:

1. Water

   a. All water is non-potable with the exception of that in the coolers.

2. Head Facilities a. A sewage problem exists. All the sewage, as well as the shower water and the water from the sinks are pumped into

   a  5,000-gallon tank. This is pumped out at various times, so use water sparingly and adhere to the posted Head Regulations.

3.  Berthing Areas

    a.  Lying on bunks during working hours is prohibited. The one exception is from 1100-1300, but one must be in underwear only.

    b.  Personnel utilizing lockers will attach a card to their locker, showing their name and bunk number. This will be done on arrival and cards may be picked up in the Master-at-Arms office.

    c.  All lockers found untagged are subject to having locks cut and contents placed in the lucky bag.

    d.  There are women in this billet. Be courteous to them and use your heads with regard to dress while utilizing the head facilities.

4.  Departing Billet

    a.  Before departing the Annapolis for any reason, you must log out with the Master-at-Arms. Upon returning, you will log back in with the MAA.

    b.  E-6 and below who find it necessary to leave the Annapolis for any reason other than going to chow must have a signed chit.

    c.  Before departing for your ultimate duty station, make certain you have cleaned our locker.

5.  Musters

    a.  Musters are held at 0730, 1300, and 1700. Attendance is mandatory. Officers and E-7 and above are required to attend the 0730 musters only, in order to pass on necessary information.

b.    Approximately 30 minutes after checking into the Annapolis you will be required to at-tend your first lecture, held in Bay 8. At this time, all personnel will be given a security brief—informed of their next lecture.

## 6. Watches

a.    In order to defend the Annapolis in event of enemy attack and to ensure your safety, various watches have been established and men in grades E-1 thru E-6 may expect to be placed on the watch bill.

## 7. Watch Bill and Flight List

a.    Be certain & check lists once announcement has been made that they are posted.

## 8. Daily Charge

a.    You will be charged 25 piasters per day while at this billet. This fee is used for linen service and to pay the maids for services rendered. You are reminded that this fee is to be paid in piasters only.

## 9. Uniforms

a.    Civilian clothing, mixed uniforms, and camouflaged greens are not authorized in the Saigon area.

## 10. Personal appearance

a.    Long hair, sideburns, and uncleanness are not tolerated.

## 11. Lounge area (Bay 8)

a. This is a reading and TV viewing area only. Do not sleep there, nor put your feet on the furniture or the bulkheads.

## 12. Movies

a. Movies are shown five out of seven evenings from 1900-2000 in the Muster Bay.

## 13. Lobby and Quarterdeck

a. Pass quickly through this area. Do not congregate.

## 14. Outside area

a. Tables, chairs and trashcans have been put there for your convenience. Keep this area clean by putting waste and cigarette butts in the cans provided.

## 15. Annapolis Master-at-Arms Force

a. The purpose of the MAA is to enforce rules and regulations and to maintain security throughout the building.

b. Strict discipline will be adhered to while you are onboard and rowdiness and unruly conduct will not be tolerated.

c. We solicit your cooperation doing your part in order to make your stay enjoyable.

(1) Willingly follow commands and regulations.

(2) Relate all problems such as lack of supplies, water pressure, uncleanness, etc. to the duty MAA.

(3) Conduct yourself in a courteous manner at all times.

## 16. Security and Theft

a.  All gear adrift will be confiscated and placed in the lucky bag.

b.  At no time should valuables such as watches, wallets, and radios, etc., be left adrift.

c.  Personnel are reminded that it is unwise to carry or possess large sums of money.

## 17. Messing

a.  Officers will mess at the Idaho BOQ, which is located directly behind the Annapolis

b.  Enlisted personnel will mess at the Montana BEQ, which is located about three blocks down the street from the Annapolis.

## 18. Liberty

a.  There is no authorized liberty for transients in the Saigon/Cholon area; however, you are allowed to utilize the facilities at Idaho BOQ and Montana BEQ.

## 19. RIVFLOT ONE & Naval Advisory Personnel Assigned to DaNang

a.  RIVFLOT ONE personnel do not draw field gear or weapons from the Annapolis.

b.     Naval Advisory personnel being assigned to DaNang
will not draw a weapon from the Annapolis armory,
but will draw field gear from the Annapolis.

## 20. DON'T CONGREGATE!

a.     At no time will anyone congregate around the entrance
to the building and the front bunker. Standing outside
the protected area and gathering groups is extremely
dangerous—Charlie is watching! ! !

# ALL HANDS INFORMATION
# WELCOME TO NAM

# OFFICERS' IN-PROCESSING INFORMATION

All NAVSUPPACT and other officers administratively supported by COMNAVSUPPACT, Saigon will report immediately upon arrival in-country to the Annapolis BOQ/BEQ in Saigon for In-processing. All officers assigned to Naval Advisory Group, COMNAVFORV, MACV and other commands will proceed to their respective commands upon completion of In-processing at the Annapolis. RIVPATFLOT FIVE officers designated as Squadron Commanders and Division Commanders will proceed to Binh-Thuy for briefing when released by the Annapolis. All others will proceed to their respective units.

NAVSUPPACT officers will generally spend one night in the Annapolis and will attend a Personal Response briefing prior to going to Nha-Be to check in with Headquarters. All NAVSUPPACT Supply Corps Officers will report to NAVSUPPACT Saigon Supply Department where they will meet with the Assistant to the Supply & Fiscal Officer and the Supply & Fiscal Officer, at which time they will be informed of their ultimate assignment.

NSA and COMNAVFORV officers will draw greens and weapons while here at the Annapolis. MAC officers will draw greens and weapons from MACV. NSA officers will take all gear with them to Nha-Be, unless otherwise advised.

# ALL HANDS INFORMATION
# WELCOME TO NAM

# NAVSUPPACT OFFICERS

Upon arrival at Nha-Be, you will report to the Officer Personnel Office, Headquarters, Building C. You will turn in your records to the Officer Records Yeoman, and then have your picture taken. From there you will meet the Admin Officer who will then set up an appointment for you to meet the Chief Staff Officer and the Commander.

After meeting with the Chief Staff Officer and the Commander, you will be briefed by appropriate departments and transportation will be arranged to your ultimate duty station if located outside the Nah Be area.

## DO'S AND DON'TS

A few DO's:

1. Conduct yourself as gentlemen.
2. Remain in a complete, clean, and neat uniform.
3. Pay all bills.
4. Treat all persons with due respect.

A few DON'Ts:

1. Don't become intoxicated.
2. Don't become involved in political discussions.
3. Don't "talk shop" or discuss classified matters ashore.
4. Don't make tactless comparisons between conditions in Vietnam and the United States.

# Appendix I

## ANNAPOLIS BOQ/BEQ CHECK-IN SHEET

Annapolis BOQ/BEQ Check-In Sheet
For Personnel Inprocessing for Duty in Vietnam

Name: Rate: _____ Rate: _____ Ser.# _____
Duty Station: _____

THE IN-COUNTRY CHECK-IN PROCESS REQUIRES THAT YOU REPORT TO THE ABSOLUTE MINIMUM OF STATIONS. THESE FEW STATIONS ARE ESSENTIAL AND IT IS IMPORTANT THAT YOU COMPLETE THE CHECK-IN PROCESS AS EXPEDITIOUSLY AS POSSIBLE. ALL PERSONNEL MUST SIGN THE <u>CERTIFICATE OF UNDERSTANDING</u> AT THE BOTTOM. THIS WILL BE FILED IN YOUR SERVICE RECORD.

YOU ARE DIRECTED TO CHECK IN WITH THE FOLLOWING OFFICES/PERSONNEL PRIOR TO DEPARTING FOR YOUR ULTIMATE DUTY STATION. (PERSONNEL ORDERED TO 7TH FLEET SHIPS, NAG AND MACV NEED <u>NOT</u> CHECK IN WITH ANNAPOLIS ARMORY AND FIELD ISSUE.)

PERSONAL RESPONSE (Koepler Compound)

_____

(Stamp and Authorized Signature)

FIELD GEAR ISSUE (Annapolis BOQ/BEQ)

_____

(Signature)

ARMORY (Annapolis BOQ/BEQ)

_____Weapons Issued: Yes____No____

(Stamp and Authorized Signature)

POSTAL LOCATOR CARD

_____

(Personnel Office)

Disbursing officer, NAVSUPPACT

_____

(Signature)

CERTIFICATE OF UNDERSTANDING        DATE:_____

I UNDERSTAND THAT I AM TO COMPLETE CHECK-IN PROCESSING AS QUICKLY AS POSSIBLE AND RETURN THIS CHECK-IN SHEET TO THE TRANSIENT PERSONNEL OFFICE IMMEDIATELY THRERAFTER. I CERTIFY THAT I HAVE ATTENDED ALL INPROCESSING EVOLUSIONS AND HAVE RECEIVED IN-COUNTRY SECURITY LECTURE, DISBURSING LECTURE AND ADMINISTRATION LECTURE AND HAVE RECEIVED ONE MACV RATION CARD AND ONE MACV CURRENTY CONTROL PLATE.

_____

(Signature)

WITNESSED:

_____

OIC, ANNAPOLIS BOQ/BEQ, SAIGON

# Appendix J-U

I discovered the following items on the Internet.
I found them to be most interesting
and included them below.

These two sites are well worth the visit:
**USSSATYR.COM**
**&**
**MRFA.COM**

Appendix S06:   Good Conduct Medal & Ribbon
Appendix S07:   Presidential Unit Citation Ribbon
Appendix S08:   Navy Unit commendation Ribbon
Appendix S09:   Meritorious Unit Commendation Ribbon
Appendix S10:   Medals, Ribbons & Stars

Appendix T:   Statistics about the Vietnam War
Appendix T01:   The misunderstood war in Vietnam
Appendix T02:   Most American soldiers were addicted to drugs, guilt-ridden about their role in the war, & deliberately used cruel & inhumane tactics.
Appendix T03:   Most Vietnam veterans were drafted
Appendix T04:   The media have reported that suicides among Vietnam veterans range from 50,000 to 100,000. 6 to 11 times the non-Vietnam veteran population.
Appendix T05:   A disproportionate number of blacks were killed in the Vietnam War.
Appendix T06:   The war was fought largely by the poor and uneducated.
Appendix T07:   The average age of an infantryman fighting in Nam was 19.
Appendix T08:   The domino theory was proved false.
Appendix T09:   The fighting in Vietnam was not as intense as in WW II.
Appendix T10:   More helicopter facts:
Appendix T11:   Air America, the airline operated by the CIA in Southeast Asia, and its pilots were involved in drug trafficking.
Appendix T12:   The American military was running for their lives during the fall of Saigon in April 1975. The picture of a Huey helicopter-evacuating people from the top of what was billed as being the U.S. Embassy in Saigon during the last week of April 1975 during the fall of Saigon helped to establish this myth.
Appendix T13:   Facts about the fall of Saigon:

# Appendix J

## MURPHY'S LAW ON COMBAT

If the enemy is in range, so are you.
Incoming fire has the right of way.
Don't look conspicuous; it draws fire.
The easy way is always mined.
Try to look unimportant; they may be low on ammo.
The enemy invariably attacks on two occasions:
when you're ready for them, and
when you're not ready for them.
Teamwork is essential; it gives them someone else to shoot at.
If you can't remember, then the claymore is pointed at you.
The enemy diversion you have been ignoring,
is the main attack.
A 'sucking chest wound' is nature's way of telling you to—
slow down.
If your attack is going well, you have walked into an ambush.
Never draw fire; it irritates everyone around you.
Anything you do can get you shot, including nothing.
Make it tough enough for the enemy to get in, and
you won't be able to get out.
Never share a foxhole with anyone braver than yourself.
If you're short of everything but the enemy,
you're in a combat zone.

When you have secured an area, don't forget to tell the enemy.

Never forget that your weapon was made by the lowest bidder.

When in doubt, empty your magazine.

All 5-second grenade fuses will burn out in 3.

If you are forward of your position,
the artillery will always fall short.

No combat ready unit ever passed inspection.

Things that must be together to work,
usually can't be shipped together.

Radios will fail as soon as you need fire support desperately.

Tracers work both ways.

The only thing more accurate than incoming enemy fire,
is incoming friendly fire.

When both sides are convinced that they are about to lose,
they are both right.

Beer math is 2 beers times 37 men equals 49 cases.

Body-count math is 3 guerrillas + 1 probable + 2 pigs,
equals 37 enemy killed in action.

If it's stupid but works, it isn't stupid.

The important things are always simple.

The simple things are always hard.

Admit nothing, deny everything, and make counter-accusations.

Any ship can be a minesweeper . . . once.

Combat will occur on the ground between two adjoining maps.

Don't ever be the first, don't ever be the last and don't ever
volunteer to do anything.

Don't run, you'll only die tired.

If you find yourself in a fair fight,
you didn't plan your mission properly!

It is generally inadvisable to eject directly over the area you
just bombed.

Mines are equal opportunity weapons.

Never tell the Platoon Sergeant you have nothing to do.

Never trust a private with a loaded weapon, or an officer with a map.

Odd objects attract fire—never lurk behind one.
Peace is our profession, killing is just a hobby.
Push to test, Release to detonate.
Retreating?! Hell no, we're just attacking from the other direction!
The side with the simplest uniforms wins.
There are two kinds of ships, submarines and targets.
When the pin is pulled, Mr. Grenade is not our friend.
Murphy was a grunt.

# Appendix K

## USMC RULES FOR GUN FIGHTING

Bring a gun. Preferably, bring at least two guns.
Bring all of your friends who have guns.
Anything worth shooting is worth shooting twice.
Ammo is cheap. Life is expensive.
Only hits count.
The only thing worse than a miss is a slow miss.
If you're shooting stance is good,
you're probably not moving fast enough,
nor using cover correctly.
Move away from your attacker.
Distance is your friend.
(Lateral and diagonal movement are preferred.)
If you can choose what to bring to a gunfight,
bring a long gun and a friend with a long gun.
In ten years, nobody will remember the details of caliber,
stance, or tactics. They will only remember who lived.
If you are not shooting,
you should be communicating, loading, or running.
Accuracy is relative.
Most combat shooting standards will be more dependent
on "pucker factor" than the inherent accuracy of the gun.

Someday someone may kill you with your own gun,
but they should have to beat you to death with it because it was empty.
Always cheat; always win.
The only unfair fight is the one you lose.
Have a plan.
Have a back-up plan, because the first plan won't work.
Use cover or concealment as much as possible.
Flank your adversary when possible. Protect yours.
Don't drop your guard.
Always tactical load and threat scan 360 degrees.
Watch their hands. Hands kill.
In God we trust,
everyone else, keep your hands where I can see them.
Decide to be aggressive ENOUGH, quickly ENOUGH.
The faster you finish the fight, the less shot you will get.
Be polite. Be professional. But, have a plan to kill everyone you meet.
Be courteous to everyone, friendly to no one.
Your number one Option for Personal Security,
is a lifelong commitment to avoidance, deterrence, and de-escalation.
Do not attend a gunfight with a handgun,
with a caliber of which does not start with a "4."

# Appendix L

## NAVY RULES FOR GUN FIGHTING

Go to Sea.

Send in the Marines.

Drink Coffee.

# Appendix M

## HOW TO SIMULATE BEING A SAILOR

Buy a steel dumpster, paint it gray inside and out, (Green for BrownWater Navy ships) and live in it for six months.

Run all the pipes and wires in your house exposed on the walls.

Repaint your entire house every month.

Renovate your bathroom. Build a wall across the middle of the bathtub and move the showerhead to chest level.

When you take showers, make sure you turn off the water while you soap down.

Put lube oil in your humidifier and set it on high.

Once a month, take all your major appliances apart and then reassemble them.

Raise the thresholds and lower the headers of your front and back doors so that you either trip or bang your head every time you pass through them.

Disassemble and inspect your lawnmower every week.

On Mondays, Wednesdays, and Fridays, turn your water heater temperature up to 200 degrees. On Tuesdays and Thursdays, turn the water heater off. On Saturdays and Sundays, tell your family they used too much water during the week, so no bathing will be allowed.

Raise your bed to within 6 inches of the ceiling, so you can't turn over without getting out and then getting back in.

Sleep on the shelf in your closet. Replace the closet door with a curtain. Have your spouse whip open the curtain about 3 hours after you go to sleep, shine a flashlight in your eyes, and say "Sorry, wrong rack."

Make your family qualify to operate each appliance in your house—dishwasher operator, blender technician, etc.

Have your neighbor come over each day at 5 am, blow a whistle so loud Helen Keller could hear it, and shout, "Reveille!"

Have your mother-in-law write down everything she's going to do the following day, then have her make you stand in your back yard at 6 am while she reads it to you.

Submit a request chit to your father-in-law requesting permission to leave your house before 3 PM.

Empty all the garbage bins in your house and sweep the driveway three times a day, whether it needs it or not.

Have your neighbor collect all your mail for a month, read your magazines, and randomly lose every 5th item before delivering it to you.

Watch no TV except for movies played in the middle of the night. Have your family vote on which movie to watch, and then show a different one.

When your children are in bed, run into their room with a megaphone shouting that your home is under attack and ordering them to their battle stations.

Make your family menu a week ahead of time without consulting the pantry or refrigerator.

Post a menu on the kitchen door informing your family that they are having steak for dinner. Then make them wait in line for an hour. When they finally get to the kitchen, tell them you are out of steak, but they can have dried ham or hot dogs. Repeat daily until they ignore the menu and just ask for hot dogs.

Bake a cake. Prop up one side of the pan so the cake bakes unevenly and then spread the icing on real thick to level it off.

Get up every night around midnight and have a peanut butter and jelly sandwich on stale bread.

Set your alarm clock to go off at random during the night. At the alarm, jump up and dress as fast as you can, making sure to button your top shirt button and tuck your pants into your socks. Then run out into the backyard and uncoil the garden hose.

Every week or so, throw your cat or dog in the pool and shout, "Man overboard, port side!" Rate your family members on how fast they respond.

Put the headphones from your stereo on your head, but don't plug them in. Hang a paper cup round your neck on a string. Stand in front of the stove, and speak into the paper cup, "Stove manned and ready." After an hour or so, speak into the cup again, 'Stove secured." Roll up the headphones and paper cup and stow them in a shoebox.

Place a podium at the end of your driveway. Have your family stand watches at the podium, rotating at 4-hour intervals. This is best done when the weather is bad, January is a good time.

When there is a thunderstorm in your area, get a wobbly rocking chair. Sit in it and rock as hard as you can until you become nauseous. Make sure to have a supply of stale crackers in your shirt pocket.

For former engineers: bring your lawn mower into the living room, and run it all day long.

Make coffee using eighteen scoops of budget priced coffee grounds per pot, and allow the pot to simmer for 5 hours before drinking.

Have someone under the age of ten give you a haircut with sheep shears.

Sew the back pockets of your jeans on the front.

Every couple of weeks, dress up in your best clothes and go to the scummiest part of town. Find the most run down, trashiest bar, and drink beer until you are hammered. Then walk all the way home.

Lock yourself and your family in the house for six weeks. Tell them that at the end of the 6th week you are going to take them to Disney World for "liberty." At the end of the 6th week, inform them the trip to Disney World has been canceled because they need to get ready for an inspection, and it will be another week before they can leave the house.

# Appendix N

## LESSONS OF A
## VIETNAM HELICOPTER CREWMAN

1. Once you are in the fight, it is way too late to wonder if it was a good idea.
2. Helicopters are cool!
3. It is a fact that helicopter tail rotors are instinctively drawn toward trees, stumps, rocks, etc. While it may be possible to ward off this natural event some of the time, it cannot, despite the best efforts of the crew, always be prevented. It's just what they do.
4. NEVER get into a fight without more ammunition than the other guy.
5. The engine RPM, and the rotor RPM, must BOTH be kept in the GREEN. Failure to heed this commandment can affect the morale of the crew.
6. A billfold in your hip pocket can numb your leg and be a real pain in the ass.
7. Cover your Buddy, so he can be around to cover you.
8. Letters from home are not always great.
9. The madness of war can extract a heavy toll. Please have exact change.
10. Share everything. Even the Pound Cake.

11. Decisions made by someone over your head will seldom be in your best interest.
12. The terms "Protective Armor" and "Helicopter" are mutually exclusive.
13. The further away you are from your friends; the less likely it is that they can help you when you really need them the most.
14. If being good and lucky is not enough, there is always payback.
15. "Chicken Plates" are not something you order in a restaurant.
16. If everything is as clear as a bell, and everything is going exactly as planned, you're about to be surprised.
17. The B.S.R. (Bang, Stare, Read) Theory states that the louder the sudden bang in the helicopter, the quicker your eyes will be drawn to the gauges.
18. The longer you stare at the gauges, the less time it takes them to move from green to red.
19. It does too get cold in Vietnam.
20. No matter what you do, the bullet with your name on it will get you. So too can the ones addressed "To Whom It May Concern."
21. Gravity may not be fair, but it is the law.
22. If the rear echelon troops are really happy, the front line troops probably do not have what they need.
23. If you are wearing body armor, the incoming will probably miss that part.
24. It hurts less to die with a uniform on than to die in a hospital bed.
25. Happiness is a belt-fed weapon.
26. If something hasn't broken on your helicopter, it's about to.
27. Eat when you can. Sleep when you can. Visit the head when you can. The next opportunity may not come around for a long time. If ever.
28. Combat pay is a flawed concept.
29. Having all your body parts intact and functioning at the end of the day beats the alternative.
30. Air superiority is NOT a luxury.

31. If you are allergic to lead, it is best to avoid a war zone.

32. It is always a bad thing to run out of airspeed, altitude, and ideas all at the same time.

32a. Nothing is as useless as altitude above you and runway behind you.

33. While the rest of the crew may be in the same predicament, it's usually the pilot's job to arrive at the crash site first.

34. When you shoot your gun, clean it the first chance you get.

35. Loud sudden noises in a helicopter, WILL get your undivided attention.

36. Hot garrison chow is better than hot C-rations, which, in turn is better than cold C-rations, which is better than no food at all. All of these, however, are preferable to cold rice balls (given to you by guards) even if they do have the little pieces of fish in them.

37. WHAT is often more important than WHY.

38. Boxes of cookies from home must be shared.

39. Girlfriends are fair game. Wives are not.

40. Everybody's a hero on the ground in the club after the fourth drink.

41. There is no such thing as a small firefight.

42. A free-fire zone has nothing to do with economics.

43. The farther you fly into the mountains, the louder the strange engine noises become.

44. Medals are OK, but having your body and all your friends in one piece at the end of the day is better.

44a. The only medal you really want to be awarded, is the Longevity Medal.

45. Being shot hurts.

46. Thousands of Vietnam Veterans earned medals for bravery every day. A few were even awarded.

48. Running out of pedal, fore or aft cyclic, or collective are all bad ideas. Any combination of these can be deadly.

49. NOMEX is NOT fire proof.

50. There is only one rule in war: When you win, you get to make up the Rules.

51. Living and dying can both hurt a lot.
53. While a Super Bomb could be considered one of the four essential building blocks of life, powdered eggs cannot.
54. C-4 can make a dull day fun.
55. Cocoa Powder is neither.
56. There is no such thing as a fair fight, only ones where you win or lose.
57. If you win the battle, you are entitled to the spoils. If you lose, you don't care.
58. Nobody cares what you did yesterday or what you are going to do tomorrow. What is important is what you are doing NOW to solve our problem.
59. If you have extra, share it quickly.
60. Always make sure someone has a P-38.
61. A sucking chest wound may be God's way of telling you it's time to go home.
62. Prayer may not help . . . but it can't hurt.
63. Flying is better than walking. Walking is better than running. Running is better than crawling. All of these however, are better than extraction by a Med-Evac, even if this is technically a form of flying.
64. If everyone does not come home, none of the rest of us can ever fully come home either.
65. Do not fear the enemy, for your enemy can only take your life. It is far better that you fear the media, for they will steal your HONOR.
66. A grunt is the true reason for the existence of the helicopter. Every helicopter flying in Vietnam had one real purpose: To help the grunt. It is unfortunate that many helicopters never had the opportunity to fulfill their one true mission in life simply because someone forgot this fact.
67. "You have the right to remain silent" is always EXCELLENT advice.

# Appendix O

## PATCHES

# Appendix P

## P-38 & CONCUSSION GRENADE

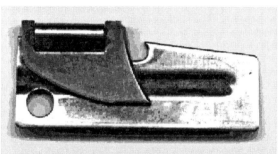

# Appendix Q

## CONTROL PASS

U.S. ARMED FORCES CONTROL PASS

| | | |
|---|---|---|
| _____ | _____ | _____ |
| NAME | RANK | ORGANIZATION |

IS AUTHORORIZED TO VISIT ON LIMITS FACILITIES AND COMMERCIAL ESTABLISHMENTS IN LONG XUYEN AREA OF MR4.

THIS PASS IS NOT VALID DURING HOURS OF CURFEW. IT WILL BE RETURNED TO ISSUING UNIT UPON TERMINATION OF PASS.

/s/ D. S. MELROSE
MAJOR GENERAL, USA
ZONE COORDINATOR MR4

| USS SATYR ARL23 | / | / | /s/, | USN, | LT |
|---|---|---|---|---|---|
| CONTROL HCS | DATE VALID | | UNIT CMDR | | COUNTERSIGN |

- - - - - - - - - - - - - - - - - - - - - - - - - - - - - - -

TO EACH SERVICEMAN ON PASS IN THE DELTA:
YOU ARE BEING TRUSTED TO GO ON PASS. YOUR LEADERS EXPECT
YOU TO BE WORTHY OF THAT TRUST.
WE EXPECT THAT YOU WILL STAY AWAY FROM HEROIN AND OTHER
DANGEROUS DRUGS.

WE EXPECT THAT YOU WILL SUPPORT YOUR FELLOW MAN BY HELPING
HIM HAVE A GOOD TIME WITHOUHT USING HEROIN AND SIMILAR
SUBSTANCES.

WE EXPECT YOU TO HELP US IDENTIFY THE PUSHERS AND OTHER VILE
PERSONS WHO SELL FOR PROFIT THIS HEROIN MONSTER THAT THRIVES
ON MEN'S WEAKNESSES TO DESTROY THEIR BODIES AND MINDS. WE
ASK YOU TO REPORT THESE WORMS TO THE MILITARY POLICE, AND WE
EXPECT YOU TO BE WELL BEHAVED, IN CORRECT UNIFORM,
CONSIDERATE OF THE VIETNAMESE ARMED FORCES, AND ABOVE ALL A
CREDIT TO THE UNITED STATES OF AMERICA.

/S/ D. S. MELROSE
MAJOR GENERAL, USA
COMMANDING

_____
SIGNATURE

# Appendix R

## SHIP PHOTO

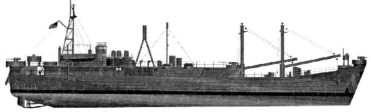

GEO. MESA 2002 NO. 6636

**ACHELOUS CLASS LANDING CRAFT REPAIR SHIP**

In my story, I called her the USS Summit(ARR23), in reality, it was the USS SATYR(ARL23)

# Appendix  S

## MEDALS and RIBBONS

Note:

3/16" Bronze Star     Worn to indicate second and subsequent awards for service or campaign medals.

3/16" Silver Star     Worn in place of five bronze stars.

# Appendix S01

## National Defense Service Medal

This medal was authorized by Executive Order 10448, "Establishing the National Defense Service Medal," as amended by Executive Order 11265, January 11, 1966.

## Eligibility requirements

Honorable active service as a member of the Armed Forces of the United States for any period between June 27, 1950 and July 27, 1954, or between January 1, 1961 and August 14, 1974. During those periods, Service members in the following categories shall NOT be eligible for the NDSM:

1. Members of the Guard and Reserve Forces on short tours of active duty to fulfill training obligations under an inactive duty-training program.

2. Any Service member on TDY or TAD to serve on boards, courts commissions, and similar organizations.

3. Any Service member on active duty for the sole purpose of undergoing a physical examination.

Honorable service as a member of the Armed Forces of the United States for any period between August 2, 1990, and November 30, 1995. Service members on active duty, members of the Selected Reserve in good standing, and members of other than the Selected Reserve who were called to active duty shall also be eligible. During that period, Service members in the following categories shall NOT be considered eligible:

1. Any Service member on active duty for the sole purpose of undergoing a physical examination.

2. Any member of the Individual Ready Reserve, the Inactive National Guard or the Standby or Retired Reserve whose active duty service was for training only, or to serve on boards, courts, commissions, and similar organizations.

Exceptions to policy criteria in the paragraphs above may be granted by the Military Departments.

Midshipmen attending the Naval Academy during the above periods are eligible for this medal. NROTC Midshipmen are only eligible if their summer cruise was in an area, which qualified for a campaign medal.

Notwithstanding these limitations, any member of the United States Coast Guard or the Reserve or Guard Forces of the Armed Forces who, between January 1, 1961 and August 14, 1974, became eligible for award of either the AFEM or the Vietnam Service Medal or between August 2, 1990 and November 30, 1995, became eligible for award of the Southwest Asia Service Medal shall be eligible for award of the NDSM.

## Subsequent Award

A bronze service star shall be worn on the suspension and service ribbon of the NDSM by Service members who earned the medal during two different periods of eligibility (e.g., during the period 1961 through 1974, and during the period 1990 through 1995).

# Appendix S02

## Republic of Vietnam Campaign Medal

The Secretary of Defense approved a request for approval of foreign awards to US Military personnel on 7 February 1966. As a result of this approval, the Republic of Vietnam Campaign Medal with device bar (1960-) was awarded to US Armed Forces personnel by the Government of the Republic of Vietnam per Republic of Vietnam Armed Forces Order No. 48, dated 24 March 1966. The acceptance, criteria and description was announced in the Federal Register, Volume 31, No. 147, 30 July 1966 (Title 32, Code of Federal Regulation 47).

The Republic of Vietnam Armed Forces Memorandum 2655 prescribed there were two devices to be worn on the ribbon. The first device was for the period 8 March 1949-20 July 1954 and is not authorized for wear by American Military Personnel. The second period was from 1 January 1960 with the last period to be decided after the war was over. The ending period remains blank, since the Republic of Vietnam Government ceased to exist before the ending period was established. The devices for the medal are in two sizes—the large size is 1 13/64 inches in width and is worn on the suspension ribbon of the full size decoration. The regular size is 19/32 inch wide and is worn on the miniature decoration and service ribbon bar.

Since the Republic of Vietnam Campaign Medal is a foreign award, it is not issued by the United States Government. The medal may be purchased from commercial sources.

1. Description: A gold six pointed star with rays, 32cm in diameter, superimposed by a White enameled star, 42cm in diameter, overall in center a Green disc, 18cm in diameter, with the outline of the Vietnamese Country with a Red flame of three rays between North and South Vietnam. On the reverse of the medal is a circle with a designation band containing the word "CHIEN-DICH" (Campaign) at the top and "BOI-TINH" (Medal) at the bottom. Across the center of the circle is the word "VIET-NAM."

2. Criteria: The Republic of Vietnam Campaign Medal is awarded to personnel who meet one of the following requirements:

   a. Served in the Republic of Vietnam for six months during the period of 1 March 1961 and 28 March 1973.

   b. Served outside the geographical limits of the Republic of Vietnam and contributed direct combat support to the Republic of Vietnam and Armed Forces for six months. Such individuals must meet the criteria established for the Armed Forces Expeditionary Medal (for Vietnam) or the Vietnam Service Medal, to qualify for the Republic of Vietnam Campaign Medal.

   c Six months service is not required for individuals who were wounded by hostile forces; killed in action or otherwise in line of duty; or captured by hostile forces.

# Appendix S03

## Republic of Vietnam Service Medal

The Vietnam Service Medal was authorized by Executive Order 11231 "Establishing the Vietnam Service Medal," July 8, 1965

It is awarded to all Service members of the Armed Forces who, between July 4, 1965, and March 28, 1973, served in the following areas of Southeast Asia:

1. In Vietnam and the contiguous waters or airspace, they are over.

2. In Thailand, Laos, or Cambodia or the airspace, there over, and in direct support of operations in Vietnam.

Service members qualified for the AFEM by reasons of service between July 1, 1958, and July 3, 1965, in an area for which the Vietnam Service Medal was authorized subsequently shall remain qualified for that medal. Upon application, any such Service member may be awarded the Vietnam Service Medal instead of the AFEM for such service. However, no Service member shall be entitled to both awards.

## Personnel Eligible

To be eligible a Service member must be as follows:

1. Attached to or regularly serving for one, or more, days with an organization participating in or directly supporting ground (military) operations.

2. Attached to or regularly serving for one, or more, days aboard a naval vessel directly supporting military operations.

3. Actually participate as a crewmember in one or more aerial flights directly supporting military operations.

4. Serve on temporary duty for 30 consecutive days or 60 nonconsecutive days.

Those time limitations may be waived for personnel participating in actual combat operations.

## Limitation on Medal

The medal shall be awarded only for operations for which no other U.S. campaign medal is approved. No Service member may be issued both the Vietnam Service Medal and the AFEM for service in Vietnam, and furthermore they shall be entitled to no more than one award of the Vietnam Service Medal.

## Stars

A bronze service star shall be worn on the suspension and service ribbon of the Vietnam Service Medal for the Service member's participation in additional approved campaign.

# Appendix S04

## Purple Heart Medal

Established by General George Washington—known as the "Badge of Military Merit"—on August 7, 1782.

Revived as the Purple Heart in 1932 by General Douglas MacArthur.

It is awarded to any member of the Armed Forces of the United States or any civilian national of the United States who, while serving under competent authority in any capacity with one of the U.S. Armed Forces, after April 5, 1917, has been wounded, killed, or who has died or may hereafter die of wounds received under any of the following circumstances:

1. In action against an enemy of the United States.

2. In action with an opposing armed force of a foreign country in which the Armed Forces of the United States are or have been engaged.

3. While serving with friendly foreign forces engaged in an armed conflict against an opposing armed force in which the United States is not a belligerent party.

4.  As a result of an act of any such enemy of opposing armed forces.

5.  As the result of an act of any hostile foreign force.

6.  After March 28, 1973, as a result of an international terrorist attack against the United States or a foreign nation friendly to the United States.

7.  After March 28, 1973, because of military operations while serving outside the territory of the United States as part of a peacekeeping force.

8.  A Service member who is killed or wounded in action as the result of action by friendly weapon fire while directly engaged in armed conflict, other than as a result of an act of an enemy of the United States, unless (in the case of a wound) the wound is the result of willful misconduct of the member under Section 1129, title 10, United States Code, March 1995.

9.  Before April 25, 1962, while held as a prisoner of war (or while being taken captive) in the same manner as a former prisoner of war who is wounded on or after that date while held as a prisoner of war (or while being taken captive under Section 521, DOD Authorization Act for 1996, February 10, 1996.

While clearly an individual decoration, the Purple Heart differs from all other decorations in that an individual is not "recommended" for the decoration; rather he or she is entitled to it upon meeting specific criteria.

A Purple Heart is authorized for the first wound suffered under conditions indicated above, but for each subsequent award an Oak Leaf Cluster for Army and Air Force personnel and a 5/16" gold star for Navy, Marine Corps and Coast Guard personnel will be awarded to be worn on the medal or ribbon. Not more than one award will be made for more than one wound or injury received at the same instant or from the same missile, force, explosion, or agent.

# WOUND

A wound is defined as an injury to any part of the body from an outside force or agent sustained under one or more of the conditions listed above. A physical lesion is not required, however, the wound for which the award is made must have required treatment by a medical officer, and records of medical treatment for wounds or injuries received in action must have been made a matter of official record.

When contemplating an award of this decoration, the key issue that commanders must take into consideration is the degree to which the enemy caused the injury. The fact that the proposed recipient was participating in direct or indirect combat operations is a prerequisite, but is not sole justification for award.

# QUALIFIED RELATED INJURIES

Examples of enemy—related injuries which clearly justify award of the Purple Heart are as follows:

> Injury caused by enemy bullet, shrapnel, or other projectile created by enemy action.
> Injury caused by enemy placed mine or trap.
> Injury caused by enemy released chemical, biological, or nuclear agent.
> Injury caused by vehicle or aircraft accident resulting from enemy fire.
> Concussion injuries caused as a result of enemy generated explosions.

# UNQUALIFIED INJURIES

Examples of injuries or wounds which clearly do not qualify for award of the Purple Heart are as follows:

> Frostbite or trench foot injuries.
> Heat stroke.
> Food poisoning not caused by enemy agents.
> Chemical, biological, or nuclear agents not released by the enemy.
> Battle fatigue.
> Disease not directly caused by enemy agents.
> Accidents, to include explosive, aircraft, vehicular, and other accidental wounding not related to or caused by enemy action.
> Self-inflicted wounds, except when in the heat of battle, and not involving gross negligence.
> Post traumatic stress disorders.
> Jump injuries not caused by enemy action.

It is not intended that such a strict interpretation of the requirement for the wound or injury to be caused by direct result of hostile action be taken that it would preclude the award being made to deserving personnel. Commanders must also take into consideration the circumstances surrounding an injury, even if it appears to meet the criteria.

Note the following examples:

1. In a case such as an individual injured while making a parachute landing from an aircraft that had been brought down by enemy fire; or, an individual injured as a result of a vehicle accident caused by enemy fire, the decision will be made in favor of the individual and the award will be made.

2.  Individuals wounded or killed as a result of "friendly fire" in the "heat of battle" will be awarded the Purple Heart as long as the "friendly" projectile or agent was released with the full intent of inflicting damage or destroying enemy troops or equipment.

3.  Individuals injured as a result of their own negligence; for example, driving or walking through an unauthorized area known to have been mined or placed off limits or searching for or picking up unexploded munitions as war souvenirs, will not be awarded the Purple Heart as they clearly were not injured as a result of enemy action, but rather by their own negligence.

## POSTHUMOUS AWARDS

A Purple Heart will be issued to the next of kin of each person entitled to a posthumous award. Issue will be made automatically by the Commanding General, PERSCOM, the CNO, and the CMC upon receiving a report of death indicating entitlement.

# Appendix S05

## Combat Action Ribbon

The Combat Action Ribbon was authorized by the Secretary of the Navy, February 17, 1969.

It is awarded to members of the U.S. Navy, the U.S. Marine Corps, and the U.S. Coast Guard, operating under the control of the U.S. Navy, in the grade of O-6, or below, who have actively participated in ground or surface combat. Upon submission of evidence to their commanding officer, personnel who earned the Combat Infantryman Badge or Combat Medical Badge while members of the U.S. Army maybe authorized to wear the Combat Action Ribbon instead.

The principal eligibility criterion is that the individual must have participated in a bona fide ground or surface combat firefight or action during which he was under enemy fire and his performance while under fire was satisfactory.

The following is provided as guidance:

1. Personnel in Riverine and coastal operations, assaults, patrols, sweeps, ambushes, convoys, amphibious landings, and similar activities who have participated in firefights are eligible.

2. Personnel assigned to areas subjected to sustained mortar, missile, and artillery attacks actively anticipate in retaliatory or offensive actions are eligible.

3. Personnel in clandestine or special operations such as reconnaissance and SEAL teams are eligible when the risk of enemy fire was great and was expected to be encountered.

4. Personnel aboard a ship are eligible when the safety of the ship and the crew were endangered by enemy attack, such as a ship hit by a mine or a ship engaged by shore, surface, air or sub-surface elements.

Personnel eligible for the award of the Purple Heart would not necessarily qualify for the Combat Action Ribbon.

The Combat Action Ribbon will not be awarded to personnel for aerial combat since the Strike/Flight Air Medal provides recognition for aerial combat exposure; however, a pilot or crewmember forced to escape or evade after being forced down could be eligible for the award.

A Service member, whose eligibility has been established in combat in any of the following listed operations, is authorized award of the Combat Action Ribbon. Only one award per operation is authorized. Subsequent awards will be indicated by the use of a Gold Star on the ribbon.

# Appendix S06

## Good Conduct Medal

The Navy Good Conduct Medal, originally in the form of a badge, was the first award specifically designed to recognize the military service of an individual.

Established by the Secretary of the Navy, April 26, 1869.

The medal was originally awarded to recognize the 'all-around' good Navy enlisted person, well qualified in all phases of conduct and performance. Effective 1 February 1971, commanding officers were delegated authority to award the Good Conduct Medal and subsequent awards and to issue medals and certificates.

Awarded on a selective basis to recognize 3 years of continuous active duty, above average conduct, and proficiency by enlisted Service members in the regular U.S. Navy or U.S. Naval Reserve.

## ELIGIBILITY

### Service

After 1 November 1963 any 4 years of continuous active service as an enlisted person in the Regular Navy or Naval

Reserve. For first enlistments, this requirement may be fulfilled by:

1.  Continuous active service during a minority enlistment provided the member concerned served on active duty to the day preceding his 21st birthday even though he extended his enlistment and remained on active duty.

2.  Continuous active service during a minority enlistment provided the member concerned served on active duty within 3 months of the day preceding his 21st birthday.

3.  Continuous active service during a first enlistment for 4 years from which the member concerned has been discharged or released to inactive duty within 3 months of the date of expiration of enlistment. (This does not apply to those members who are discharged for the purpose of immediate reenlistment.

## Conduct

Within the required period of active service, the individual must have a clear record (no convictions by courts-martial, no non-judicial punishments, no sick-misconduct, no civil convictions for offenses involving moral turpitude).

1.  If confinement as result of conviction by any courts-martial (general, special, or summary) is involved, a new 4-year period shall begin with date of restoration to duty on a probationary basis. If confinement is not included in approved sentence of the courts-martial, a new 4-year period shall begin with date of convening authority action.

2.  If the service record contains a non-judicial punishment, a new 4-year period shall begin with next date following the date of the offense.

3. If convicted by civil authorities for an offense involving moral turpitude, a new 4-year period shall begin with date of return to active duty status.

4. If the record contains a disqualifying mark which is not the result of a non-judicial punishment, the new 4-year period shall begin with the next date following the date of the mark.

## Performance marks required during period of eligibility:

1. Subsequent to 31 August 1983 no mark below 3.0 in Military Knowledge\Performance, Rating Knowledge\Performance, Reliability, Military Bearing, Personal Behavior and Directing.

2. Prior to 31 August 1983:

   a) E-4 and below. No Mark below 3.0 in any trait.
   b) E-5 and E-6. No Mark below EEL (Typically Effective-Lower) in Directing, Individual Productivity, Reliability, or Conduct.
   c) E-7, E-8, and E-9. No Mark below the bottom 50 percent in Performance, Reliability, Conduct, or Directing.

If an individual receives a disqualifying trait mark, a new period of eligibility would begin on the day following the ending date of the performance evaluation report which contains the disqualifying trait mark.

Subsequent to 17 May 1974, for the first award only, the Good Conduct Medal may be awarded in the following cases provided conduct and performance requirements are met:

1. For those individuals who are killed in combat action against an opposing armed force, or die as a direct result of wounds received in combat action against an opposing

armed force, the award may be presented posthumously to the next of kin.

2. For those individuals who are separated from the naval service for physical disability as a result of wounds incurred in combat action against an opposing armed force, or in the line of duty where such wounds were directly related to action against the enemy.

3. For those individuals who die while in a Prisoner of War (POW) status, the Good Conduct Medal may be presented posthumously to the next of kin, provided it has been determined that conduct while in a POW status was acceptable.

A certificate shall be prepared for each award, when earned. The member's rate, name, branch of service, and the number of the award shall be centered in the appropriate spaces. The ending date of the period of service for which the award was earned shall be centered after "Awarded for service completed on." The commanding officer's name, rank, and branch of service shall be typed above "Commanding Officer and his/her signature affixed.

## ATTACHMENTS

A Bronze Star, 3/16 inch in diameter will be worn on the suspension ribbon and bar to denote subsequent awards.

## NOTES

1. For personnel who are serving in a first enlistment of 4 years or a minority enlistment and who have met the eligibility requirements except for length of service, the Good Conduct Medal may be presented 3 months prior to the eligibility date. In the event that the member fails to

fulfill the requirements during the remaining 3 months of the eligibility period, the commanding officer may revoke the award.

2. A member not eligible for the Good Conduct Medal under the foregoing criteria who reenlist or reports for active duty within 3 months after his/her discharge or release to inactive duty is considered to be serving under "continuous active service" conditions. While the time between the date of separation and date of return to active duty is not counted as an interruption of active service, it may not be included in computing time served. A member who reenlist or reports for active duty after 3 months must begin a new 4 year period on the date of reenlistment or reporting for active duty.

3. An enlisted member appointed a temporary warrant or commissioned officer is entitled to include such temporary service upon reverting to an enlisted status for any purpose (including for discharge to accept appointment as a permanent officer). Naval Academy midshipmen who are not commissioned, but are retained in the service in an enlisted status, may include such midshipman service for the purpose of earning the Good Conduct Medal. Except as provided above, service in warrant, commissioned or Naval Academy midshipman status may not be included in computing time served.

4. Active service in a Reserve status credited toward the Naval Reserve Meritorious Service Medal may not be credited for the Good Conduct Medal Award.

5. When the requirements have been met, but it is evident that the individual is not deserving of this award due to a repeated record of valid letters of indebtedness, or other

acts which are not in keeping with the high moral standards required of all Navy personnel, the commanding officer will make appropriate recommendations to CNO (OP-09B33) stating the reasons.

6. If there is insufficient evidence in a member's service record to determine eligibility for the Good Conduct Medal or subsequent award, a copy of page 9, Enlisted Performance Record, NAVPERS 1070/609 should be requested from Chief of Naval Personnel in order to complete the service record and determine the member's eligibility for the award.

7. Effective 12 March 1969 the minority enlistment program was terminated.

# Appendix S07

## Navy Presidential Unit Citation Ribbon

The Navy Presidential Unit Citation was authorized by Executive Order 9050.

It is awarded in the name of the President of the United States to units of the Armed Forces of the United States for extraordinary heroism in action against an armed enemy occurring on, or after, October 16, 1941, for U.S. Navy and U.S. Marine Corps units. The unit must have displayed such gallantry, determination, and esprit de corps in accomplishing its mission under extremely difficult and hazardous conditions to have set it apart and above other units participating in the same campaign. The degree of heroism required is the same as that which would be required for award of a Distinguished Service Cross to an individual.

## Devices

Navy and Marine Corps Service members shall wear the 3/16-inch bronze and Silver Star to denote subsequent unit awards. In addition to oak-leaf clusters and bronze and silver stars, the following devices are authorized specifically for wear on the service ribbon of the Presidential Unit Citation:

# Appendix S08

## Navy Unit Commendation Ribbon

It was authorized by the Secretary of the Navy, December 18, 1944.

It is awarded by the Secretary of the Navy to any unit of the U.S. Navy or U.S. Marine Corps which, subsequent to December 6, 1941, distinguished itself by either of the following:

1.  Outstanding heroism in action against the enemy, but not sufficient to warrant award of the Presidential Unit Citation.

2.  Extremely meritorious service not involving combat, but in support of military operations that was outstanding when compared to other units performing similar service.

The Navy Unit Commendation may be awarded to other units of the Armed Forces of the United States and of friendly foreign nations serving with the Armed Forces of the United States provided such units meet the standards established by the Department of the Navy.

To justify this award, the unit must have performed service of a character comparable to that which would merit the award of a Silver Star Medal for heroism or a Legion of Merit for meritorious service to an individual. Normal performance of duty or participation in a large number of combat missions does not in itself justify the award. An award will not be made to a unit for actions of one or more of its component parts, unless the unit performed uniformly as a team in a manner justifying collective recognition.

Navy and Marine Corps Service members, when authorized shall wear a Bronze Star to denote second and subsequent awards.

# Appendix S09

## Meritorious Unit Commendation Ribbon

It was authorized by the Secretary of the Navy, July 17, 1967.

It is awarded by the Secretary of the Navy to any unit of the U.S. Navy or U.S. Marine Corps that distinguished itself, by either valorous or meritorious achievement considered outstanding when compared to other units performing similar service, but not sufficient to justify award of the Navy Unit Commendation.

Service maybe under either combat or non-combat conditions.

Bronze stars are worn by Navy and Marine Corps personnel to denote second and subsequent awards.

# Appendix S10

## Medals, Ribbons & Stars

National Defense
Service Medal & Ribbon

Republic of Vietnam
Service Medal & Ribbon

Republic of Vietnam
Campaign Medal &
Ribbon

Purple Heart Medal &
Ribbon

Combat Action Ribbon

Good Conduct Medal &
Ribbon

Bronze
Star

Silver
Star

Presidential Unit Citation
Ribbon

Navy Unit Commendation
Ribbon

Meritorious Unit
Commendation Ribbon

# Appendix T

## STATISTICS ABOUT THE VIETNAM WAR

# Appendix T01

## The misunderstood war in Vietnam

"No event in American history is more misunderstood than the Vietnam War. It was misreported then, and it is misremembered now. Rarely have so many people been so wrong about so much. Never have the consequences of their misunderstanding been so tragic." [Nixon]

The Vietnam War has been the subject of thousands of newspaper and magazine articles, hundreds of books, and scores of movies and television documentaries. The great majority of these efforts have erroneously portrayed many myths about the Vietnam War as being facts. [Nixon]

# Appendix T02

## Myth:
**Most American soldiers were addicted to drugs, guilt-ridden about their role in the war, and deliberately used cruel and inhumane tactics.**

The facts are:

91% of Vietnam Veterans say they are glad they served. [Westmoreland]

74% said they would serve again even knowing the outcome. [Westmoreland]

There is no difference in drug usage between Vietnam Veterans and non-veterans of the same age group. (Veterans Administration study) [Westmoreland]

Isolated atrocities committed by American soldiers produced torrents of outrage from antiwar critics and the news media while Communist atrocities were so common that they received hardly any attention at all. The United States sought to minimize and prevent attacks on civilians while North Vietnam made attacks on civilians a centerpiece of its strategy.

Americans who deliberately killed civilians received prison sentences while Communists who did so received commendations.

From 1957 to 1973, the National Liberation Front assassinated 36,725 South Vietnamese and abducted another 58,499. The death squads focused on leaders at the village level and on anyone who improved the lives of the peasants such as medical personnel, social workers, and schoolteachers. [Nixon]

Vietnam Veterans are less likely to be in prison—only 1/2 of one percent of Vietnam Veterans have been jailed for crimes. [Westmoreland]

97% were discharged under honorable conditions; the same percentage of honorable discharges as ten years prior to Vietnam. [Westmoreland]

85% of Vietnam Veterans made a successful transition to civilian life. [McCaffrey]

Vietnam veterans' personal income exceeds that of our non-veteran age group by more than 18 percent. [McCaffrey]

Vietnam veterans have a lower unemployment rate than our non-vet age group. [McCaffrey]

87% of the American people hold Vietnam Vets in high esteem. [McCaffrey]

# Appendix T03

## Myth:
## Most Vietnam veterans were drafted

The facts are:

2/3 of the men who served in Vietnam were volunteers. 2/3 of the men who served in World War II were drafted. [Westmoreland] Approximately 70% of those killed were volunteers. [McCaffrey]

# Appendix T04

## Myth:
The media have reported that suicides among Vietnam veterans range from 50,000 to 100,000. 6 to 11 times the non-Vietnam veteran population.

The facts are:

Mortality studies show that 9,000 is a better estimate. "The CDC Vietnam Experience Study Mortality Assessment showed that during the first 5 years after discharge, deaths from suicide were 1.7 times more likely among Vietnam veterans than non-Vietnam veterans. After that initial post-service period, Vietnam veterans were no more likely to die from suicide than non-Vietnam veterans were. In fact, after the 5-year post-service period, the rate of suicides is less in the Vietnam veterans' group." [Houk]

# Appendix T05

## Myth:
## A disproportionate number of blacks were killed in the Vietnam War.

The facts are:

86% of the men who died in Vietnam were Caucasians, 12.5% were black, 1.2% were other races. (CACF and Westmoreland)

Sociologists Charles C. Moskos and John Sibley Butler, in their recently published book "All That We Can Be," said they analyzed the claim that blacks were used like cannon fodder during Vietnam" and can report definitely that this charge is untrue. Black fatalities amounted to 12 percent of all Americans killed in Southeast Asia—a figure proportional to the number of blacks in the U.S. population at the time and slightly lower than the proportion of blacks in the Army at the close of the war." [All That We Can Be]

# Appendix T06

## Myth:
## The war was fought largely by the poor and uneducated.

The facts are:

Servicemen who went to Vietnam from well-to-do areas had a slightly elevated risk of dying because they were more likely to be pilots or infantry officers.

Vietnam Veterans were the best-educated forces our nation had ever sent into combat. 79% had a high school education or better. [McCaffrey]

Here are statistics from the Combat Area Casualty File (CACF) as of November 1993.
The CACF is the basis for the Vietnam Veterans Memorial (The Wall):

Average age of 58,148 killed in Vietnam was 23.11 years. (Although 58,169 names are in the Nov. 93 database, only 58,148 have both event date and birth date. Event date is used instead of declared dead date for some of those who were listed as missing in action) [CACF]

| Deaths | Total | Average Age |
| --- | --- | --- |
| | 58,148 | 23.11 years |
| Enlisted | 50,274 | 22.37 years |
| Officers | 6,598 | 28.43 years |
| Warrants | 1,276 | 24.73 years |
| E1 | 525 | 20.34 years |
| 11B MOS | 18,465 | 22.55 years |

Five men killed in Vietnam were only 16 years old. [CACF]
The oldest man killed was 62 years old. [CACF]
11,465 KIAs were less than 20 years old. [CACF]

# Appendix T07

## Myth:
## The average age of an infantryman fighting in Vietnam was 19.

The facts are:

Assuming KIAs accurately represented age groups serving in Vietnam, the average age of an infantryman (MOS 11B) serving in Vietnam to be 19 years old is a myth, it is actually 22. None of the enlisted grades have an average age of less than 20. [CACF] The average man who fought in World War II was 26 years of age. [Westmoreland]

# Appendix T08

## Myth:
## The domino theory was proved false.

The facts are:

The domino theory was accurate. The ASEAN (Association of Southeast Asian Nations) countries, Philippines, Indonesia, Malaysia, Singapore, and Thailand stayed free of Communism because of the U.S. commitment to Vietnam. The Indonesians threw the Soviets out in 1966 because of America's commitment in Vietnam. Without that commitment, Communism would have swept all the way to the Malacca Straits that is south of Singapore and of great strategic importance to the free world. If you ask people who live in these countries that won the war in Vietnam, they have a different opinion from the American news media. The Vietnam War was the turning point for Communism. [Westmoreland]

Democracy Catching On—In the wake of the Cold War, democracies are flourishing, with 179 of the world's 192 sovereign states (93%) now electing their legislators, according to the Geneva-based Inter-Parliamentary Union. In the last decade, 69 nations have held multi-party elections for the first time in their histories. Three of the five newest democracies are former Soviet republics: Belarus (where elections were first held in November 1995), Armenia (July 1995) and Kyrgyzstan (February 1995). And two are in Africa: Tanzania (October 1995) and Guinea (June 1995). [Parade Magazine]

# Appendix T09

## Myth:
## The fighting in Vietnam was not as intense as in World War II.

The facts are:

The average infantryman in the South Pacific during World War II saw about 40 days of combat in four years. The average infantryman in Vietnam saw about 240 days of combat in one year thanks to the mobility of the helicopter.

One out of every 10 Americans who served in Vietnam was a casualty. 58,169 were killed and 304,000 wounded out of 2.59 million who served. Although the percent who died is similar to other wars, amputations or crippling wounds were 300 percent higher than in World War II. 75,000 Vietnam veterans are severely disabled. [McCaffrey]

MEDEVAC helicopters flew nearly 500,000 missions. Over 900,000 patients were airlifted (nearly half were American). The average time lapse between wounding to hospitalization was less than one hour. As a result, less than one percent of all Americans wounded who survived the first 24 hours died. [VHPA 1993]

The helicopter provided unprecedented mobility. Without the helicopter, it would have taken three times as many troops to secure the 800-mile border with Cambodia and Laos (the politicians thought the Geneva Conventions of 1954 and the Geneva Accords or 1962 would secure the border) [Westmoreland]

# Appendix T10

## More helicopter facts

Approximately 12,000 helicopters saw action in Vietnam (all services). [VHPA databases]

Army UH-1's totaled 7,531,955 flight hours in Vietnam between October 1966 and the end of 1975. [VHPA databases]

Army AH-1G's totaled 1,038,969 flight hours in Vietnam. [VHPA databases]

# Appendix T11

## Myth:
## Air America, the airline operated by the CIA in Southeast Asia, and its pilots were involved in drug trafficking.

The facts are:

The 1990 unsuccessful movie "Air America" helped to establish the myth of a connection between Air America, the CIA, and the Laotian drug trade. The movie and a book the movie was based on contend that the CIA condoned a drug trade conducted by a Laotian client; both agree that Air America provided the essential transportation for the trade; and both view the pilots with sympathetic understanding. American-owned airlines never knowingly transported opium in or out of Laos, nor did their American pilots ever profit from its transport. Yet undoubtedly, every plane in Laos carried opium at some time, unknown to the pilot and his superiors. For more information, see http://www.air-america.org

# Appendix T12

## Myth:
**The American military was running for their lives during the fall of Saigon in April 1975. The picture of a Huey helicopter-evacuating people from the top of what was billed as being the U.S. Embassy in Saigon during the last week of April 1975 during the fall of Saigon helped to establish this myth.**

The facts are:

This famous picture is the property of Corbus-Bettman Archives. (Appendix U) It was originally a UPI photograph that was taken by an Englishman, Mr. Hugh Van Ess.

Here are some additional facts to clear up the poor job of reporting by the news media.

# Appendix T13

## Facts about the fall of Saigon:

It was a "civilian" (Air America) Huey not Army or Marines.

It was NOT the U.S. Embassy. The building is the Pittman Apartments. The U.S. Embassy and its helo pad were much larger.

The evacuees were Vietnamese not American military.

The person that can be seen aiding the refugees is Mr. O.B. Harnage. He was a CIA case officer and now retired in Arizona.

# Appendix T14

## Myth:
## Another famous picture (Appendix U) of Kim Phuc, the little nine-year-old Vietnamese girl running naked from the napalm strike near Trang Bang on 8 June 1972, was burned by Americans bombing Trang Bang.

The facts are:

No American was involved in this incident near Trang Bang that burned Phan Thi Kim Phuc. The planes doing the bombing near the village were VNAF (Vietnam Air Force) and were being flown by Vietnamese pilots in support of South Vietnamese troops on the ground.

The Vietnamese pilot who dropped the napalm in error is currently living in the United States. Even the AP photographer, Nick Ut, who took the picture, was Vietnamese. The incident in the photo took place on the second day of a three-day battle between the North Vietnamese Army (NVA) who occupied the village of Trang Bang and the ARVN (Army of the Republic of Vietnam) who were trying to force the NVA out of the village.

Recent reports in the news media that an American commander ordered the air strike that burned Kim Phuc are incorrect. There were no Americans involved in any capacity. "We (Americans) had nothing to do with controlling VNAF," according to Lieutenant General (Ret) James F. Hollingsworth, the Commanding General of TRAC at that time. Also, it has been incorrectly reported that two of Kim Phuc's brothers were killed in this incident. They were Kim's cousins not her brothers.

# Appendix T15

## Myth:
## The United States lost the war in Vietnam.

The facts are:

The American military was not defeated in Vietnam. The American military did not lose a battle of any consequence. From a military standpoint, it was almost an unprecedented performance (Westmoreland quoting Douglas Pike, a professor at the University of California, Berkley a renowned expert on the Vietnam War) [Westmoreland]. This included TET 68, which was a major military defeat for the VC and NVA.

# Appendix T16

## Facts about the end of the war

The fall of Saigon happened 30 April 1975, two years AFTER the American military left Vietnam. The last American troops departed in their entirety 29 March 1973. How could we lose a war we had already stopped fighting? We fought to an agreed stalemate. The peace settlement was signed in Paris on 27 January 1973. It called for release of all U.S. prisoners, withdrawal of U.S. forces, limitation of both sides' forces inside South Vietnam and a commitment to peaceful reunification. [1996 Information Please Almanac]

The 140,000 evacuees in April 1975 during the fall of Saigon consisted almost entirely of civilians and Vietnamese military, NOT American military running for their lives [1996 Information Please Almanac].

There were almost twice as many casualties in Southeast Asia (primarily Cambodia) the first two years after the fall of Saigon in 1975 then there were during the ten years the U.S. was involved in Vietnam [1996 Information Please Almanac].

# Appendix T17

## POW-MIA Issue (unaccounted-for versus missing in action)

Politics & People, On Vietnam, Clinton Should Follow a Hero's Advice, Sen. John Kerrey is quoted, as saying about Vietnam, there has been "the most extensive accounting in the history of human warfare" of those missing in action. While there are still officially more than 2,200 cases, there now are only 55 incidents of American servicemen who were last seen alive but aren't accounted for. By contrast, there still are 78,000 unaccounted-for Americans from World War II and 8,100 from the Korean conflict.

"The problem is that those who think the Vietnamese haven't cooperated sufficiently think there is some central repository with answers to all the lingering questions," notes Gen. John Vessey, the former chairman of the Joint Chiefs of Staff and the Reagan and Bush administration's designated representative in MIA negotiations. "In all the years we've been working on this we have found that's not the case." [The Wall Street Journal]

More realities about war: Post Traumatic Stress Disorder (PTSD)— it was not invented or unique to Vietnam Veterans. It was called "shell shock" and other names in previous wars. An automobile accident or other traumatic event also can cause it. It does not have to be war related. The Vietnam War helped medical progress in this area.

# Appendix T18

## Myth:
## Agent Orange poisoned millions of Vietnam veterans.

The facts are:

Over the ten years of the war, Operation Ranch Hand sprayed about eleven million gallons of Agent Orange on the South Vietnamese landscape. (The herbicide was called "orange" in Vietnam, not Agent Orange. That sinister-sounding term was coined after the war) Orange was sprayed at three gallons per acre that was the equivalent of .009 of an ounce per square foot. When sprayed on dense jungle foliage, less that 6 percent ever reached the ground. Ground troops typically did not enter a sprayed area until four to six weeks after being sprayed. Most Agent Orange contained .0002 of 1 percent of dioxin. Scientific research has shown that dioxin degrades in sunlight after 48 to 72 hours; therefore, troop's exposure to dioxin was infinitesimal. [Burkett]

Restraining the military in Vietnam in hindsight probably prevented a nuclear war with China or Russia. The Vietnam War was shortly after China got involved in the Korean War, the time of the Cuban missile crisis, Soviet aggression in Eastern Europe and the proliferation of nuclear bombs. In all, a very scary time for our country.

# Appendix T19

## Personnel

9,087,000 military personnel served on active duty during the Vietnam Era (5 August 1965-7 May 1975).

8,744,000 personnel were on active duty during the war (5 August 1964-28 March 1973).

3,403,100 (including 514,300 offshore) personnel served in the SE Asia Theater (Vietnam, Laos, Cambodia, flight crews based in Thailand and sailors in adjacent South China Sea waters).

2,594,000 personnel served within the borders of South Vietnam (1 January 1965-28 March 1973).

Another 50,000 men served in Vietnam between 1960 and 1964.

Of the 2.6 million, between 1 and 1.6 million (40-60%) either fought in combat, provided close combat support, or were at least fairly regularly exposed to enemy attack.

7,484 women served in Vietnam, of whom 6,250 or 83.5% were nurses.

Peak troop strength in Vietnam, 543,482, on 30 April 1969.

# Appendix T20

## Casualties

| | |
|---|---|
| Hostile deaths: | 47,359 |
| Non-hostile deaths: | 10,797 |
| Total: | 58,156 |

Highest state death rate: West Virginia—84.1. (The national average death rate for males in 1970 was 58.9 per 100,000).

| WIA: | 303,704 | |
| | 153,329 | required hospitalization. |
| | 50,375 | did not require hospitalization. |

| Severely disabled: | 75,000 | |
| | 23,214 | were classified 100% disabled. |
| | 5,283 | lost limbs. |
| | 1,081 | sustained multiple amputations. |

Amputation or crippling wounds to the lower extremities were 300% higher than in WWII and 70% higher than in Korea. Multiple amputations occurred at the rate of 18.4% compared to 5.7% in WWII.

| MIA: | 2,338 |
| POW | 766- of whom 114 died in captivity. |

# Appendix T21

## Draftees vs. volunteers

25% (648,500) of total forces in country were draftees.
66% of U.S. armed forces members were drafted during WWII.
Draftees accounted for 30.4% (17,725) of combat deaths in Vietnam.

Reservists KIA: 5,977
National Guard: 6,140 served; 101 died.

# Appendix T22

## Ethnic background

88.4%   of the men who actually served in Vietnam were Caucasian

10.6%   (275,000) were black

1.0%    belonged to other races.


86.3%   of the men who died in Vietnam were Caucasian (including Hispanics)

12.5%   (7,241) were black

1.2%    belonged to other races.


170,000 Hispanics served in Vietnam

3,070   (5.2%) of whom died there.


86.8%   of the men who were KIA were Caucasian.

12.1%   (5,711) were black; 1.1% belonged to other races.

14.6%   (1,530) of non-combat deaths were black.

34%     of blacks who enlisted volunteered for the combat arms.


Overall, blacks suffered 12.5% of the deaths in Vietnam when the percentage of blacks of military age was 13.5% of the population.

# Appendix T23

## Socioeconomics status

76% of the men sent to Vietnam were from lower middle/working class backgrounds.
75% had family incomes above the poverty level.
23% had fathers with professional, managerial, or technical occupations.
79% of the men who served in 'Nam had a high school education or better.
63% of Korean vets had completed high school upon separation from the service).

# Appendix T24

## Winning & Losing

82% of veterans who saw heavy combat strongly believe the war was lost because of a lack of political will. Nearly 75% of the general public (in 1993) agrees with that.

# Appendix T25

## Age & Honorable Service

The average age of the G.I. in 'Nam was 19 (26 for WWII) 97% of Vietnam era vets were honorably discharged.

# Appendix T26

## Pride in Service

91% of veterans of actual combat and 90% of those who saw heavy combat are proud to have served their country. 66% of Viet vets say they would serve again, if called upon. 87% of the public now holds Viet vets in high esteem.

Helicopter crew deaths accounted for 10% of ALL Vietnam deaths. Helicopter losses during Lam Son 719 (a mere two months) accounted for 10% of all helicopter losses from 1961-1975. * Doris Jean Watkins.

# Appendix T27

## Operation BABYLIFT—The flight

The plane, a C-5A 'Galaxy', was carrying 243 children, 44 escorts, 16 crewmen, and 2 flight nurses. These numbers vary according to which news articles you read as totals vary from 305 to 319 onboard.

Eight members of the Air Force crew perished in the crash. The plane was enroute to Travis AFB in California. Most of those who perished were in the lowest of three levels in what was then the largest aircraft in the world.

A survivor of the crash stated: "Some of us got out through a chute from the top of the plane, but the children (and escorts) at the bottom of the plane didn't have a chance." Air Force Sgt. Jim Hadley, a medical technician from Sacramento, CA recalled later that oxygen masks dropped down automatically, but the children were sitting two to a seat and there were not enough masks to go around. "We had to keep moving them from kid to kid."

In an early report, the U.S. embassy indicated possibly 100 of the children and 10 to 15 adults survived, including the pilot. At least 50 of the children were in the lower cargo level of the plane.

The Galaxy had taken-off from Tan-Son-Nhut airbase and had reached an altitude of approximately 23,000 feet and was approximately 40 miles from Saigon when its rear clamshell cargo doors blew off crippling its flight controls. In what was described as a "massive explosive decompression" near Vung-Tau, the pilot lost control of his flaps, elevators, & rudder.

The pilot, with only the use of his throttles and ailerons, was able to turn the giant plane back towards Tan Son Nhut. At 5,000 feet Capt. Dennis Traynor, determined that he was unable to reach the runway safely with the crippled plane and set it down approximately 2 miles north of the airport to avoid crashing in a heavily-populated area where it broke into three pieces and exploded. The fact that many did survive such a crash was indeed a result of his flying ability.

A Pentagon spokesman at the time commented on Capt. Traynor's efforts to bring the aircraft in safely as "a remarkable demonstration of flying skill."

Victor Ubach, a Pan American World Airways pilot who was flying behind and above the crippled Air Force plane said the C-5A pilots "had done one heck of a job" to avoid a worse disaster. South Vietnamese sources said three militiamen on the ground were killed when the airplane fell.

At first, it was thought the crash may have been attributed to sabotage but later ruled-out by the USAF. The crash investigation was headed by Maj. Gen. Warner E. Newby.

The flight-recorder was recovered by a Navy diver on 7 Apr 1975 from the bottom of the South China Sea. A Pentagon spokesman said the plane had undergone minor repairs to its radio and windshield in the Philippines before flying to Saigon but added that had nothing to do with the crash.

At the time, the USAF had taken delivery of 81 Galaxy's. Wing problems had plagued this immense cargo plane but were not considered a factor in this incident. In spite of its wing problems, this was only the second crash of a C-5A after over 190,000 combined flying hours by the USAF but the first crash resulting in loss-of-life. Two other C-5A's were previously destroyed in a fire while on the ground.

Representative Les Aspin and Senator William Proxmire immediately urged the Air Force to ground the remaining 77 C-5A's, pointing to the continuing problem of weak wings.

By 8 Apr, Operation Baby Lift had resumed with the arrival of 56 orphans to the U.S. At the time of the crash, over 18,000 orphans were being processed for evacuation from South Vietnam for adoption in the U.S. and other countries. Over 25,000 orphans were in South Vietnam in April of 1975. We compiled these facts from AP & UPI articles that appeared in the Seattle Times, Seattle P-I and New York Times from 4 April to 8 April of 1975.

# Appendix T28

## Agonizing perception of Vietnam

One reason America's agonizing perception of "Vietnam" will not go away, is because that perception is wrong. It's out of place in the American psyche, and it continues to fester in much the same way battle wounds fester when shrapnel or other foreign matter is left in the body. It is not normal behavior for Americans to idolize mass murdering despots, to champion the cause of slavery, to abandon friends and allies, or to cut and run in the face of adversity.

Why then did so many Americans engage in these types of activities during its "Vietnam" experience? That the American experience in Vietnam was painful and ended in long lasting (albeit self-inflicted) grief and misery cannot be disputed. However, either the American people or their government does not even remotely understand the reasons behind that grief and misery.

Contradictory to popular belief, and a whole lot of wishful thinking by a solid corps of some 16,000,000+ American draft dodgers and their families / supporters, it was not a military defeat that brought misfortune to the American effort in Vietnam.

The United Sates military in Vietnam was the best-educated, best-trained, best-disciplined, and most successful force ever fielded in the history of American arms.

Why then, did it get such bad press, and, why is the public's opinion of them so twisted? The answer is simple. But first, a few relevant comparisons. During the Civil War, at the Battle of Bull Run, the entire Union Army panicked and fled the battlefield.

Nothing even remotely resembling that debacle ever occurred in Vietnam. In WWII at the Kasserine Pass in Tunisia, the Germans overran elements of the US Army. In the course of that battle, Hitler's General Rommel (The Desert Fox) inflicted 3,100 US casualties, took 3,700 US prisoners and captured or destroyed 198 American tanks.

In Vietnam, no US Military units were overrun and no US Military infantry units or tank outfits were captured. WW II again, in the Philippines, Army Generals Jonathan Wainwright, and Edward King surrendered themselves and their troops to the Japanese.

In Vietnam no US generals, or US military units ever surrendered. Before the Normandy invasion ("D" Day, 1944) the US Army (In WW II the US Army included the Army Air Corps which today has become the US Air force) in England filled its own jails with American soldiers who refused to fight and then had to rent jail space from the British to handle the overflow. The US Army in Vietnam never had to rent jail space from the Vietnamese to incarcerate American soldiers who refused to fight.

# Appendix T29

## Dissertation

Only about 5,000 men assigned to Vietnam deserted and just 249 of those deserted while in Vietnam. During WW II, in the European Theater alone, over 20,000 US Military men were convicted of dissertation and, on a comparable percentage basis, the overall WW II desertion rate was 55 percent higher than in Vietnam.

During the WW II Battle of the Bulge in Europe, two regiments of the US Army's 106th Division surrendered to the Germans. Again: In Vietnam, no US Army unit ever surrendered. As for brutality: During WW II, the US Army executed nearly 300 of its own men. In the European Theater alone, the US Army sentenced 443 American soldiers to death. Most of these sentences were for the rape and or murder of civilians.

In the Korean War, Major General F. Dean, commander of the 24th Infantry Division in Korea was taken prisoner of war (POW). In Vietnam, no US generals, much less division commanders, were ever taken prisoner.

During the Korean War, the US Army was forced into the longest retreat in its history, a catastrophic 275-mile withdrawal from the

Yalu River all the way to Pyontaek, 45 miles south of Seoul. In the process, they lost the capital of Seoul. The US Military in Vietnam was never compelled into a major retreat nor did it ever abandon Saigon to the enemy. The 1st US Marine Division was driven from the Chosin Reservoir and forced into an emergency evacuation from the Korean port of Hungnam. There other US Army joined them and South Korean soldiers and the US Navy eventually evacuated 105,000 Allied troops from that port. In Vietnam, there was never any mass evacuation of US Marine, South Vietnamese, or Allied troops.

# Appendix T30

## Other items

Only 25 percent of the US Military who served in Vietnam were draftees. During WW II, 66 percent of the troops were draftees. The Vietnam force contained three times as many college graduates as did the WW II force. The average education level of the enlisted man in Vietnam was 13 years, equivalent to one year of college. Of those who enlisted, 79 percent had high school diplomas. This at a time when only 65% of the military age males in the general American population were high school graduates.

The average age of the military men who died in Vietnam was 22.8 years old. Of the one hundred and one (101) 18-year-old draftees who died in Vietnam; seven of them were black. Blacks accounted for 10.5 percent the combat deaths in Vietnam. At that time black males of military age constituted 13.5 percent of the American population.

The charge that the "poor" died in disproportionate numbers is also a myth. An MIT (Massachusetts Institute of Technology) study of Vietnam death rates, conducted by Professor Arnold Barnett, revealed that servicemen from the richest 10 percent of the nation's communities had the same distribution of deaths as the rest of the nation.

In fact, his study showed that the death rate in the upper income communities of Beverly Hills, Belmont, Chevy Chase, and Great Neck exceeded the national average in three of the four, and, when the four were added together and averaged, that number exceeded the national average. On the issue of psychological health: Mental problems attributed to service in Vietnam are referred to as PTSD.

Civil War veterans suffered "Soldiers heart" and in WW I, the term was "Shell shock" during WW II and in Korea it was "Battle fatigue." Military records indicate that Civil War psychological casualties averaged twenty-six per thousand men. In WW II, some units experienced over 100 psychiatric casualties per 1,000 troops; in Korea nearly one quarter of all battlefield medical evacuations were due to mental stress. That works out to about 50 per 1,000 troops. In Vietnam, the comparable average was 5 per 1,000 troops.

To put Vietnam in its proper perspective it is necessary to understand that the US Military was not defeated in Vietnam and that the South Vietnamese government did not collapse due to mismanagement or corruption, nor was it overthrown by revolutionary guerrillas running around in rubber tire sandals, wearing black pajamas, and carrying home made weapons. There was no "general uprising" or "revolt" by the southern population. A conventional army made up of seventeen conventional divisions, organized into four army corps, overran Saigon. This totally conventional force (armed, equipped, trained and supplied by the Soviet Union) launched a cross border, frontal attack on South Vietnam and conquered it, in the same manner as Hitler conquered most of Europe in WW II.

# Appendix T31

## A quick synopsis of America's "Vietnam experience"

The following will help summarize and clarify the Vietnam scenario:

Prior to 1965; US Advisors and AID only 1965-1967; Buildup of US Forces and logistical supply bases, plus heavy fighting to counter Communist North Vietnamese invasion.

1968-1970; Communist "insurgency" destroyed to the point where over 90% of the towns and villages in South Vietnam were free from Communist domination. As an example: By 1971 throughout the entire populous Mekong Delta, the monthly rate of Communist insurgency action dropped to an average of 3 incidents per 100,000 population (Many a US city would envy a crime rate that low). In 1969, Nixon started troop withdrawals that were essentially complete by late 1971.

Dec 1972; Paris Peace Agreements negotiated and agreed by North Vietnam, South Vietnam, the Southern Vietnamese Communists (VC, NLF / PRG) and the United States.

Jan 1973; all four parties formally sign Paris Peace Agreements.

Mar 1973; Last US POW released from Hanoi Hilton, and in accordance with Paris Agreements, last American GI leaves Vietnam.

Aug 1973; US Congress passes the Case—Church law which forbids, US naval forces from sailing on the seas surrounding, US ground forces from operating on the land of, and US air forces from flying in the air over South Vietnam, North Vietnam, Cambodia and Laos. This at a time when America had drawn its Cold War battle lines. As a result, had the US Navy protecting Taiwan, 50,000 troops in South Korea and over 300,000 troops in Western Europe. This has a land area, economy, and population comparable to that of the United States.

This along with ironclad guarantees that if Communist forces should cross any of those Cold War lines or Soviet Armor should role across either the DMZ in Korea or the Iron Curtain in Europe, then there would be an unlimited response by the armed forces of the United States.

This will include if necessary, the use of nuclear weapons. In addition, these defense commitments required the annual expenditure of hundreds of billions of US dollars. Conversely, in 1975 when Soviet armor rolled across the international borders of South Vietnam, the US military response was nothing. In addition, Congress cut off all AID to the South Vietnamese and would not provide them with as much as a single bullet.

In spite of the Case—Church Congressional guarantee, the North Vietnamese were very leery of US President Nixon. They viewed him as one unpredictable, incredibly tough nut. He had, in 1972, for the first time in the War, mined Hai Phong Harbor and sent the B-52 bombers against the North to force them into signing the Paris Peace Agreements. Previously the B-52s had been used only against Communist troop concentrations in remote regions of South Vietnam and occasionally against carefully selected sanctuaries in Cambodia, plus against both sanctuaries and supply lines in Laos.

Aug 1974; Nixon resigns.

Sept 1974: North Vietnamese hold special meeting to evaluate Nixon's resignation and decide to test implications.

Dec 1974: North Vietnamese invade South Vietnamese Province of Phouc Long located north of Saigon on Cambodian border.

Jan 1975: North Vietnamese capture Phouc Long provincial capitol of Phouc Binh. Sit and wait for US reaction. No reaction.

Mar 1975; North Vietnam mounts full-scale invasion. Seventeen North Vietnamese conventional divisions (more divisions than the US Army has had on duty at any time since WW II) were formed into four conventional army corps (This was the entire North Vietnamese army. Because the US Congress had unconditionally guaranteed no military action against North Vietnam, there was no need for them to keep forces in reserve to protect their home bases, flanks or supply lines), and launched a wholly conventional cross-border, frontal-attack. Then, using the age-old tactics of mass and maneuver, they defeated the South Vietnamese Army in detail.

The complete description of this North Vietnamese Army (NVA) classical military victory is best expressed in the words of the NVA general who commanded it.

Recommended reading: Great Spring Victory by General Tien Van Dung, NVA Foreign Broadcast Information Service, Volume I, 7 Jun 76 and Volume II, 7 Jul 76. General Dung's account of the final battle for South Vietnam reads like it was taken right out of a US Army manual on offensive military operations. His description of the mass and maneuver were exquisite. His selection of South Vietnam's army as the "Center of gravity" could have been written by General Carl von Clausewitz himself. General Dung's account goes into graphic detail on his battle moves aimed at destroying South Vietnam's armed forces and their war materials.

He never once, not even once, ever mentions a single word about revolutionary warfare or guerilla tactics contributing in any way to his Great Spring Victory.

# Appendix T32

**Another Aspect—US Military battle deaths by year:**

Prior to  1966—3,078 (Total through 31 Dec 65) 1966—5,008
1967—9,378
1968—14,589 (While JFK & LBJ were on watch—32,053)
1969—9,414
1970—4,221
1971—1,381
1972—300 (While Nixon was on watch—15,316)

Source of these numbers is the Southeast Asia Statistical Summary, Office of the Assistant Secretary or Defense and were provided to the author by the US Army War College Library, Carlisle Barracks, PA 17023. Numbers are battle deaths only and do not include ordinary accidents, heart attacks, murder victims, suicides, etc.

Those who think these numbers represent "heavy fighting" and some of the "bloodiest battles" in US history should consider the fact that the Allied Forces lost 9,758 men killed just storming the Normandy Beaches; 6,603 were Americans. The US Marines, in the 25 days between 19 Feb 45 and 16 Mar 45, lost nearly 7,000 men killed in their battle for the tiny island of Iwo Jima.

By comparison the single bloodiest day in the Vietnam War for the Americans was on 17 Nov 65 when elements of the 7th Cav (Custer's old outfit) lost 155 men killed in a battle with elements of two North Vietnamese Regular Army regiments (33rd & 66th) near the Cambodian border southwest of Pleiku.

## Parallel point

During its Normandy battles in 1944 the US 90th Infantry Division, (roughly 15,000+ men) over a six week period, had to replace 150% of its officers and more than 100% of its men. The 173rd Airborne Brigade (normally there are 3 brigades to a division) served in Vietnam for a total of 2,301 days, and holds the record for the longest continuous service under fire of any American unit, ever. During that (6 year, 3+ month) period the 173rd lost 1,601 (roughly 31%) of its men killed in action.

# Appendix T33

## Further Food For thought

Casualties tell the tale. Again, the US Army War College Library provides numbers. The former South Vietnam was made up of 44 provinces. The province that claimed the most Americans killed was Quang Tri, which bordered on both North Vietnam and Laos. Fifty four percent of the Americans killed in Vietnam were killed in the four northernmost provinces, which in addition to Quang Tri were Thua Thien, Quang Nam, and Quan Tin. All of them shared borders with Laos.

An additional six provinces accounted for another 25 % of the Americans killed in action (KIA). Those six all shared borders with either Laos or Cambodia or had contiguous borders with provinces that did. The remaining 34 provinces accounted for just 21% of US KIA. These numbers should dispel the notion that Vietnam was some kind of flaming inferno or a huge cauldron of burning dissent. The overwhelming majority of Americans killed, died in border battles against regular NVA units.

Looking back it is now clear that the American military role in "Vietnam" was, in essence, one of defending international borders. Contrary to popular belief, they turned in an outstanding performance and accomplished their mission.

The US Military was not "Driven" from Vietnam. The US Congress voted them out. This same Congress then turned around and abandoned America's former ally, South Vietnam. Should America feel shame? Yes! Why? For kowtowing to the wishes of those craven hoards of dodgers and for bugging out and abandoning their former ally. The idea that "There were no front lines." and "The enemy was everywhere." makes good press and feeds the craven needs of those 16,000,000+ American draft dodgers. Add either a mommy or a poppa, and throw in another sympathizer in the form of a girl (or boy?) friend and your looking at well in excess of 50,000,000 Americans with a need to rationalize away their draft-dodging cowardice and to, in some way, vilify "Vietnam" the very source of their shame and guilt.

During the entire period of the American involvement in "Vietnam," only 2,594,000 US Military actual served inside the country. Contrast that number with the 50-million plus draft dodging anti-war crowd and you have the answer to why the American view of its Vietnam experience is so skewed. Once the draft dodging gang's numbers reached critical mass, the media, and politicians started playing to the numbers.

Multi-million dollar salaries are not paid to people for reporting the news, in any form, be it written, audio, or video. Multi-million dollar salaries (e.g., Cronkite) are paid to entertainers, stars, and superstars.

One does not get to be, much less continue to be, a superstar unless one gives one's audience what it wants. Once the dodging anti-war numbers started climbing through the stratosphere, it was not in the media's interest to say something good about Vietnam to an audience that was guilt ridden with shame and a deep psychological need to rationalize away the true source of their guilt.

A good example of this number pandering can be found in a 1969 Life magazine feature article in which Life's editors published the portraits of 250 men that were killed in Vietnam in one routine week. This was supposedly done to illustrate Life's concern for the sanctity of human life; American human life.

In 1969, the weekly average death toll from highway accidents in the United States was 1,082. If indeed Life's concern was for the sanctity of American lives, why not publish the 1,082 portraits of the folks who were killed in one routine week on the nation's highways?

The most glaring example of the existence of the dodging guilt syndrome can be found in a statement made by the ranking head dodger himself. When asked for his reaction to McNamara's book In Retrospect, Clinton's response was "I feel vindicated." (Of his cowardly act of dodging the draft). Clinton is a lawyer and understands the use of English words very well. For one to "feel" vindicated, as opposed to being vindicated, one must have first been feeling guilty.

# Appendix T34

## The Battle of Xuan Loc; Mar 17-Apr 17, 1975 & The End

Xuan Loc was the last major battle for South Vietnam. It sits astride Q. L. (National Road) #1, some 40 odd miles to the northeast of Saigon (on the road to Phan Thiet), and was the capitol of South Vietnam's Long Khanh province. The NVA (North Vietnamese Army) attack fell on the ARVN (Army Republic of Vietnam) 18th Division. On 17 Mar 75, the NVA Sixth and Seventh Divisions attacked Xuan Loc but were repulsed by the ARVN 18th.

On 9 Apr 75, the NVA 341st Division joined the attack. After a four thousand round artillery bombardment, these three divisions massed, and, spearheaded by Soviet tanks, assaulted Xuan Loc; but again the ARVN 18th held its ground. The NVA reinforced with their 325th Division and began moving their 10th and 304th Divisions into position. Eventually, in a classic example of the military art of "Mass and Maneuver" the NVA massed 40,000 men and overran Xuan Loc.

During this fight, the ARVN 18th had 5,000 soldiers at Xuan Loc. These men managed to virtually destroy 3 NVA Divisions, but on 17 Apr 75 sheer numbers and the weight of the "Mass" overwhelmed them. Before overrunning Xuan Loc the NVA had committed six full divisions, plus a host various support troops.

In the Sorrow of War, author and NVA veteran Bao Ninh writes of this battle: "Remember when we chased Division 18 southern soldiers all over Xuan Loc? My tank tracks were choked up with skin, hair, and blood. And the bloody maggots. And the fucking flies. Had to drive through a river to get the stuff out of my tracks." He also writes, "After a while I could tell the difference between mud and bodies, logs and bodies. They were like sacks of water. They'd pop open when I ran over them. Pop! Pop!"

# Appendix T35

## The Irony

It's ironic that in spite of all the hype and hullabaloo about the "Viet Cong" and the "American Soldiers" both were absent from the final battles for South Vietnam. The Viet Cong had been bludgeoned to death (During TET 1968) on the streets of the cities, towns, and hamlets of South Vietnam. The Americans had left under the terms of the Paris Peace Agreements, and then were barred by the US Congress, from ever returning. The end came in the form of a cross border invasion. Two conventional armies fought it out using strategies and tactics as old as warfare itself.

A quick word about the South Vietnamese government lacking support from the people, and of the so-called "Popular support" for the Communists. During the 1968, TET Offensive the Communists attacked 155 cities, towns, and hamlets in South Vietnam. In not one instance did the people rise up to support the Communists. The general uprising was a complete illusion. The people did rise, but in revulsion and resistance to the invaders. At the end of thirty days, not one single communist flag was flying over any of those 155 cities, towns, or hamlets.

The citizens of South Vietnam, no matter how apathetic they may have appeared toward their own government, turned out to be overwhelmingly anti-Communist. In the end, they had to be conquered by conventional divisions, supported by conventional tanks and artillery that was being maneuvered in accordance with the ancient principles of warfare. But then, as with mathematics, certain rules apply in war, and, military victories are not won by violating military principles.

# Appendix T36

## Closing Comments

For those who think that Vietnam was strictly a civil war, the following should be of interest. With the collapse of Communism and the Soviet Union along with the opening up of China, records are now becoming available on the type and amount of support North Vietnam received from China and the Soviet Block. For example: China has opened its records on the number of uniformed Chinese troops sent to aid their Communist friends in Hanoi. In all, China sent 327,000 troops to North Vietnam.

Historian Chen Jian wrote, "Although Beijing's support may have fallen short of Hanoi's expectations, without the support, the history, even the outcome, of the Vietnam War might have been different." In addition, at the height of the War, the Soviet Union had some 55,000 "Advisors" in North Vietnam. They were installing air defense systems, buildings, operating and maintaining SAM (Surface to Air Missiles) sites, plus they provided training and logistical support for the North Vietnamese military.

When I asked a well-known American reporter why they never reported on this out side Communist support. His answer was essentially that the North Vietnamese would not let the reporters up there and that because "We had no access to the North during the war and that meant that there were huge gaps in accurately conveying what was happening north of the DMZ."

By comparison, at the peak of the War there were 545,000 US Military personnel in Vietnam. However, most of them were logistical / support types. On the best day ever, there were 43,500 ground troops actually engaged in offensive combat operations, i.e., out in the boondocks, "Tiptoeing through the tulips" looking for, or actually in contact with, the enemy. This ratio of support to line troops is also comparable with other wars, and helps dispel the notion that every troop in Vietnam was engaged in mortal combat on a daily basis.

## Final Entry

General Dung's Great Spring Victory was supported by 700 (maneuverable) Soviet tanks, i.e. Soviet armor, burning Soviet gas and firing Soviet ammunition. By comparison, the South Vietnamese had only 352 US supplied tanks and they were committed to guarding the entire country, and because of US Congressional action, were critically short of fuel, ammo, and spare parts with which to support those tanks.

# Appendix T37

## Resources

[Nixon] No More Vietnams by Richard Nixon.

[Parade Magazine] August 18, 1996, page 10.

[CACF] (Combat Area Casualty File) November 1993 (The CACF is the basis for the Vietnam Veterans Memorial, i.e. The Wall), Center for Electronic Records, National Archives, Washington, DC

[All That We Can Be] All That We Can Be by Charles C. Moskos and John Sibley Butler

[Westmoreland] Speech by General William C. Westmoreland before the Third Annual Reunion of the Vietnam Helicopter Pilots Association (VHPA) at the Washington, DC Hilton Hotel on July 5th, 1986 (reproduced in a Vietnam Helicopter Pilots Association Historical Reference Directory Volume 2A)

[McCaffrey] Speech by Lt. Gen. Barry R. McCaffrey, (reproduced in the Pentagram, June 4, 1993) assistant to the Chairman of the Joint Chiefs of Staff, to Vietnam veterans and visitors gathered at "The Wall", Memorial Day 1993.

[Houk] Testimony by Dr. Houk, Oversight on Post-Traumatic Stress Disorder, 14 July 1988 page 17, Hearing before the Committee on Veterans' Affairs United States Senate one hundredth Congress second session. Also "Estimating the Number of Suicides Among Vietnam Veterans" (Am J Psychiatry 147, 6 June 1990 pages 772-776)

[The Wall Street Journal] The Wall Street Journal, 1 June 1996, page A15.

[VHPA 1993] Vietnam Helicopter Pilots Association 1993 Membership Directory page 130.

[VHPA Databases] Vietnam Helicopter Pilots Association Databases.

[1996 Information Please Almanac] 1995 Information Please Almanac Atlas & Yearbook 49th edition, Houghton Mifflin Company, Boston & New York 1996, pages 117, 161 and 292.

[Burkett] Stolen Valor: How the Vietnam Generation was Robbed of its Heroes and its History by B.G. Burkett and Glenna Whitley, Verity Press, Inc., Dallas, TX, 1998. Book review.

# Appendix U

## FAMOUS PICTURES

Huey helicopter evacuating people form the top of what was billed as being the US Embassy in Saigon.

Kim Phuc, the little nine year old Vietnamese girl running naked from the napalm strike near Trang Bang

# Appendix V

## CONTRIBUTIONS AND CREDITS

The following U.S. Navy Veterans have most graciously contributed photographs and other items to enhance and better visualize my story. For that, I am most grateful.

Harold Best
Tony Bour
Jay S. Brown
Steve Elicker
Rick Erwin
Jimmy Estes
Kent Hawley
Wayne Higdon
Artie Kitchen
Tom Lefavour
Roderick King
Steve McAvoy
Richard E. Pettit
Charlie Prather
Ken Strickland
Mike Urbom

Special thanks to Don West SK2, USN,
Naval Support Activity, Saigon October 1967-May 1969
for his review and editing of my story.

# CHAPTER ONE

My private room with twelve beds.

# CHAPTER TWO

Miss America ladies with the USO visiting the hospital.

# CHAPTER TWO

More Miss America ladies.

# CHAPTER TWO

The Miss America's line up for a photo shoot.

# CHAPTER TWO

Flying in formation.

# CHAPTER TWO

Nice view looking past the M-60 mounted in the doorway. However, it was a little difficult to appreciate the bombed out area below.

# CHAPTER THREE

Helo on the helo pad, aft of the ship.

The author, Samuel C. Crawford tanning.

# CHAPTER THREE

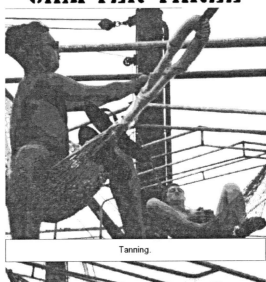

Tanning.

# CHAPTER FOUR

The aft pontoon was a busy place for helos. Getting a ride out should be easy.

# CHAPTER FOUR

LST tied along side. Real close like.

# CHAPTER FIVE

A striptease show.

M-60, a loaded M-60, next to a bunch of drunks.

# CHAPTER FIVE

We circled the YRBM while on Bid Patrol.

# CHAPTER FIVE

A portable fort.

# CHAPTER FIVE

A storm is on the way.

# CHAPTER SEVEN

Parts of downtown Saigon across from the Annapolis BEQ.

# CHAPTER SEVEN

More of downtown Saigon.

# CHAPTER SEVEN

This lady was selling snakes.

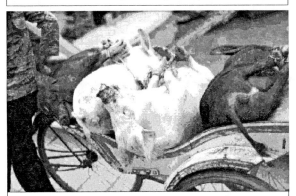

An old man with his little cart filled with four dead pigs.

# CHAPTER EIGHT

Guns, guns, and then more guns.

This may seem like a harmless boat, but don't get the crew mad.

# CHAPTER EIGHT

The bus was waiting on the Vietnamese officer from our boat. Looking across the river, we could see some kids with their pet water buffalo's.

# CHAPTER EIGHT

Below us, there were a few kids swimming along with a few momasans doing laundry. The, down river, there was a guy taking a dump.

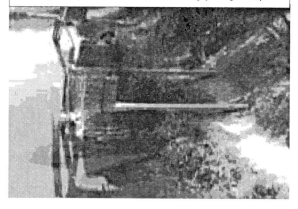

# CHAPTER NINE

Our bridge to guard.

Friend or Foe?

# CHAPTER TWELVE

Tan San Nut Air Force Base terminal.

# CHAPTER THIRTEEN

She was either his girlfriend or his rental.

These guys must have been here all day by number of empty beer bottles on the table. You can get them to bring you beer all day long, but no one will pick up the empties.

# CHAPTER FIFTEEN

View of Sydney Harbor.

# CHAPTER FIFTEEN

Sydney Harbor

# CHAPTER FIFTEEN

Hyde Park

Girls, girls, and more girls.
All of them with round eyes.

# CHAPTER SEVENTEEN

Marked crosswalk and a double decker bus.  I thought they were red in color.

# CHAPTER SEVENTEEN

Getting my hair combed at the beach.

# CHAPTER NINETEEN

KFC over here?

# About the Author

**SAMUEL C. CRAWFORD** was born October 1949 and
enlisted in the US Navy in 1968 after graduating from Baltimore
City College.

His first assignment out of boot camp was to the Mobile
Riverine Task Force 117, onboard the USS Satyr (ARL 23). After
a number of tours in Vietnam with the Mobile Riverine Force,
Sam served a tour of duty with VQ4 (Fleet Air Reconnaissance
Squadron Four) and VP30 (Patrol Squadron Thirty) at the Naval
Air Test Station, Patuxent River, Maryland.

Honorably discharged and is a current member of the Mobile
Riverine Force Association and a Life Member of the Veterans of
Foreign Wars (VFW). Awards and Decorations include, National
Defense Service Medal, Vietnam Campaign Medal w/60 device,
Vietnam Service Medal w/four Bronze Stars, Navy Unit
Commendation Ribbon while serving with River Assault Flotilla
One, Meritorious Unit Commendation, Combat Action Ribbon,
Presidential Unit Citation for Extraordinary Heroism, and the
Good Conduct Medal.

Samuel C. Crawford
South Vietnam, 1971